THREE AND OUT
BOOK THREE OF THE LOVE AND SPORTS SERIES

MEGHAN QUINN

CHAPTER ONE

Mason

"Seriously, stop acting like a damn vagina and get in the bath," Mason chastised Ryker, as he pussy-footed around the ice baths.

"Fuck off; you weren't the one who got frostbite on his dick last time," Ryker replied, as he tested the water with his pinky.

Mason shook his head and laughed, "You did not get fucking frostbite. Just because you couldn't get it up at the strip club the other night, it wasn't because of 'frostbite' from the ice bath."

Ryker spun on his heels and shout-whispered to Mason. "Seriously, say it a little louder, fuckwit, I don't think the defensive line heard you." Ryker shook his head and turned around. "Damn, man, you can't keep anything to yourself, can you?"

Mason chuckled. "Don't be such a princess. Face the facts; you have a limp noodle because you can't get your head out of Hannah's ass long enough to take note that there are other woman swarming at your gnarly testicles, ready to take the oblong marbles in their mouths."

"Is that all you talk about?" Jesse, the Stallion's quarterback, asked, as he walked into the ice room. "If you weren't bringing

1

home girls almost every night, I'd swear you were into men with all your ball talk."

"Who's to say I'm not?" Mason asked with a cocky grin.

"Is that so?" Jesse asked, as he quickly submerged himself under the ice cold bath. He always got in like a champ, one quick movement, unlike Ryker who danced around for ten minutes, occasionally dipping his hand in the water and swearing about how the temperature kept getting colder. "So, the big question is, me or Ryker?"

Mason looked at both men. He wouldn't say it out loud, but they were both attractive fucks…both had brown hair and were bulky like him, but where Jesse was a macho man, Ryker was your prissy metrosexual with a "frostbite" complex.

"Jesse…" Mason answered.

"What?!" Ryker practically shouted, as he finally got in the bath and hissed through his teeth from the cold ice water hitting his skin.

"What can I say? I like my men like I like my coffee, dark and bitter."

Jesse's eyebrow rose at Mason's comment. "Bitter, really?"

"Well, if you're not bitter, then what the hell are you? There's no way a man like yourself doesn't go out and pick up women just because he doesn't want to. There has to be a reason why you choose to be a hermit. What is it? Relationship with some hot piece of ass turn sour, making you into a bitter man? Hell, welcome to my life. Bitter is like fucking underwear to me, I almost always wear it, but can shuck it when I want sex."

Laughing at Mason, Jesse said, "We can't all be Casanova man-whores like you."

Jesse bowed his head and examined his hand as Mason watched him. Mason was all kinds of fucked up, thanks to tweedle-slut and tweedle-whore, but he was still able to have fun. Jesse didn't seem like he had fun…ever, unless he was on the football field, then the man knew how to have a hell of a time. When they were on the field…that was when Mason really saw Jesse come alive. Other than that, he was very quiet and reserved. Mason really wanted to break the shell he was living under and figure out what his problem was.

"Come out with us tonight," Mason suggested.

"Nah, I'm good. Thanks, man."

"My fucking nipples are purple...purple!" Ryker complained. "Fuck this; I'd rather be sore than lose my dick again." Ryker climbed out of the bath and grabbed a towel from the shelf to dry himself off.

Ryker had been a moody little bitch ever since Hannah found out Todd was actually a lying ass and was married. Mason didn't dig too deep into the situation because, frankly, he didn't give a fuck, but what he did know was that Ryker hadn't seen or heard from Hannah since he left the bar that one fateful night when both of their lives were flipped upside down.

Mason didn't think of that night very often, because it was one of the biggest mistakes of his life. He was a hurting bastard the minute he heard Piper was engaged to Jax, Mason's coach, and he turned to the wrong person, the completely wrong person. Brooke was a mistake, sleeping with her was a mistake, and now he was paying for it. He hadn't seen or heard from Piper since he slammed the door in her face, and he had never felt emptier. He tried to convince himself that he was better off without her, that he didn't need her, and he didn't want her, but that was a lie. His body still craved her.

Rage and spite were the only things currently getting him through life, and of course the occasional fuck with a random girl. He never really felt anything when he was with another woman, it was just the act of sex, of releasing all of his pent up emotions that helped him. On the outside, he put on a front so it seemed like everything was okay, but on the inside, he was a broken and battered man. To have one woman screw him over was a blow to the old nuts, but to have two women screw him over was devastating to his ego and his mind.

"Where are we going tonight?" Ryker asked, as he toweled

off.

"I know where we're not going," Mason said under his breath. They hadn't been to their old stomping grounds in a while. Frankly, Mason missed going to Piper's bar, watching her float around with her red hair swaying behind her. He shook his head from his thoughts.

"How about Number Nine," Mason suggested, as his body finally hit numb status from the ice bath.

"Is that where you met that one girl, what was her name?" Jesse thought to himself.

"Margie," Ryker helped out.

"Yeah," Jesse smacked the water. "Margie, what ever happened to her? Wasn't she the best sex you'd had in a while?"

Mason smirked as he thought about Margie. She was really good in bed. She did this thing with her thighs that clenched so tight around him he thought he was going to explode.

"Marge in charge," Mason reminisced. "Damn, I don't know what happened to her. We had one great night, and she just took off. It was probably my donkey dick that scared her away," Mason said with a smirk.

"Or maybe you're just not as good at fucking as you thought you were," Ryker shimmied in his towel as he looked at Mason, making Mason raise his eyebrows at his best friend.

"I'm not even going to answer that, because you know it's a lie. So, you in? Number Nine? Maybe you can invite Ashlin?"

"No, she wouldn't want to go. The media has blown things up between us, of course. Shocker…I doubt she'll be up for fending off paparazzi."

"Anything happening between you two?" Jesse asked, as he looked down in the water. The question was odd, coming from the guy who could care less about everyone's relationships.

"No. I mean, she wanted to start something, and I thought about it because, damn, she is a good fuck, but I don't think we would do well in a relationship. The sexual chemistry is there, though, that's for damn sure."

Mason laughed as he said, "Clearly, since you popped a chubb every time you were in a photo shoot together."

Ryker flipped Mason off and said, "I'll meet you at the club, dickhead. Try wearing something decent."

Ryker left the ice bath room and went out to the lockers.

"He's such an ass nugget," Mason said, as he eyed Jesse, who, all of a sudden, turned very quiet. "Dude, you okay?"

Jesse nodded his head as he got out of the ice bath. "Yeah, just a lot on my mind."

Jesse was very reserved, always kept to himself. He was a damn king on the football field, but off the field, he kept to himself. Mason wished that Jesse would go out with him and Ryker, but it was never his scene.

"I'm not much for talking, but if you ever need to talk…" Mason offered, like the good teammate he was.

"I'm good, seriously. Have fun tonight. I'll see you later." Jesse fist-bumped Mason and said, "Have a good night; don't get any STDs or anything tonight."

"Wouldn't dream of it."

Jesse

Jesse got back home to his empty apartment, put his gym bag away, and went to his kitchen to make himself some dinner. As he cracked some eggs to make himself an omelet, he looked around his place and was happy he was home. He loved being home and out of the spotlight. He was portrayed in the media as a self-absorbed ass because he very rarely did interviews and was never really seen out on the town, but that was because he was shy as hell. He hated public speaking, and he hated the spotlight. The only reason he was able to flourish on the field was because he had his men with him, he was in the zone, and there was one goal in mind: winning. When he was by himself, with a million cameras flashing in front of him, he got tongue tied, sweaty, and turned into a hot mess. He preferred to be home, where the anxiety of being swarmed by people and onlookers didn't bother him.

Occasionally, he would go out with his boys, and that was a rare occasion, but he only stayed for an hour or two and never drank alcohol. His dad was an alcoholic and died from liver poisoning, so drinking never appealed to Jesse, plus his body was a fine-tuned machine; he didn't want to put toxins in it that would hinder his ability to play.

If he did go out, he also never brought home a girl. He wasn't a one-night stand kind of guy; he preferred being in a relationship. He'd only had one girlfriend, Katie, his entire life, and they broke up right before he was drafted. She wanted to travel the world, and he was being drafted. They still were close friends; she was teaching English in some foreign country, and he was throwing footballs around for a living.

As Jesse was pulling his omelet off the stove, his phone rang. While placing his omelet on a plate, he answered his phone.

"Hello?"

"Hey, man. Good game today," Jesse's brother and best friend, Johnny, said.

"Thanks, bro."

"Sorry I couldn't be there. We think Daisy has the flu, and Jenny was called in to work tonight."

Daisy is Johnny and Jenny's three year old daughter who practically owns Jesse's heart. He loved her with everything in him. Johnny had the perfect life. He had a wife, a house, the cutest daughter ever, and he was happy; his life was fulfilled. Jesse knew he had no reason to complain, but he couldn't help being jealous; he wanted what his brother had…he wanted a family.

"Don't worry about it. Is Daisy going to be okay? Do you need me to come over and help?"

"No, I got her down a couple of minutes ago, and the clothes I was wearing that she just puked all over are currently being soaked in the laundry room sink."

Chuckling to himself, Jesse asked, "Was it projectile?"

"Isn't it always?" Johnny responded.

"Damn, that's sick, dude."

"Tell me about it," Johnny blew out a long breath. "So, I'm assuming you're home, since I don't hear any background noise. Why didn't you go out with everyone? I'm assuming they're all out celebrating the win."

"Not my scene, you know that."

"But how the hell do you plan on ever meeting a girl?"

Jesse laughed. "Do you really think I'm going to meet my wife out at a bar with a bunch of professional football players? You're delusional. The only women I would meet there are money-grubbing mooches. Not interested."

"Your dick has to at least be interested."

Jesse shook his head at his brother. He always said what was on his mind. Johnny, Ryker, and Mason would all get along quite nicely; that was why Jesse kept his brother far, far away from his teammates…they would be lethal together.

"Is this why you called? To talk about my dick?"

"No, but seriously, whatever happened with that girl that you thought was gorgeous?"

Shoving a huge piece of omelet in his mouth, Jesse said, "Can't answer, eating."

"What was her name?" Johnny continued. "I think it was Ashley, no Ashlin. That's it. Whatever happened with her?"

Jesse blanched at her name. He always did. Ryker brought Ashlin to a game once, and she had on-field passes that allowed her access to everything. Jesse had a hard time concentrating that day, because he couldn't take his eyes off of her. She was, by far, the most gorgeous woman he had ever laid eyes on, and now he was regretting ever telling his brother, because he always asked about Ashlin.

"Nothing. How many times do I have to tell you that?"

"You couldn't stop talking about her. You're just going to let it go? Why not ask Ryker for her number."

Shaking his head, Jesse said, "No, there is no way I can do that. Ashlin and Ryker have some kind of weird relationship, plus, the idiot would never let me live it down."

"You're not going to ask for her number because you don't want to be picked on? What the hell is wrong with you?"

"Just drop it, Johnny, okay? I'm not in the mood."

"Damn. Maybe you'd be in the mood if your dick wasn't only mating with your hand."

"I'm hanging up now. Take care of my baby girl, Daisy. I'll come over tomorrow."

Jesse hung up the phone with his brother and rinsed off his plate. Once the kitchen was clean, he sat on his couch, and started watching sports highlights as he thought about Ashlin. He would give anything to just go on one date with the goddess, but he knew there was no way he would get the chance because of Ryker and because of how damn shy Jesse was. Ashlin needed an outspoken guy like Ryker, not a hermit like him.

Jax

"No, not the supreme plus, just the supreme," Jax said, as he pulled out his credit card.

"But, sir, for only an additional eight dollars, you can get a body gloss and tire dressing."

Jax raised a quizzical eyebrow at the pimply-faced, overeager sales boy. Jax handed his credit card over to the boy and said, "Just the supreme. Thank you."

The boy leaned in and looked a little closer at Jax. The boy's eyes widened as he took in Jax's appearance.

"You're Coach Ryan! Holy shit! Man, I love the Stallions. Dash is my favorite player, that guy is a total stud. I bet he gets all the ladies."

At the mention of Mason's nickname, Jax cringed. He hated Mason with a deep passion, but he couldn't lie, the dickhead was damn good at catching a football, and one of the reasons why they were doing so well this season.

"He was out with some brunette the other night," the boy

8

continued, "I saw pictures on one of those chick websites. My friend posted it on Facebook, and whenever there's news about Dash, I'm all over it. Anyway, that girl was damn fine. Seriously, he is the man."

Jax tried not to snarl as the boy went on and on about the one man Jax couldn't stand. Jax saw the same pictures the other day. It made Jax want to rip heads off…seeing Mason with someone other than Piper. Not that he wanted Mason and Piper together, but the fact that Jax went through all that pain and suffering for nothing made him want to blast heads right off.

"Yup, he's a pretty cool guy," Jax said, while tamping down the bile that started to rise in his throat.

"You can say that again. Hey, you sure you don't want the supreme plus? You can afford it," the boy said with a shit-eating grin.

Jax was seconds from telling the butt plug to fuck off, but instead, he just smiled politely and said no thank you. He knew what a rip off the "body gloss" was, he wasn't going to pay an extra eight dollars for crap.

Handing his keys off to one of the washers, Jax went into the waiting area, grabbed a Coke and a Three Musketeers bar, and went to sit down in one of the chairs that overlooked the cars running through the car wash conveyor belt.

The Stallions had the day off today, and instead of cuddling with a warm body like he would have enjoyed, he decided to run errands…fucking errands! He had no life, at all. He was either at the stadium, on the road with the team, or at home sleeping. There wasn't much to his days now that Piper was gone.

Piper.

Damn, did she do a number on him. It had been three months, and even though the pain had lessened from losing her, his rage was still very much present. He was mad for being fucked over, lied to, and losing to the infamous Dash. Jax rolled his eyes just from thinking about the nickname.

Jax heard the click of heels walk by him as he shoved the last bit of his candy bar in his mouth. Red pumps walked by him, attached to toned bronze legs. Just as he was about to look up to see if the rest of the woman's body matched the mouth-watering legs, the woman slipped on the floor where it was just mopped and started falling backwards.

Not even thinking, Jax fell to his knees and caught the woman before her butt hit the ground. Her brunette hair fanned over his arms as he held onto her back. He was rewarded with a flowery scent as he breathed her in.

"Whoa, careful there."

"Damn, wet floor. Like mopping is going to make it any better looking."

Jax's ears perked up at hearing a familiar voice. He lifted them both up so they were standing. The woman was brushing off her navy blue, hip-hugging skirt, so he couldn't tell who it was, but when she looked up, Jax instantly knew why he recognized the woman's voice.

"Brooke?"

Her eyes widened, and then recognition fell over her features.

"Jax. Wow, never thought I would ever cross paths with you again. How's it going?"

"Alright, and yourself?"

As Brooke talked about her new clothing line and her little apartment in downtown Denver, Jax took her all in. Her hair was short now, just below chin length, and styled to frame her face. Her body was the same rocking figure he remembered from when he met her at the bar, that awkward night his boys and Jake Taylor all hung out before a pre-season game, and for some reason, her eyes were brighter than he remembered, as if she was breathing a new life.

"Here, let's sit down," Jax offered.

They both sat down in two chairs in the waiting room that had a side table sitting between them. Brooke crossed one of her legs over the other, drawing Jax's attention to her lower limbs. Had it really been that long since he'd been with a woman that he couldn't help but stare at her?

"It sounds like you're doing great. That's good to hear," Jax said absentmindedly, as he continued to peruse Brooke's body.

"Yeah, it took some time, but once I pulled my head out of my ass, grew up a little, and decided to do something for myself, I was able to really put together some sketches and make my dream a reality…with some help from my dad, of course, but I'll be paying him back. How about you? How are you doing?"

In an offhanded way, Jax knew she was asking about his break up with Piper and, for once, he knew he could talk to someone about it who would truly understand.

"I'm doing better. I don't believe I miss her anymore. I know she wasn't the girl for me, and I've come to accept that, but I still can't get over the anger that boils up inside of me when I think about everything that happened."

"That's understandable," Brooke said, as she placed her hand on his arm. "I was a part of that whole clusterfuck of a love….square? And I made some choices that I wish I could take back, but it's in the past now. I'm moving forward with my life and forgetting about what happened back then. I figure, if I dwell on the past, it's going to get me nowhere, so I'm just going to move forward."

Jax was surprised by the new and improved Brooke that was sitting before him. She was different then when he last saw her. She was more confident in herself, and not just in her looks. She was sexy as hell, but not in an obvious way like she used to be with her short shorts and low-cut shirts. Now, she was classy, but still gorgeous.

"Black escalade," called one of the workers, letting Jax know that his car was done. Jax got up and let the man know he would be right there.

Taking a huge leap of faith, Jax said, "This might be really weird, but do you think I could have your number? I would love to take you out."

A big smile spread across Brooke's face as she reached into

her purse and pulled out a business card.

"I would love to go out. Give me a call anytime."

"I will. We're home this week, so maybe we can go out Wednesday night?"

"Sounds great to me. I look forward to it, Jax."

"Me too."

With that, Jax gave her a small, dorky wave and headed to his car. Who knew he was going to pick something up while he was running errands that he didn't have on his list? As he drove to the grocery store, he felt his chest start to loosen at the prospect of starting new, just like Brooke said. He needed to forget the past and move on; maybe Brooke was the person to help him do that.

Brooke

Brooke watched Jax walk out the door, and she couldn't help but stare at his jean-clad ass. When they first met, she apparently was so distracted by keeping Mason's attention that she never did a full once-over on Jax, because, damn, he was hot. He had a charming southern voice that she knew would make her toes curl in bed, his shirt clung to his defined biceps, and his jeans were tight in all the right areas. Seeing Jax confirmed Brooke's opinion of Piper, she really was a dumb hooker. Oh well, her loss and Brooke's gain.

Pulling her phone out, she dialed up her good friend, Lexi.

"Hey girl, I was just thinking about you," Lexi answered. "Jake has this event he has to go to, and it's kind of fancy, do you have a dress that would do this body justice?"

Brooke laughed and said, "You know any dress will do that body of yours justice, but yes, I think I have something that would work perfectly for you. I'll take a couple of pics and send them over, so you can see if you want me to send it over to you."

"Ahh, I love you. Thank you! Of course I'll be telling everyone I'm wearing an original Cali B design."

Cali B was the name of Brooke's clothing line. She was unsure of what to call her line, so she went with California and her first initial. She shortened it, and bam, Cali B was born. It was starting to catch on, and her hot pink logo was starting to show up all over clothing blogs and magazines. It was amazing to see something she dreamt of actually come to fruition.

"You better!"

"I always do, pretty. So tell me, why do I get to hear your lovely voice today?"

"Well, I just had to call you. You'll never guess who I just ran into."

"Hmm," Lexi paused. "Man or woman? Wait, don't answer that, you wouldn't be calling all excited if it was a girl. Is he attractive? Oh, my God, is he a celebrity?"

"Um, I guess he is a celebrity to some people?"

"Some people? That doesn't make any sense, why just some people? A celebrity is a celebrity. Yeah, some people might not know who they are, but they…"

"It was Jax," Brooke interrupted Lexi, who would have kept going on forever.

There was silence on the other end of the line as Lexi processed what Brooke just told her.

"Lex, you there?"

"Yeah, sorry. You mean Jax Ryan? The Stallions' offensive coordinator?"

"Yup, and guess what? He asked me out."

"He did not!" Lexi practically shouted. She screamed as Brooke pulled the phone away from her ear. "Jake! Jax Ryan asked out Brooke. Yes, he did!" There was mumbling on the other side of the phone, and then Brooke heard Lexi say, "She's on the phone right now. I'm not lying, Jake!"

"Brooke?" Jake's deep voice came over the phone.

"Hey, Jake."

"Did Jax Ryan really ask you out? My wife seems to be mistaken."

"She's not; Jax actually asked me out."

"No shit."

Brooke heard Lexi's voice in the background, "I told you!" which made Brooke laugh.

"Isn't that a twist? Jax Ryan, going after Mason's other girl. I wonder what was running through his mind."

Brooke's smile broke for a second, as she thought about what Jake was implying. She never considered the fact that Jax might have been asking her out to get back at Mason, not that she'd even talked to Mason after Piper showed up at his apartment, declaring her love for the man. After that, Brooke was done; she couldn't stand to be near the man who could be so hot and cold with her…she deserved better.

"Oh, do you think he only asked me out because of Mason?" Brooke said quietly.

"No!" Jake started backtracking. "Not at all. He probably was, like, wow, this chick is hot, I need a piece of her ass."

"Nice try, Jake, put your wife back on the phone."

"For what it's worth, Brooke, I think Jax would be lucky to go out with you. You have really turned your life around, and we couldn't be prouder."

"Thanks, Jake."

There was some shuffling of the phone, and Lexi came back on. "Sorry about that, Jake can be an idiot sometimes. Don't listen to what he said. Jax is definitely interested in you for you, not because of Mason. I mean, how could he not be? You're sexy and sweet and you have a good head on your shoulders…now." Brooke knew Lexi was smiling to herself.

"Smart ass. A girl loses her mind for a second, and her friends won't let her live it down."

"It was longer than a second, sweetie."

"Whatever. That section of my life is in the past, and just think, when we're older and talking to our grandchildren, we can tell them what a moron grand-mammy Brooke was, thinking she could make it big as a singer."

Lexi barked out in laughter. "I'm sorry, I don't mean to laugh, but Jesus, what the hell were you thinking?"

Brooke smiled to herself and shook her head. "Who knows, I want to say I was drunk, but I know I wasn't. I guess temporary insanity. Anyway, it looks like my car is about done being washed, so I'm going to go. Before I do, do you think I should go for it? Go out with Jax?"

"I think you should do whatever makes you happy, and if that means spreading your legs for Coach Ryan, then I say game on, Brooke."

"Spreading my legs, really? I'm a lady."

Lexi snorted and said, "I love you, but we both know that's not true."

"Bitch," Brooke said playfully. "I'll talk to you later."

CHAPTER TWO

Mason

"What about that one?" Ryker said, as he took a sip of his beer. "You can't tell me those are real tits."

Mason looked at the girl by the bar that Ryker was pointing to and examined her. She was talking to her friend, who looked like she'd spent too many hours in the tanning bed. Mason noticed that the girl Ryker pointed out had a really good rack...that was being elevated by a dangerously low-cut shirt. The way she talked with her hands made her boobs sway back and forth. They were real, no doubt in Mason's mind.

"They're real," Mason confirmed.

"No fucking way."

Mason pushed back his sleeves, drained the rest of his beer, and said, "There's only one way to find out."

"Watch out, ladies, donkey dick is on the prowl," Ryker practically shouted as Mason got up. Mason flipped his obnoxious friend off and ignored the comment about his dick; the man couldn't seem to get over the fact that Mason had his fair share of a vagina stuffer.

Walking up to the women at the bar, Mason caught their

attention as he stood right in front of them.

"Hey ladies, I'm Mason."

Big tits' eyes widened as she recognized who he was, and her friend, oven-baked, gasped as well.

"Mason Dashel, wow. It's nice to meet you," big tits said, as she held out her hand.

"It's my pleasure," Mason grabbed her hand in his and kissed the back of it. "I'm not going to bullshit you. I saw you across the bar, and I needed to know if those tits of yours are real."

A small smile spread across the girl's face, and she said, "Why don't you see for yourself?"

Mason raised his eyebrows as he took in the full package she was offering. He could fuck her for sure. She had a good body, her tits were tempting him to bury his face in them, and her face was decent. He could totally fuck this chick.

"How about we go somewhere more private?"

Big tits looked over at oven-baked and scanned for the secret girl-nod of approval. Mason looked over at oven-baked and noticed she wasn't very subtle at all, she was shaking her head, yes, like it was a damn maraca.

Big tits turned back to Mason and said, "Where to?"

"Follow me."

Mason guided big tits to the apartment above the bar that he had rented out. He had become good friends with the owner, who knew Mason didn't like taking girls back to his place, so instead, he took them to the apartment above the bar. It was quick, convenient, and when he was done stuffing them, he could leave them behind, on his own terms.

Turning on the lights to the apartment, Mason lit up the room just enough so he could faintly see big tits. She was good looking, but that was also in the dim light of the bar; Mason wanted to continue the illusion. The last thing he needed was to realize he'd brought up a fucking wart faced witch, when all he really wanted to do was titty fuck the bitch, blow his load, zip up, and go home to his big warm bed.

"Is this your place?" she asked, while looking around.

"Sure," Mason said, as he led her to the bedroom. He didn't want to start chit chatting. "Get on the bed, I'm going to plow my fucking dick through your tits until I come all over your face."

The girl squealed and took off her shirt as her back was toward Mason. He kept the lights off in the bedroom, so the only light filtering in was coming from the living room. There was just enough light that Mason could see everything, but nothing in detail.

She flopped her body on the bed, wearing only her jeans and bra...that was all he needed, just her big old tits.

"Take your bra off." She did as she was told, and that was when Mason got a good look at her saucer-sized nipples. Fuck, they were huge, almost a turn-off, but he wasn't going to let that deter him. Big nipples weren't a terrible thing.

When he walked closer, he almost laughed to himself, because he wished Ryker could see this girl. The girl's fucking nipples almost took up her entire breast, and the damn things were starting to get thick as hell.

Mason unbuttoned his shirt, but kept it on, because this was going to be a quick release for him. After seeing her saucer nipples, he knew this was going to be a one blow and go. He shucked his jeans as big tits licked her lips and stared at his impressive body. He knew he was ripped, he knew he had it going on, and this was the luckiest night of this bitch's life, but little did she know, he was just going to take what he wanted and get the hell out of the apartment.

He took his boxer briefs off and started massaging his cock. The sight of big tits in front of him was alright, but nothing that would have his dick poking him in the eye from excitement, so he closed his eyes for a second and, unfortunately, thought of a certain redhead's tight ass and perfect breasts. Once Piper came into his mind, he was instantly hard. Pleased with his dick, but mad at himself for relying on Piper's image to get him up, he walked toward big tits and straddled her stomach.

"Push your tits together, sweetheart." She nodded and pushed them together. He had to admit, if it weren't for the fucking pizza pie nipples, her tits would be amazing to stare at. He leaned down and pinched her nipples that were already hard as hell. The damn things were so thick, it felt like rubbing a baby carrot between his fingers. If he wasn't in such a rush, he would have bent down to get a better look, but his dick wasn't going to stay hard forever, especially with what he was working with.

Lowering his dick to her chest, he worked it between her breasts and started fucking her. His knees sat right below her armpits and his ass sat on her stomach. It was awkward as hell for her, but frankly, he didn't give a flying cow turd how she felt. Mason grabbed the headboard and braced himself as he plowed his dick through her breasts.

"That's it, just like that," Mason said. "Keep up that pressure."

As he thrust into her, he noticed something was tickling his knees, and it was starting to become distracting, but wanting to get this over with and find his release, he kept plowing forward.

"Let me lick you, Mason. I want to suck you off."

Mason considered finishing off in her mouth, but he wanted to keep this clean; he didn't know where her mouth had been, so he kept plowing forward. For all he knew, big tits had some fucking disease that would turn his dick green.

"Press your tits together, harder," Mason demanded, as he started to feel his balls tighten, which he was thankful for, because the tickling on his knees was starting to get really annoying.

"Let me know when you're going to…" At that moment, Mason blew his load all over her. "Come," she finished as Mason finished off.

He decorated her, straight up bedazzled her with his jiz, and damn if he didn't make her look good.

He got off her stomach and off the bed in one fell swoop. His job was done here. As he reached around for his pants, she turned on the lamp on the bed side table, making his eyes fight off the light as his pupils adjusted.

"Damn, woman, give a guy a warning before you blind him

with light."

"Oh, like you gave me a warning before you came all over my face."

"Listen, sweetheart," Mason turned around to face her, and when he did, he felt like dry heaving.

Big tits was laying on the bed, man paste scattered across her chest and neck, with her hands behind her head as she looked at him. She was actually pretty attractive, and she wore his cum well, but what had him pulling his jeans on as quickly as possible and not caring if he zipped up his dick were the thick-ass jungle armpits she was sporting.

Man hairs, actual man hairs sprouted from her armpits, and at that moment, he prayed to Jesus and his disciples that he did not just titty fuck a drag queen. Her tits were real, her tits were real, he kept saying to himself, but were they? .

"Holy fuck," he said out loud, not meaning to.

"Is everything okay?" she asked, while getting up and sauntering toward him.

She undid her pants and dropped them to the ground, revealing a thick patch of lap broccoli and sweater legs. There was hair...everywhere, hair spreading down her legs, swinging down from her armpits and sprouting out from under her thong.

Holy shit, he'd just titty fucked Sasquatch.

Ryker

Ryker sat in his booth as Mason took big tits up to his apartment, the man whore. Ryker knew Mason was losing himself completely in other women ever since Piper left, which was concerning, not because Ryker really cared too much about Mason's relationship, but at the rate Mason was going, his donkey dick was bound to contract something, and that would be a damn shame.

Looking around the bar, Ryker noticed there were some pretty good looking women, but no one he was particularly interested in taking home. Since the last time he talked to Hannah, which was about three months ago, he'd slept around a little, but just to get a fucking release, nothing that really pleased him…which was bothersome. He used to be the fun-loving bachelor, now he was the depressed Debbie Downer that no one wanted to be near. He couldn't blame them; he barely wanted to be near himself.

Taking a sip of his beer, he pulled out his phone and sent a text to Ashlin.

Ryker: What you up to, babe?

Luckily, Ryker and Ashlin were done with their photo shoots for C.C. Morris and the campaign was wrapped up. Posing and modeling clothes was supposed to be fun for Ryker, but instead, it turned into this intense sexual experience where he had to let Russell the Love Muscle learn to calm himself and not misbehave. Now, he was dealing with the after-effects of posing practically nude with Ashlin. To the world, they were a couple, but to them, they were just friends.

There was one night after a photo shoot where they got a little drunk and they might have slept together, but the next morning, when they were sober and the air in the room was awkward as hell, they both knew what they did was a huge mistake. They were meant to be friends, and that was it. Ryker wouldn't lie though, from what he could remember, she was a good fuck, but that was it; there was no emotional connection between them.

His phone beeped back.

Ashlin: Sitting in my room, looking at pictures of hot men. What are you up to?

Ryker smiled to himself as he responded.

Ryker: Sitting at a bar as Mason takes another girl up to his lair.

Ashlin: He is going to get a disease.

Ryker: Tell me about it. So I'm guessing I can't persuade you to come join me.

Ashlin: Not tonight. My face is off and my hair is a mess.

Ryker: Damn, I wouldn't want to see you without a face. That would be some scary shit. Alright, well, have a good night. I'll talk to you later.

Ashlin: Night Ryke.

Ryker put his phone away and thought about how damn lonely he was. He was pathetic. He knew he was the one who left Hannah to work out her shit on her own, but damn if he still didn't want her. He wanted to hold her, listen to her sweet laugh, and suck in her alluring scent.

Ryker's thoughts of Hannah were disturbed as Mason pulled up next to Ryker.

"Dude, let's get the fuck out of here." Mason was fidgeting with a look of panic crossing his features.

Draining his beer, Ryker left some money on the table and followed Mason out the door.

"What the hell is going on? Why are you acting like you just saw a ghost?"

Mason looked behind them as they walked to grab a cab. "Those were real tits…"

"Okay…" Ryker said, while trying to figure out what was wrong with his friend.

"And so was the damn hair all over her body."

Stopping on the sidewalk, Ryker looked at Mason and said, "Hair, what are you talking about?"

Mason turned around and said, "I'm not fucking with you when I say, Tarzan could do a couple of laps from her armpits with the damn coarse vines running down them. I'm pretty sure I threw up in my mouth."

Barking out in laughter, Ryker threw his head back and thought about big tits with the hairy pits.

"Oh, fuck, that is awesome," Ryker said, while wiping a tear.

"That's not even the worst of it." Ryker raised an eyebrow in question and waved for Mason to continue. "After I blew my load all over her and saw the fucking rat's nest in her armpits, I started getting the fuck out of there, but apparently she wasn't done, so she took her pants off…"

"Oh, fuck, please tell me there wasn't a serious case of burnt Ramen noodles down there…"

"Like she was trying to feed a fucking family of five…"

More laughter erupted from Ryker's belly as Mason went on to tell him about big tits' legs. "Oh, that is just too fucking good."

"And the fucking nipples on this girl, damn dude, I thought aliens were going to pop out of her nipples and take me away. They were fucking saucers."

Ryker was practically crying as they hailed a cab. "That's what you get for being a man whore. You have to choose wisely, man, or else you end up with big tits with hairy pits trying to abduct you with her alien nipples."

Mason flipped Ryker off and told the cabby where to go. Ryker couldn't have imagined a more perfect way to end his night.

Hannah

Dick's Last Chance, the bar Hannah worked at, was packed full for a Tuesday night, especially since there were no football games playing. Word must have gotten out that the Stallions' star players, Mason Dashel and Ryker Lewis used to frequent the bar, and now it was the place to be for every belching, nacho-eating, football fanatic.

"Leela, did you get that last table in the back?" Hannah asked the girl who took Piper's place permanently after she just up and left, without even saying goodbye. Hannah hadn't heard from Piper in three months. She even tried contacting Lexi, Piper's best friend, but Lexi hadn't heard from Piper either. They were all very concerned, but Lexi did say this was what Piper did; she just up and left when she wanted to. Apparently, Lexi had gone months without hearing from Piper, but she always popped back up, so Lexi wasn't too concerned, at least not yet.

"Yes, they would like two draft beers," Leela called out as she dropped off a couple bowls of nuts on a couple of tables. Currently, Leela was the one friend Hannah had in Denver. Leela was still going to school and working at night, trying to earn her degree while being paid under the table. Hannah didn't care, as long as she had someone to talk to.

Her life took a turn for Shitville the minute Todd's wife showed up at Dick's Last Chance and confronted Hannah. Shortly after that, she blew up at Ryker because she was mad, so mad that she was so incredibly stupid; she needed to take it out on someone, and unfortunately, Ryker was it.

Shortly after her blow up in the bar, she went back to her place, tossed everything of Todd's and everything he ever gave her into boxes and put them outside for free. Todd had yet to contact her or visit, which was fine by her; she didn't want to talk to the two-timing bastard. Instead of connecting with him, she just envisioned the irate look on his face when he found out that she put all his expensive, shoes, suits, cufflinks and colognes out on the curb for free. The image kept her moving forward with a smile on her face.

"You have those beers ready for me?" Leela asked, as she sidled up next to the bar.

Hannah shook her head, trying to get rid of her thoughts as she said, "Sorry, give me one second."

"You need to get your head out of the clouds," Leela said with her little Italian accent. How she was still single was beyond Hannah.

"Yeah, I know."

"You still thinking about that boy? What is his name? Ryker?"

Hannah had made the mistake of telling Leela all the sordid

details of her messed up life, and was now regretting it because, almost every day, Leela asked about Ryker. She picked up on the fact that Hannah had feelings for the man, and even though Todd lied to her about his…marriage, she still felt more of a loss from Ryker being out of her life.

"Yes and no," Hannah said shyly, as she handed Leela the two pints of beer she needed.

"Do you want to talk about it later, while we're closing up?"

"No, that's okay. There's really nothing to talk about. Just the same old same old. You don't need to hear me talk about nothing that is ever going to happen, or how bad I screwed everything up. Plus, you've seen the magazines, he's moved on."

Leela tisked her finger at Hannah. "You should know better. Those magazines do not speak the truth."

Hannah nodded her head as Leela walked off. She knew Leela was right, but it was hard not to believe what she saw. Ryker and Ashlin looked so perfect together; how could she not believe that they were together? Plus, she hadn't heard one word from Ryker, not that she should have; she'd royally screwed up where he was concerned.

Sighing to herself, she walked up and down the bar as patrons placed their orders and she fell into her normal routine. This was her life, this was as far as it was going to go. She had zero prospects in her love life because she was a massive idiot, and she had no other job opportunities presenting themselves to her for her to get out of tending bar. At least she hadn't taken Todd up on his offer and quit, then she would have been up a creek with no paddle.

CHAPTER THREE

Jesse

"Blue seventy two, blue seventy two. Hut, hut."

The center snapped the ball as Jesse fell into the well-formed pocket his offensive line had created for him. Turning to his right to throw off the defense, Jesse watched from the corner of his eye as Mason button hooked to the left and darted in front of the defense. Snapping the ball quickly, Jesse connected with Mason instantly and watched Mason run to the end zone for a touchdown.

Coach Ryan came out on the field clapping his hands as Jesse undid his chin strap.

"Perfect. Just like that. I think the fake to the right will throw the defense off, giving Dash enough time to get free of his defenders." Coach Ryan looked over to Ryker and said, "Good screen, Ryke. Mason, good catch." It almost pained the man to pay Mason a compliment, but at least they were cordial on the field. Few of the players knew what happened between Coach Ryan and Mason, but Jesse was one of the few; he kept it to himself, because he didn't need his team crumbling apart because one little redhead couldn't make up her damn mind.

"Huddle up, men," Coach Ryan said, as the team took their

helmets off and jogged into the center of the field. "You guys are looking sharp, let's end on a good note. Some of you need to meet me in the video room…you know who you are. As for the rest of you dickheads, get a good night's rest. I'll see you tomorrow morning for lifting."

Coach Ryan was one of the rare coaches who actually worked out with the guys in the weight room. The man did his own cardio, but he was always in the weight room with all of them.

Jesse didn't have to review video, because he'd done it earlier in the morning, so he was done for the day. As he was walking off the field, Ryker ran up behind him and hopped on his back.

"Oh, Jesse, You're my hero!"

"Get off of me," Jesse laughed, as he tried to wiggle Ryker off of him…who was trying to lean in and kiss him. He walked by Mason and called out, "Can you get this dick off of me?"

"He's your problem, dude. Not mine."

"Ryker, get off of your quarterback."

Jesse's head snapped up from the sweet voice that called out to Ryker. Ashlin was standing on the sidelines wearing a short pair of denim shorts, a Stallions T-shirt jersey and a pair of sandals. Her hair was pulled back into a ponytail, and she looked damn fine. It was a warm fall day in Denver, which was good news for Jesse, because he got to see Ashlin in shorts. She was a knockout. Completely frozen, Jesse stood in place, as if someone had shocked him and he couldn't move.

Ryker flew off of Jesse's back and ran to pick up Ashlin, who he spun around. Once he put her down, he gave her a noogy, a fucking noogy. Ashlin swatted away his hands as she tried to fix her hair.

"You ass! Why do you always have to mess up my hair?"

"Because it's fun," Ryker responded, as he started checking out Ashlin. "Why the hell are you wearing Jesse's number on your back?"

Jesse's already listening ears picked up as he listened to her answer, desperately wanting to know why she was wearing his number.

"Because he's hot." She looked over at Jesse and gave him a wink, making him weak in the knees. He was so beyond pathetic. "Plus, it was the only size that fit me."

The shirt clung to every part of her body…she thought that fit?

"Stop shopping in the kids' section, and maybe you'll find something that fits you."

"You're a real jokester today, aren't' you?"

Jesse didn't want to be the creeper watching them interact any more than he was, so he nodded toward Ryker and started walking toward the locker room as he called out, "See you tomorrow, bud. Good practice."

"Hold up, Jesse. Have you met Ashlin?"

A smile spread across Jesse's face as he walked over to Ryker and Ashlin. He could kiss Ryker right now, but instead, he held out his hand to Ashlin and said, "I don't believe we've met. Jesse, nice to meet you."

Ashlin placed her small hand in his and smiled brightly up at him. "Ashlin, it's good to finally meet a good looking Stallion."

"You're really looking to get yourself into trouble today, aren't you?" Ryker playfully scolded.

"What are you going to do about it? You know I own you."

Ryker thought about it for a second and said, "Yeah, you do, but only because you have incriminating photos of me from our childhood."

"And don't you forget it," she pointed at Ryker and then looked back up at Jesse. Her eyes were gorgeous, the brightest green Jesse had ever seen; he couldn't help but stare. "It was really nice to meet you, Jesse. Hopefully, I'll see more of you around."

"I'll hold you to that," Jesse said, as he walked away.

Finally taking a deep breath, he noticed he was sweating, not from practice, but from being so close to the girl that had been haunting his thoughts for a while.

He shook his head at himself as he thought back to his

conversation. He would hold her to it? What the fuck was he saying? Did he sound like a total corn dog back there?

Wanting to shove his head through a wall for acting like an idiot, well at least in his mind he thought he was acting like an idiot, he grabbed his towel and went to the showers. Quickly cleaning himself, toweling off and putting some clothes on, he bent down to put on his shoes when Mason came up next to him and sat down.

Mason got in his face and said, "So, you like Ashlin."

Jesse's head snapped up and looked at the shit-eating grin Mason was sporting. Dickhead.

"What? I don't know what you're..."

"Cut the crap," Mason interrupted. "I saw you staring at her and Ryker. You were a total creeper, practically drooling."

"I was not drooling," Jesse fought back. He looked down at his feet and quietly said, "Was it that obvious?"

"Uh, yeah buddy. I think you need to learn to be more subtle."

"Fuck," Jesse ran his hand down his face. "Is Ryker going to kill me?"

Mason raised his eyebrow in question, "Why would Ryker kill you?"

"Because I was staring at his girl." Jesse wanted to smack Mason in the head and say "duh," but he held back.

Mason looked at Jesse for a second and then threw his head back in laughter, making Jesse want to shove his foot in the wide receiver's ass.

"There are so many things wrong with that sentence. First of all, Ryker, kill you? Please, I'm surprised the boy can even play football. That dude is a total dweeb; he wears pink shirts with boat shoes, for fuck's sake. Secondly, Ryker is so hung up on this girl, Hannah, that he would never be in a relationship with Ashlin; they're just friends, Jess. That's it."

Perking his head up, Jesse said, "Seriously? They seem like they're more than friends."

"They're close, I'll give them that, but there's nothing

there. I believe they fucked once, but that was it."

"Great." Jesse threw his hands up and stood up to grab his keys and phone.

Mason stopped Jesse and said, "Listen, if you like her, go for it. There should be nothing holding you back. It would be nice to finally see you do something about the single life you lead."

"Oh, this advice coming from the biggest man whore in the world, who apparently likes to fuck girls with hairy armpits."

Mason clenched his fists and said, "Fucking Ryker," as he shook his head.

"You know, I've never been with a hairy Mary, tell me...was it good?"

"Fuck off," Mason said while walking away. "I'm in for your party on Saturday. I'll be sure to make sure Ashlin is there, and that's because I love you, man," Mason said, playfully holding his heart.

"You're just bribing me so I pass to you more."

"I don't have to bribe you, man. You don't have any other choices if you want the pass complete."

"What faith you have in your teammates," Jesse smiled.

"Can't pass up the mother fucking best, Jesse."

Cocky son of a bitch.

Brooke

"What the hell am I doing?" Brooke said to herself as she looked in the mirror. She was wearing a pair of dark colored jeans, brown boots and a yellow sweater with a matching scarf.

She was going out with Jax to a casual burger joint for dinner, and she could not be more nervous. She hadn't been out on a date in quite some time, not since she and Mason were actually dating, and that was a while ago. Jax was a nice guy, and he was hot as hell, but then again, he was connected to Mason, and Brooke really wanted to cut all ties with the man, especially after all the crap they had gone through.

Regret from agreeing to go out with Jax started to settle in as she finished up her mascara.

"This was a bad idea," she said to no one.

She was about to take out her phone and cancel her date, when there was a knock on her door. He was here. She quickly put her mascara away and told herself she would just fake a stomachache and ask to reschedule. There was no way she could go out with the man.

Answering the door and getting ready to fake sick, she made eye contact with Jax, and all the tension and nerves she was feeling instantly vanished when she took the man in. He was wearing jeans with white Nikes and a white polo shirt that stretched across his muscular chest and clung to his biceps. What really caught her eye was the big smile that was spread across his face. He was truly happy to see her, and hell if she could let the man down, plus…he was so damn handsome. Maybe she could do this.

"Hi," she said, as she smiled back.

"You look great, Brooke."

"Thank you. Are you ready?"

"Yeah, do you mind if I drive?"

"Of course not."

Brooke locked up her apartment and followed Jax out to his truck that was towering over the curb. She looked up at him with a questioning eye. He shrugged his shoulders and said, "Southern boys love their big trucks."

"Apparently."

Jax held the door open for her and then helped her climb in by offering a hand. Once she was settled, he asked, "Have you got your pretty self all buckled up?"

Smiling down at him, she said, "Strapped in and ready to go."

They drove to The Cherry Cricket, where Jax claimed they had the best burgers in Denver. Brooke had never been, so she was ready to be blown away.

Once they were seated, Jax grabbed her menu away from her and asked, "Do you trust me?"

Brooke crossed her arms over her chest and said, "I don't know. I don't really know you all that well."

"Have I given you any reason not to trust me?"

Brooke smiled and said, "Well…you did date Piper…"

Jax barked out in laughter and said, "Touché, but you can't hold that against me. Call it a momentary lapse in judgment and, hey, you dated Mason and were engaged to the man."

"You were engaged to Piper!" Brooke playfully said back.

"For a day, you were engaged for a while…"

Brooke held up her hand, "Fine. Let's call a truce."

"Works for me. So…do you trust me?"

Brooke leaned back in her chair and looked Jax up and down. He was so damn cute it was hard not to give in to him.

"I guess so," she answered, just as the waitress walked up.

"Good." He looked up at the waitress and said, "Can we get two cheeseburgers with bacon, egg and peanut butter on them, a basket of fries, and two Cokes?" He handed the menu back to the waitress as she nodded her head and walked away.

"Peanut butter and egg? On a burger? Are you insane?"

Laughing, Jax said, "I swear, you're going to love it."

"Alright…" she dragged out.

"So, tell me a little about yourself," Jax said, while placing his forearms on the table and leaning forward, as if she had the most intriguing story to tell.

"Well, I'm from San Diego…that's where I met Lexi, Jake, and unfortunately, Mason. We all went to school together at Cal U. I temporarily lost my mind…"

"We'll blame it on Mason," Jax interrupted with a smirk.

"Good idea. So, Mason made me temporarily insane, and I thought I could be a singer, when in fact," she leaned forward like she was telling a secret, "I can't carry a note to save my life." Jax laughed and waved her on to continue. "So, after some soul searching, I decided to pull my head out of my ass and make something of myself."

"Well, you've done a good job. Is that one of your designs?"

Jax said, while gesturing to her off-the-shoulder sweater.

"Yes, it is. It's part of the fall collection."

"Well, it's hot."

A bright smile spread across Brooke's face. "Thank you."

"Can I be honest with you?" Jax asked.

"Of course."

He leaned forward some more and said, "I changed my clothes probably about five times because I was so nervous about what to wear to dinner with a designer. I'm no Ryker Lewis, that's for sure."

Brooke couldn't help but chuckle. "Oh, God, you're so cute. If you wore what Ryker wore, I don't think I could get past the front door with you." Ryker was well known to experiment with patterns, colors and textures. The man was insane when it came to pairing clothes together, but for some reason, it always worked. The man had style.

"So, you don't think orange shirts with seahorses and Bermuda shorts would look good on me?"

"Ha! No," Brooke shook her head while laughing. "What you're wearing is perfect. Tight and sexy and all male."

A devilish grin spread across Jax's face. "You think I'm sexy?"

"Don't push your luck," Brooke said, while pointing at him. "We'll see how I feel about you after this burger arrives."

They were talking about their favorite dessert places in downtown Denver when the waitress brought their plates out.

Looking at the concoction on the plate in front of her, she lifted her head and eyed Jax.

"I promise you'll like it. Just give it a try."

"And if I don't like it?"

"Then I will get you whatever you want."

"Anything?" she asked, while wiggling her eyebrows.

Jax shifted in his seat and cleared his throat, making Brooke laugh to herself. "Watch yourself little lady; it's not good to tease a southern man."

"Oh, and why is that?"

"Because we are only gentlemen for so long."

"Hopefully, that's the truth," Brooke said, while taking a bite of the gigantic burger that was on her plate.

She hated to admit it, but her taste buds were rejoicing over the delectable burger. She hated to admit Jax was right, but damn it, he was.

"Damn," she said, while shaking her head.

"What's wrong?" Serious concern stretched across Jax's face.

"I was really hoping to get whatever I wanted, but damn, this burger is good."

Jax winked and said, "Told ya, but just because I'm a good sport, I'll still give you whatever you want."

"Of course you would." Brooke shook her head at the adorable man that sat across from her and took another bite of her burger. She was thankful she didn't chicken out on their date, because she was having a great time with Jax.

Mason

Stretching out on his couch, Mason grabbed the last bite of his sandwich and shoved it in his mouth as his phone began to ring. Muting *Sports Center*, Mason grabbed his phone and answered it.

"Hey, ass wipe," Mason answered with a mouth full of sandwich.

"Please tell me your mouth is full of food and not pussy," Jake, Mason's best friend, responded.

"Jake Taylor!" Lexi scolded in the background, making both of them laugh.

"What do you think?" Mason asked.

"I think your sorry ass is stretched out on your couch, wearing a pair of shorts, drinking a beer and watching highlights."

Mason assessed himself and had to hand it to his friend, he'd nailed it.

"It disturbs me how much you know about me," Mason

responded.

"Who would I be if I didn't properly stalk you? Those red shorts you have on really bring out your eyes, by the way."

"Nice try, dickhead. They're black."

"Damn," Jake laughed. "That would have been the fucking tits if I got that right."

"Has married life really been that boring? You have to dream about what I'm wearing? I know you miss me, man, but come on, you have a hot blonde lying next to you. Play with her."

Jake laughed and said, "She is pretty hot, isn't she?"

Mason rolled his eyes and said, "Is there a reason for this phone call?"

"I just wanted to see how my best man was doing. Your Stallions seem to be killing it lately. I'm impressed."

"That's what happens when you have Dash the Donkey Dick on your team."

Jake barked out in laughter. "Jesus, I think that thin mountain air is starting to go to your head."

"Look at the numbers, baby! I'm fucking killing it, but I'm sure you don't want to talk about that, given the fact that your fucking Thunder are sitting at a sad second to last place in your division."

Jake blew out a frustrated breath. "Seriously, try fucking throwing to a bunch of fairies floating around with their heads cut off. I swear to God, I'm going to kill them."

Mason laughed as Jake went on about his wide receivers, who were by far the worst in the league. The only reason the Thunder were not in last place was because they had an amazing running back.

"Seriously, can I please just tell you, my fucking favorite highlight of all time is when your receivers were crossing paths as you threw the ball, they ran into each other and the ball bounced off one of their helmets and into the other team's hands? Holy fuck, I don't think I have ever laughed so hard in my life."

"Yeah, that fucking clip is still number one on *Sports Center's*

Not So Top Ten. I don't think the two assholes will ever live it down."

"Hey, at least it wasn't something you did. You could have had the infamous butt fumble."

"Let's not go there," Jake said, while laughing. "So, how's it going, dude? I heard you titty fucked a hairy beast?"

"Fucking Christ! I'm going to chop Ryker's dick off." Jake was laughing in the background as Mason continued. "I can't tell that prick anything."

"I'm surprised you're just learning that. He gossips more than the girls in our lives."

"Sure fucking does, and don't you mean girl in your life? There is no girl in my life."

"Yeah, and why is that?"

"Don't need one," Mason said, matter of factly.

"Apparently, you do if you're trying to fuck the nipples off of Cousin It."

"Once again, is there a point to this phone call?" Mason asked, while waiting impatiently for *Sports Center* to show their Not So Top Ten again.

"Have you heard from Piper?"

Damn, the man had balls, Mason had to give Jake that. At the mention of Piper's name, Mason's stomach flipped. He was hurting, badly, but he still wanted her; he wanted her so damn much.

"No," Mason said, getting straight to the point.

"No one has," Jake said with concern in his voice.

"What do you mean?" Mason said, as he sat up on his couch.

"Lexi's finally starting to get worried, because it's not like Piper to go this long without talking to anyone, so she called Piper's parents to see if they had heard from her, and they didn't even know she was in Denver for a while. She has disappeared, man."

Mason ran a hand over his face as his heart started to beat rapidly against his chest. Instantly, his mind went to the worst, as thoughts of what possibly could have happened to Piper ran through his head. He shouldn't care; he shouldn't have this aching feeling in the pit of his gut, but he couldn't help it. The damn girl drove a wedge in his heart and left it there.

Putting on a front, not wanting to show his true feelings, Mason said, "Well, that's just something that I don't give a fuck about."

"Mason…"

Mason cut Jake off. "Listen, man, you're my best friend, and I get what you're trying to do, but your concern is doing nothing but making me irate, so just drop it. If she wants to jump off the face of the earth and disappear, then so be it. It's not my responsibility to worry about her. She dug herself a grave, she can live in it now."

There was silence on the other end of the line and Mason wondered if he might have gone too far.

"I don't believe a single piece of crap that has spewed from your mouth. I know you, Mason, and I know you care about her; I know you love her…"

"I'm going to stop you right there. Love is nonexistent in my world."

"Stop being a stubborn fuck. I know you love her, Mason. You just can't stop loving someone. It doesn't work like that."

"Well, it does in my world. Now I'm going to go, because frankly, I love you, man, but you're pissing me the fuck off. Say hey to Lexi for me. Talk to you later." With that, Mason hung up his phone and tossed it to the side.

Placing his forearms on his knees and leaning forward, he grabbed his head and thought about what Jake had said. Piper was missing. No one had heard from her. Was she dead? Did she need help?

Mason chastised himself for caring; he shouldn't care at all. He fucked her over, so he shouldn't care…right? He went to his fridge and grabbed a six pack of beer. He was going to need to drown himself in sorrow as he headed back to his couch to get lost in the micro-brew.

Jax

Jax couldn't remember the last time he laughed so much. Not only was Brooke gorgeous and charming, but she was funny, something he didn't know when they first met, probably because she was fighting for Mason's attention.

They pulled up to her apartment and Jax got out of his truck to help Brooke out on the other side. He opened her door and held out his hand so she could get down. She took it and jumped down from the high cab.

"Careful there." Jax steadied her as she slightly wobbled.

"Could you have gotten a bigger truck?" she asked playfully.

"I could have. Should I go truck shopping again?"

"No!" Brooke said, as she shut the door and started walking to her door.

"Are you not going to say goodbye to me?" Jax asked, as he stood next to his truck with his hands in his pockets.

She turned around and smiled at him, "Are you not going to be a gentleman and walk me to my door?"

Jax laughed and said, "I told you the gentleman act only goes so far. There is a limit."

Brooke turned around and sauntered back to him. She placed both of her hands on his chest and pushed him against the truck.

"Since the gentleman in you is gone, does that mean you're willing to fuck me tonight?"

Holy Shit.

Jax pulled on his neck as he looked down at Brooke. Damn, he wanted her. He wanted her badly, but did he want to take things slow? He thought about Piper and how they waited…and look how that turned out. He looked down at Brooke and saw the lust in her eyes, at that moment, that's all he cared about, nothing else.

"Show me the way, darlin'," Jax said with a strong southern accent.

Brooke smiled brightly, grabbed his hand, and rushed him up to her apartment. She quickly unlocked her door, threw her things on the ground, and took him to her room.

Her bedroom was decorated in black and white fabrics with a big bed in the middle that was calling to him. There were little personal touches everywhere in her room, but he chose to look at them later, because right now, there was a sexy woman waiting for him.

"I like your room," Jax said awkwardly, as he looked around.

Brooke looked up at him in question. "Seriously, Jax? Is that the best you've got?"

Jax laughed and walked toward her until she was pressed up against her bedroom door. "Don't sass me."

Without even giving her a chance to respond, Jax grabbed her head with his hands and brought his lips down on hers. With the first contact of their lips melding together, Jax could feel himself slipping away. She was so soft, so sweet, and he couldn't get enough.

"Mmm," she moaned, as he glided his tongue across her lips.

"Open for me," he said against her lips.

She opened her mouth and he slipped his tongue inside. Her tongue matched his strokes as his hands started to slowly glide down her body. She wrapped her hands around his neck and pulled him in closer as she pressed her body up against his. His arousal was already pressing against her, so she knew he was more than ready and willing to take her.

Running his hands down to her ribs, right below her breasts, he started making slow circles with his thumbs. The feel of her body pressed against his and the clumsiness of the sweater she was wearing had Jax feeling very eager to rip all her clothes off.

"Take this thing off," Jax said, as he started lifting the hem of her sweater.

She put her arms in the air, allowing Jax to take the sweater off of her, which revealed a perfectly pink bra that pushed her breasts up to an impossible height, making his mouth water.

Running a hand over his mouth, he took a step back and looked at her.

"You're so beautiful."

"Your turn," she said, as she grabbed the hem of his shirt and brought it over his head as well, dropping it right next to her sweater.

Her eyes widened as she took in the expanse of his chest. Her hands started roaming his muscles as she took in his strong build.

"Fuck, you're sexy," she smiled up at him. "For an old man, who knew you could be so ripped?"

"Old man?" Jax scolded playfully. "I don't think being ten years your senior makes me old."

"Don't say 'your senior.' Saying things like that makes you sound old."

"What did I say about sassing me? Respect your elders!"

Brooke rolled her eyes, causing Jax to grab her, pick her up, and toss her on her bed. He took her boots, socks and pants off, leaving her in nothing but a small set of pink lingerie.

"Did you wear those panties to drive me crazy?"

"Is it working?"

"Fuck, yeah."

"Then, yes, I did."

"Smartass," Jax said, as he leaned down and placed both of his hands on either side of Brooke's face. He hovered above her lips as he asked, "Are we moving too fast?"

"Well, we went on one date and now we are practically naked in front of each other. I would say we are, but then again, I've never wanted anything more in my life than right now."

Jax knew he shouldn't mention it, but he had to, just to make sure. "You're not doing this to get back at Mason, are you?"

The look of shock on Brooke's face let Jax know he was wrong, completely and utterly wrong.

"Is that what you really think of me, Jax? You know, I could ask you the same thing…are you doing this to get back at Mason?"

Jax pushed away from her and said, "Does it look like I'm the type of guy who would do that?"

"I don't know. I don't know you at all."

"You're right, you don't. This was a mistake," Jax said, as he bent down and grabbed his shirt. He threw her door open, put his shirt on, and walked toward her front door. He wanted Brooke, but he didn't want her like this. He didn't want her thinking his liking her had anything to do with Mason.

"Jax, wait," Brooke said, as she ran up behind him. "I'm sorry." She pressed her hand against his back, letting him know that she wanted him to turn around.

Slowly, Jax turned around as he ran his hand through his hair. "No, I'm sorry Brooke. I shouldn't have brought it up. Please excuse me for being a paranoid fuck, but I've been screwed over before, and it's kind of hard for me to trust any woman right now."

In understanding, Brooke nodded her head and pulled away. "I'm not going to lie, that sucks, and it sucks that you can't trust me, but I understand."

"It doesn't mean that I can't ever trust you. I just have to get my head straight first."

"Okay."

Jax ran both his hands over his face in frustration. "God dammit!" He pushed his hands down and then looked at Brooke. "Ahh, fuck it!"

Not giving Brooke a chance to think, he grabbed her little body, took her to her couch, tore her underpants down, and buried his face between her legs, surprising the hell out of her and himself. He spread her legs like a crazed man and swiped his tongue through her already slick folds. He looked up to see Brooke leaning against the back of her couch with her eyes closed and her arms gripping the back of the cushions.

"Ah, shit!" she screamed, as he stuck two fingers in her entrance. "Feels so good," she mumbled.

Spreading her even wider and pulling her pelvis out from the couch, he continued to taste her, nibble, and lick the fuck out of her. Her body seized and he was instantly rewarded with the cry of his name and the surge of wetness from her orgasm. He rode every wave with her, not letting up until she couldn't take it anymore.

When she finally came down from her orgasm, she slowly opened her eyes and looked up at him with sated eyes. His job here was done.

Leaning down, he placed a kiss on her lips and said, "I will call you, got it?"

She nodded her head and pulled on his neck to bring his lips back. She kissed his lips slowly and said, "Got it."

"Good."

CHAPTER FOUR

Ryker

"Where the hell are the damn beans?" Ryker said out loud, as he looked around the canned food section. "This should not be that difficult."

He hated going to the grocery store, and not being able to find anything was one of the main reasons why; the other main reason, he hated cooking. He did bump into Hannah once while he was in the grocery store, and that was one of the best days he'd had in a while because, not only did she help him get food for dinner, but she went back to his place and helped him cook it. He could never look at tacos the same way again.

"Fucking tacos," Ryker mumbled, as he stared at a can of kidney beans. "These are not what I'm looking for."

Throwing a temper tantrum, Ryker grabbed his phone and started typing a text to Jesse that he was not going to bring anything to his damn party, because he couldn't find the damn beans. As he was wrapping up his text and heading out of the aisle, he ran into a cart that crippled him to the ground. The corner of the cart hit him right in the junk, making him double over in pain.

Dropping to his knees and holding onto his crotch, he

bellowed, "Ah fuck, my dick," not even caring that there were children around.

"Oh, my God, I'm so sorry."

Ryker's head snapped up as he looked into a set of pale, light blue eyes.

Hannah.

"Ryker?" Hannah's brow crinkled as she looked down at him. "Oh, I'm so sorry. I didn't see you there."

"Clearly," Ryker grunted out, as he rolled on the floor while silently apologizing to Russell the Love Muscle.

"Well, you were looking at your phone…"

Ryker flashed her a look of death and she backed up. She reached into her cart and held out a bag of peas. "Do you want to ice…it?" A small smile spread across her face.

"I'm taking these peas," Ryker said, as he shook the bag at her, right before icing off his balls and dick. Hannah stood above him, trying to hide her snickering. "It's not that funny. I could punch you in the tit, and we could compare the pain."

"You're being a baby."

Ryker glanced up and tried to contain the sigh that was threatening to escape him. Even after three months, seeing Hannah gutted him. She was so beautiful, so innocent.

Trying not to look at her any more than necessary, he scooted his body against the shelving and held the package of peas to his crotch. A store clerk walked by and eyed Ryker up and down.

"Sir, are you going to buy those peas?" A chuckle escaped Hannah, who turned away to hide her smirk.

"Nope!" Ryker tossed the peas down the aisle and got up…slowly. "I'm the creep who comes into stores and presses peas to his penis." Ryker eyed the cart that almost took out Russell and flipped it off. "Fucking cart." As he was turning around, he saw what was in Hannah's cart, and he rejoiced. He reached down and grabbed the baked beans that were in there. "I'm taking these," he held them up as he looked at Hannah.

She just smiled and let him limp away. Another not-so-successful trip to the grocery store. Jesse owed him big time.

As Ryker climbed into his car after checking out, he turned his car on and was about to pull out of the parking spot when his phone chimed with a text message. He looked down at his phone and saw that it was from Hannah. He banged his head against the steering wheel in defeat.

"Why?" he said as his hand opened the text message. He didn't want to see her, to hear from her. He was trying to move on from the practically nothing they'd shared together.

Just running into her at the grocery store nearly took his breath away. She was just as gorgeous as she was a couple of months ago. She was just too perfect, and even though he wanted to rebel against his feelings, he couldn't. He couldn't let go.

Hannah: Sorry about your...area. I hope it feels better. P.S. I paid for the penis peas. The clerk did not seem happy.

A small smile spread across Ryker's face as he thought about Hannah texting penis. She was very much an innocent girl who never swore and barely talked about sexual things. Not even thinking about what he was doing, he texted back.

Ryker: It was the least you could do since you nearly castrated me.

Hannah: Once a drama queen, always a drama queen...

Smiling to himself, Ryker put his phone down and pulled out of his parking space. For the first time in three months, his chest felt a little lighter. He didn't want to feel happy about seeing Hannah, but at the moment, he knew he couldn't help himself. She was his girl, and even though she hurt him terribly, he still needed her.

Ryker pulled up to Jesse's house, which was more like a mansion on a ranch on the outskirts of Denver. Ashlin was meeting him here, so when he saw her car was pulling up behind

45

him, he was relieved they'd showed up at the same time. He got out of the car, grabbed his two cans of beans, and walked over to Ashlin. She got out of her car, wearing tight jeans, riding boots, and a navy blue sweater.

Placing a kiss on her cheek, Ryker said, "You look good."

Ashlin rubbed his hair and said, "You look a little disheveled."

That was when Ryker looked down at his clothes and realized his crotch shot from the cart had untucked his shirt. He was wearing a pair of orange pants, cuffed at the ankles, a white button up shirt and a blue bow tie.

"Damn," he said, while handing the beans to Ashlin and tucking everything back in place. "Long story. Did you bring something?"

"Root beer." She held up a six pack of a local brew.

"Are you trying to win our host's heart?"

"Just trying to be a gracious guest."

They started walking toward the house as Ashlin said, "What's with the smirk?"

"Smirk? I'm not smirking."

"Yes, you are." She pressed the side of his mouth with her finger and said, "You're smirking. Did you just get laid or something?"

"No..."

"Then what?" Ashlin stood still and placed her hand on her hips, not moving forward until he told her.

"Ugh, God, you're so fucking stubborn." Ryker straightened his cuffs as he casually said, "I ran into Hannah at the grocery store. Well, more like, she ran into me."

A girly squeal came out of Ashlin's mouth as she clapped her hands. "Oooh, Ryker and Hannah sitting in a tree..."

"Shut the fuck up," Ryker playfully said, as he dragged Ashlin forward by the hand. "It was just good to see her, that's all."

"Don't lie to me. I can read it all over your face. You are so fucking giddy."

"I'm not giddy!"

46

"Oh, okay…"

"I hate you," Ryker said, as he knocked on the door.

Jesse opened the door with a giant smile adorning his face. The quarterback never smiled at Ryker like that, so there was only one reason why he was smiling, and he was staring right at her. Ryker put that new-found information in the back of his mind for later and shoved the beans into Jesse's hand.

"Here are your beans, moose knuckle."

Ryker started walking by Jesse when he said, "Dude, you were supposed to bake them."

Ryker waved his hand in the air and said, "You're lucky you even got beans. You have an oven, bake them yourself. I'm grabbing a beer."

"Charming," Ryker heard Jesse say as he closed the door.

Ashlin

Jesse towered over her. She noticed how tall he was when they met at Ryker's practice, but standing in his entryway made him seem much taller.

"I'm glad you could make it," Jesse said, as he smiled down at her. He was almost too handsome, Ashlin thought, as she looked up into his almost-black eyes. He was definitely her type. Strong, athletic, dark complexion, dark hair, and dark eyes. Tattoos were scattered over his arms like Mason, and he had a little scruff on the end of his chin. He was hot, really hot…on the field and off the field, wearing jeans and a long-sleeved Henley shirt, he was giving her a little lady wood.

"Thanks for having me over. I know this is a team thing…"

"Not at all. I just like to hold a mid-season party for everyone, a little barbeque in the fall."

"I brought root beer," she said lamely, as she held up the six pack.

Jesse eyed the root beer and grabbed it from her, "Yeah, I'm not sharing this with anyone."

Laughing, Ashlin said, "Hey, I should at least get one."

"We'll see about that," he said with a wink. "Follow me."

As Ashlin followed Jesse through his house, she took in their surroundings. From the outside, his house seemed very extravagant, but on the inside, it wasn't. It was very homey. There were pictures on the walls of people who she could only assume were his family, since they all looked alike. His colors were very neutral, and his furniture was accommodating and looked very comfortable. They walked into the kitchen and she was surprised to see that there were used dishes in the sink…like he'd actually cooked.

"You didn't get the party catered?" she asked, as she looked at all the casserole dishes waiting to be taken outside.

"Never do. That's why I asked Ryker to bring beans, but the idiot can't even do that right."

Ashlin laughed as she said, "You can only count on one thing where Ryker is concerned, he will be looking good."

"You call that good?" Jesse teased as he pointed at Ryker, who was struggling to get his beer cap off.

"Well, if you're into that sort of thing."

Jesse nodded and put the beans on the counter. "You guys are close, aren't you?"

"Yeah, he's my best friend."

Jesse nodded his head and then pointed to the tented-off back yard. "Help yourself to food, games, and drinks. Let me know if you need anything."

The mention of Ryker's name had kind of blown the mood, as Jesse excused himself to tend to the beans that Ryker had handed him.

"Do you need any help?"

"I'm good. Go have fun."

Ashlin nodded and walked out to the back yard. There were heaters placed strategically around the tent, since it was autumn in Denver, and there were chairs with tables scattered around, as well as bar-height tables that some players were already leaning over and having conversations. Games like ladder ball, washers, and corn toss were also placed around the tent. Ashlin smiled to herself as she thought about the man who put this altogether. It was like the Stallions' own personal tailgate party.

Spotting Ryker and Mason, Ashlin walked over to them.

"Is he telling you all about seeing Hannah?" Ashlin teased, as she poked Ryker in the side.

Mason stood up straight and said, "You saw Hannah?"

"Thanks, big mouth," Ryker said as he rolled his eyes.

"Hey, it's the least I could do, since you're spreading around Mason's encounter with big tits, hairy pits."

"Fucking hell!" Mason said, as he punched Ryker in the arm, who immediately started rubbing it. "I can't tell you anything. Did you tell all the opposing teams too?"

"Not on the east coast, but I'll get there."

"You're a dick, you know that?"

"Yeah, but that's why you love me."

"Try again...pal," Mason said, as he turned to Ashlin. "So, he ran into Hannah?"

"Yeah, and he was smiling like a buffoon."

Mason nodded his head and took a sip of his beer as he said, "Sounds about right."

"I was not smiling like a buffoon. Way to over-exaggerate everything!" Ryker said, as he threw his hands up in the air.

"Yeah, I'm the one over-exaggerating," Ashlin countered, as she smiled a devilish smile at Ryker.

"Why did I bring you here again?"

"Because Jesse invited her," Mason said absentmindedly.

"He did?" Ashlin asked, as Mason froze with his beer halfway to his mouth.

"Uh, yeah. He invites everyone."

"What are you not telling me, Dashel?" Ashlin threatened.

Mason straightened up and cleared his throat. "Settle down, Harris. There's nothing to look into. He casually invites everyone." Mason shrugged his shoulders, but Ashlin wasn't buying it. She saw

49

the slight panic in Mason's eyes when he let the fact that Jesse invited her slip out of his mouth.

She looked back at Jesse, who was putting out a couple more dishes and laughing with some of his team mates. Did he really invite her? He looked up and made eye contact with her. Giving her a shy side smile, he turned around and went back in the kitchen. The very popular, Goliath of a man on the football field was a shy man on the inside…very unusual for a professional football player.

Jesse

Gripping the kitchen counter, Jesse took a deep breath before grabbing the last casserole to take out to the buffet. Having Ashlin so close, in his house, was making him nervous. He was a damn six-foot-three professional quarterback, and a model was making him nervous. A gorgeous model, but a model, nonetheless.

Mason walked into the kitchen and patted Jesse on the back. "What are you doing in here, man? Shouldn't you be out…talking to people?"

Jesse looked out and watched Ryker and Ashlin laughing together. They were so close, almost too close. They couldn't be just friends, could they?

"Just making sure everything is put together."

"Dude, stop being a pussy and go talk to her. I got her here, so go make your move."

"She just got here. I'm letting her settle in. I don't want to attack her. I know what I'm doing."

"Do you? Because I can't even recall the last time I saw you with a woman."

"Drop it," Jesse said sternly, as he walked out of the kitchen, leaving Mason behind. He didn't need the dickhead on his back right now when he was already a damn wreck. It was so easy for guys like Ryker and Mason who were overly confident when it came to the opposite sex. Jesse had never had to worry about having to date, because he always had Katie, but then when they split, he was at a loss.

Jesse floated around for a while, talking to his other team mates, their wives and girlfriends, as well as some of his buddies from high school, who he always invited. Lucky shits. His friends dreamed of his mid-season party every year, because it granted them the opportunity to mingle with the Stallions, which was any football fan's dream…to casually drink a beer with one of their favorite players.

After a couple of root beers, some amazing barbeque, and some good laughs, Jesse finally allowed himself to look around for Ashlin. He had been avoiding her for the past hour, because he didn't want to look too desperate, and because he didn't know what the hell to say to her.

There was a bunch of ruckus over at the ladder ball "court," so Jesse headed over there and saw Ashlin teasing Ryker.

"I don't want you on my team. You're awful at ladder ball. You'll just bring me down."

"But there's no way I can beat Mason without you."

"No, we almost lost the last couple of games because you can't simply toss the balls."

"I don't toss balls, sweetheart, women toss them for me."

Ashlin rolled her eyes as she spotted Jesse in the crowd. She waved her finger at him and said, "QB, you're on my team. Get that fine ass over here."

The boys around him cheered him on and slapped his back. Thank God for his darker complexion, because he could have sworn he was blushing like an idiot.

"You're sticking me with, Ryker, aren't you?" Mason said.

Ashlin looked at Jesse and raised her eyebrows in question, asking him silently if he was going to join her. Gathering himself, he walked over and grabbed the balls from her hand and said, "She is sticking you with Ryker, sorry dude."

Mason gave Jesse an approving grin as he grabbed Ryker around the neck and pushed him toward the other side. With ladder ball, each team separated so they were facing each other. Jesse stood next to Mason, and Ryker stood next to Ashlin…not ideal, but Jesse would have to put up with it.

"What are we betting on?" Jesse asked, getting into the competitive spirit.

"Loser strips and runs around the tent in only their underwear," Mason said, as he grabbed a beer for all the players, except for Jesse, who didn't drink.

"Dude, its cold out," Ryker complained like a little bitch.

"You scared of shrinkage?"

"No, dickhead. I just don't want to freeze my nips off."

"God, you're such a lady," Mason chastised.

"Sprint around the tent it is," Ashlin called out, while wiggling her eyebrows.

Ryker turned to Mason and said, "You know we should just start stripping now, right?"

Mason ignored Ryker as he popped his beer open and took a swig.

"Team meeting," Ashlin called out as she ran up to Jesse, grabbed his hand and pulled him away from Mason and Ryker. Her hand was so small in his, but he liked it…a lot.

Looking up at him, she smiled and said, "We're going to destroy them."

"Yeah, you just partnered yourself up with the ladder ball king."

"Oh, is that right?" Ashlin asked, while putting her hands on her hips.

"Yup," he said simply.

"Care to wager?"

"You know we're on the same team, right?"

Laughing, she said, "Yeah, but might as well make it a little fun."

"Fine, what do you have in mind?"

"Whoever scores the most points gets to decide what the other person has to do."

"That's really vague, care to elaborate?" Jesse asked, as he watched her green eyes light up. She was absolutely adorable, especially when she got competitive. A girl who was gorgeous, into sports, and brought him root beer…what more could he ask for?

"Nope. Deal or no deal?" she asked, while holding out her hand.

Jesse eyed her suspiciously for a second before shaking her hand and saying, "Deal." She smiled at him and pranced away.

"Why do I feel like I just shook hands with the devil?" he called out to her.

She just spun around while walking backwards and said, "Let's go QB, time to light up the ladders."

Damn.

Jax

Three days, and he still felt paralyzed. It had been three days and he had yet to contact Brooke. After he got home from their date, Jax felt different…a different that he couldn't figure out, which scared him. When he first met Piper, all he wanted to do was hang out with her, be next to her, and hold her, but with Brooke, he was more hesitant, and he wasn't sure if it was because of what happened with him and Piper, or just because he didn't know Brooke all that well. He told Brooke he would call her, and he knew his timeline was running out to make that call, but he was having one hell of a time trying to convince himself to pick up the phone.

He was invited to Jesse's mid-season party, but he knew Mason was going to be there, and he didn't want to be put in an awkward situation, so he decided to stay home. His first instinct should have been to call Brooke, but instead, he sat frozen on his couch.

Knowing he needed to do something, he sucked up the weird feelings that were running through his body and picked up his phone. Given the amount of time Jax had let pass since he said he would call Brooke, he assumed she wouldn't pick up her phone just to teach him a lesson, but when she answered his call, his stomach flipped from nerves.

"You have some explaining to do," she said into the phone.

Jax blew out a long breath of relief at the easy tone she used. "I know, I'm sorry."

"I'm going to assume you were working hard every night, and didn't want to disturb the angelic way I was sleeping. I choose to believe that you weren't avoiding me…right?"

"Would you believe me if I said I was working late?"

"No," she answered honestly. "But I will forgive you for being a dick and not calling earlier."

"I'm sorry, Brooke. I really am a dick."

He could hear her settling herself in a seat. "Sounds about right. Tell me why."

"I don't know," he said, while running his hand over his face. "I think I'm really fucked up. You make me feel different."

"Different good or bad?" she asked, a little hesitant.

Wanting to be honest, he said, "I'm not sure."

"Okay…" she dragged out. "I don't know how that is supposed to make me feel." She paused for a second, and then said, "You know what, actually, I do. That makes me feel awful, Jax. If anything, I should make you feel happy."

Jax was speechless; he didn't know what to say.

"Alright, well, thanks for the pity call, Jax. For what it's worth, I hope you can pull your shit together. I know you were hurt, but everyone gets hurt at some point. The best way to live your life is to move forward, not live in the past. Believe me, I know. Have a good one."

With that, she hung up the phone, making Jax feel like a total asshat. Not living in the past…that was one of the first things she said to him when they were at the car wash. Why couldn't he just tattoo that across his forehead?

Fuck.

Quickly getting off the couch, throwing on a shirt and a pair of sandals, he took off for his truck and drove to Brooke's apartment. During his drive, he tried to think about what he was going to say, but his mind went completely blank. He had no clue what he was doing; he just knew he couldn't let Brooke hang up on him like that. He couldn't just let Brooke go, especially with the way he just made her feel.

Getting to her apartment in record time, he got out of his truck and was knocking on her door in seconds.

The look on her face when she opened the door was priceless. She was wearing a pink silk robe that grazed her thighs, and her shorter brown hair was pulled to the side by a bobby pin.

"What are you doing here?" she asked, confused.

"I don't know."

She put her hand on her hip and said, "You don't know a lot of things these days."

"I know I want to come in."

"What if I don't want you to?"

He shrugged his shoulders and said, "I guess I'll leave then."

"Ugh, I hate myself right now." She stepped aside and let him in her apartment. A small smile crept across his face.

"Thank you," he said, as he passed her and stroked her face with his hand.

They walked to the living room and sat down. She sat on a single chair, giving him a clear idea of how she currently felt about him, so he parked it on her couch. An awkward silence settled between them as the television provided background noise. Jax looked up and saw that Brooke was watching *Full House* before he came over. Classic.

Looking over at Brooke he asked, "*Full House?*"

"What? Uncle Jesse is hot."

Laughing, Jax held out his hand and said, "Come here," glad that the tension had dissipated, thanks to Uncle Jesse.

Watching her toned legs, Jax was rewarded with a saunter from Brooke as she made herself comfortable on his lap. Placing a hand on her thigh, he looked up at her and said, "I don't even really know you, but I do know that, right now, with you on my lap, I'm happy."

"You don't need to lie to me Jax. If you just want to fuck, I can do that."

"I don't want to just have sex, I'm not that guy."

"What kind of guy are you?" she asked, while stroking the five o'clock shadow on his jaw.

"I'm the kind of guy who likes to have a girl in his arms after a long day on the field. I'm the kind of guy who likes to spoil the girl in his life and take care of her. I like to know that, when I'm having a bad day or when I want to just throw caution to the wind and do something crazy, I have an amazingly beautiful girl next to my side to experience that with me."

Brooke nodded her head as she continued to stroke his jaw. "Think you want to give this girl a chance at providing all of that for you?"

"I think I do," Jax said without pausing, kind of surprising himself. "I just think that what we have, the foundation that we are building off of, is tainted. What brought us together, how we met is all very negative, and there are trust issues that we've developed, not just with other people, but with each other. We both have motives to enter this relationship with all the wrong reasons in mind, and I don't want to do that. I like you, Brooke, and I want to see if we can make something happen, but I don't know if it's possible, given the way we came together."

She nodded her head in understanding. "I get that."

"But I want to try," Jax said, before she could continue. "I just need to know you're in this because you like me, because you want to be with me, and not because of any other ulterior motives."

"I know I don't have the best track record, being a manipulative bitch in the past and all, but I can honestly tell you, I've changed. Mason is nothing to me now, absolutely nothing. He is my past, and I'm looking for my future."

Jax nodded and leaned forward. He pressed a gentle kiss on her lips and said, "Alright, so what's next?"

"Do you want to watch a movie?"

"Depends on the movie…" Jax said with a smirk.

"*Lethal Weapon*?"

"Seriously?" Jax asked, shocked.

"Oh, what fun you're going to have learning all about me."

"I guess I am."

Knowing he was making the right decision, he settled himself on her couch and waited for her to join him. Once the movie was in, she sat next to him, curled her legs under butt, and placed her head against his chest as he wrapped his arm around her shoulders. It was such a simple thing, but he could get used to this. He just hoped, in the long run, they weren't going to screw each other over.

Jesse

There was no way he was going to beat Ashlin, she was leading him by seven points, and he only had one shot left. They were destroying Ryker and Mason and, by now, the two idiots were already starting to strip down for their lap around the tent.

"Why are you even going to shoot? You know you won. You just want to rub it in," Ryker whined. "You're a giant dick."

Jesse laughed as he shot the balls and didn't score any points. Ashlin fist pumped the air and smiled at him. Yup, she was fucking adorable.

"You want to see a giant dick?" Mason asked, as he thrust his pelvis in Ryker's direction.

"Get out of here, donkey dick," Ryker said, as he swatted Mason away.

Both of his wide receivers were standing in their skivvies, giving everyone at the party a great view. He loved his boys, and couldn't imagine having anyone else on his team. The dynamic between Mason and Ryker was hysterical to watch, and Jesse was just happy that they were the life of the party. That way, Jesse could focus on Ashlin.

"Alright, boys, hit it," Jesse said, as they dropped trou and prepared to take off.

Mason and Ryker dashed out of the tent and around it. All the partygoers stopped what they were doing so they could watch the shadows of Mason and Ryker sprint around the tent as they pushed and swatted at each other. Jesse was laughing at the two idiots when Ashlin sidled up next to him.

"So, what do you say, QB, do you want to get out of here?"

"What?" Jesse asked, looking down at Ashlin, who was inching closer and closer every second.

"You owe me. I won, so whatever I want, you have to do."

"But, it's my party," he said with a chuckle.

"You won't be gone very long, now come on." She grabbed his hand and started exiting him out of the tent, just as Mason and Ryker entered at the same time.

"Beat...you...dick...smack," Ryker said, out of breath.

"Fuck...off," Mason breathed.

"I won!" Ryker shouted.

"Keep dreaming!" Mason retorted.

"Jesse, who...won?" Ryker asked, still out of breath.

"Jesse has more important things to attend to at the moment than babysitting you morons. Come on, Jesse."

Both Mason and Ryker's eyebrows shot up to their hairlines as Ashlin guided Jesse out of the tent, making Jesse laugh.

"They are never going to let me live this down, you know that, right?"

"Not my problem," she said with a smile.

They walked out to his pool, where there were lounger chairs set up to look the stars. She sat them both on a lounger and sat right next to him.

Jesse looked around and said, "So, you didn't come out here to kill me or anything, did you?"

"Please, I wouldn't take you to the pool to kill you."

"Um, the way you answered that question makes me think you have another way in mind that you might kill me?"

"Not just you, people in general. It's common knowledge that a wood chipper is the best way to get rid of someone..." she deadpanned.

"Uh..."

She pinched his chin with her thumb and said, "You're too easy. Loosen up, Jesse."

Not wanting to be a wet blanket, Jesse loosened his shoulders and straddled the chair, so he was facing her completely.

"That better?"

"Yes, it is."

"Now, what do I owe you?"

"Hmmm...there are so many things I want. A new car would be nice, maybe some clothes, this house..." she said, while looking around.

"Easy..."

"Fine, all I want is a kiss."

"A kiss?"

"Yeah, you know, when two sets of lips come together and start making smacking noises. Like this," she demonstrated with her hands as she made noises.

"Wow, that was so hot," Jesse teased.

"Like you can do better?"

"I can," Jesse admitted. He brought his hands together and made them make out, while making a moaning sound. Ashlin laughed out loud and pushed his hands down.

"Stop, God that was disturbing."

"My hands were more turned on than your hands, don't get jelly."

"It's because you're a guy; you all are disgusting. And don't say jelly!"

He laughed and said, "That's true, we are a disgusting gender."

Jesse was impressed with his ability to banter with Ashlin. He hadn't talked to a girl like this in a while, and he was really enjoying it, plus, he was bantering with Ashlin...Ashlin! The girl that he could see sharing a life with.

"So, I'm waiting," she said, while leaning forward.

"Well, if I have to…"

"You do. I won fair and square, and none of this cheek kissing crap. I want it on my lips, and if there's a little tongue, then so be it."

Jesse laughed and wrapped his arm around her waist, bringing her closer.

"I can't kiss you when you're all the way over there." He ran his hand up her neck and cupped her jaw as his other hand put her hair behind her ear. He looked her in the eyes and said, "You're beautiful, Ashlin, absolutely beautiful."

Before she could respond, he brought her lips closer, and right before he kissed her, he took in a deep breath, sucking in her essence, and then brought his lips down on hers. The moment their lips connected, Jesse knew he was done; this was it for him, she was it. She was made for him; it was so easy for him to see. The feel of her was right, just perfect.

Pulling her in closer, Jesse wrapped his arm around her waist and held on tightly. A light moan escaped her mouth as her tongue swept against his, causing heat to spread through his body.

Reluctantly, he pulled away, because he knew if he didn't, he was going to be laying her out on the lounge chair in no time. Looking down at her, he kissed her nose and smiled at her.

"Is my debt paid off?"

Her eyes were lazy with lust as she said, "No, you owe me a date."

"Is that right? I thought it was just a kiss."

"You didn't read the fine print, a date was included with the kiss."

"Ah, I see. Well, I guess since I didn't read the fine print, I owe you a date and probably another kiss."

"I think you might be right with that."

Jesse pulled his phone out of his pocket and handed it to Ashlin. "Put your number in there so I can set up a date with you.

Don't want there to be any miscommunication."

"Definitely not."

She grabbed his phone, typed her number in, and handed it over to him. He looked down, and his brow creased at what she had entered as her name.

"LBQ?"

"Ladder Ball Queen, duh Jesse." She patted his cheek and got off the lounge chair.

"Not for long. I challenge you to another game."

"I would, but I don't want to embarrass you, plus, don't you have a game tomorrow? You better save that arm of yours."

"True, are you going to watch?"

"The game?"

"Yes," he replied, hoping that she would say yes. Knowing that she was going to watch him play tomorrow would give him that extra boost that he was looking for, to have someone cheering for him who meant something to him.

"I always do. Don't forget, your name is the one I wear on my back every time the Stallions play."

She winked at him and walked back to the tent, leaving Jesse speechless.

CHAPTER FIVE

Ryker

He was whipped, beyond tired. He spent the rest of his time at Jesse's party debating with Mason as to who was faster in their little run around the tent relay. It came down to the fact that they had to race again…in their underwear. They raced in a straight line, and had Jesse hold his hands out, so whoever tagged his hand first, won. Surprisingly, they tied. Ryker believed that he hit Jesse's hand first, but the fucker would never admit it, so Ryker had to settle with being tied with Mason. Apparently, it didn't matter that he had a donkey dick propelling him forward; Ryker was just as fast.

Pulling his shirt off and settling into a pair of shorts for the night, Ryker got ready for bed. They had a home game tomorrow and Ryker could really use some rest. Maybe he was an idiot for racing Mason, since he was going to be sore from not warming up beforehand, but pride got in the way.

Overall, he had a good day, and even though Hannah's face was floating around in his mind, he was able to push her aside and have a good time with friends.

He still couldn't believe he ran into her. Denver was a huge city; they shouldn't have run into each other, right? He had to admit, she looked pretty good…like the angelic beauty he'd seen for the first time at Dick's Last Chance. Damn, he missed that bar. Life was so simple a couple of months ago. Now he was flagged everywhere he went, thanks to the C.C. Morris campaign, and they hadn't even used all of the pictures yet, so the fight against the crowds was only going to continue.

Ryker was settling into bed when his phone chimed with a text message.

Hannah: Hey Ryke, just wanted to make sure you got home okay, given your accident and everything.

Damn her, Ryker thought, as he smiled to himself. He wanted to be mad at her; he needed to be mad at her. She didn't trust him, she insulted him by comparing him to Todd, of all people; she compared him to tiny testicles Todd. What a douche; he didn't know a good thing when he had it.

Ryker flipped through his phone until he came to his pictures, he opened up a picture of him and Hannah at the bar. He took the picture one night when she was actually giving him the time of day and not pushing him away. He told her friends always took pictures together, so she obliged and took a picture with him. Smiling brightly at the camera, she easily showed off her beauty while he had his head turned, looking at her like she was the damn love of his life. He didn't know why he tortured himself by looking at the picture occasionally; it was like he enjoyed twisting a knife into his gut. It was almost as painful, but there was no way he would ever delete the picture. He couldn't bring himself to do it, so instead, he just stared at it and wondered what would have happened if Todd had never been in her life.

Looking over her text again, he wondered why she was trying to reach out. Why now? It had been three months. Had enough time passed for her to have had a change of heart? Or was she just trying to reach out to be a friend? But, he shouldn't care because she was the one that hurt him…that turned away from him. He should be wondering if he'd had a change of heart, not her.

Running his hand over his phone, he realized that, even though she hurt him, terribly, he craved her. He wanted just a tiny piece of her, even if it was temporary or just as friends; he still needed a part of Hannah in his life, because no Hannah was fucking miserable. He typed a message back to her.

Ryker: I made it home, thanks. Hope the peas didn't set you back.

She texted back almost instantaneously.

Hannah: I wasn't able to buy milk and eggs this week, but I will survive.

Ryker: Those are some expensive peas...

Hannah: They went up in price after the great Ryker Lewis touched them.

Ryker quirked his eyebrow as he read her text message.

Ryker: Are you trying to butter me up, Hannah?

Hannah: Is it working?

Fuck, it was, Ryker thought, as he texted back his response.

Ryker: I think I will withhold that information for now.

There was a pause in their texting as Ryker waited for her to message back. He was now lying down in his bed, on his side, staring at his phone like a prepubescent teenage girl. In the back of his head, he was telling himself to stop being a pussy and turn off his phone; he didn't need her, but his heart was winning out right now. He just wanted a little taste, a little nibble of Hannah, and then he could go back to normal...not thinking about her.

His phone chimed with a text notification, making him

scramble to open up the message. He was so gone.

Hannah: Ryker, this is not how I want to have this conversation, but you practically ran out of the grocery store, so I don't think you want to talk to me, but I just have to say, I miss you and I'm sorry.

"Fuck!" Ryker shouted, as he put his phone down and ran his hands down his face. He should have turned his phone off when he had the chance. He didn't need this right now; he didn't need Hannah fucking with his head right in the middle of the season, when he already had the stress of the clothing campaign gnawing away at him.

He wasn't ready to forgive Hannah, to let go, and maybe, possibly, dive back into his pursuit of Hannah's hand. He didn't think he was strong enough to go after such an endeavor. He wanted to, damn it, but he didn't think he was strong enough. He'd already exhausted all of his energy three months ago; he didn't think he had anything else left in him.

Instead of texting back, he turned his light and phone off, and closed his eyes. He would sleep on it, no need to make any rash decisions right now. She could wait for him, just like he'd waited for her.

Mason

"Fuck, I'm fired up and ready to piss all over these cocksuckers," Mason said, as he wrapped tape around his wrists to keep them sturdy.

"What kind of range do you have with that fire hose down there?" Ryker asked, as he eyed Mason's crotch.

"Dude, fucking eyes up here," Mason said, pointing to his eyes. "Damn, man!"

Ryker laughed as he said, "Well…"

"You know well and good what kind of range I get."

"I know, but fuck, can you tell the story again? I don't think

Jesse knows it."

"Knows what?" Jesse asked, as he sat down on the chair that was placed in front of his locker.

"About the pissing contest Mason's football team held in college."

Jesse stopped tying his cleat and looked up at both of them. "This is something I have to hear."

Rolling his eyes, Mason said, "In college, I played with a bunch of idiots and they thought it would be a great idea to drink as much beer as we could and then have our own pissing Super bowl. We drew a mini football field in the grass, probably seven feet long and eight feet wide, so multiple guys could piss at the same time, and we measured how far each guy could piss. We handed out awards for furthest stream, most accurate spray, hardest sprinkler and longest pisser."

Jesse threw his head back and laughed as Mason continued, "I was bound and determined to win, given my reputation, and the fact that I wanted to let it be known that I was the king of all dicks…"

Jesse raised his eyebrows up at Mason, who shrugged his shoulders. "I was a total asswipe in college; I'm surprised I even made it through. Anyway, I drank a fucking twelve pack without pissing, and when the clock started and the whistle blew, I fucking took the mother fucking cake and cleaned house. I have never pissed so hard, so long, and so accurately in my life. It was as if the dick gods were shining down upon me and made my cock the epitome of all cocks for those three and a half glorious moments. I don't even remember holding my dick up; it was guided by little phallic fairies as they peppered my cock with their penis pixie dust. From then on out, I was the king of all dicks."

Mason stared off into space as he relived one of the most shining moments of his college career.

Slapping him in the stomach, Jesse got up and said, "No, man, you're the king of all douchebags. Good story, though." Jesse took off toward the stadium and said, "Let's get em', boys."

Ryker walked up next to Mason and said, "You're still my dick king, man."

Punching Ryker in the stomach, Mason said, "Get out of here, you creep!"

Game time.

The crowd roared as the Stallions took the field. Smoke billowed out of the tunnel as music thumped through the speakers. Mason lived for this moment. When he was on the field, nothing could touch him. Not his shitty love life, which was non-existent, not the pain of knowing Piper was nowhere to be found, or the fact that, after the game, he would go home alone. He was really good at putting up a front when people were around, but when he was home, that was when he truly felt alone…when he truly sulked about what a shitty life he was leading.

Going out to bars, hooking up with random girls, and living in a fog was all him overcompensating for not wanting to go home, to face that fact that, once again, he'd failed at keeping a girl, failed at letting her know that she was the most important person in his life, and that he would do anything for her.

After the opening ceremonies and coin toss, Mason stood in position on the field as the opposing team got information to deliver the opening kick. Carefully, Mason watched the kicker run up to the football and pelt it across the field. The ball was kicked off directly in Mason's direction. With finesse, Mason caught the ball and zig-zagged his way through the defense, bringing the ball to the forty yard line before he was tackled. The offensive line of the Stallions ran out to the field and patted Mason on the helmet as they huddled to receive the first play from Jesse.

"Bootleg to the right and I'll find you downfield, Dash. Got it?" Jesse asked, as he called out the play.

The players nodded and clapped their hands together to break.

Mason set himself up along the line as the opposing defense did the same. Jesse called out in his deep voice random numbers and colors, trying to throw the defense off with false snap calls.

Once Jesse sounded off the third hut, the ball was snapped and Mason took off, running down the field. After he hit the thirty yard line, he switched gears and curled to the right, the same way Jesse was running. Mason lifted his head and found the ball was placed exactly where it needed to be by Jesse's precise throwing.

Catching the ball and cradling it into the crook of his arm, Mason turned toward the end zone at the same time the defender grabbed him from behind and another player tackled him from the side. The split tackle from both defenders twisted Mason's body in an unnatural way, causing a loud pop to explode from his right knee that was bearing all his weight as he turned.

Pain exploded through Mason's leg as he fell to the ground with both defensive players falling on top of him.

"Mother fucker!" Mason shouted, as he scrambled under the players. "Get the fuck off of me." The anger and pain radiated from his face, indicating to the other players that he was hurt.

Once they were off of him, Mason sat up and gripped his knee, knowing right then and there that his season was over. There was no doubt in his mind that he had just ripped every tendon in his knee.

The Stallions' medical team came running out on the field as Mason writhed in pain on the field with thousands of onlookers watching him go through one of the most painful injuries he had ever experienced.

After a decent amount of time on the field, Mason was lifted onto a cart and driven off of the field as both teams and everyone in the stadium clapped for him. He didn't want their praise, because he wasn't walking off the field; he was being carried out, which is a player's worst nightmare. He was taken to the medical room where they X-rayed his knee and put it through an MRI, followed up by the doctor wrapping up his knee and bracing it.

Once the X-rays and pictures were analyzed, the team doctor came to the conclusion that Mason had torn both his ACL and MCL, closing down his season and setting him up for surgery in a week with an extensive rehab program once he was able to start moving around. He was fucked.

He was completely toast for the rest of the season.

Jax

"Come in," Jax called out, as the knock on his door rang through his office.

Jesse walked in and sat down in the chair across from Jax. The look on his face gutted Jax, because he knew Jesse was blaming himself for what happened to Mason.

Jax had watched the whole play in slow motion, and once he saw the other defender come in from the right, Jax knew Mason was cooked. Mason's knee was locked and ready to turn when he got hit from both sides; there was no way he was getting out of the tackle unscathed. Jax just hoped, for the team's sake, that the injury wasn't going to be too terrible, but no such luck; Dash was out for the season, with a long road of recovery ahead of him.

"I shouldn't have thrown the ball. I saw the other tackle coming in, but I just assumed Mason would turn on his afterburners and blow right by them," Jesse said, as he shook his head.

Jax leaned forward on his forearms and said, "Jesse, you can't blame yourself for this. Players get hurt all the time in this sport. The man was in the wrong place at the wrong time. He has a long road of recovery, but he'll be starting next season."

"But he should be fucking playing this season."

Jax sat back in his chair, took off his hat, and ran his hand through his hair. "Believe me, I want Dash on the field more than anyone. He's a leader and a damn fine receiver, but right now, we have to move forward and figure out how to connect you with one of your younger receivers." Even though it pained Jax to say good things about Mason, he meant them. Losing Mason was a huge hit to the team, not just because of his talent, but because of the leadership he provided on and off the field.

Jesse nodded his head as he blew out a loud breath. "I just

keep replaying the route in my head over and over again. I should have gone to Ryker who was down field. I should have switched it up."

"Stop," Jax said in a stern voice. "You can't dwell on this, or it's going to eat you alive on the field. Drop it and let it go. Don't second guess yourself, because the minute you start doing that, you're going to be the one being wheeled off the field. You have to listen to your instincts and keep moving forward. Do not think twice about your decisions; what's done is done. You hear me?"

"Yes, Coach," Jesse said, as he got out of the chair.

"Get some rest, Jesse. We have a long week of practice ahead of us."

Nodding and leaving the office, Jesse retreated back to the locker room…leaving Jax to himself, thinking about how he was going to continue their almost-perfect season without their star wide receiver.

Ashlin

She watched the game from her apartment, and the minute Mason was tackled, she knew it wasn't good; then when the camera zoomed in on Jesse's face, her heart broke in two for the man that was on her mind. The Stallions ended up losing, and Ashlin knew why; Jesse's head wasn't in the game after Mason was driven off the field.

She didn't know Jesse very well, but she did observe him when she watched the games, and after Mason was taken off the field, his whole demeanor changed from a confident quarterback to a hesitant one. His throws were not as accurate as they usually were, and his head hung low throughout the game, as if he kept playing the play that ended Mason's season over and over in his head.

Unfortunately, she didn't have Jesse's number; he only had hers, so she couldn't call him. That meant one thing…she had to call Ryker, and she knew he was going to make a big deal out of her wanting Jesse's number, but she was going to suck it up because she needed to know how he was doing.

After their entirely too short kiss at his little gathering, she felt connected to him, and seeing him in pain, pained her. There was no denying the fact that she liked the guy, but was she ready for a relationship? Hell no, but that didn't stop her from wanting some hot sex and making sure the man was okay.

Pulling out her phone, she sent Ryker a quick text.

Ashlin: Don't give me crap, please send me Jesse's phone number.

Ryker's text came back instantly.

Ryker: Ooooh, Ashlin and Jesse are getting it on *pelvic thrust*

Ashlin shook her head as she read Ryker's text. The man was impossible.

Ashlin: Just give me the damn number, asshole.

Ryker: A little testy tonight. Is that why you need a little late night booty call?

Ashlin: Next time I see you, your dick will be cut off and shoved down your throat.

Ryker: Now, why would you do that to Russell? He had nothing to do with any of this.

Ashlin: Losing my patience very quickly.

Ryker: I'm sorry, I didn't know you were menstruating and couldn't take a joke.

Ashlin: That makes absolutely no sense. Just give me the damn number.

After a little more coaxing and more intimidating threats of cutting off Russell, Ryker finally handed over Jesse's phone number. Ashlin quickly plugged the number into her contacts, filed Jesse in her phone as Sexy QB, and hovered her finger over the call button. It was the truth; he was damn fine.

Taking a deep breath, she dialed his number. After three rings, he finally picked up.

"You know, I wasn't going to answer my phone, and then I saw LBQ come up on the screen and thought, I can't pass up the chance to talk to a Queen."

Ashlin laughed into the phone. "Is there a reason you're trying to flatter me?"

"Nope, just being honest."

"How are you doing?" Ashlin asked honestly.

Jesse blew out a frustrated breath. "Could be doing better. I feel like I just ruined the season for me and my boys."

"Why do you say that?" Ashlin asked, as she got comfortable in her chair.

"I saw it all happen right in front of me," he said, referring to Mason's tackle. "I could have avoided it. I could have thrown the ball down to Ryker, but instead I went with Mason, which ended in him being carted off the field. I fucked up big time."

Ashlin's heart broke for the man. His voice was so weak, so broken. He was so strong and confident on the field, maybe a little shy in person, but she had never seen this side of him before.

"You know you couldn't have predicted what was going to happen, right? It's not your fault Jesse; you can't put this on yourself, and it's not like he's dead," Ashlin tried to put a spin on it.

Jesse lightly chuckled. "I bet Mason would rather be dead. The man lives for football, and he's had such a shitty year that I'm sure this is just the fly on the pile of crap that his life has turned into."

"Yeah, but you can't blame yourself for that. Who's to say he wouldn't have gotten injured on a different play or driving to the stadium? No one can predict what happens to people, so when something does happen, we just have to roll with it and grow from our experiences."

There was a pause on the other end of the line before Jesse said, "It sounds like you speak from experience."

"I do, but that's a story for a different day."

"You sure?" he asked, trying to change the subject.

"Positive. Now tell me, how hot is the new receiver that will be taking Dash's place? Do I need to get a new T-shirt jersey?"

"You wound me," Jesse said jokingly. "And just so you know, he's hideous, total train wreck of a face, might as well just stick with the jersey you already have."

Ashlin laughed. "Train wreck of a face? Wow, I didn't know you were able to say such cruel words."

"When it means that I might lose a fan, I'm willing to throw a teammate under the bus."

"Just any old fan?"

"Well, I get a little more rabid when it's a beer belly, belching bald fan, but that's a given."

Chuckling, Ashlin said, "I never knew that was your type. We have more in common than I thought. Can't get enough of those hairy-bellied men, mmm pure sex on a stick."

"Is that right? I guess I better start hanging out at the all you can eat buffets and putting Rogaine on my stomach."

"Yes, and if you can wear crocs with pajama pants out in public, that will up your sex factor as well."

"Noted," Jesse said, laughing.

An awkward silence fell between them. Ashlin didn't know what to say; her mind went completely blank. One thing she did know was that she didn't want their phone conversation to end; she was having fun with someone other than Ryker, and it surprised the crap out of her.

Right before she was going to ask Jesse a question, he said, "Well, thanks for calling Ashlin. You brightened my night."

Feeling slightly disappointed that their conversation was ending, Ashlin said, "Any time. If you ever need to talk, I'm only a phone call away."

They said their goodbyes and, as Ashlin hung up the phone, she leaned her head back on the couch and thought about how the man she always had a curious eye on was slowly starting to work his way into her life…and the strange thing was, she didn't mind.

CHAPTER SIX

Mason

"Fucking crutches," Mason muttered to himself as he pushed his crutches to the side and sat down in the bistro chairs that were far too small for his body.

He needed to get away from Jake and Lexi and their smothering. After his surgery, he needed to go somewhere where people could help him out. Unfortunately, that meant Jake and Lexi's house, since he had no one in Denver and his parents were on a two week cruise.

There were three things wrong with staying with Jake and Lexi. One, they were all over each other, and it was sickening for Mason to watch, especially since he was on a hiatus when it came to relationships. Two, they enjoyed smothering Mason like he was their damn kid. Jake even tried giving him a bath at one point…that was where Mason drew the line. Thirdly, they were leaving tonight for an away trip, so there really was no point in Mason coming to San Diego, except to escape Denver and the talk that surrounded the Stallions.

Leaving his team wasn't an issue, since he needed to recover, but even if Mason was supposed to stay, he didn't think he could have. This was the first injury he had ever really had, and it just happened to occur during one of the best seasons of his life. At least he went all out when it came to injuring himself. Nothing says injury like tearing every last ligament in his knee.

The metal of his chair was already boring into his ass after sitting on the damn bistro chair for five minutes. He didn't want to go to the bistro, but it was the closest restaurant to Jake and Lexi's house that he could crutch to. Unluckily, Mason injured his right knee, making it impossible for him to drive. He tried to tell everyone that he could drive with his left foot, no problem, but when he went to grab his keys, they all miraculously disappeared, leaving him almost completely stranded.

Currently, he was a pathetic fuck with the inability to drive, no woman by his side to push his worries away, and two best friends that couldn't leave him alone for two damn seconds. He was miserable.

Mason's phone rang, disrupting him from his thoughts. As he looked down at the caller ID, he saw Jake's name pop up. Shaking his head, Mason answered the phone.

"Hey," he said casually, as he could already hear Jake's heavy breathing.

"Where the fuck are you? Did you get a car? I swear to God, Mason..."

"Settle down...Dad. I'm at the corner bistro."

"How the hell did you get there?"

"I crutched my way here."

A scream from a child behind Mason sounded off, making Mason cringe. Mason's nerves were already bordering on making him jump off a cliff, he didn't need a child screaming right behind him.

"That's almost a mile away. Have you lost your damn mind?" Jake asked as his voice rose.

Almost a mile? That could explain the chaffing in his armpits and the shortness of breath Mason was experiencing when he finally sat down. He was so determined to get away from Jake and

Lexi's hovering that he plowed down the street and made it to the bistro in record time.

"Whatever, I'm fine. You happy now?"

"How do you expect to get home?"

"I'll call a cab. Jesus, Jake, don't you have some packing to do? I'll be fine." The child behind him continued to wail as Mason tried to hear what Jake was saying. "What did you say? I can't fucking hear you because a God damn child is screaming its head off," Mason said loudly, as he turned around to eye the noisy beast.

When he turned around, he didn't see a child right away, but what he did see was a head full of red curly hair and silver eyes that were as wide as his good old friend's saucer nipples.

"I need to fucking call you back," Mason said, as he turned off the phone while Jake was trying to talk to him.

Turning around slowly, Mason took in the sight before him. Piper was sitting at the table next to him, wearing a yellow shirt and teal scarf. Her hair was in a mess of curls, framing her face and making her look absolutely perfect. But the sight that really disturbed him was the child in her arms with bright red hair and chocolate eyes, just like his.

"What the fuck? Did you have a kid and not fucking tell me?" Mason skipped the niceties and went straight for the kill.

Piper's eyebrow quirked at him as she shoved a pacifier in the kid's mouth. He could see the wheels starting to turn in her head as she geared up her response. This wasn't going to be pretty.

"Are you a fucking moron? We haven't even known each other for ten months. How the fuck would I have had a kid with you? They say football players aren't the brightest crayons in the box, but your asinine question really takes the cake."

Yup, seemed about right, Mason thought to himself, as he took in what Piper said. He'd definitely had a jock moment, but he was so thrown off by seeing her that time wasn't even a question when he saw a baby that looked like it could have been theirs.

That would have been all kinds of fucked up.

"Whose kid then?"

"Why does it matter? You plan on harassing its parents as well?"

"I see that you still wear a tight pair of bitch pants," Mason replied, as he looked her in the eyes...the eyes that had haunted him for months. He hated that his draw to her was just as strong as it was three months ago.

"Ah, and I see that you are still a misogynistic asshole, but to my delight, a one-legged one."

Flames sprouted in Mason's eyes as a smirk spread across Piper's face after mentioning his injury.

Mason was about to respond when Piper fake pouted and said in a baby voice, "Oh, is poor Dash out of commission? Poor baby."

"Fuck you," Mason muttered.

"Still so eloquent," Piper retorted, as she swayed the baby back in forth in her arms. The sight of her with a baby pained Mason, because he once saw a future where Piper was holding their baby and, clearly, that wasn't what was in their future now.

Mason shifted his chair so he was facing her, and when he did, his crutches fell to the ground, making Piper laugh.

"What's so damn funny?"

Piper picked up one of the crutches and started poking Mason with it. "The big bad Mason can't stand to be laughed at."

"What are you, fucking twelve?" Mason asked, as he snatched the crutch out of her hand. "Damn."

"Look who has the menses now," Piper said, referring back to when Mason called her out for being temperamental on the airplane when they first met.

Scowling, Mason stood up, placed his crutches under his arms, and pushed the chair he was sitting on into the table with his crutch.

"I'm out."

He needed to get out of the bistro before he did something stupid, like either try to throw a fork at Piper's eyeball, or fall to his knees and beg for her to be with him. He would rather do the fork stabbing, even though his heart was aching to have her near him.

Talk about one fucked up…relationship? Is that what they had? Whatever it was, it was so screwed up, but it held some of the best moments in his life, having her in his arms, curling her hair around his finger, and listening to her talk to him softly. Deep down inside, he knew he would blow his other knee out just to steal another moment like that with her, but the stubborn man on the outside was flipping her off in his head in every which way possible.

"Did you drive here? I hope not, because that's very dangerous." her voice came, ringing sincere.

Was that concern that laced her voice? Surprising, Mason thought. He didn't know the spawn of the devil had a heart.

Turning around slowly on his crutches, Mason faced Piper for what was hopefully the last time and said, "Listen, your pity concern for me is nauseating and, frankly, insulting, since three months ago you could have cared less about my wellbeing…"

"That's not true," Piper said, cutting him off.

Mason held up his hand. "Cut the crap. If you cared one ounce about me, you never would have agreed to marry that piece of southern shit."

"I was doing it for you," Piper shouted, drawing attention from everyone around them.

A maniacal laugh escaped Mason's mouth. "Wow, if that's what you do to help people, please, for the love of God, do not try fucking helping me again. You broke me, Piper, simple as that. You fucking broke me."

With that, Mason turned and crutched his way out of the bistro, never getting that peace and quiet that he needed.

Piper

She couldn't move. Seeing Mason and hearing his words felt like she'd been hit by a brick wall, a six-foot-something, brown

79

haired, scruffy faced, handsome as hell brick wall.

Never did she think she would see him again, in person that was. She saw him all over the media, but in person, she didn't think it was possible, especially during the season. Unfortunately, she was babysitting for her cousin, who lived a mile away from Jake and Lexi. It was risky, because she could be spotted, but right now she would give anything for a little bit of money and to get the hell out of her parents' house, so that meant she needed to babysit.

Once she left Mason's place, after being told to fuck off, she packed everything up and just started driving. She ended up in Las Vegas where she drank, fucked, and went on a damn bender, expending every last cent she had in her bank account. It wasn't the finest moment of her life, but she sure as hell forgot; she forgot every last thing that happened between her and Mason...the one man she couldn't get out of her mind, even though they never had the chance to get close enough.

Not having any money or friends that weren't already in Mason's circle, she had only one place to go, and that was her parents' house. Gritting her teeth and sucking up her pride, she'd walked up the elaborate granite steps to her parents' house and asked if she could stay with them for a while, until she could get back on her feet. Her mom was barely present, given the amount of prescription drugs rolling through her body, so she was no help. That meant she had to listen to her dad lecture her for at least a week about poor decisions after she told them a condensed and less-slutty version of what she had just gone through. She asked both of her parents to not mention to anyone that she was with them, and that meant Lexi, who Piper knew would call at some point, and she did.

Not talking to Lexi pained Piper, because more than anything, she could have used Lexi's shoulder to cry on, to talk to, and to help her through the shit show her life had turned into.

Alex, her cousin's baby, started getting out of hand and, frankly, Piper couldn't take it anymore...the whole babysitting thing that is, so she put Alex back in his car seat, grabbed his items and headed out to her car. Her cousin was home doing yoga, which she liked to do without the baby, so Piper didn't mind taking Alex back, especially since she thought she was going to have a panic attack from seeing Mason.

Quickly driving to her cousin's house she dropped off the baby in the midst of the warrior pose, called out her apologies, and got back in her car. Pushing her hair back and out of her face, she tried to gain control of her breathing from the thought of seeing Mason again. Her body tingled as she thought about the rough scruff on his face and the way his chocolate brown eyes bore through hers. She still needed him, after everything they went through, she still needed him.

Because she was a glutton for punishment, she stealthily drove by Lexi and Jake's house as she peered out the window, wanting to catch any kind of glimpse of the dark, brooding man she'd grown to love. But there was nothing; the house was dark and there was no movement. Piper pulled out her phone and quickly checked the San Diego Thunder's schedule. They were heading into an away game, meaning Jake and Lexi weren't home. Was Mason staying there by himself?

She shouldn't even care; she should just drive away and peace out, but curiosity and a broken heart were causing her to be a little crazy, so she drove her car down the road to the bistro. Sure enough, Mason was on the sidewalk, tossing his crutches to the side as he yelled at them. She watched him sit on the lawn, like a little boy who'd lost his ice cream cone and look up at the sky as he shook his head.

He needed help; she could see that, but was she ready to offer help? Was she ready to put herself out there for ridicule from a burly bear of a man who seemed to have had his hair ruffled from a season-ending injury?

Considering her options, she would rather be blasted by Mason and his smart mouth than by her dad and his condescending one. There was no contest.

Taking a deep breath, she drove up right next to Mason and

rolled down her window.

"Need a ride?" she called out, as Mason's head snapped up.

The lines in his forehead creased as he made eye contact with Piper. So far, her chances of her offer of help being accepted were not looking good.

"No, I don't," he said, full of pride.

"Looks like it. That was quite the lashing you were giving those crutches."

Mason looked at his crutches that were scattered on the ground, but didn't change his expression.

"That's how I fucking talk to them," Mason paused, as he most likely thought about the ridiculousness that was coming out of his mouth. "Stop stalking me!"

"I was just in the neighborhood, don't flatter yourself," Piper lied, as she felt a slight pink shade grace her face from doing just that, stalking him.

"How convenient for you."

Blowing out a frustrated breath, Piper asked, "Do you need a ride or not?"

"No, I don't," Mason said defiantly, as he ran his hands over the grass. "This is my thinking spot, and you're disturbing the deep thoughts that are running through my head."

"Is that right?" Piper asked, as she suspiciously eyed Mason. "Trying to solve world hunger over there?"

"As a matter of fact, yes," Mason replied, as he lay back on his elbows, exposing his tight chest that his shirt was stretched across.

Rolling her eyes, she said, "And how's that going for you?"

Mason eyed her and said, "Very well, actually. I have a brilliant idea."

"Is that right?"

"Yeah," he replied, using his cocky voice. "I figure if we start killing off all the dirty skanks like you, frying you up and serving it around the world, not only will your food consumption be given to someone else, but we will be feeding people with your bits."

Piper crinkled her nose. "Really, Mason. Cannibalism? I know you're a sick fuck, but I think that's a little beneath you."

"The only thing beneath me is you, so best you mosey the fuck out of here." Mason scurried his fingers in front of him, showing Piper exactly what he wanted her to do.

Instead of listening to the annoying prick, she put her car in park, got out of the car, grabbed both of his crutches, and put them in the back of her car.

"Hey, what the hell are you doing? You're going to get fucking whore dust all over those and they're going to leave me too..."

"Ha, ha, Mason. I'm a skank, I'm a whore, I've heard it all. Try something new and get in the damn car."

"Hooker?" Mason asked, still leaning back.

"You can do better," Piper said, as she stood over him with her arms crossed.

Mason looked to the sky as if he was deep in thought, and when he looked back at her, his eyes lit up as if he'd come up with the best name ever.

Licking his lips, he smiled and said, "Satan's slut?"

Nodding her head, she said, "Yup, that's me. Satan's slut. I visit him once a month to report on my accomplishments, and he pays me in hot and heavy slaps to the ass in his sex dungeon. It's fucking hotter than hell. You'll never know that kind of pleasure until you're slapped on the ass by the devil."

A small....very small smile twitched the corner of Mason's mouth as he said, "You always liked being slapped on the ass."

Blushing, Piper let the comment roll off of her and bent down to help Mason up.

"I don't need your help," Mason snapped his body away, instantly ending the somewhat-disturbing but semi-cheerful conversation they were having.

"Stop being a stubborn fuck. I know Jake and Lexi aren't home, and that's where you're staying. You're not crutching all the way back to their house, so get in the damn car." Piper really didn't know any of that, she just assumed, but she was getting tired of the little game they were playing.

"Fucking nag," Mason said, as he struggled to get up. Piper tried to help him, but he pulled away. "I got this," he said, as he grabbed ahold of a little tree to help him up. Once he pulled on the tree, his muscular build pulled the damn thing right out of the ground, making him fly back on the grass. A very un-ladylike snort came out of Piper's mouth as she watched the bewildered Mason try to grasp what just happened as he held the lifeless tree in the air.

Growing frustrated, Mason, tossed the little tree to the side, held out his hand, and said, "Just fucking help me up already."

Trying to stop the giggles that threatened to burst out of her, she grabbed ahold of Mason and helped him into her car. She tried to ignore the muscles that were flexing under her hand as she held onto his side and the masculine soap smell radiating off his body as she helped him.

Piper led him to her car and got him settled in the passenger seat. Jake and Lexi's place wasn't that far away, but for a stubborn man on crutches throwing a hissy fit, it seemed like ten miles.

They sat in silence as Piper drove to the beach house, neither one of them striking up conversation. Once they arrived, Piper grabbed Mason's crutches from the back and helped him out of the passenger seat. He was reluctant, but when he lost his balance from trying to rush out of her car, she steadied him, and he allowed it.

Small victory for her.

Following him up to Jake and Lexi's place, she waited for him to pull out a key from his pocket. Once he got the door unlocked, he said, "You can go now."

Not entirely the thank you she was expecting, but she guessed she shouldn't have thought he would have been grateful. He was, by far, the most stubborn man she had ever met.

"Can you get yourself settled in there?"

"I'm not incapable of taking care of myself. I'll be fine," Mason retorted with a testy tone.

Piper fired back, "Oh, is that right? Because last I saw, you were yelling at your crutches in the middle of someone's yard while sitting on the grass. That doesn't speak to me of you being able to take care of yourself."

"Fuck off…"

And there it was, Piper thought, Mason's instant brush off.

She watched as his back retreated into the house, watched him toss his crutches to the side, and watched him land his bulky body on the couch. He draped his arm over his face and let out an exasperated breath. His position gave Piper the opportunity to take in his body. Even three months later, she felt this indescribable pull toward him, like she needed to breathe the same air as him or she might fall apart.

He was just as moody, just as ornery, and just as handsome as three months ago. Damn him, she thought as she teetered between walking into the house to help him and just leaving him and trying to extract the memory of the man from her mind forever. After looking at him one more time, she knew the latter wasn't an option, so she stepped in the house, closed the door, and headed to the kitchen. Mason went to the bistro to eat some food, and he didn't get any, so he must be hungry. She would make him some food, and then leave…

Hannah

It had been a couple of days since Hannah texted Ryker and put herself out there, something she very rarely did. She hadn't heard anything, so the balls that she'd strapped on to text Ryker had shriveled up and buried themselves as far into her body as possible. No response from Ryker had her feeling embarrassed for saying anything to him at all. She should have sensed his moody attitude towards her in the grocery store and taken the hint to back off, but she couldn't. Her life was plummeting big time, especially in the last couple of months, and when she saw Ryker, it was like there was a little bit of light peeking through the sludge of her life. She needed to hold onto that feeling she got from being near him and milk it for all it was worth. Unfortunately, there wasn't much milk, because she was still lonely and embarrassed without a word from Ryker.

"Are you ready?" Leela asked as she sidled up next to Hannah who was sitting on a bench outside of the shoe store Leela was shopping in.

"Yeah, did you get the shoes?"

Leela held up the bag with a bright smile. "I did, I think my date is going to love them tonight."

"Date?" Hannah cheered up. "You didn't tell me you had a date. Tell me all about it. Who is he?"

Leela shook her head. "No, no, no. No details. All you get to know is that I have a date and these are the shoes I'll be wearing."

"What?" Hannah asked shocked. "Why aren't you telling me anything? I tell you all about my pathetic romantic life."

Leela patted Hannah's face and said, "Well, yes, but that's your choice, and it's not pathetic. It's just on…uh, what's the word?"

"Hiatus?"

Scrunching her nose, Leela looked at her and repeated the word, "Hi-a-tus?"

"Yes, like a break."

"Ahh," Leela said, as understanding set in. "I'm still learning all the words," she said with her cute accent.

"And you're doing a great job. If it wasn't for your hot accent, I'd forget that you're even from Italy."

"Now, don't say that," Leela said with a smile. "I need to make sure I keep my roots while I'm here in America."

Hannah laughed at Leela's accent.

"Now, tell me," Leela said, "What is going on with that Ryker boy and you? I thought you ran into him in the grocery store and talked."

"We did," Hannah huffed out as they walked around in the mall. "I kind of put myself out there, let him know that I missed him, and that I was sorry, but he didn't respond. I don't think he'll ever forgive me. I was such a hot mess back then. I mean, I still am now, but I at least have a clear head on my shoulders, unlike back then. I was so confused and so insistent upon proving everyone wrong about my relationship with Todd and working things out with him that I hurt the one person who had been nothing but kind and sweet to me."

"Maybe you tell him that," Leela suggested.

"Believe me, I want to, but he won't listen to me. He's too hurt."

"You never know until you try." Leela stopped in front of Victoria's Secret and raised her eyebrows. "Oh, do I have an idea," she smirked.

Hannah didn't like the look on Leela's face.

Grabbing Hannah's hand, she dragged her into the store and said, "We need to make you feel good inside and out. This way, when you go to see Ryker, he won't be able to help listening to you because you're going to look and feel smoking hot."

"Smoking hot?" Hannah asked. "But I never look smoking hot; I'm more the girl next door. You know, Keds and sweater sets, nothing like that," Hannah said while pointing to the itty bitty bra Leela was holding up while wiggling her eyebrows.

"Well, you're going to make a little change, girl. Time to toss those shoes to the side and put on some heels," Leela said, while pointing to Hannah's red Keds. "It's time we win that man back."

"Oh, God…"

Mason

Once the front door clicked shut, Mason let out a long breath that he'd been holding in ever since Piper spotted him throwing a temper tantrum on the side of the road. He hated that he let her help him, but in his current state, he didn't have an option, especially since Lexi and Jake already left and he was a pathetic mess, who couldn't crutch his way back to the house.

Fucking pride.

Thinking back to seeing Piper had Mason's body reeling. She was so damn beautiful, it pained him to be near her. He wished that she didn't have such an effect on him, especially after all the bullshit she put him through, but he couldn't help it. When she was around, she pulled him toward her; there was no stopping his body.

Secretly, when she was helping him to the car, he inhaled her scent of vanilla and lavender, the same scent that had played with his mind for the last couple of months. He was a sucker where Piper was concerned. He thought he could stand his ground against her, but after being near her for such a short time, he could feel the wall he put up around his heart start to break down piece by piece. She was his ultimate crutch, the one who could make him or break him.

A loud crash came from the kitchen, making Mason jackknife off the couch and hold up one of his crutches in defense.

"Who the fuck is there?" Mason called out, as he continued to hold out his crutch and hop over to the kitchen.

When he got to the kitchen, he saw a head full of bright red hair bending over and picking up a cutting board from the ground.

"What the hell are you doing here? I thought you left," Mason said, as he lowered the crutch, realizing he was trying to use it as a bullet-less gun.

Piper eyed his crutch and laughed as she picked up the cutting board and set it on the counter. She nodded toward the crutch and said, "That's one lethal weapon you have there."

Mason cleared his throat and stuck the crutch under his arm to help support his body. Ignoring her jab, he said, "I asked you a question."

"Oh, that's right," she said with her hand on her hip. "I forgot that you're a giant ass who can't seem to have any fun."

Looking her up and down while biting his bottom lip, he said, "You know better than anyone I know how to have fun."

Instantly, her face blushed from his offhanded comment. Satisfied with himself, he pushed past her on his one crutch and went further into the kitchen to grab some water. When his crutch slipped on something on the ground, he flew back and was about to hit the ground when Piper put a stop to his fall by pushing on his back. He was much bigger than she was, so he was surprised she was able to push him up.

"Go sit down," she demanded.

"I'm fine!" Mason shouted, as he tore into the fridge and grabbed a water, as he tried to calm down from the embarrassment rushing through his body from slipping. He hated feeling inferior, useless, like he couldn't take care of himself at all. He was a strong man, and right now, he felt anything but strong.

"You don't look fine. Why can't you just set your pride aside for one second and let someone help you?"

Mason turned around and leaned against the counter as he took a sip of his water. "I don't have a problem with people helping me. If I did, I wouldn't be at Jake and Lexi's house. What I have a problem with is you helping me."

Piper nodded her head and replied, "I deserve that. I fucked you over and you're pissed. I get that, but right now, I'm the only one here, and according to Jake's schedule, he won't be back in town until Sunday night...meaning you're alone for the next five days."

"Yeah, so..." Mason said indignantly.

"So...you need someone to help you," Piper dragged out.

Mason eyed Piper for a second, and then threw his head back and laughed. Really laughed.

When he was able to control himself, he looked at Piper and said, "And you think you're going to help me?"

"Who else is going to do it?"

Shaking his head, Mason said, "I'd rather army crawl my way around San Diego to my appointments and to get food than to have you take care of me. Fuck knows if you're in charge, you'll end up chewing my dick off and fucking feeding it to the seagulls outside."

Piper's eyebrow rose as she said, "That makes no sense. Face it, Mason, you're fucked without me."

Trying not to show a tell, Mason kept a straight face. She was right. He had a physical therapy appointment on Friday that he needed to go to and had no one to help him in and out of the building, let alone get him there. He'd proven to himself today that he was incapable of doing anything on his own. Why did he think coming to San Diego was a good idea? Probably because he wanted nothing to do with Denver right now; it just reminded him of the season he was no longer a part of.

She just stood in front of him with her arms crossed as if she knew it all. Cocky bitch.

"Fuck," Mason said under his breath, making her smile up at him.

"I'm glad you realize you actually need help. Now, go sit down and I'll make you lunch. I'm sure you're hungry."

"Like fucking hell you're going to make me lunch. You'll poison it; I'm not a jackass."

Quirking her lip, Piper said, "You really think I'm going to poison you? What the hell is wrong with you?"

"I've been burned before. I'm not taking any chances." Mason reached behind her, opened a cupboard, took out a package of beef jerky, and said, "This will do me just fine." He ripped the bag open and shoved some jerky in his mouth as he looked at Piper, chowing down.

"You're a pig."

"You're the devil."

They stared each other down, as Mason continued to chew on the beef jerky, making God-awful chewing noises to grate on her nerves. By the way her eye began to twitch, he knew he was getting to her.

Finally giving up, Piper threw her hands in the air and said, "Fine, I'll just make myself lunch and you can watch me eat it."

"Fine," Mason said defiantly.

Lying down on the couch, making sure there was no room for Piper to join him, he listened to her clang around in the kitchen. His beef jerky was good, but the moment he started to smell grilled cheese and soup, his stomach was roaring.

"Damn, bitch," Mason muttered. She knew what she was doing, tempting him with her grilled cheese skills; well, he wasn't going to fall for it, no way in hell.

Piper appeared in the living room with a tray full of grilled cheese and a huge bowl of piping hot tomato soup. The aromas were twisting knots in Mason's hungry stomach, but he averted his eyes from the delectable treats.

"Just want to enjoy the view outside while I eat my lunch, hope you don't mind," Piper said with a condescending smile. Damn her. He either wanted to rip that smile off her face and teach her a lesson or pull her to the ground and kiss her smile until she kissed him back. There was something seriously wrong with him. Not only was his stomach in for a ride, but his emotions seemed to have jumped on a roller coaster today as well.

Licking her lips and taking a gooey bite into the grilled cheese, Piper moaned as she started to chew the lunch staple. Mason's stomach growled at the sight of the cheesy goodness and the woman who was eating it.

Slowly, his control was slipping as she dipped the sandwich into the soup.

"Wow, this is so good. I think using the four slices of cheese on these sandwiches was a good idea…"

"You're a fucking bitch," Mason said as he leaned over, grabbed the tray, and put it on his lap. He dove into the sandwiches and started dunking them left and right into the soup, while shoving them in his mouth like a maniac.

He caught a glance of Piper as triangles of grilled cheese were flying down his gullet, and she was smiling ear to ear. She might have won this round, but she sure as hell wasn't going to win the next.

CHAPTER SEVEN

Ryker

"What are you going to do tonight?" Jesse asked Ryker, as they both put on their shirts. Practice was brutal, given the fact that Mason was out of commission and Ryker was the only one really able to catch Jesse's throws. The other receivers were alright, but without Mason, Ryker knew he was going to be getting his ass handed to him.

"Relaxing and drinking a beer. I was thinking about inviting Ashlin over for some dinner…and when I say invite her over for dinner, I mean asking her to make my sorry ass something to eat."

"I see," Jesse said as he turned away, making Ryker smirk.

It was so obvious that Jesse liked Ashlin, and kind of comical to Ryker that Jesse didn't talk to him about it, so what else could Ryker do but push Jesse to his breaking point?

"Yeah, she's been coming over almost every night since Mason's injury, making sure I'm fed and that my muscles are relaxed. She can give one hell of a massage, man. Last night's massage was so good that I almost…"

Jesse held up his hand and said, "Listen, I don't really feel like hearing it, so just keep that shit to yourself."

Ryker laughed hard as he took in Jesse's perplexed look. "Dude, you're so easy. I haven't seen her since your party. Why don't you just fucking admit it to me that you like Ashlin?"

If Jesse's skin was a little lighter, Ryker would have sworn Jesse blushed, but his mocha-colored skin made it almost impossible to tell.

"If you're worried about me, there's nothing to worry about. Seriously, we're just friends. She asked me for your number the other day. She has some little crush on you, man. I don't know why, but she does."

Jesse's head snapped up from the football that he was tossing around in his hands and he said, "Seriously? Did she tell you that?"

Laughing again, Ryker said, "No, but I can tell. Why else would she want your number? Get a clue, bud, she wants a piece of your QB ass."

Jesse nodded his head as he took in what Ryker was saying. "So, do you think I should text her, see what she's up to?"

Shaking his head in disgust at Jesse's lack of charisma, Ryker said, "Dude, I'm not going to walk you through the process of getting a girl. You had something flowing between you two at your party, run with that. She's not going to wait around forever, and she's the kind of girl that needs an assertive man to take control."

Jesse sat down and ran his hands over his face. "Funny thing is, I'm not that guy." Jesse turned away as he muttered, "Fuck," to himself, trying to hide his embarrassment.

Ryker really wasn't in the mood to get all deep with Jesse at the moment, especially since he was tired as hell and just wanted to prop a beer on his stomach as he shoved peanuts down his gullet while relaxing on his couch.

Trying to move along the conversation, Ryker patted Jesse on the shoulder and said, "You'll be fine. Just ask her out." Not his best advice, but frankly, Ryker wasn't in the mood. "Go get those titties, man," Ryker finished off, as he walked out of the locker room, not wanting to look back at Jesse because he knew if he did, he'd stay and listen to Jesse's sob story about why he was a gentle fucking giant, and Ryker wasn't interested.

On the way home, he drove through a fast food restaurant, got himself a couple of burgers and went home. Beer, burgers, and peanuts, not much more a guy could ask for.

When Ryker pulled into his driveway, he noticed there was another car parked in it and a girl standing outside his door, ringing the doorbell. Confused as to who knew where he lived and who would be visiting him right now, he cautiously got out of the car and walked to the front of the house.

He was a couple steps away from the girl when she turned in defeat from him not answering the door. When she spotted Ryker, she squealed and flew back a couple feet from being startled.

"Goodness, Ryker. You startled me," Hannah said, as she breathed heavily and held her hands to her heart.

Ryker had to do a double take, because the girl he was staring at sounded like Hannah, but looked nothing like her. She was wearing a tight, short skirt that caressed her thighs, a shirt that barely reached her waistline, showing off a smooth view of her tight stomach, and a pair of black high heels. Her hair was shorter and had light highlights contrasting with her brown hair. Her makeup was heavier than usual, but her eyes stood out like laser beams, sucking him in.

What. The. Hell?

Ryker gulped as he took her in. "Hannah?"

"Hi, Ryker," she said sheepishly, letting Ryker know that the woman he fell for was still in the knockout body that was standing before him.

"Uh, what are you doing here?" he asked, looking her up and down while scratching his head with the hand that held the bag of burgers he'd purchased for himself.

Looking at the ground, Hannah replied, "I really wanted to see you. I know this is really presumptuous of me, but I thought maybe you might want to hang out tonight?"

He was speechless; he couldn't get over the way she looked.

"Why are you dressed like that?" he asked, pointing at her

body.

"Do you not like it?" her eyes widened as she responded self-consciously. "Leela said it was the new me."

"I like the old you," Ryker said, before he could stop himself.

Her eyes widened even more as tears started to form in her eyes.

"I knew this was a bad idea. I told her I looked stupid," Hannah said, as she started to move toward the driveway. "Sorry for bothering you."

A foreign creature must have taken over his body because, in his head he was saying good riddance, but his body wasn't listening. Instead of letting her go, he grabbed her arm and stilled her. Her body was right next to his as he spoke into her ear.

"I meant I liked the old you better, but you look damn good now."

She turned her head to look at him as she said, "Really?"

Licking his lips, he responded as he looked her up and down, "Really."

A bright smile lit up her face, and that was the moment his restraint snapped. All the pent up anger, his stubbornness, and the wall he'd put up around his heart broke down with one sweet smile from Hannah. He wanted to hate her, to get her out of his head, but it was impossible with those ice blue eyes baring his soul and the sweetest smile known to man looking up at him as if she just won the best prize in the world. He was a goner.

Not even caring to think about his actions, he dropped his bag of burgers, gripped Hannah's hips and pushed her up against the side of his house. Before she could react, he grabbed her hands, held them above her head and pressed his chest against hers. They were both breathing erratically as they searched each other's eyes. No one spoke and no one moved, they just stared at each other, waiting for the other one to break, to make the first move.

Hannah's eyes went to Ryker's lips and, as she bit down on her bottom lip, Ryker knew this was it…he was jumping in head first and hell if he could stop himself.

Ever so slowly, as he held her hands above her head, Ryker moved his lips to hers, leaving only a breath between them. He looked into her eyes one last time before he finally pressed his lips against hers.

The moment they connected, Ryker let out a pent up moan that he must have been holding onto ever since he laid eyes on Hannah at Dick's Last Chance.

Their kiss was gentle and sweet, but urgent. Their lips moved in tandem as they finally gave in and explored each other. Her lips were soft and just full enough that Ryker enjoyed getting lost in them. Their bodies moved closer as Ryker continued to press her up against the wall of his house. One of his hands continued to hold hers, as his other hand rested on her hip and gradually made it up to her ribcage, right under her breasts.

A luscious whimper escaped Hannah's mouth as Ryker's hand stilled at her rib cage. His hand itched to go further, but he showed restraint, just caressing her side with his thumb, wishing and praying that soon it would be her nipple that he was pinching between his fingers.

Ryker opened his mouth slightly to see her reaction, and was pleasantly surprised when her mouth opened as well, granting him access. Taking his trip around her lips incredibly slowly, he gently licked her upper lip as he kissed her, letting her know what was to come. She let him take charge as she gave him an even wider open-mouthed kiss. That was all he needed as he slipped his tongue in her mouth. The feel of her tongue on his was something he would never be able to erase from his memory. Even though it was a simple kiss, it felt so damn erotic with the way her body continued to press against his and the feel of her soft breasts against his hard chest.

Not wanting to give the neighbors a show, he reluctantly pulled away just enough so he could look her in the eyes.

Once her eyes opened, Ryker was pleased that they were filled with lust...lust that he always hoped for from her. He kissed the tip of her nose and said, "I have some burgers, do you want to share dinner with me?"

Delivering another one of her sweet smiles, she nodded her head, making Ryker's heart flip inside of his chest.

Grabbing her hand, he entwined their fingers together and led her into his house. He pointed to the bathroom down the hallway and said, "There are some washcloths down there; wash that make-up off your face, and I'll bring you one of my shirts and a pair of my shorts. I want to see the Hannah I know, even though this Hannah is gorgeous."

Nodding her head again in embarrassment, she took off toward the bathroom, giving Ryker an amazing view of her bubble butt. He may be a fool for letting her so easily back into his life, but he couldn't help it; the moment he saw her handing beers out to other men, she stole his heart away.

Jesse

Wiping his hands against his shorts, Jesse looked down at his phone as he sat in his car and contemplated whether or not to call Ashlin. They'd had a great time at his party; he'd kissed her for fuck's sake, and then they talked on the phone the other night. This shouldn't be that hard, but for some reason, it was. He was always shy when it came to the opposite sex, so reaching out and trying to "put on the moves" was a difficult thing for him.

Taking a deep breath, Jesse pressed the call button for Ashlin as his Bluetooth connected to his call. He pulled out of his parking spot at the stadium as her phone rang through his car's speaker system. Having the phone play through his car was more intimidating to him, as the surround sound installed in his car shook the ring through his body.

Clearing his throat, he waited for her to pick up. On the fourth ring, she spoke into the phone, "Hey, I was wondering if I was ever going to hear from you."

A smile spread across Jesse's face, as his racing heart eased at her answering the phone.

"Sorry, I was just trying to come up with enough money to buy you some cupcakes," Jesse said lamely, but felt better when she laughed into the phone.

"Oh, are these cupcakes made of gold and fed to you by the Queen of England?"

"Something like that," Jesse laughed. "So, would you be able to steal a moment away from your night and have some cupcakes with me?"

"Why do I find it so adorable that a big strong man like you wants to eat cupcakes with me?"

"You think I'm strong?" Jesse teased, feeling relaxed whenever he talked to Ashlin.

"Stop fishing for compliments and tell me where to meet you. I'm dying to try these cupcakes that have kept you from calling me."

"Meet me at the stadium in an hour. I'll be waiting for you."

"How should I dress?"

"Comfortable. See you in a bit."

Jesse hung up the phone and headed over to Mermaid's Bakery off of Champa Street. He had been to the bakery a couple of times, so he knew exactly how to get there in a short amount of time. He was guilty of having a sweet tooth, and Mermaid's was the perfect place for the cure, carrying multiple flavors of cupcakes.

Quickly, Jesse picked out the cupcakes be believed Ashlin would want, grabbed some drinks from the store, and headed back to the stadium. He grabbed one of the team blankets, went out to the field, spread it on the fifty yard line, and put out a little camping light that he had in his car, as well as the cupcakes and drinks. Then he went back out to the parking lot to wait for Ashlin.

He wasn't much of the romantic type, but he thought his little idea would win him some points. He wanted to impress Ashlin, even though he barely knew her; he couldn't help thinking about her and wishing that instead of going home after a game to an empty house, that she would be there waiting for him with open arms. When she was at his house the other night, he could easily imagine her living in his place. She fit in the big home perfectly, filling an empty void he'd had for a while.

A little white sedan pulled into the parking lot and parked right next to Jesse's Range Rover. Jesse rounded her car and pulled open her door, while holding a hand out for her. The first thing Jesse noticed was Ashlin's long bronze legs step out of the car. They were mouth-wateringly delicious to look at, especially when they were displayed by little cut-off shorts. It was a warm night for Denver, but he still wondered if she was going to be cold. As she proceeded to get out of the car, he noticed that she was wearing a long-sleeved Stallions shirt, and her hair was pulled back into a ponytail. She looked amazing and fresh with barely any make-up on.

"Wow, you look good," Jesse said, as he closed her door for her.

"Thank you, but I know I look like I just rolled out of bed."

The mention of bed from Ashlin's mouth had Jesse hardening in a matter of seconds, especially since she was showing off all the curves of her body in her tight clothes.

"Aren't you going to be cold?" Jesse asked, as he cleared his throat.

"That's what you're here for," Ashlin said, as she patted his chest. "You're supposed to keep me warm." She looked around the parking lot, and said, "Are we going to go somewhere? Because it's kind of creepy out here in the dark."

Smiling to himself, he pressed his hand to her lower back and guided her to the stadium as he listened to her talk about her day. It felt so natural, to have her next to him, listening to her stories and spending time with her in an intimate setting. Jesse could only hope this was the beginning of something special.

Once they got to the field, Ashlin stopped and looked at the blanket in the middle of the fifty yard line and the camping light that was giving off the only light in the stadium. Jesse guided her to the blanket, using his phone's "flashlight" to get them where they needed to be without tripping over benches and random equipment.

Ashlin turned around and looked up at Jesse. "Aren't you the cutest?" She slipped her arms around his waist and pulled him in for a hug. Jesse relished the warmth of her embrace, but was disappointed when she pulled away too quickly for his liking.

"What do we have here?" Ashlin asked, while sitting down on the blanket and fiddling with the box of cupcakes.

Jesse stood above her and smiled as he watched Ashlin play around with the cupcake box as if she couldn't wait a second longer. She was adorable, and so damn gorgeous. Even in her casual wear with no make-up, she made Jesse want to throw all caution to the wind, man up and take exactly what he wanted.

Sitting down next to her, but with a little distance between them, Jesse said, "I got some cupcakes from Mermaid's Bakery. Have you ever been there?"

Her eyes lit up. "Please tell me you got the churro cupcake?" Without even giving him a chance to answer, she flipped open the lid and squealed as she eyed exactly what she wanted. She grabbed the cupcake and took a huge bite from it, making Jesse laugh at the shock of seeing her manhandle the sweet treat.

"Well, I guess I got what you wanted."

Her eyes rolled in pleasure as she said, "This is my favorite cupcake ever!"

"Really? Never had it. I just got it because it sounded interesting."

Ashlin stopped mid-bite, and said, "You've never had one before? Oh, my God, Jesse, you haven't lived."

"Apparently not," he joked.

She leaned into him and said in a low whisper, "Get ready for your life to be flipped upside down." Even though she was talking about the cupcake, Jesse thought how his life was already turning upside down with her in it, leaning in close to him and whispering so close to his face that is was hard to breathe. She was so erotic and sexy at times that Jesse was afraid he would burst right through his pants.

Pulling off a piece of the cupcake, she leaned so she was mere inches from his face and said, "Open up." Jesse did as he was told and let her place the cupcake piece in his mouth. "Don't forget about the icing on my fingers," she said in a seductive voice, making Jesse grow even harder, making things uncomfortable in his lower regions.

Ever so slowly, Jesse sucked on Ashlin's iced-up fingers one by one while her face was still so close to his, close enough that he could easily switch from her fingers to her mouth flawlessly. Looking into her eyes, he licked his lips and said, "Delicious." She smiled brightly and pulled away, disappointing him. Even though he wasn't a forward kind of guy, he really wished they'd re-live the kiss they shared at his house on the lounge chair.

"So, tell me, Jesse, why did you bring me here tonight?" Ashlin asked, as she took another bite of the churro cupcake.

Jesse grabbed the German Chocolate cupcake and chowed down as he answered, "Wanted to show you the stars, I guess." He looked her in her eyes and said, "And spend some time with you in my comfort zone."

Licking her fingers, she finished off her cupcake and said, "I would think the end zone is your comfort zone, giving your record, not the fifty yard line."

Jesse laughed and replied, "True, but overall, the field is my comfort zone. It's where I feel at peace, and if I'm honest with you, you tie my stomach in knots, in a good kind of way, and I knew that if I was on my field, I could be brave enough to hold your hand, maybe even kiss you again."

A slow smile crossed Ashlin's face.

Jesse finished off his cupcake, took a sip from one of the drinks he bought, gave Ashlin one, and then capped it off when she was finished.

"Want to lay down?" Jesse asked, as he looked over at her. Nodding her head, Jesse bundled up a side of the blanket to make a faux pillow and then guided them both so they were on their backs. Their arms barely caressed as they looked up at the stars, filling

Jesse with warmth.

"Here, let me turn this off," Jesse said, while turning off the camping light, putting them into complete darkness. Even though they were in a giant open stadium, looking up at the stars, Jesse felt like they were in an intimate setting, on their blanket, only a whisper away from each other.

"This is beautiful," she murmured, as she shifted closer.

"Are you cold?" Jesse asked, concern lacing his voice.

"Just a little," she admitted.

"Here," Jesse sat up and folded the blanket that was on the side of her over her legs, and then laid back down. "There, that better?"

"Could be better."

"Yeah, how so?"

She sat up, pulled out his arm that was settled on his chest and laid her body next to his so his arm was wrapped around her and her head was on his chest, snuggling up next to him.

"So much better," she said as she placed her hand on his chest.

He felt like he couldn't breathe, she was so close to him, practically wrapped up like a pretzel with him. He liked it...no, he fucking loved it. Her breasts pressed against his side and her hair tickled the bottom of his chin, releasing a lilac scent that was intoxicating. She was memorable, perfect in every way, and in his mind, made just for him.

"Now, tell me," she asked, "Why is such a strong and confident man like you on the field so shy when it comes to the ladies? Shouldn't you be a cocky bastard with women texting you every two seconds?"

Shrugging his shoulders, Jesse said, "I've always been too busy for girls. I had a girlfriend, Katie, in high school and college, but she moved away. We're good friends now, but that's pretty much it. I've never really been the player that everyone expects me to be. I'm more of a reserved kind of guy; I like being at home."

"I get that vibe from you. You seem like a really good guy and very genuine."

Jesse nodded as she nailed his personality exactly. He was just an all-around good guy. He didn't go "fishing for bearded oysters" as Ryker liked to say. Mason and Ryker always tried to get him to go out with them, but frankly, he just wasn't interested because what he wanted was a wife, a future, not a quick bang in a broom closet…that was just not the kind of guy he was. It wasn't in his blood.

"I try to be," Jesse answered. "What about you? You're gorgeous and sweet, how come you don't have a boyfriend?"

Ashlin was quiet for a second as she thought about his question. She took a deep breath and said, "I really don't want to get into that side of my life. It's complicated and fucked up, and I'd rather not taint the impression you have of me."

Slightly disturbed by her answer and sad, Jesse squeezed her tightly to let her know that even though she didn't want to talk about her past right now, he would be there for her.

"Nothing you tell me could taint what I see in you, Ashlin."

Ashlin huffed at his comment, but dropped it.

"Do you not believe me?" Jesse asked, pushing the subject for some reason.

"No, I do, and that's what makes me nervous. You're too good, Jesse."

"Too good for what?" Jesse asked, confused.

Ashlin sat up and stroked his jaw with her petite hand. "You're too good for me, Jesse. I have a lot of baggage, and I could easily bring you down." Jesse was about to disagree with her, but she stopped him from talking by placing her fingers over his lips. "That doesn't mean I'm not a jealous girl and won't take what I want." With that, she placed both of her hands on either side of his head and lowered her mouth just above his. Licking her lips, she said, "I want you, Jesse, more than anything."

Silently agreeing, Jesse wrapped his hand around her neck and brought her lips to his, igniting the burning fires in the pit of his stomach. She melted into his chest as their tongues meshed together, arousing them both.

The way she moved her mouth against his had him quaking in his shoes, pleading for her to continue. She felt so perfect, so right. She was confident and sexy and had a powerful aura about her that had him begging for more.

Her hands ran up the sides of his face and cupped his cheeks, as she continued to move her tongue in and out of his mouth, testing his restraint. He hadn't had sex in a very, very long time; it was his choice because he just didn't find pleasure in fucking random women, but now that he had the woman he wanted in his arms, he felt his will slowly ticking way with each whimper and moan that came from her mouth.

Pulling away, Jesse ran his hand over her cheek and said, "You're so damn beautiful."

Smiling, Ashlin replied, "Then kiss me again."

She didn't have to ask him twice.

Brooke

Checking her watch, she sighed as she waited for Jax to get home. He'd been working late almost every night since Mason was injured, leaving no time to go on dates. She tried not to think about how, once again, football took precedence over her...just like when she was dating Mason. She kept reminding herself that she was just getting to know Jax, so she didn't need to go all psycho girlfriend on him.

Frankly, she wasn't even sure if they were boyfriend and girlfriend; it was so juvenile to think of such a thing, but she would like to know if they were exclusive. They'd seen each other a couple of times, but Brooke really didn't like sharing, especially after everything that went down between her, Jax, Mason, and Piper.

Shaking her head, she thought about the whole fucked up situation and how funny it was that, in the end, Brooke was talking to Jax, the sweet southern man who got screwed over by the fiery, indecisive redhead. Although, if Brooke had to look at the two men side by side, she would have a hard time picking too, she thought. Mason was rough, a domineering alpha male who got what he wanted. Jax was a sweet southern gentleman with a body to die for. Not that Mason didn't have an amazing body, Jax was just different…unexpected, and she liked that about him.

Car lights glared through the dark night, indicating Jax was finally home, which was a good thing, because Brooke was starting to freeze her tits off. Denver was pretty, but damn, it was cold sometimes.

Walking up to Jax's car, she waited for him to get out as she held onto the sandwiches she'd brought over in case Jax hadn't had dinner.

Smiling, Jax got out of the car and looked her up and down. "Hey, beautiful. Why do I get the great pleasure of seeing you tonight?"

Brooke instantly melted on the spot from the way his southern voice dripped with smooth molasses as he spoke to her. It was undeniable that he could possibly give her an orgasm by just talking sweetly into her ear.

"I thought I might surprise you with some sandwiches, is that okay?" she asked, as she held up the bag.

Eyeing the bag, Jax said, "I love sandwiches. Now, let's get you out of this cold night air."

Leading her by putting a hand at the small of her back, they entered his house and went straight to the living room, where Jax started a fire by just flipping on a light switch. Ah, modern conveniences.

"Sit," he pointed to the leather chair next to the fireplace. "I'll get us some drinks and plates. Would you like a beer?"

"Yes, please."

Jax winked at her and walked off toward the kitchen. He was wearing worn jeans, a navy blue Stallions polo, his ever-present white Nike hat, and his white Nike shoes. It was a common outfit for the man, and boy, did he pull it off. He was so damn hot with his broad shoulders, slim waist, and muscular thighs that were well-displayed by his jeans. He had it all, and she was one lucky girl to be sitting in his chair right now.

Carrying a tray with some drinks, plates, and chips on it, Jax walked back into the living room and set the tray down on the coffee table, which he pulled closer to them.

"You going to hog that chair all to yourself?" Jax teased as he eyed her.

"Maybe," she replied by eyeing him up and down.

"I guess I'll just have to go to the other room…" Jax fake walked away, making Brooke laugh.

"You're such a baby," Brooke said, as she got out of the oversized chair so Jax could sit down first.

As he passed her to sit down, he cupped her chin and placed a gentle kiss on her lips, making her insides flip upside down. "You like it, and don't even lie to me," he replied, right before he tore away from her and sat down in the chair, scooting the coffee table full of food closer to him.

Patting his lap, Jax said, "Come here."

"You know you have a perfectly fine dining room table we can eat at."

"Where's the fun in that? If we're at the table, I wouldn't be able to work my hand up your thigh, now would I? Now, get over here," he said, while leaning forward and grabbing her hand. He pulled her down on his lap and tugged her legs over his so her back was against the arm rest of the chair and her legs were on top of his. "Much better," he mumbled, as he leaned in and kissed the side of her neck.

Little beads of pleasure started to pour through her body as Jax's lips worked their way up and down her sensitive skin, sending goose bumps along her arms.

"I'm so glad you're here; you have no idea." Jax pulled away and looked her in the eyes, making her sink even further into his chocolate brown gaze. "I've had a rough couple of days and you here is making everything better."

"Are you trying to sweet talk me?" Brooke teased.

"Is it working?" Jax wiggled his eyebrows.

"Wouldn't you like to know?" Brooke grabbed the sandwiches and handed him one. "When was the last time you ate today?"

Jax thought about it for a second, and then said, "I had an apple for breakfast."

"What?" Brooke scolded. "Jax, you can't just eat an apple all day. You need more food than that. I don't want to be walking around with a skeleton."

A smile crossed Jax's face which only irritated her. "What are you smiling about? I'm serious," she demanded.

Gripping her thigh and drawing small circles with his thumb, Jax said, "I like you worrying about me. It's cute."

"Well, you better eat, so there's someone for me to worry about," Brooke said, while poking his ribs.

"Noted," Jax replied, just as he took a giant bite of his sandwich. "Damn, this is good. Thank you, Brooke."

"Of course," she replied, while taking a bite of her sandwich as well.

They both sat in silence as they ate their food, occasionally stealing glances at each other and smiling like fools. They didn't have to say anything or even touch, just the heated glare in their eyes spoke enough. They wanted each other badly, and it didn't look like anything was going to stop them.

Once they finished their food and tossed the wrappers to the side, Brooke turned Jax's hat so it sat backwards on his head and straddled his lap. Placing his hands on her hips, he situated her body so they were both comfortable. Given his height and her lack thereof, their faces were evenly leveled, giving Brooke perfect access to Jax's lips.

"So, tell me, have you missed me?" she asked, hoping to get the answer from him that she wanted to hear.

"Terribly," he said, warming her heart. "I'm sorry that I've been working late these past couple of days. Believe me, I would rather be here with you, getting to know you better…everywhere."

Jax ran his hands slowly up her thighs to the juncture of her hips and legs, making her want to squirm in place. It was such an easy thing to do, to run his hands up her legs, but to her senses, it was as if he was performing magic on her nerves, igniting every last sensation in her body.

"Everywhere?"

Nodding, he continued to move his hands up her body until his hands rested right below her breasts. Her breathing started to hitch as she tried to rein in her raging hormones. They were just hands, not magical orgasm wands, she thought to herself as she continued to stare him in the eyes. His head was leaning against the chair, and he was so casual, so comfortable…as if his slight movements weren't about to make her combust any minute.

Shifting on his lap, she wondered how he could be so calm, and then she felt the bulge that was protruding from his lap. She smiled at the thought of him being turned on as well.

Reaching for the hem of her shirt, she lifted it over her head and dropped it behind her so it was out of the way. She'd made sure to wear some sexy navy blue lingerie, just in case she was presented with the situation she was in at the moment.

Nodding in appreciation, Jax took in everything about her, slowly perusing her body and making her body temperature skyrocket. She didn't know how much more of this she could take; she needed to be with him.

"You're so sexy, Brooke," Jax said in a throaty tone. He outlined her bra with his finger, making her breathe even heavier. She just wanted him to touch her, in any way, just touch her and make the pressure building up in her core float away.

"Jax, I want you to fuck me." She didn't mean to be so crude, but she was at her breaking point. All the looks he gave her during dinner, the wait of not seeing him, and the slight touches he delivered were a recipe for explosion, and she needed to explode…badly.

Raising an eyebrow at her, Jax said, "Well, I never knew a lady to use such strong language."

"Jax…" she whined, actually whined. Is that what her life had come to?

Chuckling to himself, he wrapped his arms around her back and unclasped her bra in one swift movement. Looking down at her breasts, he licked his lips and said, "Damn, I'm about to have myself a little fun."

CHAPTER EIGHT

Hannah

"Were you going to eat all these burgers by yourself?" Hannah asked, as she counted five in the bag Ryker brought back to his place.

Not ashamed, Ryker said, "Yeah, I'm a hungry boy." He lifted his shirt while patting his stomach. Hannah felt like her eyes bulged out of their sockets as she took in the extremely well-defined six pack Ryker was sporting. She never swore, but holy shit, those abs were swear worthy.

Laughing, Ryker poked her in the side and said, "Didn't your mother ever tell you not to stare? It's not very polite."

Shaking her head, she said, "I'm sorry. I just...I mean wow, Ryker. You're kind of toned for a guy who likes to eat five burgers at..." she checked her watch and said, "At nine at night."

"I've been blessed with the metabolism of a god."

"And an extreme amount of humbleness as well," Hannah added.

"Always humble," Ryker said, as he dove into his first cheeseburger. "Here, these two are for you, and I'll take these three. Fair?"

Eyeing the burgers, Hannah said, "One will be just fine for me."

"Now, Hannah, I've noticed you're looking a little thin; you better eat two burgers, or you're going to be in trouble."

He thought she was thin? She didn't think she'd lost that much weight. Yes, she missed a couple of meals here and there when she was depressed as hell when Todd broke her heart and she lost Ryker, but nothing noticeable.....right?

"I'm not thinner," she said defensively.

Ryker gave her the "You're kidding me" look and then put his burger down. "Come here," he waved his finger at her.

They were both sitting on his couch, but with a decent distance between them. After she changed and washed her make-up off, the magic that sparked between them out in his front yard had slightly disappeared, and immediately Hannah felt awkward, even though she knew she shouldn't. She was with Ryker, the one person who could make her feel the most comfortable.

Moving closer, she sat a foot away from him now.

"I said, come here," Ryker scolded, as he pulled her on top of his lap. He positioned her so she was now straddling him, making her feel even more awkward. She was by no means a virgin, but she was also a little more reserved, so that fact the that she was wearing men's clothing while straddling someone she once only thought of as a friend was a foreign thing to her.

"There, much better," Ryker said, as he looked her up and down. "You see, I've known you for a while, and I've really examined your body..."

"Ryker!" Hannah exclaimed, as her face heated from embarrassment.

"Nothing wrong with taking a look at the goods," he joked. "Anyway, you're thinner. I can tell, because I know this body like the back of my hand." Gently he started to lift her shirt, but she stopped his hands.

"What are you doing?"

"I want to make sure you're not thinner than I thought," he

said with a smile.

Getting off his lap, she replied, "Nice try, Romeo. Eat your burgers."

Laughing, he bit into his burger, but then grabbed her hand, making sure she didn't go too far. The feel of his hand on hers was overwhelming. She liked Ryker, a lot, and always thought of him as a friend…yes, she thought he was sexy, but never did she think she would be sitting on his couch, wearing his clothes, and holding his hand as she watched him take down three cheeseburgers.

"So, tell me," Ryker said with his mouth full, "What made you go out and get all gussied up? You weren't meeting up with someone else, were you?" The way he asked the question was teasing, but Hannah saw the insecurity that was right below the surface. He was a very confident man, but at that moment, she saw his confidence lacking.

Finally taking a bite of her burger, she answered, "No, the only person I was looking to see was you tonight."

A small smile grew on Ryker's face as he took in what she said. "Is that right? Well, aren't I a lucky son of a bitch?" Hannah quirked an eyebrow at him for his language. "Oh, yeah. Sorry. Why the change, though?"

She shrugged her shoulders and said, "Thought that maybe if I changed, became, you know…sexier," she practically whispered making Ryker smile brighter, "That maybe you would give me a chance, take a second look at me."

Ryker creased his brows as he listened to her. Putting down his second burger, he said, "Hannah, you have to know that I've never had a hard time looking at you, or thinking about you. You've been on my mind ever since I first saw you…"

"But we haven't seen each other in three months, and then at the grocery store, it was like you couldn't get away from me fast enough."

"Yeah, because I was mad at you," Ryker said with a firm voice. "I mean, damn, Hannah. You ripped me apart the moment you compared me to Todd. I would do anything for you…anything!" Ryker's voice kept rising, making Hannah wilt in place. "And then you go and compare me to Todd, when I'm nothing like that douche nugget. I would never cheat on you…ever, and do you know why? Because I fucking cherish you; I cherish everything about you, from the way your eyes sparkle in the sun to the way you crinkle your nose when I swear. There is nothing I don't like about you, and it fucking gutted me when you so easily turned me away…when I was trying to be there for you."

Tears started to trickle down her face as she listened to Ryker get everything off his chest. She had no excuse; she'd been terrible to him, and all she could think about was that he deserved better.

Running his hands over his face, he asked, "Why are you crying?"

"I'm just so sorry," she sniffed, as she quickly wiped her tears away. "I was so horrible to you when you've been nothing but amazing." Getting up, she said, "I need to go."

Ryker was on her so fast, she didn't know what was happening. He grabbed her hands and pulled her back down so they were only inches apart.

"You're not going anywhere. You can't just walk away, Hannah. I'm mad, yes, but that doesn't mean I want you to leave. If I wanted you to leave, I would tell you. I just…" he paused for a second, as he tried to choose his words. "I just need to regain myself, okay? I didn't think that you would ever come to my place or lay those gorgeous lips on mine," Ryker said, while moving his thumb across her bottom lip. "I have so many damn feelings running through me right now, I just need some time to gather myself, but I want you here while I do that, okay?"

Nodding her head, she relaxed back on his couch. Ryker was different than Todd in so many ways, but one of the main differences was that he actually wanted her around; he wanted to be with her. That was a feeling she never really got from Todd, and maybe it was because he had a wife and family in New York, who knew? But she liked whatever Ryker was giving her, even if it was just companionship for now. She would take it.

"Spend the night with me?" Ryker asked, as he looked over at her. "I just want to hold you."

She nodded, as she took another bite of her burger. Ryker was on number three already and eyeing the second one she probably wouldn't wind up eating.

"Good," Ryker said, as he pulled her into his chest and wrapped his arm around her shoulder. They just sat like that, in silence, as they held onto each other. In that moment, Hannah knew something was brewing between them…something great; she just hoped she would be able to hold onto it.

Ashlin

He was a good kisser. No, he was one hell of a kisser. She was lying on top of Jesse, lost in the way his body molded with hers and letting his lips control every aspect of her life. When he called and said he wanted to meet up, a little part of her stomach flipped in excitement; being able to see him again was something she looked forward to. She was never the relationship kind of person or someone who waited around for a guy to call, but with Jesse, it was different. She got excited when she saw his name flash across her phone.

As she adjusted herself on his stomach, she felt the very noticeable bulge in his pants, straining to be released. Unfortunately, he kept his hands above her shoulders, driving her crazy, so she decided to take things up a notch, because frankly, her insides were burning with need.

Moving her hand down between them, she moved past his stomach and was just about to cup him when his hand stopped hers.

Pulling away slightly, she asked, "What's wrong?"

His eyes were hazy from kissing as he looked back up at her. His brow creased as he thought about what he was going to say. "I really want this, more than I think you will ever know, but I want to get to know you better. I think it's important to get to know each other when you're starting a relationship."

Relationship?

The word rang through her head with warning bells sounding off. She knew she wanted to see him, to possibly get to know him, but a relationship? Is that what they were doing? In a matter of seconds, she climbed off of him and started searching around for her purse as the word relationship started ringing through her head. She didn't do relationships, ever. Relationships meant becoming attached, and becoming attached to someone only led to heartache and disappointment.

She could feel her breathing becoming erratic, but she couldn't steady it; she just needed to get away from Jesse as quickly as possible. She was only in this for a good lay, maybe a really fucking fantastic lay, but not a relationship.

"Ashlin, what's wrong?" Jesse said, jarring her out of her thoughts. She looked into his deep brown eyes and instantly felt terrible, because the worry and concern lacing them had her heart breaking in half. The man had no clue what he was getting himself into when he started talking to her, and that was her fault because she led him on. "Did I say something wrong?" he asked.

"Uh, no. I just have to get home. I think I left the oven on." Yup, she played the oven card, but she had nothing else in her arsenal.

"Oven? Are you brushing me off?" Jesse asked, almost offended.

"No," she got up and started walking toward the tunnel, or at least she thought she did until she realized it was pitch black. She fumbled around in her purse, trying to find her phone, while she heard Jesse behind her gathering up everything.

"Ashlin, wait," he called out. "If you really have to get home, at least let me walk you to your car."

Knowing he was being logical, she waited for him.

They walked in silence out of the stadium; all the while, Ashlin's heart beat at an unhealthy rate. She just needed to get away from Jesse, and then she would be okay. When they got to her car, she quickly unlocked it and called out a thank you, trying to avoid an awkward goodbye, but Jesse was having none of that.

"Hey, why are you running away from me? I'm sorry; I just didn't want to move too fast. Please know that I think you are so incredibly sexy, and I want nothing more than take you back to my bed."

He held on tightly to her arm, not letting her go.

"It's not that, Jesse…"

"Then what is it? Whatever it was, please let me know; don't shut me out."

Growing frustrated, she just blurted out, "I don't do relationships."

As if she'd smacked him, he stepped back from her and let go of her arm. A look of dejection crossed his face.

"Then, why are you here?"

Not wanting to sound like a total sex-crazed groupie, she said, "Because I like you and I think you're hot."

Jesse nodded his head as he stepped back again. "I see. Well, I'm not that guy, Ashlin. I'm not the guy who is just going to have random sex for the hell of it. I'm sorry. I thought that maybe you wanted something more; I guess I was wrong." Handing over the box of cupcakes, he said, "For what it's worth, I had a nice time. Take these; I won't eat them."

With that, he turned on his heel and walked to his car, leaving her alone like she wanted, but for some reason, she felt worse off.

Jax

Brooke's breasts floated in his face and all he could think about was getting out of the chair they were sitting in and to his bed. His first time with her was not going to be uncomfortable as they tried to position themselves correctly in his chair.

Scooping her up, he placed a kiss on her mouth and said, "We're going to do this right."

"I don't care how we do it; all that matters to me is that we're doing it."

Jax rushed her to his room and tossed her on the bed. She looked up at him with a saucy smile as he tore his shirt off, followed by his shoes, socks and pants, leaving him only in his boxer briefs.

Shaking her head, she said, "I really can't get over how hot you are, especially for an old man."

Smiling, Jax pounced on her and said, as he was inches from her mouth, "I'm not an old man."

"Prove it," Brooke pushed.

"Gladly."

Not giving her a chance to retort back, Jax took her lips with his, relishing the way they were so plump and soft against his. Immediately, her hands found his back as he ran his hands up to her breasts. The moment he'd released her bra, he'd needed to get his hands on her; he knew they were going to be just perfect for his hands, and he was right. They were so damn perfect. Just full enough, but not too big.

A low moan escaped Brooke's mouth as Jax squeezed her breast and massaged her nipple with his thumb. Her little pink nipples were erect and aroused, waiting for him to take control, which he did. Leaving her mouth, he moved his way down to her chest and sucked in one of her nipples, while his hand continued to massage the other breast.

Her chest lifted from the bed, letting him know she wanted more. Lightly biting down, he nipped her, making her joyously cry out his name. Pride surged through Jax's chest as he watched the ever-confident Brooke turn into a pile of mush on his bed. He knew she had to be ready; there was no doubt in his mind…for fuck's sake, he was ready to explode. Wanting to find out, he moved his hand down to her pants and started undoing them. She sensed his struggle and quickly let go of his hand to help him.

Once she was completely naked, he kneeled before her and took in the picturesque naked woman in front of him. Her skin was smooth and soft, her eyes were lustful and her curves were plentiful in all the right places. She was every man's wet dream, and he was the one who got to fuck her; he was one lucky ass.

"Are you wet for me?" Jax asked, feeling like she would be one who enjoyed dirty talk, especially since she'd begged him to fuck her in the living room.

"Find out for yourself."

Leaning over her body, he whispered in her ear, "One or two fingers?"

"It better be two," she said breathlessly.

"Believe me, it's more than two," and with that, he put two fingers into her heated center, confirming that she was more than ready for him. "Mmm, you're so wet, and all for me."

"Only for you, Jax," Brooke moaned, as he pushed his fingers in and out of her with a come-to-me motion. It was so erotic to watch such a beautiful woman writhe from the simple work of his fingers.

"I'm going to fucking come," Brooke shouted right before she gripped the sheets of the bed and screamed his name. Jax continued to press up, hitting her G-spot and making her lose all control. She continued to vocalize her pleasure, which pleased Jax greatly. Some women could be obnoxiously loud and overdo it, but Brooke was sexy and hot and the way her voice strained when she came was something Jax would have in his mind for a while.

"I'm not done with you," Jax said, as he leaned over and started kissing her again as she recovered. "Spread your legs."

She did as she was told, giving him an all access pass to her arousal. Slowly lowering his head, he started pressing kisses down her stomach, making her intake of breath quite noticeable. He got to her pubic bone and kissed it lightly, letting her know his intentions. He moved his hands under her ass and brought her arousal to his mouth. She smelled like heaven as he drove his tongue inside of her. This was his second time eating her out, and he was fucking loving it.

Her orgasm made her even wetter than before, making his

tongue slide around easily. He flicked and sucked, making sure to hit every part of her delicious pussy. He was not much of an oral man, he did it to please his woman, but with Brooke, it was turning into a necessity. He needed to see the way he controlled her entire body with just the flick of his tongue. The way she closed her eyes tightly, held on for dear life to the sheets and moaned and whimpered as he took what he wanted. It was intoxicating, and before he knew it, she was screaming his name again as her pelvis flew into his mouth, making him smile. He continued to suck on her until she was sated.

Happy with himself, he took off his boxers and grabbed a condom from his night stand. Brooke looked up at him and gave him a shy smile as she took in his powerful erection. He didn't think he had ever been so hard in his life.

"Touch yourself," she said with lustful eyes.

Wanting to please her, he grabbed ahold of his erection and started pumping himself. The strain from not having a release yet and the beautiful woman lying naked in front of him had him shaking as he fought off his release.

"Brooke, I want to come inside of you."

She spread her legs even more and said, "Then do it. Fuck me, Jax."

Not giving her a second to change her mind, he grabbed her legs, put them on his shoulders and surged inside of her, so fucking deep.

"Ahh, fuck, you feel good," Jax strained as his dick was encased in her warmth. He had never felt anything so perfect before in his life. He couldn't hold off any longer, he drove into her, not letting up once.

Her cries of pleasure echoed through his room as he felt her starting to contract around him, once again giving into her orgasm. The strength of her arousal around him had his balls tightening and his dick aiming for release. With one last thrust, he belted out her name as he came inside of her.

"Christ," Jax said, as he made slow thrusts, trying to regain himself. "Fucking hell, that was good."

"So good," Brooke said, as her arm was draped over her eyes, as if she couldn't take any more.

Jax released himself from her, threw out his condom and cleaned himself up in his bathroom before returning to Brooke's side. Scooping her up, he cuddled her on his bed and said, "Stay the night?"

"I didn't plan on leaving."

"Good."

He kissed her ear and nuzzled into the crook of her neck. Happiness surrounded him as he held onto a woman he never saw coming into his life, but he couldn't be happier about her being with him.

CHAPTER NINE

Mason

"Will you stop fiddling around with the radio and just leave it?" Piper chastised as Mason kept switching the radio stations, pretty much just to annoy Piper. Mission accomplished.

She had been over at Jake and Lexi's house every day since she picked him up on the side of the road. They never talked, except for the obligatory conversations they had to have...like how you're feeling and can I get that for you? She would come over around noon and make lunch and dinner for Mason to heat up later. She would also re-fill his ice packs and wrap his knee back up in compression, if needed. Along with feeding him and tending to his knee, she cleaned up around the house. He told her she didn't need to keep showing up, but every day, but without blinking an eye, she stood at the front door around noon, and to Mason's chagrin, every day he let her in.

He started to worry because he was getting used to having her around, depending on her feedings and the way she made his bed. It wasn't good...he knew it wasn't good at all, but hell if he could stop it. He craved her. He was an addict.

When she was busying herself around the house, Mason acted

like he was reading or watching TV, never letting her see him staring at her, even though that was all he did. He watched her float around the house as if she owned the place, tending to his every need. The whole situation was odd, especially given the way they ended things between them with the classic, "fuck off" and "go to hell." They were demented.

Having Piper in the house with him was like having a giant pink, glitter dildo in the room that no one talked about or touched. Clearly, they were both bitter and angry, but neither of them talked about it. Instead, they just lived and went through the motions of taking care of Mason's knee. It was all very odd to him.

"Don't be so sensitive," Mason said, as he finally picked a Spanish station that was really meant to push her over the edge.

"For fuck's sake," Piper scolded, as she switched the radio off, making Mason smile to himself. "You think you're so funny, don't you?"

"Nope, I know I'm funny, and you're a hothead, so it's way too easy to mess with you."

"I'm not a hothead!"

Laughing, Mason dragged out, "Riiiight, that's why you're about to grab ahold of the steering wheel with your teeth like a fucking rabid dog."

"You're a dick."

"Tell me something I don't know."

"Are we going to discuss what the doctor said today? How you need to go back to Denver to start rehab with your trainers?"

Mason quirked an eyebrow at her, even though he knew she couldn't see him. "I'm sorry, I didn't know that concerned you. I must have missed something during that exam which you so rudely barged in on. I don't remember the doctor bringing you into the conversation once. "

"Don't be an ass; someone had to pay attention. You couldn't take your eyes off the new issue of the *Sports Illustrated*, swimsuit edition, so who knows what you paid attention to."

"That's because Isabel Gomez has the fucking sweetest tits

I've ever seen. Fucking tan melons begging me to bite into them. I bet Ashlin will have her number if I ask."

Piper was silent at Mason's comment. Old Mason would have felt bad, given the fact that, hands down, Piper had the best breasts he had ever held, but new and ornery Mason didn't give a shit about making the girl that ripped his heart apart feel bad.

"What, you can't talk now? Just because I talked about someone else's tits? News flash, you're not the last girl I fucked."

"No, that was Brooke..." Piper spat out with such venom that Mason thought she might just dump him on the side of the road and leave him.

Why she was getting mad at him, he had no clue. She was the one who couldn't decide between him and Jax; she was the one who went and got engaged to another man when she promised to be with Mason...she was the one who fucked everything up, not him.

"Really? You want to go there, Piper?" Rage started to boil in Mason's blood, gearing him up for a fight...something they were really good at. "Because I have a whole shit storm of things we can talk about."

Letting out a frustrated breath, Piper sighed and said, "I'm not here to fight with you, Mason, I just want to make sure you're okay."

"I'm fine," he shouted, not knowing why he was getting so damn emotional. Piper brought it out in him, fucking females. "I'm fine," he announced more calmly. "I don't need your help."

"Is that right? Then why do you keep letting me in every day when I show up?"

Silence met them in the car. She was right, why did he keep letting her in? Technically, he could take care of himself; it would be hard as hell, especially on crutches, but he could do it. He would most likely beat his head with his crutches to end his misery, but damn it, he would be able to do it. Maybe he just kept letting her in because it was easier; he didn't have to work as hard. He chalked it up to that, because if he thought about the other reason, of actually enjoying her company…that would go against everything he promised himself the minute she walked away from him.

Clearing his throat, he said, "You can just drop me off here, we're close enough to the house."

"I'm not going to drop you off on the corner. Are you insane?"

"Just drop me off here!" Mason shouted, slowly losing control of his emotions. He didn't want Piper near him; he couldn't handle it…not with her asking questions, not with her actually giving a shit about him. He couldn't handle it; he would lose the Piper-free barrier he'd put up around his heart if he stayed near her any longer.

"I'm not going to pull over," she shot back.

Losing his mind, Mason grabbed ahold of the steering wheel and brought her car to the sidewalk, making her scream and slam on the brakes.

"Are you fucking insane?" she asked as she held onto the steering wheel.

Not answering her, Mason got out of the vehicle, grabbed his crutches and started walking away from her, turning his back on the life he once wanted. Anger seared through him as he crutched his way to Jake and Lexi's house.

He was mad at himself for letting her back in his life; even if it was a small part of his life, he'd let her in. He let her take care of him, and he hated that he found himself depending on her to stop by…that he looked forward to having her come over. He tried to tell himself that he was just lonely, but if he thought about it, he was lonely for her, for her soft caresses, her exotic scent, and the way she could make him feel like he was floating on air. She was an addiction that he was having one hell of a time kicking.

Mason didn't pay attention to the outside world as he made it back to Jake and Lexi's house. It wasn't until he spotted Piper's car parked in the driveway that he realized she must have sped past him.

"Motherfucker," he mumbled, as he worked his way to the

front door where Piper was sitting, waiting for him with her arms crossed, making her breasts look more delectable than ever. Damn devil woman.

"You done having a hissy fit and almost trying to kill us?" she asked in a snarky tone.

"Nope, you're still here."

"I'm not leaving Mason; you need my help, and don't even deny it."

"I don't want your help," he responded, as he unlocked Jake and Lexi's house. He didn't even try to fight her not to come in, because only having one working leg put him at a disadvantage, and he didn't feel like injuring himself any more while trying to get rid of her.

"I know you don't want it, but you need it. I know I'm not your favorite person in the world," Mason guffawed. "But…let's be honest, you don't have anyone else right now. You need me, and frankly…I need you."

Her words caught Mason off guard as he took up residence on the couch. She needed him? That was new information to him. Last thing he knew, she needed another man. The thought of her needing him tore at the walls blocking her away. She needed him…that was all he wanted, to be needed. After all the bullshit he'd been through with Brooke and Piper, all he wanted was to be needed, and with those few simple words, she gutted him.

Trying not to show the way she affected him, he nonchalantly said, "You need me? For what?"

"I know that you really don't care, but I've had to move back in with my parents. I don't want to get into it, but it's just not a good situation. Coming here, helping you, has been the saving grace in my life recently," she admitted solemnly.

Mason gritted his teeth as he tried to contain the expletives that wanted to escape from his mouth. He didn't want to feel bad for her, but damn it, with the way she looked at him with those silver eyes of hers and the sadness that surrounded them, he could feel himself falling apart, wanting to help her.

"Sometimes you get what you deserve," Mason said without thinking, but happy with himself for not giving in.

"I guess you're right." She got up and went to the kitchen. "I'll make you a big batch of spaghetti tonight so you have it for the weekend. Jake and Lexi get back on Sunday night, right?" Mason nodded. "Alright, I have two boxes of noodles, so that should get you through the weekend. I'll be in the kitchen if you need anything, and then I will be out of here." She turned around to the kitchen, but called over her shoulder, "For what it's worth, Mason, I appreciate you opening that door every day, you really made my days brighter."

"Fuck me," Mason muttered, as he tossed his head on a throw pillow and turned on the TV to *Sports Center*.

Ryker

"Hand me the oven mitts," Hannah said as she opened the oven, letting a deliciously scented breeze of lasagna out of the oven. Ryker invited her over for dinner, but the only concession was, she had to cook. They hadn't seen each other since the night she spent after the cheeseburgers, because Ryker had practice and he wanted to really think about what he was getting himself into, but it was the night before his game and he really wanted to "carbo load," at least that was what he told Hannah.

Willingly, she came over and started cooking away in his kitchen. She had to bring over a couple of her kitchen supplies, because he didn't have much to cook with, but she didn't mind. Watching her float around in his kitchen was heaven. She fit in his home, in his life, and slowly, he was starting to realize that, even though she hurt him, he could not deny himself any longer. He was done fighting; he needed her in order to breathe, to move, to be.

"Here," he said, as he stared at her cute cherub face with her hair tied up into a bun on the top of her head. She was wearing her normal Hannah clothes this time and minimal makeup. She'd donned a pair of leggings, red Keds, and a striped navy blue, off the shoulder sweater. She was comfortable and fucking huggable.

"What are you looking at?" Hannah said as her face blushed.

"Just you," he answered honestly.

"Well, stop, you're making me nervous," she said, as she took out the lasagna and put it on top of the stove. He watched her check the top and then smile, pleased with her cooking abilities. "It just has to cool off and gel and then we can dig in. It will probably be about ten to fifteen minutes."

She turned around and faced him as she put the oven mitts on the counter. "What shall we do?"

Ryker knew what Russell the Love Muscle wanted to do, but Ryker wasn't quite ready for that. Instead, he pulled Hannah to the couch and said, "Let's talk."

They sat across from each other on the couch, both angling their bodies so they were facing each other. Ryker put his arm along the back of the couch and played with Hannah's sweater.

"I like you like this, comfortable and cute."

"So you've told me. I guess I'm just the kind of girl who can't pull off the sexy look," Hannah said, while picking imaginary lint off of her leggings.

Lifting her chin so she was looking Ryker in the eyes, he said, "You know that's not the truth. You are the sexiest woman I know, but what's special about you is that you don't need the fancy make-up or designer clothes to be sexy; all you need is you."

"You really think that?" she asked self-consciously. If it was any other girl, Ryker would have thought she was fishing for compliments, but not Hannah; she was sincere and she never lied, ever.

"Yes, I really think that. You know that I thought that the moment I saw you. By far the sexiest, smartest, most beautiful soul I've ever met. You should know that by now."

Nodding her head, she said, "I was just so lost back then, Ryker. I was lost in Todd, in making us work, in wanting to move forward with him; I lost myself along the way and I pushed you away." She grabbed his hand and spoke into his eyes. "I don't think

I can tell you how sorry I am. I can't believe I treated you so terribly."

Right there, at that moment, all the resentment and anger that had built up from Hannah's past actions dissipated, and he parted ways with the wall that blocked him from moving forward. She was so sincere, so honest, that all Ryker wanted to do was move forward now.

Ryker moved his hand to her cheek and brought her closer. "I forgive you, Hannah, I really do, and all I want is to move forward; will you do that with me? Move forward, maybe see where this will take us?" he asked, while waving between the two of them.

A tear pricked her eye as she nodded her head with an endearing smile on her face. "I would love that."

"Just you and me," Ryker said, as he brought her even closer, so their lips were only inches apart.

"You and me," Hannah repeated, as she put her hands on his cheeks.

Licking his lips, Ryker leaned in and was about to touch her magnificent lips again when there was a knock on his door.

"Ah, hell," Ryker said, angry that someone was disturbing his precious moment with Hannah.

Giving Hannah a light peck on the nose, Ryker said, "Hold that thought; I'll be right back."

Reluctantly leaving Hannah hanging on the couch, Ryker went to the front door and was surprised that the door opened before he could even get to it. In came a distraught Ashlin with her hair all askew, her clothes on inside out, and her eyes looking hazy. She was hammered.

"Ryker!" she slurred, as she tossed her arms around his neck and hung on to him like he was the last thing keeping her from floating into the dark abyss.

"Did you drive here?" Ryker asked, worried that she could have harmed someone in her drunken state.

"No, but can you pay the taxi driver...pah-wease," she said in her drunk voice.

Rolling his eyes, he set Ashlin down in the entryway of his home, jogged out to the cab, threw some cash at the driver, and jogged back. He thought he was pretty quick, but apparently not quick enough, because when he walked in, Ashlin was on the floor, now only wearing her lingerie, and Hannah was standing in the hallway, looking down at her.

"Ashlin, where the hell are your clothes?" Ryker asked as he went to his couch, grabbed a blanket, and tossed it at her so she could cover up.

"In your umbrella stand…" she said, pointing to her apparently new dresser.

Not bothering to ask why her clothes were in his umbrella stand, Ryker said, "What are you doing here and why are you so drunk?" Ryker looked up at Hannah, who looked stunned, and he sent her an apologetic smile.

Ashlin laid the blanket on the ground and started rolling herself up like a burrito while she was talking. "He doesn't want me," she said, while looking up at Hannah, making Ryker's gut twist. "He doesn't want to just fuck; he wants a relationship, but I can't give him that."

The stricken look on Hannah's face made panic set in Ryker's belly. She quickly grabbed her purse, and said, "I think I should go. It looks like you two have some talking to do…"

Before she could get anywhere near the door, Ryker stopped her and gripped her shoulders, forcing her to look him in the eyes. "Look at me," Ryker said sternly. She looked up, and that was when Ryker noticed her eyes were watering. "She's not talking about me, Hannah. She's talking about Jesse." Looking down at Ashlin, who was petting her own head now and laughing, Ryker said, "Tell her, tell her you're not talking about me; tell her there is nothing between us, Ashlin," Ryker demanded, nudging her with his foot to get her attention.

Ashlin looked up at the mention of her name and smiled, "Nah, Ryker and I only fucked once."

Fucking Ashlin.

Hannah stiffened, but stood in place.

"He's right, though," Ashlin continued, as she now started rolling back and forth on the ground in her human tortilla. "It's all about Jesse. He doesn't want anything to do with me. He doesn't want to just fuck."

Ryker pulled Hannah's eyes off of Ashlin and made her look at him. "Let me get her into a guest bedroom so she can pass out, and then we'll have dinner, okay?" She looked unsure, which made Ryker nervous; he didn't want to chase after her anymore. He was so close. "Hannah, do you hear me? Give me a couple of minutes; I'll be right back." Nodding slowly, Ryker brought her lips to his and gently gave her a kiss, just letting her know she was the one he wanted, no one else. "Can you cut the lasagna and pour the wine? I'll be right down." Once again, she nodded and turned away from him.

Still feeling uneasy, but wanting to get back to Hannah as soon as possible, Ryker grabbed Ashlin off the ground, threw her over his shoulder and took her to the downstairs bedroom, as far away from his room as possible.

She mumbled a bunch of gibberish as he carried her, occasionally smacking him in the ass and yelling, "Yahoo!" at the top of her lungs.

Ryker plopped her on the bed, shoved her under the covers, grabbed a glass of water and a trash can, and gave them to her.

"You're really fucking with my life right now, Ash."

"At least someone is fucking…"

"I'm not even going to go through this with you again. We talked last night; Jesse wants a relationship…if you want to be with him, you're going to have to give him that."

"You know I can't." Ashlin said feebly, making Ryker feel bad for her. She was not much of a relationship person, given the fact that everyone who ever was supposed to love her had walked away. She wouldn't put herself in that kind of position again. Ryker got it, but he also felt bad for his friend, because she was missing out on a good thing by living in the past.

"I know, sweetie." Ryker bent over and kissed her forehead. "But maybe Jesse might be the exception. Don't worry about that now, just get some sleep. If you need anything, get it yourself; I'm with Hannah tonight," Ryker said jokingly, but kind of meaning it.

He got off the bed and was about to shut the door when Ashlin called out to him, "I'm happy for you, Ryker. She's perfect for you."

"I know," Ryker replied, as he shut the door.

Hannah

She didn't think she could breathe; her mind was running a mile a minute the second Ashlin rolled into Ryker's house and then stripped off her clothes, as if it was the most natural thing in the world to do. She couldn't be jealous; she shouldn't be jealous. She was never with Ryker, ever, so whatever he did on his own time was his business. That was what she kept telling herself, but she couldn't help but feel pained from the knowledge that Ryker and Ashlin had been together intimately.

Knowing that she needed to believe Ryker, believe in what he said, and that he was just being a good friend and helping out Ashlin, Hannah cut the lasagna and placed it on two plates with a little side salad, and then poured some wine for the both of them. She set the plates and glasses at the table and took a seat. She waited patiently for Ryker to come back, trying not to bog down her mind with thoughts of what Ryker and Ashlin were doing in the other room.

Jogging into the room, Ryker stopped in his tracks when he saw Hannah sitting at the table with dinner laid out and wine poured. Relief crossed his face as he walked toward her. He was wearing jeans and a light blue T-shirt, very un-Ryker-like, given his sense of style, but Hannah liked his dressed down appearance.

His eyes flashed her a smile, letting her know he was happy that she was still at his house. Even though she felt uneasy about everything between her and Ryker, the way he was looking at her relieved some of the aching feeling that was gnawing at the pit of her stomach.

"You stayed," he said breathlessly, as he reached her seat.

"You told me to," Hannah said, as he knelt down in front of her.

Grabbing her hands in his, Ryker brought them up to his lips and gently kissed them. "Thank you. I was afraid you were going to leave while I was taking care of Ashlin. I was afraid I was going to have to start my chase again."

"Chase?" Hannah asked, not quite understanding what Ryker was saying.

Nodding his head slightly, he said, "Yes. Ever since I met you, I've been chasing after you, trying to keep you in one place, and I feel like I finally was able to do that, tonight. Then Ashlin came over and fucked everything up."

"Does she come over often?" Hannah knew she should stay away from the question and try to enjoy the rest of the night they had together, but she couldn't help herself. She had to know.

"Depends." Ryker shifted in his spot, as he considered what to say. "We grew up together, Hannah. We were each other's safety blankets in the shitty world we were living in. We had rough childhoods, which I won't go into, and unfortunately, we lost touch, but when we found each other again, it was like finding that safe spot again, finding home again."

Hannah tried not to feel hurt by the fact that Ryker thought Ashlin was his home, because she hadn't even given him a chance to call her his home, but it still sent a pang of jealousy through her body.

He continued, "We've been through a lot together and have spent a lot of time together, especially since what happened between you and me; she was there for me."

"So, she hates me then," Hannah said, as she looked down into her hands, feeling like an idiot for how she treated Ryker.

"Not at all," Ryker lifted her chin so she was forced to look at him. "She's happy that you're back in my life, and she thinks you're perfect for me."

"How can she think that? She doesn't even know me."

"But she knows me," Ryker countered. "She knows the effect you have on me, how you make me feel. She knows you through me and is supportive. Believe me when I say this, you have nothing to worry about when it comes to Ashlin. She's only a sister to me, I promise."

Hannah nodded, but still had a hard time with the feelings that were rolling around in her body. She believed Todd, she believed that she owned his heart...that he loved her and her alone, but, boy, was she wrong. Ryker seemed genuine as well, and she knew she could trust him, but there was always that feeling in the back of her mind that was telling her, Ryker could be like Todd. She would never voice that thought, because the last time she compared Ryker to Todd, she hurt him and drove him away, but she couldn't help but wonder. That's what happened to a damaged girl; she never quite trusted anyone ever again. She always waited for someone to break her trust.

"Thank you for letting me know," Hannah croaked out, her throat feeling dry from holding back tears.

A gentle smile crossed Ryker's face, as he placed the palm of his hand against Hannah's cheek. "You're my girl, right? You're my boo?"

Smiling back at his hopeful eyes, Hannah said, "Yes, I'm your boo."

Ryker fist pumped the air like a dork, and then kissed her on the nose, apparently his new favorite place to kiss her. He sat down on his chair and rubbed his hands together, "Now, this looks good. With you being my boo now, I'm going to have to watch what I eat, because with meals like this, I'm going to turn into a fat motherfucker..."

"Ryker..." Hannah teasingly chastised him for swearing.

Clearing his throat, he said, "I mean a fat...uhh..." he scratched his head as he tried to think of a word, and then laughed. "Damn, I can only think of insults."

"You could say fat man, or football player," Hannah suggested.

"Where's the fun in that?" he asked, as he shoved a large piece of lasagna in his mouth. In an instant, he opened his mouth wide and spit it back out, making Hannah cringe from the half mashed piece of lasagna on his plate. Quickly grabbing the wine, he guzzled it down. "Shit, that's hot," Ryker swore, as he panted like a dog.

"That's what you get for swearing," she winked, blew on her lasagna, and then took a bite.

Mason

Fuck, he was lonely. Almost too lonely. He didn't realize how much he enjoyed having Piper over until she was actually gone. Mason was so sick of pasta by now, but he kept eating it because he reminded himself that Piper made it for him, and he was holding on to every last thing that reminded him of Piper.

What a douche, he thought. He put on a front that he was a non-emotional ass, but deep down, he was a pussy. He had feelings, and it bothered the hell out of him. He didn't want to feel; he didn't want to yearn. All he wanted was a quick fuck and a good beer, or at least that's what he tried for, but deep down, he knew that would never be satisfying enough.

Mason's phone rang him out of his thoughts.

"Hello?" he answered.

"Well, if it isn't my second half," Jake announced.

"Hey, dickhead. Why are you calling me when you should be getting ready for a game?" Mason had the TV tuned in to watch Jake play first, and then the Stallions game afterward, but was still deciding whether to watch that game, because it was still painful to know that in fact, his season was over.

"Just wanted to call my boyfriend for good luck before I went out on the field," Jake said in a girly voice.

"There's something wrong with you, you know? You and Ryker have some kind of sick obsession with me."

"Can you blame us?"

"Not really," Mason laughed.

"So, how are you doing? Are you holding down the fort or blowing the place up?"

"I'm doing fine, and no I have not blown the place up, but I am pissed at you for hiding the car keys."

Jake laughed. "I was wondering how long it was going to take you to start to get stir crazy and try to take out one of my cars."

"You're a dick; I would have been careful."

"Yeah, okay. Keep telling yourself that. So, when we get back, are we going to see massive amounts of takeout boxes scattered everywhere?"

Mason had talked to Jake almost every night since he'd been gone because the man was a damn pest, but Mason never told him about Piper coming over to help out. He didn't know why, but he just wasn't ready to tell Jake, but now, he needed someone to talk to because he was a damn woman and couldn't suppress his feelings.

"Well, not really," Mason said hesitantly.

"Dude, you've been eating, right?"

"Yes, Mom," Mason retorted annoyingly. "I've just had someone making me food…"

"Oh, for fuck's sake," Jake said into the phone. "I swear to God, if you hired a hooker into my house to fuck and feed you, I'm going to kick your ass. I don't want strangers knowing where I live!"

"Settle down. Damn, man," Mason said, cutting off Jake. "It's not what you think."

"So, you hired a personal chef?"

Getting annoyed, Mason finally said, "No, Piper has been helping out."

Silence.

And then more silence.

"Jake?" Mason asked, wondering if his friend had actually hung up on him.

"I'm sorry, I think I misheard you. It sounded like you said Piper."

Okay, he was in shock, Mason thought, as he decided on how to talk to his friend about Piper and the way he'd been feeling lately.

Slowly, Mason told Jake how they ran into each other, how she refused to leave him alone, and just came over to help him out by herself. Jake let Mason talk, and by the time Mason finished telling him about Piper's surprise appearance in his life, Mason was on edge waiting to hear what Jake might say.

"Well, I'm happy for you, man," Jake finally said, shocking Mason.

"What do you mean? We're not together or anything; we haven't even fucked or played around."

"Clearly, or else you wouldn't be so tense," Jake teased. "Seriously, though, I think this is a good thing. You both have so much pride that neither of you will give in, but I think her coming to you means something."

"She's lonely...I'm lonely," Mason admitted.

"How do you feel about possibly having her back in your life again?"

"I don't know. A part of me is excited, especially my dick," Jake laughed on the other end of the phone. "But I'm still so fucking pissed at her. She strung me along, man, used me and made me believe she loved me."

"She did love you..." Jake interrupted.

"People in love don't do that to each other...what she did to me. She ripped me apart!" Mason shouted, getting way too emotional, way too quickly.

"I know," Jake said gently. "But you have to think, she was trying to help you with your career."

"That's bullshit and you know it. We could have worked something out. She didn't have to go running off with the Southern Shithead."

"Is that his new name?" Jake asked.

"Yes, has a good ring to it."

"Besides all that, Mace. In her head, she was trying to help. You have to give her that. It may have been fucked-up, but she was trying. I think if you really want to see where things go, which it seems like you do, you need to put the past behind you and move on. You need to start new and start from the beginning. You two never had a chance to actually get to know each other. Maybe that's what you need to do, start from ground zero and work your way up. You'll only know after that if you two really belong together."

Mason thought about what Jake was telling him. Maybe he was right; maybe Mason needed to start from the very beginning with Piper. He knew he couldn't keep doing what he was doing, because all he thought about was her, and her smile and silver eyes and the way her hair bounced softly when she walked. She consumed his thoughts, and denying himself of her was not working. He needed to do something.

"I fucking hate it when you're right," Mason admitted, making Jake let out a hefty laugh.

"You can pay me for my services later."

"You can fuck off," Mason said jokingly. "Good luck today, man. Keep the interceptions under ten."

"Ha! You wish. I haven't thrown an interception in three games."

"And now you'll throw five this game. Way to jinx yourself, fuckwit."

Laughing, Jake said, "Damn, you're right."

Mason said his goodbye to Jake, feeling a little lighter, and wondering what his next step was going to be when it came to Piper.

CHAPTER TEN

Piper

It was finally Sunday, and Piper was really starting to feel lost. The last couple of days, when she was taking care of Mason, visiting him and making sure he had everything he needed, she felt wanted again; she felt fulfilled. Now, as she lay on her childhood bed, listening to her dad yell at her mom on the other side of her wall, she wished she hadn't gotten jealous about Brooke. If she hadn't opened her stubborn mouth, her spat with Mason wouldn't have escalated, and she could be over at Jake and Lexi's watching the game with him. Instead, her head was buried under her pillow, like she used to do as a child and she tried to not think about the life she could possibly be living if she wasn't so indecisive.

She was probably at her lowest point. She had never felt so lost, so bitter, and dejected. Slowly, she felt herself starting to slip into the deep depression that used to eat her up when she was young. Living with her parents again, living with the constant demands and yelling was eating her alive. That was why she felt so terrible. She couldn't handle the wrath of her father any more, and now that she was back in his house, the state of her life had only gotten worse.

While she was slipping into darkness, her phone buzzed next to her. She picked it up and saw that she had a text message from Mason.

Mason: Want to watch the game with me?

Piper sat straight up in her bed and held her phone like it was a block of gold. Mason texted her? He invited her over? Last time she saw him, he wanted nothing to do with her. Was he drunk? She didn't care; she would take advantage if he was. She was not going to stick around in her dad's house any more. She texted back.

Piper: Sure, do you need me to bring anything?

Mason: Food, anything but pasta.

Laughing, Piper thought about Mason eating pasta for the last couple of days. It was easy to heat up, but she could see him getting sick of it. She sent him a quick text back, saying she would stop and get some food and then be right over.

She needed to get ready quickly, because she knew the game was starting at one, so she threw her hair into a messy bun, put on a pair of yoga pants and a tight long-sleeved shirt that said, "Bitches be hoes" on it; quite fitting, she thought, and put on her sneakers.

Piper was very quick getting food and headed on over to Jake and Lexi's house in record time. She picked up a bountiful amount of Chinese food, enough to feed a family of ten, as well as some ice cream for later, since Chinese food always seemed to fill you up for two seconds and then you were ready to eat again.

She pulled up to Jake and Lexi's house and gave herself a little pep talk before she went in. She wasn't going to get too excited that he'd invited her over. She wouldn't read too much into it, and she sure as hell wasn't going to get jealous over any past sexual encounters Mason might have had.

Feeling ready, she grabbed the food and walked up to the door. She knocked and instantly heard Mason call her in from the other side.

The moment she walked in, she was hit by the fresh scent of Mason's body soap and the delectable man stretched out across the couch in nothing but a pair of Nike shorts. His chest was bare, showing off his chest and sleeve tattoos, and the well-defined sinew gracing his body. He was the epitome of male perfection…there was no doubt about that. Her eyes traveled down the length of his body, to the V of his hips and to the slight bulge in his pants. The man was hung and always had a bulge, which he had no problem showing off.

"My eyes are up here," Mason teased as he sat up, shaking Piper out of her perusal of his body.

Clearing her throat, she said, "Yes, uh sorry. I wasn't expecting you to be shirtless." She fumbled around with the food as she ran to the kitchen to set everything down. Where was her head at? She never acted like a spaz. It's not like she'd never seen Mason without his shirt on.

Piper heard Mason's crutches coming her way, so she quickly pulled herself together and grabbed two plates.

"What did you get?" Mason asked, poking his head into a bag. Piper was so confused by his instant mood change. The man could be a seriously moody bastard most of the time, but right now, his smile was light and his attitude was actually fun. His face wasn't crinkled together like he was trying to think of the next insult to throw at her. Whatever the change was, she wasn't going to mention it, because that would be a perfect way to spoil the mood.

"Chinese. I got a lot of different options, so if you tell me what you want, I'll put it on a plate for you and bring it out to you."

"Give me some of everything," Mason said, as he hobbled over to the fridge. "I can get the drinks." He popped open the fridge and grabbed two beers.

"Mason, I can carry those…"

"I got it," he interrupted her and said, "See?" He put the beers in his short pockets, which tugged his shorts down to a dangerous level. His black Under Armour briefs peeked out, making her gulp.

He was hot...just too damn hot for Piper to keep clean thoughts in her head.

She turned around quickly and started opening all the Chinese food boxes. "I'll be right out," she called to him, just quickly dumping as much Chinese on the plates as possible, as she tried to steady the pounding of her heart.

For the first time in a while, she felt alive, and the darkness that was trying encompass her was pushed back; she was starting to see some light again. She knew she'd brought all the bad things that happened to her upon herself, but she was grateful for the reprieve in her shitty life. She was grateful to have found Mason again. She was grateful for being invited over today, even though the possibility of him being hyped up on Vicodin might be the reason, which she didn't think was the case, because he seemed so clear in his thought and his eyes told her he was lucid. Whatever, she would take a drugged up Mason if she needed to.

"Here you go." Piper set a pile of Chinese food on the TV tray sitting in front of Mason. He wasn't kidding about wanting to watch the game. The surround sound was on, the TV was blaring, and he had Jake's jersey on now, covering up his beautiful body. "Are you allowed to wear another team's jersey?"

"When it's my best friend, yeah." He leaned into Piper and said, "Plus, no one can see me, so who gives a fuck." His eyes widened as if he just thought of something. He pointed his fork at her and said, "I know we've had our Instagram wars, but don't go posting this." He smiled, stuck his fork into the lo mein noodles, and took a hefty bite. He smiled at her as noodles hung out of his mouth, making her laugh.

"Don't worry. I think I left my phone in my car."

"Why would you do that? How are you going to update your Facebook status every two seconds when something happens in the game?"

Groaning, Piper said, "I despise when people do that. God, game stat updates, workout statuses, and invites to play Candy Crush rank as the top most annoying and obnoxious Facebook activities."

"You're right about that, but I will admit, Ryker got me hooked on Candy Crush Saga. That shit is addictive. But, just so you know, you're looking at the Stallions reigning Candy Crushing champion."

"Ryker would," Piper said, as she shook her head and laughed, then added, "It's a little concerning that you're so proud of being the champion."

"I take pride in being the champion in everything, babe," Mason said nonchalantly, as he shoved some beef in his mouth, followed by a swig of his beer.

Piper tried to disregard the term of endearment as she watched the columns of Mason's neck work up and down as he swallowed. What she wouldn't give to lick him there, taste the musk on his skin, the salt from the light sweat they were both accumulating from being so close together, well at least she was accumulating.

"Might want to eat up before your food gets cold," Mason said, as he caught her staring. Her cheeks instantly flamed at being caught.

They ate in silence for the rest of their meal as they watched Jake easily push the ball down the field. Every time there was a completed pass, Mason would silently fist pump for his friend. It was endearing to see Mason be so supportive, even if they were on separate teams.

Lexi cut onto the screen to tell viewers to stay tuned for the after game reports and interviews. She looked gorgeous, like always with her blonde hair pulled back, and a fresh face of make-up. She looked happy, and Piper was glad to see that. Lexi deserved Jake; they were perfect for each other. At the thought of their two friends, Piper wondered if Mason had talked to them about her being in town.

Getting some courage to open the gates a little, Piper asked, "Have you talked to Jake and Lexi recently?"

Mason sat back on the couch and rubbed his belly as he said, "Yeah, just talked to them today. Told them you were strutting around their house naked and feeding me grapes all day long." His lips tugged at the corners of his mouth, letting her know he was joking.

"You're an ass."

He laughed and said, "Truthfully, I talked to Jake this morning and I did mention you coming over to help me out. I'm sure, by now, the information has been relayed to Lexi, so for your health, it might be best to try to call her tonight before she has a conniption about where you've been and why you haven't been talking to her. You know how she likes to butt into everyone's business."

"True," Piper said, while thinking about Lexi's reaction. What would she think? Would Lexi be mad at her for not communicating with her? Would she be supportive of Piper helping out Mason?

"I'm sure she will be relieved to hear from you," Mason cut in her thoughts, knowing her so well. "Nothing to worry about." Mason gave her leg a gentle squeeze, which shocked her lady parts into full alert. It was a small touch, but it ignited every lost flame in her body. "I need another beer, do you want one?" he asked, as he started to get up.

"No, I mean yes, but I'll get them. You sit." Piper quickly got up and grabbed their empty plates to take to the kitchen.

"You know, I can do things," Mason said, almost annoyed.

Being patient, Piper said, "I know, but I would feel better if you continued to let me help. I don't need you slipping on those damn things on my watch." With that, she went to the kitchen, rinsed the plates, and put them in the dishwasher. Once they were cleared, she gripped the counter to gain control of her heart. Everything seemed so easy. Why was he being so nice? Why wasn't he giving her any shit? Was he trying to play her for everything she did to him? If she were to be honest, she didn't fully trust the man, especially not to break her heart…since she'd done exactly that to him.

"You okay?" Mason asked from the kitchen doorway.

Straightening up, Piper said, "Yes, sorry. I'll just put away these boxes of food and then be right out." She busied herself with packing everything up, but was stopped when Mason grabbed her hands and made her look at him.

"Stop. Why are you avoiding me right now?"

"I'm not avoiding you," she squeaked out. He was too close, way too close. She could rub the stubble on his jaw, lick the sweet full lips that were gracing his face, nibble on his ear lobe; he was just too damn close.

"Yes, you are. You'll do anything to keep yourself busy so you don't have to be near me for that long."

"That's not true, it's just…this is going to sound terrible, but why are you being so…nice to me?"

Mason studied her face for a second, and then said, "I want to start from the beginning."

"Start what?"

"Start us, from the beginning. The way we met on the airplane, instantly aggravating each other, and then the wedding…we were bound to fail from the very start, but we still had that unbelievable pull that brought us together. We never were given the chance to get to know each other, to go on dates, to learn each other's likes and dislikes."

"What are you saying?" Piper asked, wanting to actually hear the words from his lips, afraid that she might be hallucinating.

"I want to try dating, Piper."

He was still holding her hands, thankfully, because she felt like she was going to pass out.

"But, I hurt you…"

"And I hurt you too. We both hurt each other, and we are both to blame for what happened."

"But, if I hurt you, why do you want to date me? Shouldn't you be tossing my ass out on the pavement right now?" She felt very uneasy. Mason was not the kind of guy to just forget the past and move forward. No, he was a stubborn ass with the vengeance to seek revenge. So to see him so easily switch gears after lashing out at her had her feeling very skeptical.

Mason let go of her hands and ran his through his hair, making the ends stand straight up in the air. "I'm not happy, Piper. I'm here on this earth, going through the motions, but I'm not really living; I'm not experiencing anything. The only time that I really felt alive was when we were together. I might be a giant idiot to trust you, but I can't help it; I'm drawn to you, and I just need to give this a proper chance. And, frankly, I'm just not over you. I never was and I don't think I ever will be, no matter what I say; I will never get over you. I need to see if we were really meant to be pulled together by the universe."

His words sliced through her heart as she thought about what he said. She wasn't over him either, not by a long shot, but he didn't trust her. Well, that was a given, but she didn't trust him either. It would be a big deciding factor in their relationship if they gave it a go…would they ever be able to trust each other?

"I don't know if it will work. We both have trust issues and we both said some awful things to each other."

"That's the past, Piper. Let's leave it behind and move forward. We need to give this a chance; if anything, do it for Lexi. She was so distraught that we didn't work out."

A sharp laugh escaped Piper's mouth, as she thought about her little blonde friend bumming hard that she wasn't able to make things right with Mason.

"Well, if it's for Lexi, then we'll have to give it a go, I guess."

Smiling, Mason said, "Perfect, but there is only one problem."

"What's that?"

"I leave for Denver on Wednesday. I have to start rehab."

"Oh…" She had never done a long distance relationship, and the thought of having to stay with her parents while Mason was in Denver made her sick to her stomach. "Long distance might be hard."

"Long distance?" Mason asked, confused. "Oh, fuck no, you'll be coming with me."

"With you? I thought we were taking things slow, starting from the beginning. Moving to a different state for a guy doesn't seem very slow to me."

"Do you have anything tying you down here?"

"Well…no, but…"

"Good, it's settled then," Mason said, cutting her off.

"No, it's not settled. You can't just go around making demands, thinking they are going to come true." A spark lit inside her as she spoke. "People have lives, you know."

"Keep talking, sweetheart, I know you have no life here. Otherwise you wouldn't be babysitting and volunteering to come take care of the one man who could make you pull your hair out one minute and then have you praising God while I'm buried ten inches deep inside of you the next."

Piper blushed just from the thought of Mason being hard and inside of her. It was probably one of the best feelings she had ever experienced.

Laughing, Mason pointed at her face that was smirking, and said, "See, you can't deny it. You want to be with me; you're coming to Denver."

Putting her hands on her hips, knowing defeat when she saw it, she put up one last fight. "Let's get one thing straight, I don't take well to demands. You should know that, given the childhood I had, but if you wanted to ask me to go with you, I would consider it."

Giving her a delightful smirk, he grabbed her hand and held it to his heart as he said, "Piper, will you please come with me to Denver and help me with rehab while we get to know each other?"

"Well, since you asked so nicely…"

Rolling his eyes, he dropped her hand and crutched back out to the game as he muttered, "Stubborn woman," under his breath.

Inwardly smiling, Piper thought about how she couldn't wait to get back to Denver, not just because she would be as far away from her parents as possible, but she would be able to go back to the life she loved in Denver, minus Jax, the crazy love triangle, and the annoying bitch, Brooke.

Life was finally starting to look up.

Jesse

"Hit me baby one more time," Ryker sang at the top of his lungs, as he whipped a towel around and danced to the song that was obviously by Britney Spears that he was listening to through his earbuds.

Jesse took the opportunity to take what Ryker was singing literally and hit him in the shoulder to shut him the hell up. He couldn't deal with Ryker's obnoxious behavior right now; he was not in the mood. He was barely in the mood to take the field, and that spoke volumes about the kind of rage that was searing through him.

"Dude!" Ryker complained, as he rubbed his shoulder. "I don't have my pads on yet, can you lay off until then?"

"You know the dickheads out there are going to hit you harder than that, especially when you're carrying the ball down field, right?"

"Nah, they're a bunch of fart nuggets; they have nothing on me."

"Okay, Jamal Jackson has about fifty pounds on you. He's normally paired up with Mason, but he's coming after you today."

"No shit. You weren't the only one at practice when Coach Ryan was announcing that. I got it covered. The fucker is weak on his left. I can do a quick spin to my left and lose the sucker, no problem," Ryker said, as he demonstrated his spin move off of an unsuspecting teammate walking by.

Shaking his head, Jesse said, "You're a confident little fuck, you know that?"

"You have to be, man, especially when you're put up against one of the best defensive tight ends in the league."

Jesse nodded his head as his phone beeped with a text message. He pulled it out from his locker and saw it was a text from Ashlin. Once she pretty much blew him off, he thought about deleting her contact information, but couldn't bring himself to do it, so instead of being Ladder Ball Queen in his phone, he just changed it to Ashlin. Ignoring Ryker's non-stop chatter, he read the message.

Ashlin: Good luck today. I'm sorry about the other night. I hope we can still be friends.

Jesse shook his head as he snorted. Yeah, friends wasn't going to happen.

"You still all tied up about Ashlin?" Ryker asked as he leaned over, clearly trying to read Jesse's text message.

Jesse tossed his phone behind him in his locker and said, "No."

"Liar. You like her," Ryker said, while tickling the side of Jesse's face.

Jesse grabbed Ryker's wrist and said, "Unless you want to be getting surgery on your wrist today, I suggest you keep your extremities to yourself."

Ryker backed off, holding his hands up in defeat. "Fuck, dude. You need to calm down."

Jesse pinched the bridge of his nose, wondering why his locker was right next to Ryker's.

"Can I just fucking focus before the game without you getting in my face and my business? Damn, dude, get a fucking hobby."

Ryker was silent for a second, and then said, "I'm not going to take offense to that, since you're clearly on the brink of destruction, but for what it's worth, she's not doing well. She likes you, but doesn't know how to process her feelings. She's damaged and doesn't trust very easily, but that's not my story to tell, it's hers. Before you shut her out, maybe give her the chance of being her

148

friend. Gain her trust, and then who knows, maybe it will develop into something else. All I know is that you are both miserable fucks right now, so why not be miserable together?"

Ryker patted Jesse on the shoulder and then grabbed his pads and jersey and headed toward the sinks. The self-centered ass loved to make sure he was looking good before he headed out onto the field.

Jesse didn't feel like listening to Ryker, but deep down, he knew Ryker was right. Jesse could tell that there was something deep-rooted in Ashlin that was scaring her away. There was no denying the attraction or connection they had with each other. She just needed to let go of her past and move forward, but was he strong enough to let her do that? What if he decided to let her in his life, be her friend, and in the end, it was useless? What if, in the end, she still didn't want him? He didn't think he could take it.

He grabbed his phone and looked at her text message again. Would he be able to say no, though, and give up an opportunity that might change his life forever? Would he always wonder, if he had given their friendship a chance, would things have been different?

As he thought about it, he knew he would. He would easily regret it because, even though Ashlin liked to remain aloof with him, he felt like he knew her; he felt like their souls connected, and he couldn't give up on that gut feeling. There was no way he could, even if it meant facing a broken heart in the end.

Jax

"Would you say you have anger issues?" a reporter asked Jax as he fielded questions from the media about their brutal loss.

Anger issues? No. Frustration at losing his best receiver and having to put rookies in the game because Ryker was burned out in the first half? Yes, fucking beyond frustrated. Slamming his clipboard on the ground and tossing his headset to the side after the fourth fumble from a receiver in the game might not have been the best reaction, but without going long, that left them only playing the short game, and running the ball wasn't ideal when you needed to gain a lot of yards.

This game was probably the most frustrating three hours of his life. There was nothing he could do but yell at his rookies to get their heads out of their asses, but the dandies were sensitive and didn't respond well to a screaming tyrant...at least that's what Jax found out from Jesse afterwards. Jax didn't care, though, because they were in the NFL; they needed to grow up...it was time.

Losing Mason was more detrimental to the team than Jax could have thought. He hated the man, absolutely despised him, so admitting that the team actually needed the asshole was twisting his balls, but damn if it wasn't true. Mason and Jesse had a special connection on the field that was undeniable, and without that connection, the Stallions were going to struggle to make it to the playoffs, if today's game was any indication of their season's future.

Clearing his throat, Jax said, "No. Next question."

"What would you call the way you treated your clipboard?" the nagging reporter asked.

"I call it being frustrated with the fact that my star receiver is out with a busted knee. Unless you have any other questions that pertain to the game and not my supposed anger issues, then I'm going to leave."

"Will Ryker be able to carry the team with the long ball?" a different reporter asked.

"Ryker is a stellar wide receiver, but he can't do it alone, just like Mason couldn't do it all by himself either. Ryker will be the leader, and hopefully his seniority will rub off on the rookies. It's going to take a little bit of time, but hopefully we can pull it together quickly, because we're still looking forward to the playoffs. That will be it for tonight; have a good night."

Jax walked off the stage and pulled out his phone. He sent a quick text to Brooke, letting her know he was coming over. He needed to decompress, and the only way he could do that was if he was with Brooke. She made him feel light and needed, something he hadn't felt in a while…since his wife died.

She happily replied with a "Can't wait to see you." The drive to her place wasn't too long, but it seemed like forever to him because all he wanted was her in his arms. The team was driving him crazy. He wasn't sure what he was going to do if his backups couldn't get their shit together, and this was all happening when he was trying to prove to everyone that he was one hell of a coach.

Jax parked his car and practically jogged up to Brooke's place, because he couldn't wait to hold her in his arms. Knocking on the door, he waited impatiently for her to answer.

The door swung open and Jax didn't get a chance to take in her appearance because he had her wrapped up in his arms before she could say hi. He closed the door and continued to hold onto her. He buried his head in the sweet scent of her hair and held on tight as her arms did the same.

"Hey," she said softly as she rubbed his back. "I'm sorry about the loss today."

"Mmm…" was all he said as he continued to hold her. She was a breath of fresh air, just what he needed, because ever since the final seconds of the clock had ticked down on the scoreboard, Jax felt like a giant dark cloud was hovering over him as he tried to figure out what his next move was going to be. Because he was a younger coach, he had a lot to prove, and he would do anything to make sure he kept his job.

"Are you hungry?"

Reluctantly pulling away, Jax cupped her face with his hands and brought his lips down to hers, pressing gently against her mouth. She was wearing cherry ChapStick, and the taste of it infused with the strokes of her tongues on his lips was exhilarating. Immediately, he wanted to take her back to her bedroom or even take her up against the wall, but he restrained himself as he pulled back away. He could use a shower first, that was for damn sure.

Holding up his gym bag, he said, "Do you mind if I take a shower?"

She eyed the bag and said, "Not at all. I'll cook something up for us while you're cleaning up. I made pineapple upside down cake in hopes that you would come over after the game."

"Is that what the delicious smell is? I thought it was you," Jax said with a grin.

"So cheesy." Brooke rolled her eyes and went off to the kitchen. "Bathroom is down the hall to the right. Towels are under the sink."

"Thanks darlin'," Jax called off as he headed down toward the bathroom.

Brooke's place wasn't too overly girly, but it was girlier than his place, that was for sure. Even though there was definite chick décor going on in her place, Jax felt comfortable, which threw him off for a second. He still didn't know Brooke all that well, but he felt like he knew her better than anyone else. They'd both been hurt in previous relationships, they'd both been used, and they both just wanted to be number one in someone's life. Jax felt like he got that from Brooke. She made a pineapple upside down cake with him in mind, for fuck's sake; Piper never did anything like that.

He stopped himself right there; he had to stop comparing Brooke to Piper, because that could be dangerous. He didn't want Brooke thinking he thought about Piper at all, because he didn't...ever. She was a distant memory. Even though the pain she caused still hung around, he was done with her.

Jax turned on the water to the shower and let it get warm as he stripped down to nothing. He was using the guest bathroom, and he wondered why Brooke didn't let him into her master bathroom. Was she self-conscious? Or maybe she didn't want him looking through her things like he was right now. He had no shame; he wanted to know what he was getting himself into. The only things in her spare bathroom were an unopened toothbrush, towels, and some head cold medicine. Nothing too revealing, except for the fact that she bought store brand items.

Jax got in the shower and pulled out his soap that was pretty much for his whole body. Being a guy was so much easier than being a girl. Jax had one soap for his hair and body, simple. Girls had a million different bottles with fragrant scents in them for all different parts of the body.

Just as he was rinsing off, he heard the door to the bathroom open and quietly close, like Brooke was trying to be sneaky, but she couldn't pull one over on him. Whipping open the curtain, he said, "Can I help you?"

Brooke jumped out of place and held her heart as she looked him up and down. "Jesus, you startled me." Her gaze trailed down to his erection, which was now sprouting from her perusal, and she licked her lips like she was about to have the most delightful treat.

"Keep looking at me like that, and you're going to get yourself into some trouble," Jax said, as he felt himself grow larger on the spot.

Brooke took her clothes off in a matter of seconds, threw her hair up in a bun, and got into the shower. She shut the curtain and placed her hands on Jax's chest.

"What do you think you're doing? I'm trying to get clean here," Jax teased.

"Do you want me?" she asked, while she ran her fingernails over his pecs and down his stomach, making him harder than fucking stone.

"You know I do," he replied, while peeking down at his erection.

"Say it."

"I want you, Brooke. I want you so fucking bad."

"Good." She pushed him up against the wall, angled the shower head so the water was hitting his shoulders, and then went down on her knees.

God, he hadn't been sucked off in a while, and the mere thought of Brooke wrapping her perfect little lips around his cock had him ready to explode already.

She placed her hands on his thighs and gently licked the tip of his cock, which only made it jump from the pleasure that rolled from him. Jax relaxed his head back, which made the water splash off his chest. If this was going to happen, he was going to relax and enjoy it.

Her hands moved from his thighs to the base of his dick and his balls. One hand gently cupped his balls, as the other stroked the base of his dick. The pressure she applied as she wrapped her hand around him was perfect, just enough to make him wiggle in his stance as she played around with his balls.

"Damn..." he mumbled as she continued her torture, never going any further than the middle of his dick. It felt like she was maneuvering everything to the tip of his arousal, so when she finally touched him there, he would explode instantaneously.

Jax looked down at Brooke and saw her beautiful green eyes stare up at him right before she rolled her tongue around the head of his cock.

"Fuuuuck," he breathed out as his head flew back again. The sensation of her warm tongue around his hard tip made his head spin. His knees started to feel weak as she continued to swirl her tongue around him while working her hands. It was almost all too much to handle at once. He needed to grip something, but there was nothing but cold tile and water.

Running her tongue down the underside of his dick, she stroked the very sensitive skin as her mouth landed at the base of his balls. In one swift movement, she opened her mouth and allowed his balls to sit in her mouth, or at least tried to, as her tongue made gentle swipes against his sensitive skin.

"Christ," he panted, literally panted like a damn dog. "Brooke, you're killing me."

All she did was chuckle, which vibrated his balls, sending him into a frenzy. He was going to lose it any second. He could feel his balls tighten up and his toes start to curl.

As if she could read his body, she placed her hands back on his balls and, in one swift movement, took his entire cock into her mouth until it hit the back of her throat. The woman showed no signs of a gag reflex as she pumped him in and out of her mouth; it was every man's dream. Sparing a glance, he looked down at her as she wrapped her lips around him and pumped him.

"Motherfucker!" With one last squeeze to his balls, his stomach tightened, his legs went numb, and his eyes shut as he exploded into her mouth. Not caring about what kind of crazed man he looked like, he pumped in and out of her mouth until every last drop was released.

Breathing heavily, he sunk down to the tub, onto his knees and into Brooke's waiting arms.

"That was because you lost today," she said into his ear.

"What do I get when I win?" Jax asked jokingly.

"You'll just have to wait to find out," she replied, as she leaned over and turned off the shower.

"Something to look forward to," Jax said, as he grabbed the towel that she handed him. They both toweled off side by side, and Jax couldn't help but relish the company of having someone with him while he completed such an easy task, like a shower…well, and a blow job.

"I ordered pizza, I hope that's okay. I had more important things to do than cook," she winked.

"Fine by me."

As they grabbed their clothes, Brooke led him into her bedroom so they could both get changed. She grabbed a pair of striped pajama shorts and a tank top, not wearing anything under them; just what he liked, easy access.

Jax put on a pair of sweats and decided to leave his shirt off; he liked watching Brooke's eyes wander about his body. It made him feel energized.

He noticed Brooke's bathroom door was closed, and he nodded toward the bathroom. "Why is the door closed…you have a dead body in there or something?"

She blushed as she looked at the door. "Uh, that bathroom is out of commission right now."

Smiling, Jax was about to tease her when she held up her hand. "It's not what you think; I didn't blow it up or anything, the toilet water is just not working."

"What do you mean?" Jax asked.

She twisted her hands nervously, which Jax thought was adorable. "Well, a little bit ago, I got a little drunk one night and, well, kind of got sick…you know," Jax nodded in understanding. "And when I went to flush, it was like the toilet turned off."

"Let me take a look at it," Jax started walking toward the bathroom, but she ran in front of him and placed her hands on his bare chest, stopping him in his tracks.

"No, that's okay. The plumber will be here tomorrow…"

"You're lying. I can tell."

"Jax, there is old puke in there, like really old puke; I don't want you to see that."

Jax laughed as he said, "I'm a professional football coach, you don't think I haven't seen my fair share of gross shit? The guys on the team like to spread their ball sacs on their pants and say they have gum stuck on their jeans, okay? I can handle a little puke."

Brooke scrunched her nose in disgust as she said, "Do they really do that?"

"All the fucking time," Jax replied, as she opened the bathroom door. There was a faint smell of something nasty in there, but he ignored it and went to the toilet. He lifted the back lid and saw that there was no water in it. He put the lid back down and bent down to where the water hose connected to the toilet. He noticed the knob was twisted to off, and that was when he started chuckling to himself.

"What? What is it?" Brooke asked, while leaning over him trying to see what he was seeing.

"When you were puking your guts out the other night, did you happen to play with this knob?"

She looked at it and realization set in. "Yes! I thought it was pretty, so I was trying to twist it off to take to bed with me."

"What?" Jax shook his head as he tried to understand her. "I don't even want to know." He flushed the toilet, and water started flowing through, making Brooke clap her hands in glee.

"You're such a man!" she exclaimed, as she threw her hands around his neck and gave him a giant kiss on the lips.

"You're just figuring that out? Apparently, I haven't done a good enough job proving that to you."

"Oh no, you're all man, but who knew you were a handyman too?"

"Not really handy, just perceptive."

"Well, I'll be thanking you later tonight."

Jax squeezed her ass and said, "Any form of payment is accepted, and tips are suggested."

"Perfect. I know just the way to tip you," she squeezed his balls and then walked away, making him crouch over for just a second as he watched her hips sway away from him. Even though his team lost today, he kept thinking how he still felt like he'd won, now that Brooke was in his life.

CHAPTER ELEVEN

Piper

Piper had never felt more awkward in her life. It was Tuesday night and Lexi and Jake wanted to have a mini goodbye dinner for Mason before he went back to Denver to start rehabbing his knee. Piper thought it would be best if it was just the three of them, but both Lexi and Mason insisted that Piper join them.

Reluctantly, she put on grey skinny jeans and a Ramones T-shirt and joined in the festivities. Lexi greeted her at the door, practically squealing when she saw her, and then scolded Piper for not staying in touch. Piper didn't want to get into the details right there, in the entryway, so she just apologized and walked into the house.

From the back of house, Piper spotted Mason and Jake out by the grill, talking and drinking beers. They were like a tame porn site for the ladies to look out onto. They were both wearing khaki shorts that hung low on their waists, and Jake wore a green T-shirt, while Mason was sporting a black polo. Watching them joke with each other and clink beer bottles made Piper ache to run up to

Mason and claim him as hers forever, but she knew that was too fast. She was still hesitant around the man, but seeing him so carefree, so loveable, made her ache. She wanted to be fun-loving and happy with Mason, but she knew that was going to come in time…hopefully. Right now, they were lucky if they could get through a conversation without getting on each other's nerves.

Not really feeling like she belonged, she followed Lexi into the kitchen where she was cutting up watermelon. Instantly, Lexi handed Piper a beer and told her to drink up. Apparently, Lexi, the nosy one, wanted details, and she knew Piper well enough to know that a beer would help loosen Piper's tongue.

"Do you need any help?" Piper asked, as she took a big gulp of her beer, hoping for it to start to loosen her up a bit.

"Can you slice the tomatoes, please? We're having burgers, and Jake needs tomato slices on his burger…it's a requirement. Frankly, the idea of having a tomato on my burger makes me want to puke."

"I hear ya," Piper said, as she grabbed a knife and cutting board.

"So…" Lexi pushed.

"So, what?" Piper acted as if she didn't know what Lexi was fishing for.

"Cut the crap. I want the deets. Where have you been, and why are you and Mason all of a sudden able to be in a two mile radius of each other without ripping each other's heads off?"

"God, you're so nosy."

Lexi set down her knife and turned to Piper with her hand on her hip and her finger poking Piper's shoulder.

"When you're my best friend and you go disappearing on me, without a word, I get to be nosy. You hear me? You scared me, Piper. I was seriously concerned. So, don't try to block me out now. You owe me an explanation."

Knowing Lexi was right, Piper decided to confess everything.

"You're right, I'm sorry. I didn't mean to scare you. I was just going through a really rough time and I didn't think I could be around anyone that was connected to Mason. The moment I saw Brooke in Mason's apartment, I lost it. I lost it completely. I blamed him for being with her, which made no sense, because I was with Jax. I just couldn't stand to see the bitch, so when she came out into the living room wearing only a shirt, I saw red. I let my pride overtake my body and I shut Mason out. I picked everything up and took off. I didn't care where I ended up, as long as it was as far away from Denver as possible. I wound up in Las Vegas, where I made some really bad choices that I won't get into, but, needless to say, I didn't have any other place to go after that, so I had to live with my parents."

"Wait, I called them and asked about you."

"I know, and I told them not to tell you where I was," Piper said, feeling guilty.

"Wow, okay. I'm just going to drop that, because I don't want to get pissed at you right now. But, hell Piper, you couldn't have at least let me know?"

"You were connected to Mason. And, I love you, Lex, but we both know you gossip better than anyone we know. If you knew where I was, it was bound to get back to Mason somehow."

Lexi tried to defend herself, but knew it was pointless, so she just shrugged her shoulders and let Piper continue.

"It's been hell living with them...my parents. They haven't changed, and heaven forbid my dad show any kind of affection toward me." Shaking her head from the lack of parental love she was born into, she continued, "I fell into this black hole where I was just kind of moving around in the world, but not experiencing anything. To earn some cash, I babysat for my cousin, and that's when I ran into Mason at the bistro. It was like meeting him on the airplane all over again. I couldn't help but be snarky toward him, and he was a giant ass...surprise. He wound up taking off, and when I was cruising the streets to make sure that he actually made it back to your place, I saw him yelling at his crutches while sitting on the grass next to the sidewalk." Piper remembered seeing him on the grass acting like a child, and it brought a smile to her face.

"Ugh, he is such a freaking pansy when it comes to those crutches and just being hurt in general. He loves playing the 'woe is me' card. Jake feeds into it because the two are in love with each other, but I didn't fall for it. I helped Mason out, but I also let him be self-sufficient, which apparently you didn't do," Lexi said.

Shaking her head, Piper moved forward with her story. "No, I was a bad influence on his baby act. I made lunch and dinner for him and got things for him. I just couldn't stay away, even though there is still a lot of hate between us. There's always been this force that has pulled us together, though. I can't deny it anymore, and neither can he. I'm actually kind of shocked that he hasn't given me more of a cold shoulder. Makes me wonder…"

"Wonder what?" Lexi asked, as she popped a piece of watermelon in her mouth.

"It makes me wonder if he has ulterior motives."

"What does that mean?"

"It's not a secret that we both have trust issues. Mason and I have always had issues, but the physical aspect of our relationship has always powered through, which helped us realize that we do have some things in common. But, I just don't understand why, all of a sudden, he's being so nice to me. I feel like he's setting me up, and he's going to take me out to Denver and then humiliate me like I did to him."

Lexi stopped in the middle of putting a piece of watermelon in her mouth, and turned to face Piper again. "Are you kidding me?"

"No…"

"Piper, did you tell him that?" Piper shook her head no, and Lexi continued, "Well don't. I've known Mason for a long time, and he may be an ass, a giant douche-like bastard most of the time, especially now that he is a scarred man, but he would never do something as manipulative as that, ever."

"That's what I would like to believe."

"Well, believe it, because it's the truth. I love Mason and I know him; he would never do that to you, so get it out of your brain. He's been struggling these last couple of months. He tries to put up a front, but I hear the conversations he has with Jake. Even though he didn't want to admit it, he missed you. You two belong together; now all you have to do is step away from your stubborn pride and just live. Stop wondering about asinine things like revenge, because that won't happen. There is just one thing on Mason's mind, and that is to be happy again. For some strange reason, when you two were at each other's throats, he was happy. He wants that again, and knows he will only get it from you."

"Get what from Piper?" Jake asked, as he walked into the house with a plate full of burgers in one hand, and a beer in the other. He leaned down and gave Piper a kiss on the cheek and said into her ear, "It's really good to see you. Don't leave us again, you hear?" Piper nodded her head, as Lexi tried to cover up what she'd been saying.

"None of your business," Lexi sassed Jake. "I don't interrupt your boy talk, now do I?"

Jake set down the burgers and held up his hands. "Well, excuse me for living."

"You're excused, now set the table with that pathetic friend of yours."

"I heard that," Mason said, as he leaned over the bar and winked at Piper. "Hey, I didn't hear you come in."

God, her heart started beating rapidly as she took in the dark scruff of his jaw and the chocolate colored eyes that bored holes into her soul. The way he spoke to her was with a soft voice, one that she'd once heard when she told him she wanted to make things work out between them. It was a voice that affected her entire body from her toes to the tips of her hair; he could make her do anything just by using that voice.

"She got here a little bit ago, but you two morons were too busy drinking beer outside," Lexi said, as she blew past everyone and started placing bowls on the table.

Mason smiled and looked over at Piper, making her heart stop beating in her chest. His eyes were soft, and he looked genuinely happy to see her. At that moment, when their eyes connected, she knew, even if Mason might be playing her, she couldn't walk away; there was no way. She needed to soak up as much Mason as possible.

"What are you waiting for?" Mason asked, as he jerked his head, telling her to come to him, "Come give me a hug."

Jake and Lexi were in the dining room setting the table. Well, Lexi was more likely lecturing Jake on the proper table setting protocol, while he wrapped his arms around her body and kissed her neck.

Piper walked over to Mason, who had his arm up waiting for her to slip into them. She put her arms around his waist as he wrapped his arm around her shoulders. Taking a deep breath, she relished the masculine scent of Mason, and pressed her head against his chest. She felt his lips caress the top of her head, making her toes tingle from the contact.

"I'm glad you're here. I know it must be awkward, but we're all happy you're here."

"Me too," Piper said, as she gripped onto Mason just a little tighter.

"Are you all packed for tomorrow?" Mason practically whispered into her ear, keeping the intimacy of the conversation.

"Not much to pack, but yes, I'm all set."

"Perfect."

Mason nuzzled her hair again as Lexi shouted, "Time for dinner. Get your asses out here."

Letting go, Mason grabbed his crutches, smiled one last time down at Piper, and then went to the dining room. Piper watched as his back muscles rippled under his shirt from having to crutch himself around. The simple things made him sexy...the way his shirt expanded across his back, but then tapered down to his waist...the thick muscles in his calves...the way he gripped the crutches, which made his forearms pop with strength. The man was practically a cripple, and she wanted to jump his bones right then and there. Hopefully, she'd be able to soon.

Mason twisted around and called over his shoulder, "You coming, Piper?"

"Yup, be right there."

She grabbed her beer, said a little prayer for herself because she knew she was going to be going on one hell of an emotional roller coaster, and headed out to the dining room where food was already being distributed. It was funny how fast her life had changed from a dark abyss to seeing light at the end of the tunnel.

Mason

He needed to stop staring and eat his food, but it was hard when Piper sat across from him in one of her typical grey band T-shirts that made her skin look creamy as hell and her eyes pop. Those silver eyes of hers...he couldn't get enough of them, especially when she highlighted them with a nice coat of mascara. She was gorgeous.

Mason wished that they were already in Denver together and not at Jake and Lexi's house where he had to behave. He wasn't about to have sex with Piper anytime soon; they were taking things slow, but he wanted to hold her, and with Jake and Lexi's wandering eyes, Mason felt awkward. So instead, he kept his distance, except for when he said hello to her; he couldn't help himself then.

He'd stayed up the past couple of nights thinking about his decision to invite Piper back into his life. He was taking a chance on something that was never a sure thing. His relationship with Piper was always up in the air, and even when he thought it was solid, that she was going to be with him, she still changed her mind. Anxiety rolled through his body at the mere thought of her doing the same thing to him again, but he pushed back the thought, since what it came down to was that he was a miserable fuck. He needed to change something in his life, and he knew that even though she could screw him over, being with her brought him more happiness than he could ever remember. She was his addiction, his nirvana, the light of his day. Fuck him, but he needed her.

"Dude, Lexi is owning you right now," Jake said, shaking Mason out of his thoughts. He looked over at Lexi, who was now leaning back in her chair and licking her fingers.

"You got yourself a real prize there," Mason said sarcastically, as he took a bite from his burger that was only halfway gone. Was he really staring that much? If he was, Piper apparently didn't notice because her plate was almost cleaned as well.

"How is the new place coming along?" Lexi asked.

"New place?" Piper looked confused.

Clearing his throat, Mason said, "Well, I bought a condo downtown with a great view of the mountains."

"Oh…" Piper said, as she looked down at her plate.

"It should actually be ready when I get back tomorrow. I have to do some unpacking, but all the new furniture should have been delivered."

"It should be a fresh start for you," Jake said, as he took a sip of his beer.

Glancing up at Piper, he noticed a strange look in her eyes.

"Excuse me," she said, as she got up out of her chair and walked down the hallway toward the bathroom.

Jake and Lexi both looked at Mason, confused. He had no clue what was going on, so he looked at Lexi and asked, "Should I go see if everything is okay?"

"Might be best," she said while laughing and patting his hand. "Welcome to being in a relationship again."

"Fuck…" he joked, as he got up and crutched his way down the hall.

Mason heard the water running in the bathroom and lightly knocked on the door. The water shut off, but Piper didn't say anything. Mason tested the knob and found it wasn't locked. Taking a deep breath, he opened the door and crutched his way in. Piper was sitting on the toilet seat with a towel running through her hands. Mason shut the door, propped himself on the sink, and positioned himself directly in front of her.

"Everything okay?" he asked.

She just nodded her head, not quite making eye contact with him.

"Piper, look at me."

She lifted her head and that was when Mason saw the pain that was encasing her beautiful silver eyes.

"What's going on? And don't tell me nothing. If we have any chance of making this work between us, we have to be honest with each other."

Sighing, Piper asked, "Why are you moving?"

Damn, Mason wanted to eat his words just now about honesty. He knew he had to tell her the truth, but sometimes the truth hurt, and in this case, it was going to be a slap in the face to her.

"Well, I just couldn't stand to be in my place anymore, not after everything we went through. I would walk around my place and see reminders of you everywhere; it was killing me, and I just had to leave."

"And the furniture?"

Mason winced. "I might have sold it for all new furniture."

"Because I touched it...right?"

Mason squeezed the bridge of his nose as he tried to think of the best way to put this, but then realized he just had to be truthful. There was no way of getting around it.

"Yes." Piper lowered her head, making Mason feel like a total bastard. "You have to understand that, after you left, I lost my mind. I found a new place, I put everything up for sale, and I drank myself into an oblivion. I even missed a couple of practices. I was fined, of course, because the dickhead Jax wouldn't give me a break. I was miserable, Piper, and I needed everything that reminded me of you gone, and that meant most of my furniture. I didn't think that I was ever going to see you again, so I didn't think about how you might feel..."

"I know," she waved him off. "It just reminds me of what a

terrible person I was. I mean, I hurt you so badly that you decided to change everything in your life, even your furniture. Who does that to someone?"

"I may have been a little dramatic," Mason tried to soothe.

"No, you were right in doing what you did. I did the same thing. I went on a bender, drugs, alcohol, random sex..."

The mention of Piper having random sex with strangers made Mason cringe. He didn't want to think of her doing it with anyone else but him.

"But that's all in the past," Mason suggested.

"Stop!" Piper shouted as she looked back up at Mason, making him flinch at her tone. "We need to talk about the past in order to have a fucking future. We can't just forget about what happened, because it will always be a road block in our path. We need to talk about it."

Mason started to get angry as he looked down at her. He didn't want to talk about it, because it was a very dark time in his life. Who wants to relive such a thing?

"I don't want to talk about it," Mason said in between clenched teeth.

Piper stood up and tossed her towel to the side, "Then maybe me coming to Denver isn't the best idea, if we can't even communicate with each other."

"Christ!" Mason ran both of his hands over his face. "Can't you just let it go?"

"No, we have issues, Mason, and we need to be able to work them out."

"Well, I don't want to," Mason exclaimed, sounding more childish than he anticipated.

"Fine. Have fun in Denver. I really hope your knee gets better."

With that, she walked out of the bathroom and down the hall, leaving Mason to himself and his thoughts.

CHAPTER TWELVE

Jesse

"Thanks for having me over and all, man, but you can stop fidgeting with my clothes. Damn. What's your problem?" Jesse asked, as Ryker pulled away. He was a gay man's dream, too bad he floated down the tuna canoe river.

Ever since Jesse had arrived at Ryker's place for some pizza and beer, Ryker had been telling Jesse to pop his collar, which Jesse refused to do, to tie his shoe laces, and to "fluff" his hair.

"What the hell does it matter what I look like? We're just drinking some beer."

The doorbell rang, and Ryker said, "Can you get that? I have to take a leak."

"Seriously? And let me guess, I'm paying as well?" Ryker gave him a thumbs up as he walked away. Jesse mumbled something about Ryker being a dick as he went to the door. When he opened it, he had his head down looking at his wallet as he asked, "How much?"

"I've never been paid for my services before, but I guess I could give it a shot," a very familiar female voice said."

Jesse shot his gaze up and saw Ashlin standing in the doorway wearing a pair of leggings and a tight long-sleeved shirt. Her hair was straight and hanging over her shoulders, which enticed Jesse to want to feel the strands between his fingers. She looked gorgeous and fresh, as usual.

Clearing his throat, Jesse said, "Oh, hey. Sorry about that. I thought you were the pizza guy."

"Pizza? Ryker told me to pick up Thai." Ashlin held up a brown paper bag that looked pretty full of food.

"I think we've been set up," Jesse said, as he shook his head.

Just then, Ryker's garage door opened and they heard Ryker pull his car out. He rolled down the window and said, "I'm off to see my boo; have a good night."

"Fucker," Jesse muttered, as he watched Ryker drive away with a shit-eating grin on his face.

"Well, this is awkward," Ashlin said, as she rocked back and forth on her feet. "Here, take the food. I can pick something up on my way home."

"You're leaving?" Jesse asked, as Ashlin was trying to hand him the food.

"Yeah, I mean, clearly you don't want me here…"

"That's not true. It's just, I mean…Ryker could have said something, that's all. Why don't you come in and have a seat? We can at least have dinner together."

Ashlin shrugged her shoulders and walked into the house. Jesse felt awkward for so many reasons, but one of the reasons was having a "date" in someone else's house. Being uncomfortable in someone else's surroundings wasn't ideal.

"We should do something to Ryker to get him back. Maybe string all of his condoms together, make him a nice little tree garland," Jesse suggested, making Ashlin Laugh.

"Oh, my God, we have to. Give him a little payback."

"Yeah, we can leave all the empty packets on his bed, and then for Christmas, give him the garland; it will be perfect!"

"I like the way you think QB."

Jesse wanted to tell her he liked the way she called him QB, but resisted because they were supposed to be just friends…at least he was working on it. It was hard to be just friends with someone when you saw them as something more. It was almost impossible, actually, because every smile, every look over her shoulder, and every little touch, Jesse engrained in his memory as his body reacted. It wasn't safe at all.

They went to the kitchen, grabbed some plates from the cabinets, and started divvying up the Thai food…one of Jesse's favorite cuisines, he couldn't get enough of the noodles. Jesse grabbed beers for both of them and took them to the table where Ashlin was sitting.

"Here," Jesse handed her the beer.

"Thanks."

Silence.

They both picked at their food while they casually looked around the house, never really making eye contact with each other. Well, they were eating dinner together, that was for sure.

Yup, Jesse was going to put this moment down in history as one of the most awkward moments of his life. He had so much to say to her, to ask her, but he didn't even know how to begin. He wanted to know about her life, why she was opposed to relationships, what her childhood was like.

As Jesse chewed on some well-seasoned chicken, he glanced over at Ashlin, who glanced at him at the same time. Both of their mouths were full, so they just smiled and then went back to surveying the room.

Silence.

Ashlin took a sip of her beer and then pushed her plate away. "Well, that was good, but I guess I should be going."

"Yeah, me too."

"We can always do the condom thing later," Ashlin said, as

she took her plate to the kitchen.

"Yeah. Ryker would probably whine at me forever if I did ruin all his condoms, so it probably wasn't the best idea." Why did he sound so sad? Maybe it was because he was with the girl he wanted, but couldn't think of a way to actually talk to her. He wasn't good with the opposite sex at all, and he was showing it right now.

"He can be such a baby."

Jesse silently nodded his head as they both walked to the front door.

"Big day tomorrow?" she asked, as they closed the door and headed to their respective cars.

"Just practice. What about you, any photo shoots planned?"

"Not until next week. It's been nice having a bit of a break."

"Yeah, I wish we had a break on occasion."

They both got to their cars and stood at their driver's side doors.

"Well, have a good night," Ashlin called out.

Have a good night? That was it? That was how they were going to end this night? Something inwardly possessed Jesse, and he didn't know what it was, but it was propelling him forward to Ashlin. He couldn't end their night like this. With a few steps, he had his hands on either side of her, trapping her against her car. Her eyes were wide as she took him in.

"I can't stand being like this toward you, so casual," Jesse said, as he spoke closely to her ear.

"Me either," she breathed heavily, hopefully from his proximity.

"You're anything but casual to me, Ashlin."

"I don't know how to respond to that," she admitted honestly.

He looked her in the eyes and said, "You don't need to. Just know this, I'm not done with you. I can't be done with you. I said I don't do flings, and I meant that, but I can't just walk away. You're in me; I feel you whenever you're around, and there is no way I can shake that feeling. You'll be mine at some point, Ashlin, I'm sure of it. I just have to get you to that point first."

She nodded as she watched him intently.

Slowly, he lowered his head, so his lips were a whisper away from hers.

"Have a good night, Ashlin."

He started to pull away, but she gripped his belt loops and pulled him into her. She feverishly pressed her lips against his and moved her hands up and under his shirt, caressing his bare skin...something he was not expecting, but the feeling hit him hard. His hands ran up to her face and cupped her cheeks. He kissed her, hard, like it was the last kiss of his life. He took everything she was giving him, and demanded more, not letting up.

A light moan escaped her lips as his hands wandered down to her waist. He lifted her shirt just a little, so his hands touched her bare back. She was smooth and heated and just so perfect. He pulled her closer and knew that if he didn't stop soon, he would be bending her over her car and taking everything that he wanted.

Pulling away, he looked down at her and said, "Lunch, tomorrow?"

"Don't you have practice?"

"We get a lunch break. Meet me at the stadium at noon. It's time for us to get to know each other."

With one last effort, Jesse kissed her gently on the lips, trying to convey to her that he was serious about what was happening between them, and he wasn't going to take no for an answer.

She nodded her head once he pulled away, making him smile at his triumph. Success, now he just needed to remember to use his lips when doing all the convincing.

Piper

"Stop!" Piper heard Mason shout from down the hallway. Jake and Lexi both turned their heads to see what was going on. "Get your ass back here, right now."

"Ooo, someone's in trouble," Lexi teased as she smiled.

172

"Don't make me come over there and slap you," Piper said to Lexi.

"I can take you," Lexi puffed out her chest.

Jake gave her a slap on her back and said, "That's right, babe, if anything you can suffocate her with your tits; Lord knows I've almost passed out before while getting motor boated."

"Jake!" Lexi screeched, as she playfully swatted her husband, making both him and Piper laugh.

Glancing back at Mason, Piper realized he was not feeding into the jovial mood Lexi and Jake were trying to put on.

Giving Piper the "come here" motion with his finger, Mason said, "Get back here, now. I'm not done with you."

Even though he looked incredibly sexy, Piper said, "What if I'm done with you?" as she put her hands on her hips, not really knowing why she was giving Mason a hard time and being defiant. It was just in her nature.

"Don't play with me," Mason gritted out.

Noticing that the tension in the room had started to escalate, Piper gave in and walked toward Mason, who ushered her into the guest room he had been staying in. Mason shut the door with his crutch and motioned for her to sit on the bed that was, not surprisingly, unmade. The whole room was a bit of a disaster, with clothes scattered everywhere and pillows flung about the room.

"You're kind of a pig," Piper commented, as she looked around the room, noticing an untouched box of condoms on the night stand. She nodded toward it and said, "Not getting very lucky lately?"

Mason's jaw ticked with anger as he took her in. Why she liked it when he got mad was beyond her. Maybe it was the hot sex they usually had when he was angry, or the fact that his face turned to stone and showed off his sharp features and deep brown eyes.

Instead of backing off, she continued making jabs; she couldn't stop herself, especially when he was so easy to get riled up. "You know, when you get angry, there's this little vein that pokes out on your neck," Piper motioned to her neck as she said, "Right about here. It's fun to watch…"

She didn't get to finish her barbing because Mason pushed her back on the bed and was on her so fast she didn't think she could breathe. His strong body overlapped hers and his hands straddled her head. His delicious face was mere inches from her and his chest heaved from anger and passion mixed together. His dark eyes seemed even darker as he took her in. This was the Mason she knew, the rough one who took what he wanted when he wanted it, and even though she should stand up and push him away, there was no way her body was going to allow it, because she felt comforted; she felt at peace in Mason's arms.

Mason searched her eyes as he licked his lips, making her core melt in one fell swoop. Her breathing hitched as she anticipated his next move. She would be lying if she said she didn't want him to kiss her, to feel her, to be inside of her. She wanted it more than anything. She itched for his touch, for his caress.

"Now that I've got your attention, are you going to shut that snarky mouth of yours and listen to me?" She nodded her head, unable to speak from the sexy tone that laced his voice. "Good. Now listen carefully, because I'm only going to say this once. You running away from me and walking out on me is not a right you have anymore. You got that? You lost that right the minute you chose Jax over me and crushed my heart. If you are in this, then you are in this for the long run. No more running, Piper; your running days are over."

Piper gulped as she listened to the controlling voice that Mason very easily laid upon her. Normally, she would push against him and not take his crap, because she never liked anyone dominating her, but with Mason, it was different. The way he talked to her and used his controlled voice, she could feel the comfort he was trying to convey.

He shifted slightly so his weight was balanced a little more on her, making her realize that he should be sitting, not trying to capture her.

"Mason, you should lay down…"

"I'm fine," he said in a stern voice, making her step down. She realized that he needed this; he needed to be in control, so even though she thought he might hurt his leg again, she let him do what he wanted to do. "What happened between us a couple of months ago was shitty, and I get that we have to talk about it, but not now, not here. We'll do it when we're ready and in our own space. Got it?"

Piper nodded her head as she searched his eyes. They were fierce and serious. At that moment, she knew, this was it for her. Mason was not going to let her go, and hell if she wanted to run anymore, not with this luscious and passionate man draping himself over her.

Mason leaned down even closer, just a breath away from taking her lips. He looked her in the eyes, licked his lips, and breathed heavily as he lightly brushed his lips against hers. Everything in her body froze from the contact, the very light contact, but a contact she never thought she would receive from Mason again. His scruff tickled her chin, and just when she was about to settle in for a kissing marathon, he pulled away, leaving her wanting and yearning for his touch.

"Don't look so upset. There'll be time for that, but right now, we have some friends to enjoy before we go off to Denver."

Mason stood up, placed his crutches under his arms and crutched toward the door. He nodded his head for her to follow him and said, "Let's go, devil woman."

Piper stood up, adjusted her clothing, and steadied her racing heart. Looking at Mason, she took in his delectable body and the way his arms flexed from using the crutches. He was everything a girl dreamed of, and he was willing to give her a second chance. He was right; her running days were over…it was time to be an adult.

Walking over to him, she placed her hand gently on his cheek, feeling the rough scruff of his face under her palm, and said, "No more running, Mace."

"No more running," he repeated.

Hannah

Hannah couldn't steady the nerves that were coursing through her body. Ryker was on his way to her place to make dinner with her, but little did he know, she had plans for after. She was ready to finally give herself over to Ryker, but she was unsure if he was ready. He could easily turn her down, since they were still kind of trying to figure each other out. If he turned her down, she knew she would be crushed, absolutely devastated, but she would move on.

There was a knock at her door and she knew Ryker was here. She took a deep breath, adjusted her sundress and opened the door. Ryker was standing on the other side of the door wearing a pair of navy blue pants, a checkered orange shirt, and his classic boat shoes. In his hands was an audacious display of flowers and a bottle of wine. He smiled brightly at her, which made her heart melt as she leaned against the door.

"Hey, boo," Ryker said, as he walked into her apartment. He leaned down and placed a kiss on her lips, nothing sexy, but very romantic. He handed her the flowers, and said, "These are for you. I hope you like them. I'm not sure what your favorite flower is."

"They're beautiful," Hannah said, while grabbing them and sniffing the daisies that were in her hands. "I love daisies; they're so simple and pretty."

Puffing his chest out a little at picking a good flower, Ryker said, "Well, I'm glad I did a good job. Now, what are we making tonight? I brought some wine."

"Thanks. We're going to just make something simple tonight, is that alright?"

Ryker wrapped his arms around Hannah and pulled her into his chest. "Listen, as long as I'm with you, I don't care what we do."

"Aren't you sweet? Who knew Ryker Lewis could be romantic?"

Shrugging his shoulders as if it were nothing, he said,

"Nothing to it, Boo, where you're concerned."

Hannah placed a chaste kiss on his lips and led him to the kitchen. While she placed the flowers in a vase, Ryker poured them each a glass of wine. They worked well together in the kitchen, making homemade gnocchi, which wasn't too difficult, and then heating up some store bought spaghetti sauce. Ryker had fun putting flour on Hannah's nose whenever he got the chance, and she would always squeal at him, making him laugh.

As they worked together to make their meal, Hannah thought about how idiotic she was for waiting so long to be with this man. He cared deeply about her, and it was obvious in the way he needed to be at her side, constantly touching her, and the way his eyes shone whenever he looked down at her. He made her feel special. With Todd, she never felt special like she did with Ryker; she always felt mediocre with Todd, second best. With Ryker, she knew she was number one in his life.

Once the food was ready, they sat down together, held hands, and ate their meals. It might have been cheesy, they might have even looked like goofballs, holding hands and eating their dinner together, but it was endearing to Hannah. She loved the fact that Ryker was secure with his manhood and had no problem showing affection toward her. Affection was something she'd been missing out on for a while.

Ryker leaned back in his chair and rubbed his stomach as he looked over his empty plate. "Damn, girl, we know how to make a good meal."

"We sure do," Hannah said, while smiling, because looking back at their food preparation, Ryker mainly held her and goofed around with the flour; there wasn't much making on his part, but she wouldn't tell him that. He apparently had some pride for the meal he "helped" make.

"Is there dessert?" Ryker topped off his wine glass and took a big swig. The man was a never-ending pit of food consumption. Hannah was shocked at the amount of food Ryker was able to consume in one sitting.

There was dessert, but not the kind Ryker was probably thinking about. The nerves that started racking her body at the beginning of the evening came back in full force as she started clearing their plates. She didn't know if she could be the girl that Ryker needed in the bedroom. He was the type of guy who needed someone adventurous, who would try anything he wanted, but she was a vanilla kind of girl. She didn't explore that much in the bedroom, and it wasn't necessarily because she didn't want to, but more because she was shy as hell. She liked the lights off and she liked the basic positions, because that was what she knew, but just looking at Ryker, she knew that wouldn't do; he would need more. That was why her hands were shaking as she rinsed the dishes so she could put them in the dishwasher.

In her head, she was going over her plan of attack as Ryker slipped in behind her and wrapped his strong arms around her waist.

"Hey, boo, what's got you crinkling that pretty forehead of yours?" Ryker asked, as he kissed along her neck.

The sensation of his lips trailing along her skin had her temporarily forgetting the nerves that were coursing through her body. Her head fell to the side as he continued to kiss her neck very, very slowly. If she didn't know any better, she would have thought Ryker was planning on the same thing she was.

Pulling away gently, Ryker whispered in her ear, "Did you make me pie? You know how much I like pie."

Smiling, Hannah turned in his embrace and placed her hands on his chest. She took a deep breath and said, "I didn't make you pie." Ryker pouted. "I have something else planned." She grabbed his hand and led him to the back of her apartment, to her bedroom. Ryker stopped in her doorway and pulled away, setting Hannah on fire from the distance he put between them.

"What are you doing, Hannah?"

Taking one last deep breath, Hannah grabbed the hem of her dress, pulled it over her head, and tossed it to the ground, exposing the white lace lingerie she had on underneath. She watched as

Ryker slowly took her in with hooded eyes. His chest heaved and his fists clenched at his sides. She couldn't tell if he was mad or intrigued.

"Hannah…"

"Take me, Ryker," she said, as she stood with all the bravado she could muster.

Ryker didn't say anything; he just stood there, and at that moment, she knew he was going to say no. If he wanted her, he would have been on her already. Her cheeks blushed from being turned down, and her stomach rolled from embarrassment. She scrambled to the floor and picked up her dress as she tried to put it back on. She shut the door on Ryker and ran to her bathroom as tears started to streak down her face. She was completely mortified. She knew Ryker turning her down was a risk she had to take, but she didn't think it would actually happen. Now what was she supposed to do?

Ryker

Stunned would be one word to describe the way Ryker was feeling, but completely flipped on his ass surprised could be another. Never did Ryker think Hannah would be the one to make the first move toward the bedroom in their relationship. That theory was destroyed the minute she led him to her bedroom and took off her dress. Ryker couldn't move; he was frozen in place. He couldn't believe the woman standing before him; the woman he'd claimed to marry one day was taking him by the balls and giving him everything he ever wanted. She was giving herself over to him, and it struck him to the core.

He didn't realize he was being silent and unresponsive until she started scrambling around for her dress and shut the door on him. The slam of her bathroom door woke him from the racing thoughts in his head and propelled his body forward. Not even bothering to knock, he walked into Hannah's bathroom to find her sitting on the edge of the tub, crying into her hands.

Ryker knelt down before her and pulled her head away from her hands. "Hey, why the tears?" he asked, as he wiped them away with his thumbs.

"I don't want you to see me like this. Just give me a second, okay?"

Ryker let out a little laugh, which caused her head to snap up with anger. "I'm sorry," he said, as he laughed, "but there is no way in hell I'm going to leave you in your bathroom crying. Are you crazy? Come here." Ryker sat on the ground and pulled her onto his lap. "Now, tell me why you ran away from me when you were looking magnificent?"

"You didn't do anything," she said shyly, as she buried her head into his shoulder.

Chuckling, Ryker said, "Hannah, you didn't even give me a chance. Frankly, you shocked the hell out of me; I wasn't expecting you to take your dress off."

"Oh, God. I'm so embarrassed." She kept her head tucked, so he couldn't see those beautiful ice blue eyes of hers.

"Look at me," he pulled her head out of his shoulder and made her eyes meet his. "You should not be embarrassed at all. That was so fucking hot. I was just taken by surprise. You have to give a guy time to react. I was just starting to take in your gorgeous body when you ran away."

"I thought you were going to turn me down," she admitted.

"Why the hell would I do that?"

"Because I'm so vanilla…"

"Whoa, stop right there," Ryker said, as he started to get angry. "Whoever told you that you were vanilla?"

"No one, but it's kind of obvious. I'm not like all the girls you used to date. I'm not a supermodel, I don't dress like one, and I sure as hell don't act like one."

"And that's what I like about you, Hannah, you're you. I don't want a supermodel; I want the most gorgeous woman I've ever set eyes on, and that's you. You're everything I've ever wanted, why can't you see that?"

She shrugged her shoulder and then lightly kissed his jaw. "Maybe because I wasn't good enough for someone else."

"Well, that someone else was a total fuckstick. Don't let him affect you, you're everything, Hannah."

Ryker placed his finger under her chin and lifted her mouth to his. He started out lightly kissing her lips, letting her know how much he cared about her, but the moment she opened her mouth and allowed him to deepen their kiss, he started to slowly lose control. He groaned in the back of his throat when she straddled his body and slowly started to rotate her hips. Was this the same girl he'd grown to know? Was this his Hannah? She was anything but vanilla.

Pulling away, Ryker said, "I don't want to do this here." Bathroom sex was only good in the shower, or bent over the vanity, but with Hannah, he didn't want their first time to be quick and easy. He wanted to explore every last inch of her body.

He pulled her up and worked her back into her bedroom, walking behind her with his hands wrapped around her waist, making use of her exposed neck. Once they reached her bed, Ryker kept her facing away from him and grabbed the hem of her dress. He pulled it over her head and dropped it to the ground. His hands went instantly to her shoulders, where he stroked his fingers from her shoulders, down the sides of her body until they were at her waist, just above the waistband of her thong.

Thong.

Ryker felt his dick grow three sizes the minute he saw Hannah's sweet ass perfectly displayed by her innocent white lace thong. Her color choice didn't escape him as he took in the little bubble butt that she had. Ryker bit down on his bottom lip as his hands trailed down and cupped her ass.

"Fuck, your ass is perfect."

"I'm going to allow the swearing for now," Hannah joked, as she leaned into his grasp.

Ryker ran his hands up her back to the clasp of her bra. Not thinking twice, he unhooked it and gently removed the straps off her shoulders, letting the bra fall to the ground. Her skin was so smooth, so porcelain like, it was hard to not run his hands up and down her body.

He pulled her body against his, knowing she sure as hell was going to feel how excited he was, but he didn't care. He ran his hands to the front of her waist, right to her hip bones. His thumbs stroked her skin, making her breathe heavily, eliciting a slight purr from her. She was so responsive.

Knowing he was about to go into new territory, he took a deep breath and prepared himself. He ran his hands up her stomach to just below her breasts. Her breathing hitched as she waited for his hands to encase her breasts. Just before he took her into his hands, he leaned over her shoulder and got the perfect view of her pert breasts and little pink nipples.

"Fuck..." Ryker said, as he took her breasts in his hands. "Damn, boo. Your tits are amazing."

Hannah's hands ran up her body and found their way around Ryker's neck, pulling him closer. Her hair went to one side of her body as she titled her neck to the side. Getting the clue, Ryker bent his head and started nibbling on her collarbone and neck as he continued to massage her breasts. They were the perfect size, and he couldn't get over how great she felt in his arms.

"Ryker..." she breathed out.

"Yes?" he asked in between kisses.

"Touch me."

"I am," he said with a smile, knowing fully well what she wanted.

"Not just there?"

"Where else?"

"Are you going to make me say it?"

"Yes, I am. I need to know what you want, boo."

She squirmed in his grasp as he bit down gently on her ear.

"Touch me...touch my...pussy."

Smiling, Ryker removed one hand from her breasts and lowered it ever so slowly down to right above her waistband.

"Right here?" Ryker asked, as he stroked her skin with his thumb.

"Yes," she said breathlessly. "Please, Ryker."

"Only because you used your manners," he teased.

He slipped his hand under her waistband and her legs spread instinctively, making Ryker bite down on his lip once again. She was going to slowly kill him, one innocent act at a time. His hand ran over her bare skin and down to the juncture between her thighs. With one slip of his finger, he was able to gauge how wet she was for him…she was primed and ready to go.

"Damn, Hannah…"

Her only response was a moan as he moved his fingers in and out of her. He loved the way she felt, the way she was so wet for him, but touching her wasn't enough; he needed to be inside of her.

Ryker removed his hands, making her moan out in frustration and turn around. That was when he was rewarded with a frontal view of her perfect breasts that were a little red from his squeezing.

He cupped her breasts, and in a concerned voice asked, "Did I hurt you?"

"No," she said quickly "but if you don't finish what you started, you're going to get hurt." She grabbed his pants and started unbuckling his belt. He wasn't going to stop her, so while she worked on his pants, he took his shirt off. In seconds, he found himself only in a pair of boxer briefs, with Hannah's fingers playing with the waistband.

"Go ahead, take them off," he whispered to her.

Her innocent eyes glanced up at him and then she bent down and stripped him of all his clothing. He was very comfortable in his skin, so the once-over Hannah gave him had no effect on him. It wasn't until her small hands wrapped around his erection that he started to shake.

"Do you like this?" she asked innocently, as she stroked him with one hand and cupped his balls with the other.

Clearing his throat, he said, "Uh, yeah, but I'm going to have to stop you there, boo. I need to be inside of you…now."

He grabbed her hands, pushed her back on the bed, tore her thong off and looked down at the naked beauty that lay before him. She was perfect, absolutely perfect.

"You're so beautiful, Hannah. I hope you know that."

"You make me feel beautiful, Ryker."

That was all he needed. He reached down into his pocket, grabbed a condom from his wallet that was there in case a moment like this finally occurred, and he slipped it over himself. Hannah lay on the bed, waiting for him to return.

He positioned his body over hers, and brought his erection to her entrance. Slowly, as he kissed her mouth with his, he entered her warm heat. He could feel the veins in his neck pop out from trying to contain himself. It took a lot of self-control not to quickly bury himself inside of her and take what he wanted so desperately.

Hannah wrapped her legs around his waist and threw her head back as he fully inserted himself. Through clenched teeth, Ryker blew out a breath that felt like he'd been holding onto for hours. This was it, he was finally with Hannah in the most intimate way possible, and he didn't want to leave. Just like he thought, Hannah was heaven.

"Please, Ryker…" she begged, as she started to move her hips.

"I want to savor this, boo."

Hannah gripped the sides of Ryker's face and looked him square in the eyes. "I do too, but savor it while you pump into me."

Her comment was a little brash for her, and all it did was turn him on more. Job well done, he thought, as he started to move in and out of her. Not knowing what to expect from being with Hannah, Ryker soaked everything in. One thing he didn't think he would hear was Hannah calling out his name and being very vocal as he moved in and out of her. It was genuine though, nothing fake about the way she mewed into his ear as he bent down to kiss her neck, or the way she breathed out his name when he took her breast in his mouth, or the way her jaw clenched when his hand made it down to her clit. She was natural and raw and perfect.

"Oh…Ryker!" Hannah tensed up around him and came. Her head flew back and her hips met each thrust of his as she called out his name in ecstasy. The scene of Hannah losing herself pushed Ryker right over the edge as his balls tightened and his hips thrust into her one last time before he pumped himself into orgasm.

"God damn…" Ryker groaned out, as he finished off and lay spent across Hannah. Quickly cleaning himself up, he wrapped Hannah up into his chest and held onto her tightly as they both tried to catch their breath. Her hand lay flat against his bare chest and lightly drew circles on him.

She nuzzled his shoulder and said, "I like you a lot, Ryker."

"I like you too, Hannah."

"Thank you for accepting me, even after everything."

"Shh…" Ryker cooed. "Remember, that's over with? We are only living in the here and now."

"Was I good enough for you?" Hannah asked.

"You were better than I could have ever imagined, boo. You're everything I have always dreamed of; don't ever forget that. You're everything to me."

CHAPTER THIRTEEN

Ashlin

Ashlin gradually picked at her salad as she watched Jesse devour the burger that was in front of him. She was dying for a taste, just for a small bite of the massive burger being shoveled down Jesse's throat.

He caught her staring and sat straight up in his chair, abandoning his hunched over position where he was easily able to chow down on his food.

"Everything okay with your salad?" he asked, as he wiped his mustard-covered mouth with his napkin.

"No, I hate salad."

Confusion displayed on Jesse's face as he asked, "Then why did you get a salad?"

Ashlin gave him a "duh" look as she said, "I have a photo shoot next week where I'm wearing a string bikini. I can't have the luxury of shoving a burger and fries down my face."

The corner of Jesse's mouth quirked as he picked up his burger and said, right before he took a huge bite, "So you can't enjoy this burger like me?"

She watched in jealousy as Jesse chowed down on his burger.

"You're an ass," she said jokingly.

"Live a little," Jesse said, as he offered over his burger for a bite. "There's Photoshop for a reason."

Ashlin snatched the burger away and said, "I'm a little offended that you think they need to use Photoshop on me."

Apparently, Jesse didn't think before he spoke, because he started backpedaling. "No, that's not what I meant..."

"Cool it, QB, I'm just teasing." She took a big bite of his burger and marveled at the flavors that were bursting in her mouth. "You're not getting this back," she said, as she pushed her salad toward him.

He looked at the greens and shrugged his shoulders. "I guess I need some fiber." Ashlin raised an eyebrow at him. "You know, just in a general kind of nutrition way, not that I'm backed up or anything."

Ashlin held up her hand. "I'm going to stop you right there. I know you want to be friends, but that's too much."

He smiled and they both ate their food in comfortable silence. Once they'd finished, Jesse leaned back in his seat, and said, "So, tell me about growing up with Ryker."

Ever since they'd gotten to the restaurant, Jesse had been asking questions about her childhood, showing a great deal of interest in her, and she had to give the boy credit, she was having a good time talking about herself, reliving the good memories in her life.

"He was a little puke," Ashlin laughed, and so did Jesse.

"I can see that."

"He was my best friend. We did everything together, and we were the reason each other didn't drown in the shitty lives we were living. Not many kids at school thought it was cool that we lived in a trailer park, so we got teased most of the time. Ryker was always there to defend us, though, and we had our fun getting back at some of the bullies. We pelted them with eggs from behind bushes, and Ryker used to steal their clothes from the locker rooms and I would replace them with the clothes of bitchy girls from school…a little clothes swap. We got them back, even though they didn't know it was us…we still got them back."

"It seems like you guys had a really good time."

"We did," Ashlin thought back to her childhood. There were good times and bad times. Mostly, the good times revolved around Ryker. She got quiet as she thought about the last time she saw Ryker before she was taken away from him, away from everything she ever knew.

"Hey," Jesse nudged her from under the table. "Why are you so quiet?"

Shaking her head, she said, "Nothing. Don't you have practice?"

"Not for another half hour. Talk to me, why did you get so quiet?"

She couldn't tell Jesse he came from a different breed than she did. She didn't grow up in a perfect family where family members showed love to one another every day. She grew up in a family environment where her dad beat her mom almost nightly and, one day, finally killed her. Jesse wouldn't understand, hell, she didn't understand herself. The only person who knew was Ryker, and she knew she could trust him with that information.

"Don't worry about it. Listen, this was fun but I have to get going." Ashlin got up from her seat and grabbed her purse. Jesse laid down some money on the table and quickly followed her outside.

They walked to her car and stopped in front of the door as she dug in her purse for her keys. Her hand was stilled by Jesse's and her face was lifted to meet his eyes.

He smiled down at her and said, "I get it, you don't want to share just yet. That's fine, but just so you know, I'll always be here for you when you're ready to talk. I'm not going anywhere." Ashlin exhaled, not out of frustration, but more of relief. She didn't want Jesse going anywhere, oddly enough. She didn't want to become attached, but she didn't want him to leave either. He was different than any guy she had ever met, even Ryker. He was sensitive, sweet, and caring…all things she craved in her life.

"Now, I'm going to let you leave because I have to run back to my house before I head back to the stadium, but how about a date at the zoo on Friday? Bring some glasses, a hat, and a wig; we're going incognito," he winked, as he placed a gentle kiss on her cheek. "I'll text you the details later. Have a good day, Ashlin."

Jesse pulled away and walked toward his car. She couldn't help but stare at the handsome man as he walked away. Everything about him was mouth-watering good, and what was most important was the fact that he actually seemed like he cared about her, and that went further than any built body in the world.

Mason

He unlocked the door and was happy to see that his new furniture was all in place amongst the boxes of his personal items. He took in his new dwelling, and was excited to start a brand new chapter in his life; this go-around, he hoped Piper stuck by his side.

He crutched to the side, and turned around to see Piper's reaction to his new place. He was able to purchase a condo on the west side of downtown Denver that gave him a picturesque view of the Rocky Mountains. The condo itself was modern, but also had a Colorado-esque feel with the oak-colored hardwood floors and cabinets, plus the exposed beams in the ceiling. He was happy with his purchase, but for some reason, he wanted Piper to be happy as well.

Stepping back, he watched Piper take in his new digs. She walked up to the window that was wrapped around his living room, showing off the great view of the Rockies. He crutched up behind her and said, "What do you think?"

"It's unbelievable, Mason. This place must have cost a fortune just because of the view."

"Don't worry, babe, I can afford it." He pinched her butt,

making her squeal, and started crutching toward the kitchen, where he hoped there was a beer chilling for him.

He opened the fridge and was happy to see a fridge stocked full of food.

"Does someone have an assistant up here I don't know about?" Piper asked, as she grabbed a beer from the fridge as well.

"Not really, just hired some people temporarily to make things easier for me. Do you want to see the rest of the place?"

"Sure, I'll hold your beer for you."

They walked around Mason's condo as he showed her where his office would be where he would keep all his memorabilia. He showed her the game room, where there was a pool table already set up, eliciting past memories of them together, and then he took her to his bedroom. The bed he ordered looked much bigger in person, but he loved it. The headboard and footboard would be perfect for when he was ready to strap Piper down and take what he wanted.

"This place is amazing, Mace. I'm really excited for you."

"Thanks. Will you help me unpack and decorate? I'm not really good with that kind of stuff."

Piper laughed, "And you think I am? I barely know how to hang curtains." Mason gave her a "please" look, and she continued, "But I will try my best. It should be fun."

"That's what I like to hear." Mason pulled her into his chest and kissed the top of her head. "I'm really glad you're here, Piper. I know we have a lot to work on, but I'm happy we're trying."

"Me too, Mace," she said as she held onto him.

Mason cleared his throat and said, "I do have something awkward to talk to you about."

Piper pulled away and said, "Okaaay."

"Come here." Mason pulled her onto his bed, so they were both sitting and facing each other. He hated standing on his crutches for long periods of time, plus he felt like a douche with them, so he would rather sit. "Sleeping arrangements..."

Piper looked around, and said, "I think this bed is plenty big for the both of us, buddy."

Mason slightly winced. "That's the thing; I think we need to sleep separately for now."

Mason wished he could have taken a picture of the look of shock that crossed Piper's face; it was kind of comical.

"What do you mean…separately?" The look of heartache that crossed Piper's face hit Mason in the stomach.

"Don't get upset," Mason said quickly. "I really want this to work between us, and I know that last time, well, we kind of let the physical part get in the way…"

"You had a huge part in that," Piper accused.

"I know, that's why I'm trying to rectify that. Believe me when I say I want nothing more than to strip you down and make love to your entire body. I want to fuck you more than anything, taste that sweet pussy of yours, and have your hands wrapped around my cock, but I know that won't do anything to build our relationship."

"It will help ease the tension," Piper said, as she scooted closer to him and placed her hand on his thigh.

Mason cleared his throat and tore his gaze away from her hand. "It would ease the tension, but I don't want to get things mixed up."

"It won't get mixed up if we're careful," Piper said, as she moved even closer and leaned forward, showing off her cleavage and making Mason's mouth water. Piper, by far, was the best sex he had ever had, and the enticing package she was showing him right now was extremely hard to resist.

Licking his lips, he took a long glance down her shirt. Her breasts weren't very big, but they were just big enough to drive a man crazy. Her hand ran up his thigh and cupped him through his jeans. A smile spread across her face when she realized he was hard. How could he not be? Piper was sitting next to him; she made him hard whenever she was in the room.

"There's nothing wrong with a little touching, Mason." She straddled his lap and pushed his back against the mattress.

Slowly, Mason was losing his self-control as Piper started to move her hips on top of his. In his head, he knew what she was doing needed to be stopped, but at the moment, his head wasn't making the decisions...especially since it had been so long since he'd been with Piper.

She leaned forward and placed her hands on either side of his head, giving Mason a clear shot down her shirt. The memory of taking her breasts into his mouth ran through his head as he stared at them, while her hips slowly continued to move on top of his. Her center was rubbing him just the right way, which had him squirming in his shorts. He never let a woman take control, ever, but right now, he was enjoying the way Piper was owning him.

Her mouth came down to his and was mere inches from taking his lips when his phone started to ring in his pocket. Mason rolled to the side, breathing heavily, and pulled out his phone, leaving Piper with a confused look on her face.

He ran his hand through his hair and answered his phone. "Hello?"

"Hey, man. It's Jake. Did you get in alright?"

Mason blew out a frustrated breath, but then thought how grateful he was that Jake had piss-poor timing. The little vixen next to him was going to need some taming.

"Yes, got in fine. Thanks for checking in, Mom." Piper looked over at him and mouthed, "Jake?" Mason nodded his head. She smiled and pressed herself back down on the bed, stretching out her gorgeous body. Mason turned away, so he wasn't tempted to touch her.

"Good to hear, how's the new place?"

"You know you're going to be here soon, right? We play your sorry ass on Sunday. You can just see the place on Saturday."

"I know, but I just wanted to make sure everything was alright...you know."

"Jake, I love you man, but you have to let up a little. I can handle my life."

"I know you can. It's just, you and Lexi are the only family I have. I want to make sure you're okay." Jake had lost his parents his freshman year in college, and Mason took him in when he had nowhere else to go, so they really were family. They were brothers, and over the years, Mason grew used to Jake's mothering, but right now, when Mason was trying to get his life back on track, he needed Jake to lay off.

"I get that, but I'm doing fine, alright? I'll see you on Saturday. Thanks for everything…letting me stay at your place…and give that hot blonde of yours a kiss and hug for me."

"Just a hug," Jake replied.

"Little do you know, we make out in the closet when you're not around," Mason teased.

"Nice try, I'd know if that diseased mouth of yours touched my girl. Now, go spend some time with Piper, but watch out, man, okay?"

"Yup," Mason said, hoping Piper couldn't overhear his conversation with Jake; he didn't need anything steering Piper away from him.

"Is she right next to you?"

"You have a good one too," Mason replied back, trying to avoid the awkward conversation Jake was trying to have.

Jake laughed into the phone and said bye right before hanging up. Once their conversation ended, Mason hung his hands between his knees and thought about how close he was to taking Piper the way he'd wanted to for so long. He needed to muster a little bit more control.

He turned to see her beautiful red curls spanned across the bed and her looking at him with complete lust in her eyes.

"You're in trouble, you know that?" She nodded her head, making him laugh. "Let me show you where you'll be sleeping."

He grabbed his crutches as she pouted out of the master bedroom muttering, "We'll see how long this lasts."

Mason showed her the bedroom she would be staying in, which was down the hall from his. The space between their bedrooms would give him a little bit of breathing room, but after what just transpired in his bedroom, he wouldn't be staying away from her for too long. There was no way he would be able to.

"Mind if a take a shower, and then we can get started on unpacking your kitchen and maybe making some dinner?" she asked.

"Sounds good to me, babe."

Piper

The only reason she needed a shower was because she needed to cool off. She was hot and bothered to the point of actually considering taking things into her own hands in the shower, but she resisted. Her next orgasm she wanted to be with Mason's fingers, tongue, or dick; she didn't care…just one of them.

The man was irresistible; she couldn't keep her hands off of him, and when she was practically dry humping him on his bed, she remembered just how big Mason actually was. God, she missed him, and his cock, and his hands, and everything about him. She should never have left him. She had good intentions when it came to accepting Jax's proposal; she wanted to save Mason's career, but now that she looked back at it, there was no way she could have made a difference, because the Stallions loved Mason…they most likely would get rid of Jax before they got rid of Mason.

As she washed her hair, she thought about what a huge mistake she'd made and how she was going to try her hardest to rectify her relationship with Mason. It seemed so easy right now, he was too easygoing, they weren't fighting…it was like they were just skimming the surface of their relationship, never really diving too deep, because once they did, shit would hit the fan. She knew it was going to happen at some point, and the sooner the better.

She got out of the shower and realized she didn't have a towel, and there were none in the bathroom because Mason had just moved in. There were no bathroom boxes in the bathroom, which meant everything was out in the living area where Mason was.

Smiling to herself, she brushed her hair with her wide-toothed comb, and took her blow dryer to her body to dry some of the water off and to fluff her hair a little more. Then, she twisted the bathroom doorknob, and walked out to the living room...naked.

As she walked toward the living room, she heard Mason talking to someone, which made her freeze in place. Was someone in the condo? She peeked around the corner, and saw Mason with his back toward her, and his phone up to his ear. Sighing in relief, she walked in the room and said, "Are there any towels in this joint?"

Mason turned around, and the minute he saw her, his jaw flew open and he said into the phone, "Got to go," and hung up.

He turned around fully and looked her up and down. His eyes burned holes into her skin as he licked his lips and stared blatantly at her breasts.

"Uh, towels," she said, trying not to shrink under his gaze.

"Get over here, right now."

"Now, Mason, we're supposed to be staying away from the physical stuff, I just want a towel..."

"Get the fuck over here, right now," he gritted out, shooting fluttering nerves through her belly.

Slowly, Piper sauntered over to him, and the whole time, Mason watched her with those dark eyes of his. When she stood before him, he grabbed her hand and pulled her down on the couch. Now that she was naked and sitting right next to him, she started to feel a little self-conscious...since he was still fully clothed.

"I'm going to get your couch all wet," she complained, as he started to lay her back.

"The only thing I care about getting wet is that pussy of yours, now spread your legs."

"Mason..."

"Spread them, Piper."

When he used that dominant voice, she was putty in his hands. She spread her legs, exposing everything. Mason's eyes glazed over as he took her in.

"Not good enough," he said, as he took her leg and put it up on the back of the couch, spreading her even more. "Good, now hold on to the armrest, because my tongue is going to fuck the hell out of that pretty pink clit of yours."

Piper gasped as his head went down on her, not giving her a chance to react. His tongue instantly flew out and started attacking her clit like a madman. His entire mouth was over her mound, sucking, licking, and torturing her with sweet pleasure.

"I thought we weren't doing this," Piper said breathlessly, as Mason pushed at her legs, spreading them even farther apart.

He lifted his head and said, "You really think you can walk in here, naked, and not get your pussy licked? Nice try."

With that, he went back down on her and continued his deep and lengthy torture. He spread her lips apart with his fingers and pressed his tongue right against her clit, moving it up and down so very slowly that she didn't think she could last another moment.

The hand that was now spreading her completely open ran down her center and entered her in one quick thrust, at the same time he put more pressure on her clit with his tongue.

"Oh God!" she practically screamed as she felt herself become even wetter than before. She threaded her hand through Mason's hair as she looked down at him. His eyes were fixed on hers as he continued his tongue lashing. If she didn't know any better, she would have thought he was smiling while making her squirm. His fingers curved up with each stroke, hitting her just in the right spot, making her toes curl and go numb.

Mason pulled away and said, "Are you going to come?"

"Yes..." she panted, as she threw her head back and waited for one more stroke of his tongue, but was shocked when he pulled completely away from her, leaving her hanging on the edge, not letting her fall over.

Her head shot up as she looked at the devilish man smiling down at her. "What the fuck are you doing?" she asked, as the bottom half of her body cried for release.

"I think you need to learn a little lesson."

"Mason, I swear to God, if you leave me like this, I will chop your dick off while you're sleeping."

"My, my, my, a little feisty, aren't we?" Mason danced his fingers just above her pubic bone, making her so sexually frustrated that she wanted to cry. Her pussy was pounding, begging for one last touch to release everything that was built up.

"Please, Mason," she begged, getting emotional.

Mason leaned down and whispered in her ear, "No need to cry, Baby. I would never leave you hanging, but I want you to know, this will not happen again until we've talked and we're ready. Do you understand? No more walking around naked, no more teasing me on my bed, none of that. We will fuck on my terms, and then we will make love, but only when it's time. We have a lot to work through."

Piper nodded her head as her stomach flopped from Mason saying, "make love."

"Good, now, where was I?"

He bent back down and continued to work her clit until her vision went black and her orgasm took over her entire body. She moaned and called out his name, as he didn't let up until she was spent, until she couldn't form a coherent thought.

She felt light, like she was floating as Mason gathered her up on his lap, his very hard lap, and held her in his arms. He kissed the side of her head and said, "We have some talking to do, babe."

She nodded her head and tucked herself into his nook. "For now, can you just hold me, Mace?"

"Anything you want, Piper. I'll literally give you anything you want," he whispered.

CHAPTER FOURTEEN

Jax

Warmth fell over Jax as Brooke's naked body wrapped around him. Life with Brooke in it had changed dramatically and fast. He thought his relationship with Piper had moved fast, but Brooke proved that theory wrong the minute he saw her at the car wash. She either spent the night at his place or they went over to hers; there wasn't a night they were separated, unless he had to go on an away trip. Every night, she had him stripping down to nothing, and she would have her wicked way with him. She was insatiable.

He was slowly starting to realize that Brooke was taking control of his heart, just like Piper did, and it scared the shit out of him. It was like déjà vu; he was losing himself quickly in a woman, and it was happening all too fast. He talked to Brooke every night. They talked about their likes and dislikes, and what they wanted in life, but they never really talked about the elephant in the room, Piper and Mason. Jax didn't really want to talk about them, because frankly, he only thought it would bring down what he and Brooke shared.

Brooke stirred next to him and lifted her head to look at him. Her hair was flying in all different directions, giving her that "I just had amazing sex" look, and Jax knew that she had. She smiled at him and said, "I always doze off after you get me off."

Laughing, Jax said, "Just lets me know I did my job."

"You always do," Brooke leaned over and kissed him on the lips. "You make me happy, Jax."

"You make me happy too, darlin'."

She rested her hands and chin on his chest and said, "Tell me something I don't know about you."

"What do you want to know?"

"I don't know, just anything."

Jax thought about it for a second, and decided to make a giant leap. "Did you know that I'm a widower?"

Brooke's head perked up at his words, and her eyes grew large with concern. "Are you serious? Oh, my God, Jax, I had no clue."

"Yeah, her name was Kiera. She was killed by a drunk driver."

"Wow. How do you even get over something like that?" she asked with curiosity.

"You don't, really. You kind of just live with the pain until it stops hurting as much. Piper was the first girl I was with after my wife's death. She kind of helped me see that there was life after such a tragedy."

"Oh," Brooke said as she sat up, taking the warmth she'd spread through Jax's body with her.

"Don't be upset," Jax said, as he sat up as well.

"I'm not upset." Jax could tell she was lying.

"Yes, you are. I can tell by the way your forehead is all crinkled together," he said, as he pressed his fingers against her skin.

"I'm not. How did you meet your wife?" Brooke asked, a little forced.

Not wanting to argue with her, Jax went on to tell her about Kiera, how they met in college and what kind of person she was. Brooke sat on the bed with him and listened intently, asking questions here and there, truly accepting his past. The fact that she cared so much about Kiera and what kind of person she was made Jax's heart soar. He'd told Piper about Kiera, but she was never really curious about her as a person.

"She sounds like she was an amazing person."

"She was. We still have the foundation she started that raises money to help prevent dogs from going to kill shelters. It's not as well-known as it used to be, when Kiera was around, but once I get settled, I plan on helping build it back up. I would hate to see her pride and joy disappear because I don't have enough time to handle it."

"Let me help," Brooke offered, without missing a step. "I'm all about not using furs and animal skins in design. It would be a perfect way for me to help give back to the community. I would love to be a part of it."

"Are you serious?"

"Of course, Jax. In the past, I might have been a self-absorbed, daddy's little girl, but I've changed, and I want to do more with the community now that I'm a little more established here. I would love to help carry on Kiera's dreams."

Jax sat there shell-shocked. "Wow, Brooke. I don't even know what to say. You're amazing." Jax pulled Brooke onto his lap, and kissed her on the forehead. "Thank you so much."

"Don't act so surprised," she teased.

"It's just, I mean, wow. When I told Piper about Kiera, she didn't show any interest whatsoever. I mean, she felt sorry for what I went through, but she never asked about her, not really."

Brooke just nodded her head as she gritted her teeth, which confused Jax.

"What's going on?"

Brooke got off his lap and grabbed his button up shirt off the ground and wrapped it around her body. She walked off to the bathroom.

Jax threw on a pair of shorts and went to the bathroom. He opened it to see Brooke sitting on the counter with her hands gripping the edge.

"Brooke, what's going on?"

"Don't compare me to her," she seethed.

"Who? Kiera? I didn't think I was comparing her to you."

"No, not Kiera, Piper. Don't compare me to that skank. She was a terrible person to do what she did to you, and every time you compare her to me, it slowly eats at my heart."

"I don't ever remember comparing you to her, except for just now," Jax said, confused, as he thought back to all their conversations.

"You talk about her all the time!" Brooke flung her hands up in the air as she got off the counter and headed toward the bedroom. She grabbed her leggings and put them on, followed by her flats.

"Where are you going?" Jax asked, as he followed behind her.

"I'm getting out of here. It's been a long night, and I have an early morning tomorrow."

"Why are you leaving? We always spend the night together."

"Maybe we should just take a second away from each other for now, because frankly Jax, I'm annoyed with you right now."

"Annoyed? Because I mentioned Piper?"

"Yes!" Brooke shouted. "Because you mentioned Piper. It's not the first time, either. I feel like I'm in some kind of crazy love triangle relationship here with a non-existent person, someone in your mind. I don't want to be with you and Piper, Jax. That's not fair to me. I just want to be with you, and clearly, you're not ready for that, because you're not over her yet."

"That's not true!" he shouted back, as he followed her to the front door. "I would never go back to her. I want nothing to do with her."

"Then why do you keep bringing her up?" Brooke asked, as she grabbed her purse and keys.

"She is someone who was in my life in the past, am I not allowed to talk about my past relationships?"

"No, you're allowed to do so, but funny thing is, Jax, we've been dating for a while now, and today is the first time I'm hearing about Kiera…from day one, you've been talking about Piper."

Jax was about to reply, but he had nothing to say; she was right, today was the first time he had talked about Kiera, but he did remember mentioning Piper a couple of times.

Shit.

"It's only because it was so recent, what happened with her."

"Spin it how you want, Jax, but I'm not ready to be with you if you're not ready to let go of that manipulative red head."

"Brooke, you can't just walk out right now. Let's talk about this."

Brooke looked him in the eyes, and said, "I like you a lot, Jax, like scary a lot, but I don't want to share. Think about what you want tonight, and let me know when you're ready to forget everything and move on."

"You're not being reasonable," Jax said, right before she opened the door.

"I think I'm being plenty reasonable. Sorry if me wanting to be your number one and the only woman you think about is not reasonable. I guess I just know what I'm worth and what I want. Stop comparing me to her, Jax, and stop bringing her up, simple as that."

She leaned over to him, gave him a light kiss on his cheek and then took off, wearing his shirt. Jax slammed the door shut and let out some obscenities as he walked to his fridge for a beer.

"Women!" he shouted, as he sat on his kitchen counter and drank his beer.

Ashlin

Jesse parked his Range Rover and turned in his seat to look at Ashlin. "Are you ready for this?" he asked, as he reached behind his seat for a bag.

"Oh, I'm ready, but it might have helped if we hadn't driven here in your super flashy car."

"Flashy?" he faked offense. "There is nothing flashy about this vehicle. This is all male."

Ashlin let out a laugh. "Okay, keep thinking that, big guy." She patted his arm and then peeked in his bag. "What do you have there?"

"Well, I told you we were going incognito. Did you bring a hat and glasses?"

She nodded her head, as she pulled both items out of her purse.

"Perfect!" He pulled out a couple of wigs and fake mustaches. "Should I take the long blonde hair and you take the mustache?" he asked seriously.

"Are you kidding me?" Ashlin laughed, as she shook her head. "It will draw even more attention if we wear these ridiculous items. Plus, your giant muscular frame is going to draw attention anyway."

"Muscular, huh?" Jesse asked, while wiggling his eyebrows.

"Ugh, men!" She grabbed her hat, put it on her head, and put her glasses on as well. She reached to the back of Jesse's car and grabbed a spare sweatshirt that was back there. She looked down at it and wrinkled her nose. "You have an 'I love New York' sweatshirt? What the hell?" she laughed.

He shrugged his shoulders, "It's a great state."

"Ridiculous." She put it on, and then held her hands out in the car, "How do I look?"

He examined her and then said, "Like a hobo."

"Okay, not quite what I was going for, but I'll take it. Now, what are we going to do with you? You can't wear that ridiculous mustache, it's so fake."

"I have a hat and glasses and another sweatshirt." He pulled one out, and on the front it read "USA."

"You're so American," she teased.

"I know." He faked fluffing his non-existent hair, since his hair was buzzed.

Ashlin laughed as they both went incognito and made sure they looked inconspicuous as possible, but after she looked at both of them, she realized they just looked like frumps in glasses.

"What size is that sweatshirt?" she asked Jesse, as they walked toward the entrance. "It's like three sizes too big for you."

"It's Meatloaf's sweatshirt. He let me borrow it."

"Meatloaf? Is that a dog?"

Jesse threw his head back and laughed. "No, Meatloaf is one of my linemen. He is a bit...fluffy."

"Ohhhh," Ashlin said in understanding. "Well, then he's the American one."

"Yeah, I'm pretty sure he got this sweatshirt specially made by Omar Tents, but I love the man; he keeps my ass safe on the field."

"And we're all happy for that," Ashlin replied, as she patted him on the cheek.

Jesse paid for their tickets, grabbed a map of the zoo, and then led her to the entrance. So far, no one was staring, but they were also at the zoo in the fall/winter time so there weren't many people there.

"Don't worry, I'll get you some hot chocolate to warm you up later," Jesse leaned over and said as they started making their way past all the zoo merchandise.

Ashlin decided she didn't need hot chocolate to warm her up, she just needed Jesse whispering in her ear, because, good God, she thought her lady parts were going to melt. She saw what he was doing, he was slowly trying to work his way under the wall she put up around her heart by texting her, taking her out, and saying things no other man had ever said to her, and holy hell was it working. He was chipping away at her wall, and she couldn't help but let him in...inch by inch.

She'd had boyfriends in the past, but they were nothing like Jesse. Yes, they were handsome, strong, and your typical male, but with Jesse it was different; he actually cared about who she was as a person, and not just what she had to offer when it came to her body. She understood that she sold sex for a living, so she was stereotyping herself, but the fact that Jesse was able to look past that and find who she really was as a person was impressive.

"So, someone told me that elephants are your favorite." He looked down at his watch, his obnoxiously expensive watch, and said, "We should head on over there now, because I have a little surprise set up for you."

"What are you up to, QB?" she asked, as he grabbed her hand and guided her toward the Elephant Encounter. The fact that her hand fit perfectly into his didn't slip by her. Instead of responding to her question, he just looked back at her, winked, and kept walking, making her panties melt right off. He was sex on a stick, and he didn't even realize it. He was probably the least self-centered person she knew, who had every reason to be a self-centered ass, given the fact that he was rolling in millions of dollars, was the starting quarterback for the Stallions, and had the body of a Greek god.

"Excoose me," a little voice came. Jesse stopped in his tracks and looked down to see a little boy with deep brown hair, brown eyes, and a ring of dried ice cream around his mouth holding onto a Stallions stuffed animal mascot and wearing a Spiderman shirt.

"Hey, man," Jesse squatted down, still holding Ashlin's hand. "What's going on?"

"Are you Jesse Rutledge?" the little boy asked, as he tugged on Jesse's sleeve.

Jesse leaned in and said, "Can you keep a secret?" The little boy nodded his head rapidly. "Good, I am Jesse Rutledge, but do you see this pretty girl next to me?" The boy looked up at Ashlin and then back at Jesse, nodding once again. "Well, I promised her a trip to the zoo, and I want to make sure she gets that trip."

"Sorry about that," the mom said, as she tried to take her son away. "He's such a huge fan, he could spot you anywhere."

Jesse smiled up at the mom and said, "I think it's amazing he spotted me. You've got a good eye, pal," Jesse said, while patting the kid on the shoulder. "I tell you what, we're playing the Thunder this weekend at our stadium, and I have a box looking over the fifty yard line. If it's alright with this little lady," he said, while tugging on Ashlin's hand, "I would love for you to join her on

Sunday and then meet up with me after the game. I'd be happy to give you a tour of the locker room." The mom started bursting out in tears as the little boy jumped up and down in excitement. Ashlin was confused as to why she was brought into it.

"Can I? Can I go to the game with you?" the little boy asked Ashlin, eyes so bright.

"Of course," Ashlin said, as the little boy jumped into Jesse's arms as Jesse tried to quiet him.

"Remember, buddy, this is our little secret, alright?" the boy nodded, and then Jesse stood up. He grabbed the mom's contact information to give to his manager, tussled the little boy's hair, and told him he would see them on Sunday.

The mom was still crying as she walked away with the little boy, hand in hand. The mom dragged him away, but his body was still turned toward Jesse, waving his hand and smiling the biggest smile Ashlin had ever seen.

Yup, she was pretty sure she'd just fallen in love with the man next to her. Just like that, he busted through her wall and stole her heart. Jesse could have been a massive dick and walked away, but instead, he invited the little boy to his private suite with a tour of the locker room afterwards. Who did that?

"That was beyond words," Ashlin said, as she looked up at Jesse.

He just shrugged his shoulders and started walking toward the Elephant Encounter.

"Do you realize you just made that little boy's life?" Ashlin stopped him, trying to help him understand that the small act of kindness he was doing was actually a huge thing.

"Nothing to really discuss," Jesse said shyly.

"Handsome and humble, are you trying to make it impossible for me to be attracted to any other man ever again?"

Jesse smiled and said, "Yeah, is it working?"

"With flying colors."

"Good."

He pulled her into his side and kissed the top of her head. The gesture was so simple, but it made her toes curl. His strong grip, the soft laundry smell coming off of him, and the way he held onto her made her weak in the knees for the man. She didn't stand a chance against him. He was lethal.

"Hold on," Ashlin thought back to what Jesse said. "What's this all about me being in your suite on Sunday?"

Jesse looked at his watch and said, "We really have to get to the back of the elephant stalls."

"Not before you answer my question," she said playfully.

Jesse rubbed the back of his neck with his hand and said, "Well, I was hoping that maybe by the end of our little date here, you would want to possibly come watch me play on Sunday…as my girlfriend."

Hopeful man.

Ashlin let out a little laugh. "You really think it's going to be that easy? I told you I don't do relationships."

"I know, but…"

Ashlin put her hand over Jesse's mouth to stop him from talking, and said, "But if you happen to buy me a stuffed animal at the end of the day, your little plan might come true."

Pure and utter joy lit up Jesse's face as he understood what she was saying to him.

"I will buy you the biggest damn stuffed animal you want," Jesse replied, as he wrapped his arm around her shoulder, pressed a kiss to her temple, and led her to the elephants.

Scared would be a way to describe how she was feeling, but completely terrified was probably better. Jesse didn't know about her dad, about her family life, her trailer trash upbringing…and she wasn't ready to give her heart away, trust someone else with it, but she knew she didn't have a choice. Jesse crawled his way into her life and there was no turning back. She was jumping over the cliff, head first without a parachute; she just hoped Jesse was at the bottom, ready to catch her.

Piper

Two nights in separate beds, zero touching, zilch kissing, and a man made of pure steel walking around shirtless had led Piper to become a quivering mess. Any time Mason was in the room, shirtless and unaware of the effect he had on her, she had to retreat the premises and gather her wits. They spent their days unpacking Mason's things, going to physical therapy, which Piper never stayed at, and then watching a movie at night, never touching. It was absolute torture.

After one of the biggest orgasms she had in a while, thanks to Mason's talented tongue, she found herself yearning for more of him, and the bastard knew what he was doing to her, because when he saw her in the morning, frustrated and sexually charged, he would just smile and laugh to himself.

She was playing by his rules, and she was being a good girl about it, but she didn't know how much more she could take. Every time she tried to talk to him about their past history, he would change the subject; she was about to explode.

"You ready?" Mason asked, as he crutched into the living room.

Of course she was ready, she had been ready since six this morning, avoiding the man who was staring at her. She avoided Mason in the morning, doing yoga in her room and taking long showers. Avoidance helped with the yearning, at least just a little.

"Yup." She hopped off the bar counter and grabbed her purse, avoiding all eye contact.

Mason grabbed her hand and stopped her. "Hey, what's going on? You've been avoiding me."

Piper finally looked into those deep brown eyes of his and wanted to crumble to the floor and cry. She wanted him so badly, and there was nothing she could do about it.

"I'm fine, just taking care of things."

"Liar," Mason said flatly. "You're avoiding me. The question is, why?"

"We're going to be late," she said, while looking down at her shoes.

Mason lifted her chin, and said, "So, you're finally starting to realize how I felt when you were with Jax, not able to touch you, be with you, or feel you."

"What?" Piper felt like she'd been hit by a truck, she was so stunned. "Were you punishing me?"

A smirk spread across Mason's face, making her want to punch him square in the jaw, and then, unfortunately, kiss him back to health. Damn lady hormones.

"I wouldn't say punishing you…just teaching you a lesson."

"I can't fucking believe you!" Piper threw her hands up. "I thought we weren't going to play games; I thought we were going to at least try to have a normal relationship."

"We are Piper, but I had to have you see what it feels like to want something so badly, but not have it. I wanted to see if you had the same feelings for me that I do for you."

"Of course I do, you idiot! Jesus, I've been dying inside not being able to touch you, feel you, or be with you. It's not easy walking around in the same house, knowing that my heart is calling out to you, but there is nothing I can do about it…" Piper stopped in the middle of her sentence as realization dawned on her. "Oh, my God." Her eyes snapped up to Mason, who was, all of a sudden, examining his shoes. "Mason, look at me." He met her eyes, and that was when she didn't care anymore; she grabbed his face and pressed her lips against his for the first time since the dreaded day they'd separated.

He didn't step back or push her away. Instead, he wrapped one arm around her waist and brought her in tighter. His lips matched hers, and his tongue crept into hers as she fell into his embrace and molded her body against his. It had been so long, so long since she felt him the way she did now, to have him touch her the way his hand was gently stroking her back, and the way his lips felt against hers as his scruff brushed against her chin. This was what she wanted; this is what she'd been waiting for. She understood him now, what he went through, what she put him through.

She pulled away and cupped his cheeks. "I am so fucking sorry, Mason. I can't tell you how sorry I am."

Her heart ached at finally realizing the pain and torture she'd put Mason through when she was with Jax. Piper had only experienced the feeling for a couple of days; she couldn't imagine how tough it had been on Mason. He was so much stronger than she was.

"I know, babe. I'm sorry too; I shouldn't have tried to teach you a lesson when we're trying to be honest with each other. It's just…I wanted to make sure that, moving forward, you truly wanted to be with me, that you feel what I feel. I didn't want to waste my time if you didn't have the same feelings that I did."

"I do, Mason. I've been dying the last couple of days, just begging for your touch. I'm glad you 'taught' me a lesson, even though I'm a little mad at you," she pinched his side, which was all skin, since the man didn't have one ounce of fat on him.

"Hey, watch it," he said, as he started rocking a little off balance. Piper grabbed his shirt and steadied him, making him smile. "Who knew a spicy redhead would be able to grab me by my balls?"

"You have that all wrong, because there's a wide receiver with deep brown eyes that has a death grip on my lady balls right now."

Mason threw his head back and laughed. "Piper, if you have lady balls, we might need to have a little conversation."

"Let's go, we're going to be late," Piper guided him toward the door. "Oh, and just so you know, I'll be sleeping in that giant bed of yours tonight; I don't care what you say. We may not have sex, but hell if I'm not going to have your body wrapped around mine."

"We'll see about that," Mason teased.

"If you want to eat, then you'll make it happen."

"Threatening me with food? Cheap shot, babe, cheap shot."

They drove to the stadium where Piper dropped Mason off for physical therapy. She never went into the stadium for many reasons, one being the obvious…she didn't want to run into Jax. Mason got out and then bent down into the window on the driver's side and said, "Pick me up in a couple of hours?"

"Of course."

"Hold on." Mason stopped her from rolling up her window.

She pressed the down button and said, "Can I help you?"

Bending over, he grabbed her chin and kissed her softly on the lips. "Thanks for taking care of me."

"Thank you for letting me."

"What are you going to do while I'm here? Buy some lingerie? Maybe take some naked pictures for me?"

"Really, Mason? You know, when you're not around, women don't sit around fingering themselves and thinking about you, right?"

"A man can only dream."

"Despicable. No, I'm not going to go buy lingerie. I was actually thinking about going to see Hannah."

Mason's face grew serious. "Are you ready for that?"

"I have to; I owe her an explanation."

Mason nodded his head and said, "Call me when you're done."

"I will."

"Tomorrow, will you go to the get-together with me at Jesse's house? He's having me, Ryker, and Jake over for a little gathering before the game on Sunday."

"Am I invited?" Piper asked, concerned.

"Of course."

"Sure, then. Sounds like fun."

Mason gave her one last kiss before winking at her and crutching his way into the stadium. She wanted to pull him back in the car and have her wicked way with him, but knew that wasn't an option. Instead, she put her car in drive and headed to Dick's Last Chance, where she knew Hannah would be getting ready for the five o'clock crowd. She was in for a rough one, but she wanted to see her friend; she needed to see her friend.

Piper parked in front of the bar she used to work at, since it wasn't quite happy hour yet, and locked up her car. Nerves ran through her body as she entered the building. From the outside, the place looked like a total dive bar, but on the inside, it was modern and sophisticated…a real treasure in the heart of Denver.

She instantly spotted Hannah working frantically behind the bar, setting up bowls of nuts and getting ready for the rush. Maybe it wasn't the best time to visit and say, "Hey, I'm not dead," but Piper knew she couldn't wait any longer.

Taking a deep breath, Piper said, "Hey, Hannah."

Hannah's head shot up just as she dropped a bowl of nuts over the counter, spilling them everywhere.

"Where the hell have you been?"

At that moment, Piper knew she was in trouble; Hannah never swore. She took a big step forward and prayed that Hannah would forgive her for leaving.

Jesse

"I still can't believe I got to feed and pet an elephant! This day has been amazing," Ashlin exclaimed with elation. "Who knew they were so dry? We should really go into the elephant lotion business; we would make a killing." Ashlin took a bite out of the cotton candy Jesse got her and smiled, melting Jesse's heart.

This day had just solidified how infatuated he was with Ashlin. She was a breath of fresh air, just what he needed in his life.

"Not sure we would make a killing, since elephants aren't really a target consumer these days, but if I they did have wallets, I bet they would be fat."

Ashlin quirked her mouth at Jesse. "You're so corny."

"Got you to smile," he pressed the side of her mouth with his finger, which she tried to bite. "Hey, easy there, killer," he laughed as he shook his finger.

"Seriously, though, thank you for a great day. I'm glad you didn't have practice today. Seems like Coach Ryan is going easy on you guys."

"I agree. The boys have a theory that he might have someone in his life, because he's never this easy on us."

"Oooh, I wonder who it is." Ashlin plopped another chunk of cotton candy in her mouth, making Jesse jealous of the damn sugary confection. He wanted to be the one playing around with Ashlin's mouth, but he'd waited this long…he would wait a little longer. Hopefully, after today, she would actually consider having a relationship. She seemed like she was leaning in that direction, given her statement earlier on, and the way she'd been casually brushing up against him the whole day. A man could only hope.

"I could care less who it is, as long as she keeps doing what she's doing, because we're getting a sweet break."

They walked up to the main gift shop and walked straight to the back where all the stuffed animals were.

"Select anything you want," Jesse said, while holding his arms open wide.

"Anything?" she leaned up against his side. She pinched his side, making him jump in place as she laughed.

"Watch it, lady."

"Don't be a baby," Ashlin replied, as she pawed all the stuffed animals. "Hmm…well, that elephant on the top shelf that's the size of a mini cooper and costs three thousand dollars…that might be nice."

"Are you serious?" Jesse walked up to it and took a look at the price tag. "Who the hell would buy that?" Ashlin crossed her arms in front of her chest and tapped her foot. "You're serious? You want the three thousand dollar stuffed animal that's probably been sitting on the top of that shelf since this place opened?" She nodded her head, making Jesse laugh. "Well, I guess I'm really going to have to work to win your heart." A worker walked by and Jesse flagged him down. "Sir, we would like the elephant up there."

"Really?" the boy asked, "You know it's three thousand dollars, right?"

"Yes, I've been informed of the price tag by the pretty little lady over here. We'll still take it."

"Wow, never thought I would see the day. Carl!" the boy shouted, "Cletus has finally found a home."

"Cletus?" Jesse mouthed with a raised eyebrow to Ashlin, who was covering her mouth and giggling.

They watched in silence as Carl grabbed a ladder and took Cletus from the top shelf. The thing was dusty as hell, so they took it to the back and gave it a quick clean.

"You sure you want…Cletus?" Jesse asked, trying not to laugh.

"More than anything."

They got to the register, and the lady started ringing them up. The total came to a little under fifteen hundred dollars, which confused the hell out of Jesse.

"Umm, I thought it was three thousand dollars."

"Yes, but it's dirty. It's been up there for a while, and frankly, you're doing us a favor."

"Here we are," said Carl and the boy carrying Cletus and a box.

"What's that?" Ashlin asked, pointing at the box.

"Cletus has some accessories."

Ashlin poked her head in the box and laughed as she pulled out Santa and pilgrim hats.

Shaking his head, Jesse said, "What did you get us into?"

"Oh, this is fantastic."

Jesse turned back to the lady checking him out and said, "Can I make a donation as well?"

"Sure, sir, we would appreciate any sort of donation."

"Great, can you just make the total five thousand dollars and put it toward the elephants? We have to take care of Cletus' kin."

Ashlin's head popped up as she looked at Jesse. Fondness surrounded her eyes as she gazed at him, while holding onto Cletus' accessories.

Once they paid and were helped out to their car, Jesse opened Ashlin's door and helped her in. She turned in her seat so her feet were dangling outside of the car and she grabbed ahold of Jesse's belt loops.

"You're an amazing man, you know that, right?"

Jesse didn't really like attention for things he did, because he thought it came with the job. He was blessed to have the talent to throw a football down a field accurately and make money off of it, so he believed that he needed to share his good fortune, but not in a blatant way to get attention. He tried to pass along his good fortune as much as possible; it was just second nature to him now.

"Let's get you home," Jesse said, ignoring the praise.

"Hold up," she placed her hand on his chest. "You can't handle someone telling you what a good person you are, can you?"

"I wouldn't say 'good person.' I just think I do what's right, that's all. I would expect anyone else in my position to do the same thing. Nothing to praise me about."

Ashlin shook her head in astonishment and pulled him in closer. Her hands grabbed his waist and her thumbs slipped under his sweatshirt, so she was gently stroking his skin. His hands rested on the top of the car door opening and he leaned in toward her, dipping his head, so he was close to her. Her vanilla, coconut scent wafted in his direction, making it impossible not to gravitate even closer.

"I have to tell you, Jesse, you're not the person I thought you were. You are so much more, and I'm so grateful you didn't give up on me."

"What are you saying?" Jesse leaned closer with a smile plastered across his face like a giant goofball.

"Does the girlfriend offer still stand?" she asked shyly.

Yup, she just made his heart flutter like an idiot. Trying not to break his cheeks from smiling, he leaned down and pulled her chin toward him. "Hell yeah, it does." He went the last couple of inches and took her mouth with his. She was just as sweet as the first time he'd kissed her. Her lips were soft and light and demanding all at the same time. Her thumbs did wicked things to his skin as he continued to kiss her, making him want to lay her out in the front of the vehicle, but knew that wasn't the best idea, especially since they were in the public eye.

Reluctantly, Jesse pulled away and marveled at the way he made Ashlin almost look drunk after he kissed her. Her eyes were heavy, her smile was crooked, and her lips were swollen. It was a sight to make any man go weak in the knees.

"I just want you to know, I'm scared, Jesse. I don't do relationships."

"I know, doll. I haven't been in a relationship in a very long time, so we can help each other through this. We just need to be open and honest with each other. Okay?"

She nodded her head, and then said, "There's a lot you don't know about me."

"And I can't wait to find it all out," Jesse said, while cupping her cheek and rubbing his thumb along her cheekbone. "This is what I want, Ashlin…more than anything, and I've wanted it for a very long time." His admission surprised both him and her. He wasn't expecting to say that, but it came right out.

"How long?" She pulled him in even closer.

"Long enough, but we don't have to talk about that. What I do want to know is, will you come over tomorrow for a small gathering with some of the boys before the game on Sunday?" He knew it was quite sudden, but he wanted Ashlin there; it wouldn't feel right if she wasn't there.

"What kind of food are we talking?"

"I was going to order a bunch of pizza," he shrugged his shoulders.

"Mmm, I love pizza. I'm in."

"Because of pizza? Not because of something else?" he asked, while playing with a strand of her hair.

"Maybe because of something else. What are you doing tonight?"

"I have some things I have to sign that fans sent in."

"When you say some, how many is some?"

Shrugging his shoulders, he kissed her on the lips, and turned her legs so she was in the car and shut her door.

She didn't need to know that he had about a thousand pictures, memorabilia items, and jerseys to sign that had been sent in by fans. She already thought he was some kind of hero from today; he didn't need to put himself up on an impossible pedestal.

When he got in the car, she turned to him and said, "I'm afraid I won't have any room for Cletus at my place. Do you think he could stay with you?"

Jesse started his car and buckled up. "How did I know you were going to say that?"

"Don't act like you don't have a connection with him already, and hey, just gives me more of a reason to come visit you."

"You better visit me, as much as possible," Jesse squeezed her leg, making her squeal as he pulled out of the parking lot. If he had it his way, she would be practically living at his house by the end of the weekend, but that clearly was out of the question, given her relationship anxiety. Instead, he would just use Cletus as a pawn to get her to come over as much as possible.

CHAPTER FIFTEEN

Brooke

Jax: There seems to be this girl in my life that I can't get out of my head. She has brown hair and green eyes and dresses like a goddess. Do you know her?

Jax: Okay, so cute is not going to work. How about this, I don't care about anyone but you?

Jax: Brooke, Piper means nothing to me.

Jax: Brooke, I'm sorry. Will you please answer your phone?

Jax: So, I'm standing outside of your place, and I'm trying to text and call you, but you don't seem to be answering. Maybe you could cut a guy a break and let me know that you are still alive.

Jax: Seriously, Brooke, where are you? I'm starting to get worried.

Jax: I am seconds away from calling all the hospitals in the city.

Brooke locked up her car and headed toward her apartment;

she felt so lost without her phone, since she forgot it in the morning. She never knew how dependent she was on the damn thing until she didn't have it at her side. She had a long day at the studio, preparing a few accessories for a photo shoot, so all she wanted to do was put on a pair of sweats, kick back on her couch, and bury her face into a carton of ice cream.

The situation between her and Jax was less than desirable. He hadn't contacted her in a couple of days, so she was pretty sure she'd hit the nail on the head with the Piper assessment. She told herself that she wasn't bothered by the fact that she hadn't seen Jax in a while, but she was lying. She missed the damn man, and it only irritated her that she did.

So, she tried not to think about him…at all.

She rounded the corner of her apartment complex and nearly jumped out of her skin when she ran into Jax, who was sitting on her doorstep. His hair was standing on end and he looked stressed.

"Jax?" There went all her ideas about not thinking about him. It was pretty much impossible not to think about the man when he was standing on her doorstep.

His head shot up at the sound of her voice, and he had her in his arms before she could ask "What's wrong?"

"Jesus, Brooke. Don't fucking do that to me!"

"Do what?" she asked, while pushing him away, not liking the tone he was taking with her.

"Not answer your phone? I've been a fucking wreck wondering where the hell you've been and if you'd been abducted or something."

Brooke breezed past him and opened her door. "A little dramatic, don't you think?"

"A little childish not answering your phone, don't you think?" he threw back at her, while following her into her apartment and shutting her door.

Brooke set down her purse and bag and spun on her heel. "For your information, I left my phone at home by accident, so you can take your little lecture and leave. I'm fine; you can go home now."

"You forgot your phone?" Jax asked, looking sad but relieved at the same time.

"Yes, so I'll be sure to look at your messages and get back to you at my convenience." There, that should teach him. She walked over to her door and opened it to give him the hint to get out.

"I'm not leaving," Jax said, as he sat down on her couch.

Groaning and slamming her door shut, she ran her hands through her hair, and said, "Listen, Jax. I had a rough day at work today, and all I want to do is curl up on my couch and veg out. I don't want to fight; I don't want to deal with this right now."

She headed toward her bedroom to change because the pencil skirt and heels she was wearing were begging to be torn off her body. Not even thinking about Jax being in the room, she stripped down until she was only in her bra and thong and went into her closet where she found her boy shorts and a large button-up shirt that just so happened to be Jax's, but she didn't care. She wanted to be comfortable. Stripping off her bra, she put the shirt over her head, took off her thong, and replaced it with the boy shorts. She turned around to see Jax standing in her doorway, chest heaving, and sporting a nice bulge in his pants.

Ignoring the turned on man in her doorway, she grabbed her phone off of her nightstand and scrolled through the text messages from Jax. There were seven. She slowly read through them, and after each text message, her heart reached out for the man a little more. She looked over at him, and even though he was clearly excited, he still looked worried, and right then, she realized that he must have been worried that something happened to her like something had happened to Kiera.

"Jax…"

He came to her side quickly on the bed and turned her to face him.

"I'm sorry, Brooke. I promise you I want nothing to do with Piper, seriously, nothing. I'm sorry if I've mentioned her too much. It's just because, for some twisted reason, we have Mason and

Piper in common, and unfortunately, they brought us together in a weird way. I don't want to talk about her, but sometimes, it just comes out because we both know her and what she did."

Brooke stopped him from talking and grabbed his hands. "Jax, I'm sorry that you had to worry about me today. I know that might not have been easy."

Jax let out a long breath as he hung his head. Brooke's heart broke as she watched the strong man break down right in front of her. He wasn't crying, but she could feel all the pain and worry radiating off his body.

Pulling her onto his lap, Jax buried his head in her hair and said, "I was so fucking worried, Brooke. It felt just like when I couldn't get in touch with Kiera. I know we're still getting to know each other, but I truly care about you so much."

"I know. I care about you too, Jax, and I'm sorry you had to worry like that…and I'm sorry for being a brat. I just…I just can't stand that woman for many reasons, and every time I hear her name, I'm instantly put in a bad mood, but I understand where you're coming from. I get it because there have been times where I thought about bringing up Mason and things we'd done in the past, but I thought twice, given your history."

"You have a better filter than I do," Jax chuckled.

"I apparently do."

They looked at each other at the same time and smiled. "We're so fucked up," Brooke announced, making them both laugh.

"At least we're fucked up together," Jax added.

"We are." She kissed him on the lips and then brought her shirt over her head, revealing her naked breasts to Jax, who quickly went hard again under her. She scooted off his lap and went behind him so her chest was to his back. She grabbed the hem of his shirt and brought it up and over his head. Tossing it on the floor, she pressed her chest against his back, and straddled his backside, so her legs were pressed against his. The skin on skin contact was just what she needed. He grabbed ahold of her legs and leaned his head back to her shoulder for a kiss, which she granted him.

"You feel good," she said, as her hands wandered down to his pants, unzipping them and letting his erection out to breathe. "Mmm, you're so hard already."

"You do that to me darlin', easily."

She took him in her hands and started stroking him up and down, making the southern man groan as she worked his length. The weight of his excitement spurred her on as his head fell back and almost all his weight was in her arms. She held him up as she continued to stroke him from behind. It was erotic not being able to see anything, only feel and hear. Her senses heightened as she continued to feel him grow harder and harder in her hands, to the point that she started using two hands to stroke him, and ever so slightly rubbed the head of his cock, feeling his pre-cum at the tip. He was ready, and so was she.

"I want you to come, Jax, but not in my hands."

"Where then?" he teased.

Brooke scooted out from behind him, went to the front of his bed and sat down on his lap, letting him fully enter her in one smooth stroke. Her back was to his chest, and her hands fell to his knees as she leaned forward for better friction.

"Condom," Jax squeaked out as his hands gripped her breasts and pulled on her nipples.

"Pill, I'm on it," she breathed heavily, as she moved her hips rapidly up and down on his lap.

"Sweet Jesus."

A smile crept across Brooke's face as she continued to pump Jax. The man was impossible to stay mad at, especially when he was sporting an amazing erection.

Continuing to ride Jax, he pulled and massaged her breasts and brought her to the point of no return. She was falling over the edge where her vision turned dark and her toes started to turn numb. Every last feeling was focused at the center of her body as her stomach flipped and her pussy clenched around Jax. A guttural noise escaped her throat as she came around him while continuing to move up and down. A few seconds later, Jax squeezed her hips and rammed her up and down until he blew out a breath and said her name in an earthy tone.

"Ahhh, fuck!" he exclaimed as they both slowly tried to move, to squeeze out every last bit of pleasure that came their way.

Once she felt like nothing else could flutter in her body, she leaned against Jax and said, "Maybe we should fight more often. The make-up sex is totally worth it."

"The regular sex is just as good," Jax replied, while kissing her shoulder.

"You're right, but what's life without a little variety?"

Hannah

"Where the hell have you been?" Hannah asked, stunned to see Piper standing in front of her.

The moment she heard that familiar voice ring through the bar, she knew it was Piper, her best friend who had left her without a word...left her to pick up her shifts at the bar...left her during a time when Hannah needed her the most...and left her without even the decency of a good bye. She better have a good reason as to why she treated their friendship like it didn't matter at all.

Realizing she'd dropped a bowl of nuts, she quickly gathered them up and tossed them in the trash, as her face turned a nice shade of red. She was always easily embarrassed.

"Hannah, do you need help?" Piper walked toward her.

Hannah held up her arm to stop Piper from coming any closer. "Stop, answer the question." Hannah never swore, but hearing and seeing Piper threw her off, and she was bound for a slip up.

"I needed to leave, Hannah."

"Without even saying goodbye? How could you just leave me, Piper? I needed you," Hannah said softly, as Piper came around to the bar and wrapped her up in her arms. Hannah wasn't much of a fighting type, especially with friends, so she caved easily when Piper offered her shoulder to her.

"I'm so sorry, Hannah. I was going through such a rough time. I just broke everything off with Jax, I went to go be with Mason, and he was with Brooke. I lost everything in a matter of hours, and I didn't know how to react; all I knew was I needed to get the hell out of here, away from everything that reminded me of my life, and unfortunately, that meant I had to stop talking to you. I didn't even talk to my family or Lexi…no one knew where I was."

"I could have helped," Hannah offered.

"And I love you for that, Hannah, but I don't think anyone could have helped me…except for one person."

"Mason?" Hannah asked, as she wiped her eyes and stepped away from Piper.

"Yes," she nodded her head. "It's a long story, but I'm back, and there's no more running for this girl. I'm here to stay. The only way I'm leaving is if Mason kicks me out."

"Kicks you out? What are you saying?"

"We're kind of together, figuring things out."

"Are you serious? But I thought he was with Brooke, like you said, but then again, I've seen him with other girls as well."

Piper winced at Hannah's statement. "Well, he's not with them anymore. He has a new condo now, and is starting a new chapter in his life, we both are.

"I just can't believe this, he's taking you back, just like that?" Hannah snapped her fingers, not holding anything back. "You used him, Piper."

Piper hung her head as she said, "Yeah, I know. I don't know why he's giving me a second chance, but he is." She paused for a second, and then continued. "A part of me wants to believe that he truly wants to be with me, a big part actually, but there is this small voice in the back of my head that keeps telling me, he's going to fuck me over and his sole purpose in life right now is to break my heart."

"Why do you think that?" Hannah asked, feeling a little awkward that they were trying to fall back into their friend roles with each other.

"It just seems too easy. It should never be this easy. He should have never have given in like what I did to him was nothing. I just don't get it."

"Have you told him this?"

"Yes, he says it's because he never got over me. I just don't know."

Hannah didn't know what to do, so instead, she awkwardly patted Piper's hand.

"Whiskey sour, please," said a customer who came up to the counter, grabbing a handfull of nuts.

"Sure thing, Harry."

Hannah ignored Piper for a second, as she got the drink for Harry, and placed it in front of him. Harry left a ten dollar bill, winked at her, and told her to keep the change. Harry was always a good tipper, especially when the girls were working.

"Hannah, I'm sorry," Piper said, as tears filled her eyes. "I can't tell you how sorry I am about everything."

At that moment, Ryker popped through the bar door and called out, "There's my boo." Not even noticing Piper, he walked over to the bar, leaned over the counter, and grabbed Hannah by the hand. "I had to see you before your shift truly started, but don't worry, I'll be around for a while. There are some chicken wings in the back with my name on them." Ryker grabbed Hannah's face and kissed her senseless, making Hannah blush in front of everyone in the bar. "Damn, I missed you." He felt her forehead and said, "Oh no, I think you're coming down with something; I think you need to come home with me." Ryker laughed to himself and then nodded at Piper as a polite hello, but when he actually saw who it was, he stood up straight.

"Piper, what the hell?"

Hannah looked at Piper, and she didn't miss the surprised look on Piper's face either...from seeing the over-affectionate but incredibly sweet Ryker kiss her. He didn't care about PDA protocol. When he wanted to kiss her, he kissed her, same thing when it came to holding her hand, pinching her butt, and wrapping his arm around her waist. Sometimes he could get really handsy, and that was when she put an end to it.

"I guess I should say the same thing," Piper said, as she looked between the two of them.

Ryker rubbed his forehead and said, "Shit, I haven't talked to Mason in a while. Wait," Ryker's head shot up, "Please tell me Mason knows you're here."

"She's staying with him," Hannah interjected, calming Ryker's searching eyes. He smiled down at her and pulled her across the counter again for another kiss.

"Wow, you guys are kind of cute," Piper said, making Hannah beam. She agreed.

Ryker effortlessly hopped over the counter and wrapped Hannah up in his arms with her back to his chest.

"Aren't we?" Ryker said, while slightly swaying them back and forth. The man was adorable.

"Ryker, why don't you go sit in your booth? I'll bring you a beer and some wings in a few minutes, okay?" Hannah said, while tipping her head back to look at him.

"You're going to tell her how good I am in bed, aren't you?" His grin spread across his cheeks.

"Ryker," Hannah playfully slapped his shoulder and shooed him toward his booth, but not before he grabbed her one more time and pulled her in for a soul-searing kiss that made her dizzy when he let go. She watched him swagger over to his booth, putting on a show for her. That man.

"Earth to Hannah," Piper said, shaking Hannah out of her thoughts.

"Sorry. So, umm, we're together."

"I can see that," Piper said, looking back at Ryker, who waved from the booth. "God, he has not changed a bit."

"He hasn't," Hannah said with a smile. He was still the same goofy, instigating, handsome, and caring man she'd come to know.

"Are you going to tell me what happened?"

Hannah started wiping down the counter as she said, "I don't really like to talk about it."

Piper blew out a long breath as she said, "Hannah, I know I don't deserve your friendship right now, and I don't deserve your understanding, but please let me at least try to be there for you. I was a shitty person a couple of months ago. I was lost, and didn't think I had any options, but now I'm back and I want to make things right...especially with you. You mean so much to me, and I know I didn't show that by leaving, but Hannah, you really mean so much to me. Please give me another chance."

Hannah studied the worn wood of the bar counter top as she weighed her options. What it came down to was, she didn't have many girlfriends, and she was dying to actually talk to someone about everything, especially her relationship with Ryker.

Taking a leap, Hannah said, "Todd had a second life. He was married with kids in New York."

"What?!" Piper practically shouted, as her eyes bugged out and what seemed like steam came out of her ears. Hannah had seen that face before, Piper was going to kill.

"Yup, his wife came into the bar with a child on her hip and told me to quit seeing her husband. I've never been so embarrassed and brokenhearted in my life. I clearly got rid of all of Todd's things, told him to never contact me again, and then lived in a state of depression for a couple of months after pushing Ryker away. I had no one..."

"Shit," Piper pulled Hannah into a hug and held onto her tightly. Piper was taller than Hannah, and skinnier, but she was full of warmth as she wrapped her arms around Hannah and held her closely. "I'm so sorry you had to go through that alone."

"I'm sorry you had to be alone too," Hannah replied.

"So, how did Ryker happen?"

"I hit him with my cart...in his privates."

Piper snorted.

"You can say dick, boo. It's okay," Ryker startled both of them, making them jump.

"Jesus, Ryker," Hannah held her chest. "I'll be right over with your beer and wings."

"Don't worry, boo. I got it covered. Already put in my order for multiple baskets of wings, and I can just grab a beer." He reached into a cooler and pulled out a bottle, easily taking the top off by hitting it against the counter.

"How many baskets, Ryker?" Hannah asked, as she put her hands on her hips. "I know you can eat like a horse, but remember we talked about you starting to incorporate vegetables in your diet?"

"They're not just for me," he said, while taking a sip of his beer.

"I'm not joining you for dinner. I have to work, Ryker."

The door opened, and Hannah turned to see Mason, crutching his way into the bar with a huge grin on his face.

"Way to leave a guy hanging out on the road all by himself," Mason smiled as he headed over to Piper and placed a kiss on her cheek.

"You did not crutch all the way over here, did you? You know you can use your phone," Piper chastised.

"Meatloaf dropped me off. He was getting some knots rubbed out of his back. Ryker sent me a text and said there was a redheaded devil at the bar, and apparently we needed to catch up."

Piper spun to Ryker and said, "Redheaded devil? Really Ryker?"

He held his hands up in defense, "Hey, I only speak the truth. You're some kind of dangerous, but a good kind." He winked. "Beer, Donkey Dick?" Mason nodded, placed a kiss on Piper's cheek and then went over to the booth they used to sit at almost every night.

Hannah and Piper looked at their boys as they talked, clinked beers, and joked around.

"This is oddly familiar, but so different," Piper commented, as they both watched Mason throw his head back and laugh.

"It is, but good different."

"Great different."

Hannah and Piper spent the rest of the night catching up and maintaining the bar. Even though Piper wasn't employed at the bar anymore, she still helped Hannah out, so they could talk about everything that was going on in their lives. Hannah was happy, for the first time in a while. She had Ryker looking at her like she was the only woman in the world; Piper, her best friend was back in her life, and for once, Hannah could actually see a future coming together for her.

CHAPTER SIXTEEN

Piper

"Your hand is clammy," Mason said, as he held up their clasped hands, examining their connection.

They were almost to Jesse's house, and all Piper could think about was how nervous she was. She knew she didn't have the greatest track record where Mason's friends were concerned, so she was nervous to see how they were all going to react to her presence.

"Just a little nervous, that's all."

"Why? You have no reason to be nervous. Everyone loves you."

Piper glanced at Mason and gave him a sarcastic "I'm sure" look.

"Seriously. Jesse doesn't really know you, but once he sees what a sac-shrinker you are, he'll love you. Everyone else knows you."

"Ryker was eyeing me yesterday; I don't know if he's happy that I'm back in your life."

Mason shrugged his shoulders as he told her to turn right at the street coming up. "Ryker was just worried, but I set him straight last night. He gave Hannah a second chance, why can't I give you one?"

"I think the circumstances are completely different."

"They seem the same to me," Mason said, while kissing the back of Piper's hand, making her feel guilty. When she was around Mason, she either felt guilty for what she did to him, or not good enough, given his stature and personality. He was gruff most of the time but sensitive and a kind and caring man, something she was only privy to see. She was lucky, and she didn't believe she deserved him, not one bit.

"Why the frown?" he asked, while smoothing out her forehead.

"Do you ever think you could do better?" Piper asked, as she pulled into the big driveway and put the car in park.

Mason turned in his seat, as best as he could, given his bulky size. "Not now. I'm not doing this now. You know you're good enough, perfect for me, so get your ass out of this car and have a good time."

"But…"

"Piper," Mason said sternly, "I'm not fucking doing this. Where is the strong confident woman I first met? I want her back. I want the girl who told me to fuck off on a plane, who stole my clothes at a wedding, and who had me begging to take her on a pool table. I want that girl. The pity party is over; we are moving forward."

"How can I move forward if you won't talk to me?" Piper practically shouted, as she started to get angry. "I can't just forget everything, Mason."

"Fuck," Mason hit the dashboard and opened his door. "I'm not doing this now."

"When?" Piper shouted, making Mason close his door so no one heard them. "When are we going to talk about it? You can't keep avoiding this conversation. It's eating me alive."

"What is? Why is it so important to you to talk about this?"

Ryker's car pulled up next to theirs, and Hannah and Ryker got out, seeing Mason and Piper in a heated debate. Hannah waved politely and Ryker pulled his pants down and pressed his ass against Mason's side while shimmying it.

"Ryker!" Hannah said from outside while grabbing his arm, clearly realizing that Piper and Mason were in a serious conversation. She ushered him toward the front door, while he pulled up his pants and laughed. She scolded him like a child.

Mason shook his head and looked back at Piper. His temper had calmed down slightly from the interruption, and he asked again, "Why is it so important to you?"

"I need to know how badly I hurt you. I need to know everything, to get this off my chest, to be free of the guilt I've been carrying around for months. I need you to know how sorry I am, how regretful I am, how much I wish, instead of stealing your clothes at the wedding, that I had actually made love to you on the beach. I have regrets in my life, but my biggest regret was not giving myself over to you when you wanted me to, when I wanted to."

Mason nodded his head and looked out the window as silence fell between them.

Grabbing Piper's hand, he threaded their fingers together and looked down at their connection.

"You annihilated me, Piper, and I just don't mean when you walked away. I mean the day I saw you at the bar for the first time after Jake and Lexi's wedding. There was no turning back for me after that. I may have been an ass at times, I may have been a demanding fuck, but it's because you stole my breath, you stole my heart, and you stole my soul. I was functionless when you weren't around; you broke me down and glued me back together with your heart. When I heard you were engaged, after you said you wanted to be with me, I lost it. My life went cold and black; there was nothing left for me, so I turned to the one person I shouldn't have, not only because of your history with her, but because I was only using her, when clearly she wanted more from me that I just couldn't give her."

Tears rolled down Piper's face as she listened to Mason. For the first time, she was really starting to understand everything she'd put Mason through, and it gutted her.

He took a deep breath and continued. "I hated you, I wanted you to hurt, the way I was hurting. Even though I thought about you every day you were gone, and I craved your soft touch and beautiful lips, I hoped you were miserable." He shook his head as if he couldn't believe what he was saying. "You annihilated me," he repeated, "but not once did I stop wanting you or needing you…that's why you're with me now, because I need you in my life. I may be a stupid man, but I can see the hurt in your eyes, the pain you went through, the honesty of never wanting to leave me again, and it's like a fucking drug. I see a future with you in it, and I won't deny myself of that because I can be one of the most stubborn asses around."

Wiping a tear away, Piper asked, "Are you still mad at me?"

Mason thought for a second as he looked her in the eyes. His eyes were gentle, sincere, as he looked upon her. She couldn't turn away from him now, even if she tried.

"No, Piper. I'm not mad at you." He took a deep breath and looked her in the eyes. "I'm fucking in love with you."

Piper's breath caught in her throat as the words she had been dying to hear from Mason a couple of months ago came rolling out of his mouth with ease.

"You love me?" she asked, almost stunned.

A small smirk spread across his face as he said, "I don't think I have ever stopped loving you, Piper, and it kills me that I can't touch you the way I want to."

"Why can't you?"

"Because it's not good enough for me to just be in lust like we were. I want to be in love, I want a partner, and I want a best friend, and we can't have that if all we do is talk after amazing, wall-banging sex."

Piper blushed, thinking back to the time Mason took her up against the wall in the back room of the bar.

"The time will come for us, but for now, we need to learn

about each other, we need to date, babe."

Nodding her head, Piper agreed. "Fair enough. So, whenever we're together, we should ask each other at least one question so we can get to know each other."

"Okay, you ask first, and then we need to get into the house. Jesse is probably having a fucking fit because we didn't go straight into the house. He can be such a controlling host," Mason smiled, making Piper's heart skip a beat.

"We'll be quick. Tell me, what is your favorite cuisine?"

She knew it was a stupid question, but sometimes, the stupid questions are the most important when trying to get to know someone.

Mason smiled devilishly and said, "Anything I can eat off your body."

Piper rolled her eyes and said, "Seriously, Mason."

"I am being serious, but I'll tell you my second favorite is Mexican."

"Alright, good answer."

"What about you?"

"Anything Greek."

"I feel like I knew that?"

"Well, you know it for sure now."

"Sure do," he replied, as he kissed the back of her hand again. "Looks like we're in for a disappointing night."

"Why?" Piper asked, confused.

"Because the lazy dickhead inside is serving pizza." Piper laughed as Mason continued, "When we host dinner at our place, we're going to make one hell of a Greek burrito, show these lazy fucks how it's done." Mason placed a quick kiss on her lips, and got out of the car, maneuvering his crutches much better.

Piper sat in the car a second longer, trying to grasp the fact that, not only had Mason already started making plans about hosting dinner for their friends together as a couple, but he also called his house, "theirs." It was endearing and sweet, a side she rarely saw of Mason, but when she did, she soaked him up like a dry sponge.

Mason met up with her at the front of the car, and she pulled on his arm to make him stop from moving forward.

"He's going to kill us," Mason said, referring to Jesse's testiness about being on time.

"I'm in love with you too, Mason. Please don't ever forget that."

A bright smile spread across Mason's face as he grabbed her chin and brought her lips to his.

"Never will, baby."

Mason

The boys clinked their beers together as they wished each other a good game tomorrow. The Stallions had played the Thunder during pre-season, but this go around, the win counted.

The girls were all huddled around the kitchen island, picking at the leftover pizza and talking about girl shit that Mason could care less about, but that didn't mean he could stop sneaking glances over at Piper.

She wore skinny black jeans, a long-sleeved Aerosmith T-shirt, and a pair of her Chuck Taylors. Her vibrant hair was in its natural waves, cascading over her shoulders, and her smile was bright as she talked to her friends. Occasionally, she would look Mason's way and see him staring at her. She would blush and turn away, making Mason's libido take a giant step forward, but he tamped it down every time, reminding himself that friendship will build a long future with the woman you love.

"I thought you two were living together," Ryker interrupted Mason's thoughts.

"We sort of are," Mason replied, as he tore his gaze away from Piper.

"Then stop eye fucking her and pay the fuck attention to us for a couple of hours," Ryker complained.

"Ahh, honey, I'm sorry, are you feeling neglected?" Mason

asked, as he cupped Ryker's chin and brought him in close.

"Dude!" Ryker swatted him away, making Jake, Jesse, and Mason all laugh. "I know you're crushing on me, but seriously, I'm spoken for." Ryker waved his hand and called out, "Hey boo!" to Hannah who was now blushing feverishly.

"You're such a little bitch," Jake laughed, as he took a sip of his beer. "You all are so pussy-whipped, it's ridiculous."

Mason guffawed as he called out to Lexi, "Hey, Lex, did you hear that? Jake thinks he's not pussy-whipped."

Lexi laughed and said, "We'll see about that later tonight when he's begging for some action and the only way he'll get it is if he does what I want."

Mason laughed as Jake punched him in the shoulder. "Hey, wife, what happens in the bedroom, stays in the bedroom," Jake called out.

"Oh, is that right? Then why did your center come up to me the other day and ask me to teach his wife the little tongue trick you like so much?"

Jake instantly looked guilty as he said, "Uh, don't know what you're talking about." He lowered his body, as if he could hide from Lexi, as all the girls laughed and huddled together, most likely talking about the tongue trick.

"Tongue trick?" Mason asked, while elbowing Jake.

"Dude," he looked around quickly and then said in a hushed tone, "She can do this thing with her tongue on the underside of my dick that makes me seriously blow my load in seconds."

"Don't you love it when your girl can take you back to your teenage days, when the outline of a nipple would turn your clothing into cream-coated shorts?" Ryker asked, as he took a sip of his beer.

"That's just nasty, man," Jake responded, as he shook his head in disgust and then shivered. "Seriously, the image of jiz shorts being your only source of clothing is going to haunt me."

"Oh, please, like you've never crusted over your boxers when a light breeze crosses over an improperly supported nipple?"

"Hannah, Ryker is talking about other girl's nipples," Mason called out, making Ryker punch Mason in the other shoulder.

The look on Hannah's face actually made Mason feel bad for saying anything; sometimes he forgot that she could be a very insecure girl.

"Thanks, fuckhead," Ryker muttered, as he went over to Hannah to repair Mason's mistake. Piper gave him a look that said, "We will be talking about this later."

Fucking great.

Changing the subject, Mason turned to Jesse, who had been awfully quiet, and said, "So what's going on with Ashlin? I leave for San Diego and you finally make a move?"

Jesse looked over his shoulder at Ashlin, who was picking at a salad with a depressed look on her face.

"Yeah, it wasn't easy, but I finally got her to agree to go out with me. She is actually going to be in my suite with you tomorrow, and that little boy from the zoo I was telling you about."

"You can't be keeping her happy. She looks like her dog just got murdered," Jake pointed out, as they all looked at Ashlin for a second.

"She has a modeling gig next week and apparently deprives herself of food up until the photo shoot. I try to feed her different things, but she refuses. I actually don't like it. She works out a lot, and practically starves herself leading up to a gig. She's perfect; she doesn't need to do any of that."

Jesse was being very serious, so Mason held back all sarcastic comments. He congratulated himself for acting somewhat mature.

"Is it something to worry about?" Jake asked seriously.

"Nah, nothing like that. I just wish she didn't put such a strain on her body, you know?"

"Yes, but she could say the same thing about you," Mason pointed out. "You don't even drink beer, for fuck's sake, you drink root beer. Don't you ever want to let loose and have fun?"

Jesse just shook his head in silence as he looked down at his plate that was empty.

"Wow, well, this is awkward," Jake said. "You really know how to throw a rager."

Jesse smiled and said, "The strippers will be here later, no worries, it will pick up."

"Strippers?" Ashlin asked as she wrapped her arms around Jesse's waist. He put his arm around her and kissed the top of her head.

"Jake here thinks I throw a lame ass party."

"Well, he should have been at the barbeque earlier in the season when Mason and Ryker were running around in their underwear."

Jake looked at Mason and raised his eyebrows, making Mason laugh.

"We lost a bet because Ryker was my little bitch of a partner. The boy sucks at ladder ball."

"That's why I'm a receiver, dickhead," Ryker responded, as he held Hannah close to him. The women started trickling over to their group. "I can't toss worth shit."

Lexi settled under Jake's chin with ease as he wrapped his arms around her waist.

"It has nothing to do with tossing," she said. "Jake can't play that game to save his life, and he's the best quarterback in the NFL."

Ashlin snorted and patted Jesse's chest. "I beg to differ." Jesse beamed with pride.

Warm arms wrapped around Mason, who was sitting on a stool, and Piper rested her chin on Mason's shoulder. She kissed his earlobe and said, "I love you."

Fuck.

His heart literally just sped up a mile a minute at her simple statement. She rubbed his chest, right over his heart, as she realized she needed to soothe his tense muscles from all the pain she caused him.

"If we're talking bests in the NFL, then I think we have an all-time winner here," Piper said, as she looked up at everyone.

"Biggest dick in the NFL, sitting right in front of you."

The table erupted in laughter as Ryker leaned over to take a look at Mason's lap.

Mason pushed him away, and said, "Seriously, dude, you have a problem. I think you've seen my dick more times than Piper."

"It's just hard to believe. I don't get how you can run as fast as you can with a fucking tree trunk dragging behind you."

"Is that what they use to till the ground after the season is over?" Jake asked with a quizzical look on his face.

"Yup, they strap a rototiller on my dick and I do fifties up and down the field until I have aerated the fuck out of the field," Mason deadpanned, making all the men laugh.

"You see, this is why we split up into different groups. Men are so disgusting," Lexi said, as she wiggled out of Jake's grasp.

"She's just jealous she can't have a piece of this monster in my pants," Mason responded.

"Pig," Piper said, as she walked toward Lexi, but not before Mason grabbed her by the arm and sat her on his lap.

"Take it back," he smiled.

"Never," she smiled back.

He searched her eyes and asked, "Favorite body part of mine?"

"Is that even a question?"

"Confirm it for me, baby."

"Your dick, no question. What about mine?"

Mason thought about it for a second and whispered in her ear. "You would expect me to say your firm ass or your fucking gorgeous tits, but that would be a lie. It's your mouth, because it can be sassy, it can bring me to my knees with your words, and it gives, by far, the best blow job I've ever had."

"Such a romantic," she laughed, as she kissed him on the lips and got off his lap. He slapped her ass as she walked away, giving her a devilish grin as she looked over her shoulder.

Yup, he was in fucking love.

Hannah

The boys were now outside playing ladder ball, just so they could embarrass Ryker some more, while the girls huddled around the dining room table, drinking beer, and devouring a giant chocolate chip cookie that Hannah had brought to the party. Ashlin wasn't eating it, which made Hannah feel self-conscious, since she was on her fourth piece, but she tried to hide her insecurity. It was hard being around these girls; they were all so beautiful...Hannah felt like a gremlin compared to all of them. Sometimes, she really had to question what Ryker saw in her.

"Jesse is so yummy," Lexi said, as she grabbed another bite of the cookie, eating enough for her and Ashlin. Thank God for Lexi.

"He is," Ashlin said, as she peered outside. "He is so different than anyone I know, even Ryker."

A piercing pain went through Hannah's chest at the mention of Ryker's name. She still felt like there was a connection between Ashlin and Ryker that Hannah would never be able to have; it was another reason for her insecurities.

"Oh, I forgot you and Ryker knew each other beforehand," Piper said absentmindedly, making Hannah feel even more uncomfortable.

"You did?" Lexi asked.

"Yes, we grew up with each other."

"Is the chemistry between you two real, like in all those clothing ads?" Lexi asked, as if Hannah wasn't sitting right there.

Ashlin looked over at Hannah with an apologetic smile, which clued Lexi in.

"Oh crap, I'm sorry Hannah. God, I can be so blonde sometimes."

"No, it's alright," Hannah soothed. "Ryker and Ashlin have a history...even a sexual one; I'm aware of it."

Crickets.

Piper's mouth hung open in shock, Lexi looked confused as hell, and Ashlin looked outright mad.

"What? It's true and I'm okay with it," Hannah said, while swallowing hard.

"Yeah, you seem real cool about it," Ashlin replied, as her arms crossed over her chest.

Sensing an explosion about to happen, Piper stood up, grabbed Hannah by the arm, and said, "Help me get some more beers." Piper didn't give Hannah a chance to reply as she dragged her toward the kitchen.

"What are you doing?" Hannah asked, as she finally was able to remove her arm from Piper's death grip.

"What am I doing? What the hell are you doing? Why are you making Ashlin feel bad?"

"I'm just stating the facts."

"No, you're being a bit of a bitch. I thought you were okay with Ashlin and Ryker being friends."

Hannah ran both her hands through her hair and said, "I am! It's just that when we're all together, I'm just reminded how superior you all are to me. I mean, Ashlin is a super model for crying out loud, Lexi has the body of a Playboy bunny, and you're so tall and gorgeous that it's hard to be around the three of you without developing a complex."

Piper looked at Hannah for a second, and then burst out in laughter. "Hannah, are you kidding me? Have you looked in a mirror? You're beautiful."

Hannah looked down at her hands as she shrugged her shoulders.

"You need to stop with the pity party," Piper said honestly. "Ryker is the kind of guy that needs a strong woman next to him, and you are that girl, but you sometimes you get in these moods where you think you're some atrocious troll wandering around the world, when you're not at all. Accept the fact that you're beautiful and own it. You want to be with Ryker? Well then, act like you belong with him, because you do. You two were made for each other."

Nodding her head, Hannah grabbed some beers from the

fridge and said, "It's just so hard."

"Love is hard, sweet cheeks, get used to it. Believe me, I have."

"Motherfucker!!" Ryker shouted as Mason and Jesse high fived. They must have won in ladder ball, because Jake was also yelling at Ryker.

"You're going to want to come out here, girls," Mason called out.

Hannah rolled her eyes at Piper, and they followed the other two girls outside as Jake and Ryker stood next to Jesse's pool. Hannah sidled up next to Ashlin and leaned over to her.

"I'm sorry about earlier. I'm really cool with you two," Hannah admitted, even though she was still feeling a little sour about Ashlin and Ryker…but she would get over that in time.

"No need to be sorry. I would be the same way. Just know, there is nothing going on with us, and there never will be. He's my brother…I know that now, plus, I kind of have my hands full."

Hannah watched Ashlin look adoringly up at Jesse, who was laying out the ground rules for the next insane competition the boys came up with, while holding pool noodles in his hands.

"Listen up, boys, due to your lack of skills in ladder ball, you now have to compete in the great noodle race."

"This is going to be good," Lexi said, as she sat on a lawn chair and called the other girls over. Piper sat next to Lexi, so Hannah pulled up a chair and blanket for her and Ashlin. Hannah had to accept the fact that Ryker and Ashlin were friends, and she might as well make a friend while she was at it.

"Here," Hannah offered the blanket that Ashlin accepted with a smile.

Ashlin wrapped her arm around Hannah and whispered in her ear, "You are beyond perfect for Ryker. I'm so glad he has you."

"Thank you."

Jesse interrupted their little love fest and continued on with the instructions. "You two are to strip down to your skivvies, put this noddle between your legs and ride it like it's a horse across the pool and back. First one to climb out of the pool and do one lap around the pool doing his best cowboy impression, wins."

"Are yeehaas and yippees permitted?" Jake asked, with his hands on his hips.

"They are encouraged," Jesse responded seriously.

Hannah giggled to herself at the show the boys were putting on.

"What about Yippee I O?" Ryker asked.

"Yes, but anything other than that will place your man card into serious question."

Both Jake and Ryker nodded their heads, and they muttered an understanding.

"Alright, the first one to complete the course and tag Mason, who is propped up on the chair over there, wins."

Mason sat at the outdoor bar, holding his beer while laughing. Hannah enjoyed this side of Mason...easygoing and enjoying life. For as long as she had known Mason, she'd only known the dark, brooding, and hurting man, but now she got to see a different side of Mason...the fun-loving side, and she loved it. She glanced over at Piper, who was beaming with love for the man who sat across the pool. The difference in their lives from a couple of months ago was dramatic, and it almost seemed too good to be true, but Hannah was going to soak it in as much as she could, because she couldn't think of a time when she was happier to see her friends happy and to have happiness in her life as well.

"Time to strip, men," Jesse announced.

Ryker and Jake started taking off their clothes, as they swore about the chilly Denver air. Hannah felt her eyes glue to Ryker's body as he finished taking off his shoes and socks and went for his shirt. The space around her faded into black as her eyes were fixated on Ryker and the way his arms took his shirt off, exposing his extremely well-defined stomach and chest. He was smaller than Jake, not as bulky, but he was sculpted in all the right ways...almost perfectly sculpted. For the amount of food the man ate, Hannah was shocked at the fact that the man didn't have one ounce of body fat on him. He either busted his butt out on the field, or he had the metabolism of a wizard.

As he unbuckled his belt, he looked over at Hannah and his eyes lit up at her blatant staring.

"Boo, you can't look at me like that," Ryker said, as he stopped undoing his pants.

"You too," Jake called out to Lexi, who was licking her lips and staring Jake up and down.

"Keep your eyes on me," Mason called out to Piper, who was now laughing.

"Look all you want," Jesse called out to Ashlin, "I know these nuggets have nothing on me."

"You got that right, QB," Ashlin called out, as she blew him a kiss.

Hannah laughed and then looked back at Ryker, who was avoiding all eye contact with her.

"Women have it so easy," Ryker said, as he fiddled with his jeans. "They don't have to deal with the fact that a boner can happen at any point in time."

Hannah's face went instantly red from embarrassment. She didn't know why she was embarrassed, but she was.

"Aww, you made her blush," Piper teased.

"Jesus, she is adorable when she blushes," Ryker called out, now completely turned around.

"Only one way to fix that problem," Jake said, as he grabbed Ryker and threw him in the pool, jeans and all.

Coming to the surface, Ryker shook the water out of his hair and looked up at Jake as he pointed, "Christ that's cold. You're a dead man."

"Try me." Jake took his pants off, exposing his defined legs, and cannon-balled into the pool. When he came up to the surface, he called out to Jesse, "Let's get this started."

Ryker took his soaked jeans off, tossed them to the side, and then grabbed a noodle from Jesse. Both Ryker and Jake lined up against the pool wall with a noodle between their legs and one arm in the air, as if they were holding lassos. With anticipation, Jesse finally told them to start.

Water splashed about as Ryker and Jake started shouting cowboy noises at the top of their lungs, riding their noodles to one end of the pool and back. Everyone was laughing hysterically at the ridiculous game the boys were taking part in. Hannah had tears rolling down her cheeks from laughing so hard. Both Jake and Ryker popped out of the pool at the same time as water dripped down their sculpted bodies, and started to ride their noodles around the pool while galloping.

They swore at each other, now forgetting their cowboy calls, and were starting to play for blood. As they rounded the last corner, Jake took the initiative to shove Ryker to the side, right into the pool, giving him a clear path to Mason, where he stopped short and placed a gentle kiss on Mason's head. Mason punched Jake in the arm just as Ryker popped out from the water and started shouting obscenities.

"DQ, DQ," Ryker kept calling out as he charged his way up the steps.

Jake held his hands up in the air as he said, "Nowhere in the rules was it stated that we could not push each other in the pool, am I right, Jesse?"

"He has a point," Jesse agreed.

"This is crap. I was going to beat your ass and you knew it; that's why you pushed me."

"Keep dreaming," Jake said, as he patted Ryker on the face and walked over to Lexi, who was holding a towel out for him.

Mason looked at Ryker, and said, "For what it's worth, man, I DQ'ed Jake for kissing me. So, technically, you won."

Ryker fist pumped the air, and said, "Did you hear that, Jake?"

"Yeah, and I refuse to listen to it, because I know deep down inside, I ate away at Mason's heart with that gentle kiss."

Mason held his heart and said, "Yup, watch out Lexi, I'm

coming after your man."

"I'm not worried, Jake's not into hairy Marys like you are."

Mason spun around as he looked at Ryker, who had a huge grin on his face. "Seriously, dickhead, who have you not told?"

"I still think Piper needs to hear it…"

Mason chucked one of his crutches at Ryker, who sidestepped the assault and ran up to Hannah, soaked. He grabbed ahold of her, making her squeal from the cold seeping into her.

"Save me, boo. The sasquatch-lover is coming after me."

Hannah laughed as he carried her off toward the pool house, leaving their friends behind. He carried her over his shoulder, slapping her butt and calling out cowboy calls the whole time, while Hannah continued to laugh.

When they reached the pool house, Ryker set her down, pushed her against the door, and looked her in the eyes.

"You're in for some trouble tonight, boo."

"What did I do?" she asked, confused.

"Don't act all innocent. I saw the way you were eye-fucking me."

"Ryker!"

"Are you denying it?" he pressed his body up against hers, instantly starting a fire deep in her belly. The man was irresistible, especially when practically naked and wet.

"No," she shook her head.

"Damn, I wish you had, because then I would have taught you a lesson," he responded, wiggling his eyebrows.

"You still can," she drew a line down his chest to his belly button, making him suck in a deep breath of air. They both looked down and saw the excitement that she was so easily able to pull out of him.

"Don't test me, boo. You know I have no problem taking you right here, in front of everyone."

Hannah quickly pulled her hand away, making Ryker throw his head back and laugh. "You're so damn adorable, you know that?"

She just smiled up at him, wrapped her hand around his neck and brought him down for a chlorine-filled kiss. She may be insecure, but whenever Ryker kissed her the way he did, all her insecurities ran straight out the door.

CHAPTER SEVENTEEN

Ryker

Images of the night before kept rolling around Ryker's head as he stretched with his teammates before their game against the Thunder. Hannah surprised him with a yellow nightie she got specifically for him. The garment wasn't too revealing, but it showed off her body perfectly by forming to her shape with ease, like it was made for her. The garment wasn't made for a nun, but it wasn't something someone like Ashlin would wear either, which made Hannah's choice of clothing so much better. She was so innocent that it almost ate Ryker alive; he found it adorable and irresistible.

He made sure to make good use of her lingerie choice, and took his time removing it…driving her crazy. The sounds that escaped her mouth last night could keep him turned on for days. Thankfully, he was wearing a cup, because just the thought of last night was turning him on.

The team clapped their hands together, freeing Ryker from his thoughts as they all huddled up together. The coaches were on the sideline, planning out their attack for the day as Jesse took center stage in the huddle.

"Let's destroy these motherfuckers!" Jesse announced as the

team backed him up with hollering. They brought their hands together in a pyramid toward the center of the huddle and all grunted out "Whip those pussies," quickly, so no one knew what they were saying except for them.

The huddle broke up as the team went their separate ways to prepare for the game. The defense went to one side of the field, while the offense went to another. Jesse started doing rotator cuff stretches with a band, as Ryker and the other receivers did some more dynamic stretches and short sprints, trying to warm up their legs as much as possible.

Hannah was working today, so she would be watching from the bar. Before Ryker took off for the stadium, Hannah showed Ryker the jersey she got with his name on the back. The cut was a perfect fit for her, and pride surged through Ryker at seeing his girl wearing his name and number, something he would like to make legal one day.

"Lewis, get in position to run route," Coach Ryan called out to Ryker, who strapped his helmet on and got in position.

Jesse called out a play, hiked the ball and fell into an imaginary pocket as he waited for Ryker to get into position. Ryker's legs were feeling loose today, so he was able to sprint to position with ease, catch the ball, and jog into the end zone. Music pumped through the stadium as Ryker nodded his head at making a good play. Now he only needed to make the same play with a two hundred something pound man chasing and groping him.

"Good catch, Lewis," Jax called out, as he wrote something down on his clipboard. The man had to have a woman in his life, because he was being way too nice to the team. Jax's mood was oddly disturbing; they were just waiting for him to blow his lid at some point.

They finished up some practice routes and then headed into the locker room, where they went to put on their jerseys and do their final preparations for the game.

Both Jesse and Ryker sat down on their seats as they strapped on their cleats. Ryker saw Jesse check his phone multiple times while he was getting ready, and it got to the point where Ryker just had to ask, "Is everything okay, man? You keep checking your phone as if you're waiting to find out if someone went into labor."

"Just want to make sure Ashlin got to the suite alright."

"Dude, she's a grown ass woman; she'll be fine."

"I understand that," Jesse said, with a bit of edge to his voice. "She's just been so flighty lately, you know? I want to make sure that she actually made it...that she actually came."

"She's coming," Ryker said, as he patted Jesse on the back. "She likes you a lot, man, so settle the fuck down and just enjoy yourself. I swear, sometimes I think you and Hannah are cut from the same cloth."

"What does that mean?" Jesse asked, as he pulled out his eye black and started applying it under his eyes without looking in a mirror.

"You both are so insecure when it comes to relationships. Just believe in yourself and the person you're with; everything will work out."

"You don't ever worry about what might happen with you and Hannah?" Jesse asked, as he handed the eye black over to Ryker.

"I mean, I worry on occasion, who doesn't? But I don't spend every waking moment worrying. If it's meant to be, it's meant to be."

"That's not helpful," Jesse responded, just as his phone beeped. Acting like a fool, Jesse fumbled with his phone, and quickly read the message. A smile spread across his face as he held the phone out to Ryker.

Ashlin: Made it to the suite, have my QB's jersey on and I'm ready to wave my pom poms in the air. Go get 'em, tiger.

"Well isn't that so charming?" Ryker said sarcastically.

"You're just jealous," Jesse responded, as he typed back a response to Ashlin.

"Why do I need to be jealous?" Ryker held out his phone to show what Hannah wrote to him a little bit ago.

Hannah Boo: Good luck today, handsome. Score some touchdowns, but save one for me when you get home. I have some plans for you and me.

Jesse laughed and nodded his head. "Alright, that's pretty good."

"Pretty good?" Ryker laughed. "Dude, I'm getting me some Hannah pudding tonight."

"Does she know you call it that?"

"No," Ryker sat up straighter and said, "If she found out, I'm pretty sure she'd kill me, not because of the name, but because I said it to you. The girl is always ready and prepared to blush when I'm around her."

"You two couldn't be more opposite. She has a fine sense of class, and you...you know I love you, but you really know how to belch the alphabet, swear like a beast, and you don't mind being naked in front of strangers."

Ryker shrugged his shoulders. "What can I say, my girl knows how to pick them." He tossed the eye black into Jesse's locker, stood up, and grabbed his helmet. "Time to kick some Jake Taylor ass."

Fist bumping, Jesse got up as well, and the team followed suit as they walked out of the locker room, down the tunnel, and out onto the field to thousands of screaming fans. It was going to be a good game.

Ashlin

"Where's Piper?" Ashlin asked, as she popped a piece of cauliflower in her mouth from the veggie platter that was so nicely displayed on the counter in the suite. Along with veggies, there were plenty of sweets and cupcakes, of course. There was a note from Jesse telling her to eat up and that her body was perfect; she didn't need to deny herself sweets before a photo shoot. The man was impossible. Didn't he know that she looked the way she did because she watched what she ate?

"She didn't feel like coming here was appropriate just yet, given her history," Mason said politely.

"Makes sense, but she can't hide out forever."

"That's what I told her. I think she's going to go to the bar to hang out with Hannah for a while."

"Did she drop you off?"

"Nah, I had a car service bring me." Mason looked around and then said, "Sweet digs Jesse has going on here. Must be nice to be the quarterback."

Ashlin laughed, and then said, "You're telling me, as the star wide receiver for the Stallions, you don't get the same perks?"

Smirking, Mason replied, "Nope, only the ever so talented and handsome quarterback."

Leaning forward, Ashlin said, "He is gorgeous, isn't he?"

Mason fanned his face and said in a girly voice, "Sometimes when we're in the locker room, I get almost too excited when he's walking around in just his towel."

"You're ridiculous…"

"Excuse me?" came a voice from behind them, making them both stand up straight. The look on Mason's face read, "I hope they didn't hear what I just said," and the giggles coming from Ashlin's mouth were saying, "She hoped they did."

"Isaac, it's so good to see you again." Ashlin bent over and greeted the boy. "Mrs. Wilson, it's nice that you could make it today. Jesse will be so excited to see you both."

"I can't tell you how grateful we both are that Mr. Rutledge was kind enough to invite us up here."

"You can call him Jesse," Mason said, as he turned around.

The look on Isaac's face was priceless as he took in Mason. Shock, excitement, and admiration crossed his features as Mason stuck his hand out to Isaac.

"I'm…"

"You're Mason Dashel," Isaac said, interrupting Mason and making him laugh.

"I am. Do you mind if I hang out here today with you and watch the game?"

"Are you kidding? Mom did you hear that? Dash is going to watch the game with us."

"I see that. Remember our manners," she said softly.

Isaac nodded his head and turned back around to Mason. "Can I get you something to drink, sir?"

Mason's eyebrows cocked up in surprise and question as the room fell silent. Ashlin was the first one to bust out in laughter, followed by Mason. Isaac looked up at his mom to see what he did wrong.

Patting the boy on the shoulder, Mason said, "Little man, you're our guest. What can we get you to drink?"

"That's not necessary," Mrs. Wilson said.

"Ah, it's no problem. Ashlin doesn't mind, do you?" Mason winked and smirked. He would pay for that later, Ashlin thought, as she shook her head no and grabbed everyone drinks.

"Help yourself to any treats you want," Ashlin offered. "And over here, we saved you the best seat in the house. Mason thought it would be cool if you two could sit together and talk about the game."

"Awesome!" Isaac said, as he pumped his fist in the air and sat right next to Mason, who gave him a high five and then placed his arm around Isaac's shoulder. Ashlin took a quick picture of the two of them and sent it off to Hannah, who she told to show Piper, since Ashlin didn't have Piper's phone number.

A few minutes later, Ashlin got a text message back.

Ryker's Boo: I love that man – Piper

Looking over at Mason with Isaac, Ashlin had to admit, the man was sweet, and it was hard not to crush on him when he treated the little boy like he was his little brother.

Mason and Isaac lived in their own little world as they

watched the game, cheered, and fist bumped when Ryker scored two touchdowns. Ashlin spent the game talking to Mrs. Wilson and fielding text messages from both Hannah and Piper, asking how the game was from the posh seats. For a girl who had a sad and lonely life leading up to now, she was very happy with how Jesse and Ryker's friends had taken her in and made her feel like part of the gang.

The Stallions wound up scoring in the last two minutes of the 4th quarter, taking the lead and winning the game. It was a great game to watch, and in the end, the defense was what lost the game for the Thunder. Jake Taylor was on point, like always, but there's only so much one man can do. Ashlin did feel bad for Jake, but not that bad, because that meant her man won.

They waited in the suite and played cards while Jesse interviewed and took a shower before heading up to the suite. After an hour of waiting around and five rounds of crazy eights, the door to the suite opened and a freshly showered Jesse walked into the room. His presence was electrifying as his smile spread across his face the minute he saw Ashlin.

All she wanted to do was run up to him, wrap her legs around his waist, and kiss him like crazy to congratulate him on his win. It looked like, by the way Jesse was looking at her, that he wanted the same thing. Given the fact that they had company and young eyes in the room, Ashlin restrained herself and gave him a smile instead. He winked at her and then looked down at Isaac who was wiggling in place, waiting for Jesse to give his attention to him.

"So, how did I do?" Jesse asked, as he squatted down to the floor.

"You were awesome!" Isaac said, as he wrapped his arms around Jesse's neck and hugged him. Jesse was thrown off balance for a second before he steadied himself by placing a hand on the ground.

"Thanks, buddy. So, I'm taking it you enjoyed the game with my friend Dash over there."

Isaac nodded his head. "This has been the best day of my

life."

At the confession, Ashlin's heart melted as she watched the three boys talk about the game and analyze their favorite plays. A short time later, Ryker popped into the room and gave Isaac, who almost looked like he was about to pass out, a high five. They all stood in front of the counter and Jesse picked Isaac up and put him on his shoulders and posed for a picture. They did a couple of poses, the boys all holding Isaac up as he laid horizontally, and some fake tackling pictures where it looked like Isaac was tackling all three at the same time. They made sure to be careful of Mason's knee, but they had a good time, and Ashlin captured all the pictures, making sure to send every single one of them to Piper and Hannah, who gushed back.

"Let's go see the locker room," Ryker called out, as Isaac hopped on his back and continued down the hallway. Mrs. Wilson and Mason followed, talking about what a great day this was for her son and how grateful she was.

Jesse hung back, and once the room was clear, he cleared his throat as he leaned against the wall, arms crossed, and said, "Hey gorgeous."

"Hey yourself," Ashlin sauntered over to him, feeling a little weak in the knees.

Uncrossing his arms, Jesse rested his hands on Ashlin's hips and brought her a little closer to him. "Did you have a good time?" he asked in a husky tone.

"I did. You boys are seriously so amazing. I feel like my heart can't take any more."

"No? So, I probably shouldn't kiss you, should I?" Jesse asked, as he pulled her in even closer.

"Probably not, you don't want to make my heart explode."

"If it means kissing you, I think I do."

Before she could protest, Jesse spun her around so her back was up against the wall and cupped her cheeks. Slowly, he lowered his lips down to hers and pressed a very gentle kiss on her mouth. It was gentle, but there was something behind it, some kind of urgency…like he needed as much of her as possible and as soon as possible.

"You taste so good," Jesse mumbled, as he kissed along her jaw.

"You're gonna get yourself into trouble if you keep kissing me that way."

"Maybe I want to get in trouble."

"We both know that's not the truth, because you wouldn't leave Isaac alone with those two fools."

Jesse pressed his forehead against Ashlin's and said, "Damn, you're right. They've probably already corrupted him, especially Ryker."

Patting his cheek and pushing away, Ashlin freed herself from Jesse…reluctantly.

"Go save the poor boy, and maybe later tonight we can work some more on that kissing thing."

"Sounds like a plan to me," Jesse smirked, as he jogged after the boys.

Ashlin followed slowly behind, trying to catch her breath. Watching Jesse jog away in his tight jeans and form-fitting shirt had her clenching her thighs together and begging for some sweet release soon. She knew it wouldn't be tonight, because Jesse was "taking it slow," but it had to be soon. She didn't know how much more she could take. The man had sex god written all over him, and she wanted a piece of him.

Mason

"The boys smoked it today, don't you think?" Mason asked Piper as they got ready for bed. Mason was sitting on the counter, brushing his teeth and talking, while Piper washed her face.

Drying off her face, Piper said, "They killed it…at the end." Mason gave her a "please" look, but then Piper added, "Did you fail to realize it was tied up until the last two minutes of the game?"

"Technicality." Mason spit out his toothpaste and rinsed his mouth.

The boys played amazing; they held Jake on defense, which was impressive in itself, and Jesse was able to deliver in the end to Ryker. A pang of jealousy and insecurity had run through Mason's body as he watched his team play without him. They looked so smooth, like a well-oiled machine…as if they'd never need Mason back on the team. The realization hit him like a brick wall that maybe he wasn't as necessary as he thought he was.

The sound of running water and Piper ridding herself of her toothpaste fell in the background as Mason thought about his future with the team. What if they went on to the playoffs and won the whole damn thing without him, what would that mean?

"Hey," Piper rubbed his legs as she stepped in between them. "What's going on? I don't like seeing that frown on your face."

"Just thinking," Mason replied, as he tried to hop off the counter, but Piper wouldn't let him get by.

"What are you thinking about? Talk to me, Mason."

Mason took a deep breath and looked into Piper's silver eyes. "I'm just feeling like a tool bag right now?"

"Why?"

"Because my mind is running a mile a minute about how the boys don't need me anymore, and for some godforsaken reason, it's making my throat all tight…" Mason replied, as he touched his neck.

A small smirk spread across Piper's face as she figured out what Mason was trying to say.

"Are you…going to cry?"

"No!" Mason said too quickly. Taking a deep breath, he repeated, "No. I just don't like the idea of the team being able to win without me. It fucking hurts that they don't need me to win."

Piper cupped Mason's face and leaned in to him so he could feel her warmth.

"You silly man. They barely squeaked by with a win today. Can you imagine what they'd be able to accomplish if you were on the team? They wouldn't be biting their nails at the end of the game, wondering if they would be able to pull out a win. Believe me, everyone misses you and wants you back on the field. You should have heard all the fans at the bar; they're still mourning your injury."

Mason perked up a bit. "Are they?"

Laughing, Piper said, "Yes. Now stop feeling sorry for yourself, and let's go to bed. You need your rest for your long road of recovery."

Mason hopped off the counter with the help of his crutches and walked toward the bedroom. "Five questions tonight?" he asked over his shoulder.

"You start."

They both settled into bed, turned toward each other, and rested their heads on their pillows as they held each other's hands up by their faces. It was a natural position for them now.

With his free hand, Mason twirled a strand of Piper's curly hair in his finger as he asked, "First celebrity crush."

Quirking the side of her mouth, she thought for a second before answering, "I would have to say Jonathan Taylor Thomas."

"Simba?" Mason asked, a little perplexed.

"Yes, Simba. He was a hottie back then. Total stud. He grazed every *Tiger* and *Teen Beat* magazine out there."

"Did you have posters of him pinned to your walls?"

"What kind of fan would I be if I didn't?" she asked seriously.

"Damn, I'm so embarrassed for you right now," he chuckled.

"Your turn. What did you used to jerk off to in high school?"

"Seriously?" Mason laughed. "There is something wrong with you."

"Answer the question."

"Well, since you really want to know. I was blocked from using any kind of porn sites back then, since my mom made it her mission to censor everything. It was kind of pathetic for me, but I had a really good friend, Jimmy, who used to go to Vegas with his parents all the time, since they did some part time technology work out there, and he would bring me home showgirl pamphlets that he found on the street. I got a notebook, taped them all on there, and that was my stroke book."

Piper was giggling to herself with her hand over her mouth. "Oh, my God, did you label it your stroke book on the front?"

"No, I didn't want my mom to notice it."

"Oh, you poor horny little boy. Vegas showgirl pamphlets. Wow!"

"Ok, Mrs. Simba."

Not taking offense, Piper responded back, "Looks like you're losing your wit there Dashel."

Rolling his eyes, he asked, "Favorite place you have ever lived."

"Is this a trick question?"

"How would it be a trick question?"

Piper played with Mason's hand in hers as she said, "Am I supposed to say Denver because you're with me?"

Chuckling, Mason said, "No. Be honest."

"Well…" she thought. "I've lived in North Carolina, Kansas, Seattle, San Diego, and Denver. I would have to say San Diego is my favorite, because I'm a beach kind of girl and the cold winters are not my favorite thing, but I do love it here…the views, by far, beat out the ones in San Diego."

"Same here," Mason said, as he leaned in and kissed Piper on the lips.

He meant for the kiss to be a quick peck, but the moment his lips met hers, he didn't want to pull away…and from the way her body scooted closer to his, she didn't want to pull away either. Her body slowly pressed against his as their legs entwined together. Their noses touched as their kiss deepened, taking away any air that lay between them.

Normally, they would keep their distance from each other while in bed, but there was only so much anticipation Mason could take, especially when he had to sleep next to Piper every night. She was every one of Mason's fantasies come true…from her vibrant hair, to her sassy personality, to her long legs and firm ass. She was perfection, and she was all his.

A light moan escaped the back of Mason's throat as she played with his tongue against hers. He didn't mean to show her how much she affected him, but he couldn't help it.

With her small hand roaming down his back to his waistband, Mason felt himself grow hard. He was only wearing a pair of shorts, so the skin-on-skin contact from her hand roaming his back was exciting him more than it should.

His free hand explored her thin tank down to her boy shorts that were just short enough to expose a little bit of her ass cheeks. Mason's hand ran over her behind, down to where her shorts ended. The exposed skin at the bottom was such a turn-on that he grew even larger.

There was a point in time where Mason could stop all forward sexual progress, but the minute Piper slipped her hand to the front of his shorts and gently cupped Mason, he knew there was no turning back; there was no way in hell he would be able to.

Instead of pulling away, Mason moved his hips into Piper's hand, making her break out in a smile. Her mouth pulled away from his, causing a groan to escape his mouth as he tried to get closer, but she stopped him. He was teetering on losing all self-control, and her pulling away from him wasn't helping.

"Baby..." he breathed heavily as he looked her in the eyes. "What are you doing?"

"This..." she said as she sat up, took her shirt off, exposing her beautiful chest, and quickly straddled him. Her warm center pressed against his erection in just the right way that, with a couple of strokes, he knew he would lose all his dignity.

Looking up at her, in the light of the moon, Mason knew she was the most beautiful woman he had ever laid eyes on. Her skin was soft and porcelain-like, especially in the rays of the moon beaming in through the windows.

Her hips started to move against his crotch, instantly causing the best kind of friction between them. With every move of her hips, Mason slowly slipped away from his hold on control. She really was a devil woman.

Laying out her body on top of his, but continuing to casually move her hips, she pressed her bare chest against' Mason's and leaned over to kiss his mouth, gently. Her lips barely caressed his mouth as her hips barely caressed his dick. The sensation only drove him to want more...and harder.

"Fuck," he breathed out as his hands went to her hips and pressed them harder against his crotch. "I've missed you," he confessed.

"I've missed you too, Mace."

Testing the constraints of her boy shorts, Mason slipped his hands under the waistband and cupped her delectable ass, forcing her down harder on his crotch, which made him moan even louder.

"Feels so good," he said, as his hips started to move.

"Do you know what would feel better?" she asked, as she started to shimmy down his body until her head met the little tent he was popping.

She pulled down his shorts, exposing his massive erection that fell against his stomach. Piper's eyes widened with excitement as she took off his shorts, exposing his entire body. She removed her shorts, as well, so now they were both naked. She straddled his legs, making sure not to hurt his knee, and lowered her head until the tip of his cock was right before her mouth. Her little pink tongue darted out and took one swipe at his engorged tip.

Moving her hands up his thighs, she calmly ran them to the inside and parted his legs, so they were a little wider, and so she could kneel between them. He felt his balls against the cool satin sheets as she made him spread his legs just a touch farther to accommodate her body. Everything felt so incredibly good, and he questioned himself for putting this off for so long.

Her hand went to the base of his cock, as her other hand grabbed ahold of his balls, literally. She rolled them in her hand, which caused Mason to grip onto the sheets for dear life, just as she took him in her mouth. Her lips glided along his shaft as his hips pumped into her, there was no stopping them.

Mason blew out a heavy breath as he tried to gain control of the feelings rolling through his body, but there was no hope. She was fucking him with her mouth and hands like no one had ever done before.

His balls tightened as he felt himself about ready to explode.

"Fuck, baby, stop. Stop!" he panted, as his hand flew over his eyes.

Immediately, Piper stopped and pulled away from him.

"Did I hurt you?" she asked in a panicked voice. "Is your knee okay?"

"Yes," he said heavily. "I just need to be inside of you. I want to feel that wet pussy of yours around my cock."

"Oh," she said with a smile. "Where are your condoms?"

"Are you serious?" Mason asked desperately, as he thought his cock was about to fall off from too much pressure at the tip. "Just hop on, baby."

"Mason…"

"I'm clean, please, Piper. You're on birth control, aren't you?"

"Yes, but…"

"But nothing. Please, baby, you're slowly taking the life out of my dick with every pause you make."

Running her hands up Mason's body, all the way up past his pecs, to his neck, she gripped his face and kissed him on the lips. "You can't always get what you want," she whispered.

"When it comes to your sweet pussy, I get whatever the hell I want. Now you can either hop the fuck on me, or I'll pin you to this bed and fuck the shit out of your mouth."

"Well, they both seem tempting…"

Mason growled, actually growled, and was about to flip Piper on her back when her hips headed south and her hand grabbed ahold of his dick, inserting it straight into her warm heat.

"Ahh, fuck!" Mason sighed as his head flew back against his pillow.

His eyes opened to find Piper with her head back, exposing her neck, and her tits bouncing in his face. Naturally, his hands moved up to her breasts and played with her nipples, which made her moan his name out loud. Her hands found his chest as her head fell forward from his assault on her nipples and her breath hitched as she tried to gain control of the pressure starting to build between them.

"Oh, God," she hissed between her teeth as her hips started to fall harder on his with unbelievable pressure. Every time her hips slammed down on his, she swirled them at the same time, sending a sensation through Mason's body that he'd never felt before. She was hot as hell…and a fucking mastermind when it came to fucking him cowgirl style.

"Christ, I'm gone, baby," Mason cried out, as his balls seized on him and his hips rapidly flew into hers. He could feel the veins in his neck tense as he went completely numb and blew everything he had into Piper. Seconds later, as he started to slowly ride off his orgasm, Piper clamped around him, threw her head back, and screamed out his name as she came apart, making his orgasm last even longer.

Her hips continued to slowly rock as they both tried to catch their breath. There was nothing between them anymore, everything was out in the open…they had nothing left to hide.

Piper spread across Mason's chest as he rubbed her back, still connected. Occasionally, he would kiss the top of her head as she nuzzled into him. He could sleep like this, no problem.

"I love you," he whispered, wondering if she was sleeping.

He found out his answer when she whispered back, "I love you, too." She leaned up, gave him a light kiss on the mouth and then rested her head back against his chest.

"I have another question for you," she said.

"Go for it."

"Best sex you've ever had."

"Well…there was this one girl, Margie…"

Piper sat up in disbelief as he laughed and stroked her face with his thumb.

"Baby, you know it's you. That shouldn't even be a question," he added quickly, before he ruined the moment between them.

"It better be," she said, as she gave him a little tweak to the nipple.

"Damn," he shouted, as he rubbed his nipple. "Payback is a bitch, babe. Just remember that when your naked nipples are hanging out for my death grip."

"Bring it, Dashel," she replied, as she moved her body back on top of his.

They settled into a comfortable silence as he rubbed her back and she stroked his chest. It was moments like this that made him forget about the long journey they took to get to this point, because nothing could beat the feeling of having Piper, naked, and in his arms.

CHAPTER EIGHTEEN

Jesse

Thanksgiving was in a couple of days, and Jesse's brother, sister-in-law, and niece were all coming to Denver for the holiday…and to meet Ashlin. Jesse could tell she was nervous about the upcoming meet and greet, but she tried to hide it. Their relationship felt pretty solid and comfortable, despite the fact that his girl was currently in some photo studio with his friend, Ryker, taking practically nude pictures together.

Apparently, C.C. Morris wanted to redo one of the lingerie combinations and, of course, they needed both Ashlin and Ryker present. It drove Jesse nuts to know that Ryker was going to be intimate with his girl, when Jesse hadn't even been that intimate with her.

Jesse was drinking a cup of coffee on his day off when his phone alerted him to an incoming text message. He grabbed his phone and saw that Ashlin had sent him a picture. When he opened it up on his phone, he nearly choked on his coffee as he tried to sit up and cough it out. Ashlin had sent him a picture of her in her barely-there purple bra that was tied with a bow at the center of her breasts, and her matching purple thong that looked like a piece of ribbon covering her. If C.C. Morris wanted her to sell sex, then holy shit, was she doing a good job.

All of a sudden, Ashlin's face appeared on his screen as his phone started to ring. He quickly answered it, as he tried to adjust himself in his pants.

"Hey."

"Did you get my picture?" she asked.

"Uh…yeah," he cleared his throat.

"And…"

"And, I don't know how I feel about this photo shoot. You look fucking hot, Ashlin."

He could hear her smile when she said, "Thank you."

"Seriously, how many people are going to be in that room with you? I don't want them seeing you like that."

A slight chuckle came through the line, making Jesse grow even harder. "You know that this picture will be posted all over magazines and websites, right?"

"Shit," Jesse said, as he ran his hand through his hair.

"Can I confess something to you?"

"Always," he said, as he tried to bring his attention back to the conversation, rather than the picture that was still running through his head.

"Well, Hannah is here, hanging out with Ryker; they actually have been in his dressing room for a while now, and it just made me think how nice it would be if you were here."

That wouldn't be awkward at all, Jesse thought, as he tried to figure out what to say.

"Jesse?"

"Yeah, I'm here. Do you want me to come down?"

"I do," she said shyly. "I know it sounds stupid, but it would be nice if you were down here…being here for me…and you do have the day off…"

"Text me the address, and I'll be there in a little bit."

She squealed with joy, told him she would text it right away, and then hung up. Jesse went to his bedroom after he got the text and changed into a pair of jeans, a black T-shirt, black leather jacket, and threw a black baseball hat on before he took off.

On the drive over to the studio, which wasn't that far away, Jesse thought about what he was getting himself into. He was only going to get irritated and angry at seeing Ryker's hands all over Ashlin, but then again, he couldn't say that to her now. She came to his games; he needed to support her in the same way.

When he got to the studio, he was immediately escorted back to the dressing rooms, where he saw Ryker's name on one door and Ashlin's on the other. He walked past the set, which was still being put together by the set designer, but from what Jesse could tell, it was a bed with lots of pillows in an intimate looking room. Fan-fucking-tastic.

He shook his head in disbelief that he was even there as he knocked on Ashlin's dressing room door.

"Come in," she called from inside.

Jesse walked in and saw her spread out on the cream couch that was in the room, wearing a short, black, silk robe, with her hand propping up her head as she watched TV. When she saw Jesse walk in, she shot up from the couch, and wrapped her body around his.

"You made it!" She kissed his lips with so much force that Jesse had to step back to catch his balance. His hat was knocked off from her jumping onto him. He laughed at the excitement coming off of her.

"Hey, gorgeous," he whispered in her ear, as he squeezed her close.

She dropped down and stood in front of him while holding on tight to her robe ties. Her hair was curled and falling over her shoulders, and her makeup was very minimal and natural. She looked stunning.

"Damn, Ashlin, you look good."

"Thank you." She bent down, picked up his hat, and placed it back on his head. "I'm so glad you're here."

"I can see that. It looks like they're still setting things up out there. When do you think you'll be done today?"

She shrugged her shoulders, grabbed his hand, and made him sit down on the couch with her. She sat him down first, and then straddled his lap so she was facing him. He adjusted himself and coughed as he tried to calm himself down; he was way too excited right now.

"We just need to fix this one shot we took, because apparently C.C. didn't like the angle. Once that's done, we're free to go. It shouldn't be too long. All that we're waiting on is the set now."

She settled on his lap, and even though he was trying to think of his grandmother and of the nastiest, hairiest man on his team, it didn't distract him from looking at the opening of Ashlin's robe, or from the fact that she was sitting perfectly on his lap. He could feel himself grow under her, and he just prayed she didn't notice.

"Where's Ryker?" Jesse asked, trying to change his thoughts to anything that didn't deal with Ashlin in a short robe.

"In his room with Hannah. Pretty sure they've done it at least five times already."

Jesse laughed as Ashlin wiggled again. This time her eyes widened, and then a smile spread across her face, making Jesse feel a blush creep up on his cheeks.

She pressed her hands on his cheeks and said, "Are you…blushing?"

"No," he said quickly.

"You are. Are you embarrassed?"

Adjusting his hat and avoiding eye contact, Jesse said, "Well, it's not the coolest thing to be sporting a boner in public."

"I would hardly say we're in public, and it makes me so hot thinking about the fact that you want me," she said, while leaning forward, making her robe fall open more and exposing her beautiful cleavage.

Considering how many creeps there were in the world, Jesse considered himself to be an upstanding man, one who didn't need to drop his pants the minute he got a boner, but having Ashlin sitting on top of him, practically wearing nothing, had him itching to tear her robe off, and he knew she knew because the dangerous look in her eyes told him so.

"So…did you uh, eat breakfast?" Jesse asked nervously, as Ashlin's robe slid off of one of her shoulders. He gulped and tried not to stare at her bronze skin.

"Really? Breakfast? That's what you want to talk about?"

"I'm trying to be good here, Ashlin. Don't make it any harder on me than it is." A smile spread across her face, as he quickly said, "No pun intended."

"Stop trying to be a gentleman. Do you know how bad I want you? How bad I've wanted you?"

He shook his head no, not being able to talk from the way her hands were running along his chest.

"It's been too long, Jesse."

"Too long for what?" he croaked out, as she undid her robe, showing off her toned body, ample cleavage, and bronze skin. She was too much for him to handle like this. He wanted her more than anything, and was about to just take what he wanted, because he was hard as a damn rock.

"Too long for you, and don't lie to me. I know it has. Let me take care of that for you."

She slid down his lap and kneeled in front of him on the floor. His legs felt numb; his body was useless as she started to undo his pants. He knew he needed to push her away, but his brain was detached from his limbs, making him incapable of moving. The only thing on his body that was currently moving was his dick, as it pressed against his pants.

"Ashlin…" Jesse said, as he tried to stop her, but it didn't; she only smiled and continued until his jeans were completely open. The only thing between Ashlin's lips and Jesse's cock was a thin piece of fabric.

Instead of taking him in her hands like he thought she would, she stood up in front of him, grabbed her phone and started playing some music, which turned out to be pretty seductive, given the fact that she was now dancing in front of him while moving her hands all over his body. Yup, he was going to go all teenage boy on her and lose everything before she even touched him.

Taking her hands down to his pants, she scooted his jeans down to his ankles, so she could see his erection in plain view. She stood back up and then reached up to the bow that was in between her breasts. In one swift pull, she undid the front, and her breasts fell out in front of him.

"Jesus," he muttered, as he took her all in. "No fucking tan lines."

She smiled and dropped the bra as she walked closer to him. She spread his legs slightly and then sat down on his lap as she thrust her chest out toward him.

"We'll be ready in ten minutes, someone knocked on the door."

Jesse's muscles stiffened at the interruption, which made him suddenly aware of where they were and what they were doing. He started to sit up and move away when Ashlin pinned him to the back of the couch.

"Don't even think about it, QB. You're mine."

"Ashlin, you have…"

She placed her finger over his mouth. "I'm well aware of my time line, and what I have planned for you will be over way before then. Now, do something with those hands and touch me."

His hands were at his sides, but lucky for him, he was able to connect back with his limbs and run them up the sides of Ashlin's body. Her skin was so soft, so smooth that he didn't want to move too fast, he wanted to revel in the feel of her. Her breath hitched as his fingers skimmed the bottom of her breasts.

"Don't tease me," she said, as she moved her hips on top of him.

"I don't want to do this here," Jesse admitted, as he took her in.

She blew out a heavy breath and rested her forehead on his. "I can't wait anymore, Jesse. I need to touch you, to be intimate with you."

"But, why now?" he asked, not moving the extra inch to

touch her breasts.

"I want you to know how much I want you."

Jesse sat back on the couch and placed his hands on her hips. "Is this because you have to do a photo shoot with Ryker today?" She was about to answer when he said, "Don't lie to me."

"Jesse…"

He shook his head and set her on the side of the couch as he grabbed his jeans and tossed her robe at her. She was only attacking him because she had to be intimate with Ryker today. He wanted to be with Ashlin just to be with her, not to prove a damn point.

As he buckled up his pants and adjusted himself, he saw Ashlin scramble to get her robe on from the corner of his eye.

"Jesse, stop," she called, as she grabbed his arm and stopped him from moving forward.

He spun around on her and said, "How come we can't just have a normal relationship? Why does everything have to be so damn difficult or a production? It should be easy…I like you, you like me, we talk about our pasts and learn about each other, and when it comes time to be intimate, we are in it for all the right reasons."

"I am in it for the right reasons," she said.

"No, you were just doing that because you know today is going to be difficult for me, so you wanted to ease my mind. I get that you had good intentions, but I don't need you sucking my dick off to prove to me that you like me. You can just tell me, Ashlin."

She ran her hand over her forehead as she said, "You're not normal! You're not like any other man I've ever dealt with. I don't know how to handle situations with you. I think I'm doing the right thing, but then you go and point out that I'm not. I can't win with you, Jesse."

"Well, stop trying to do the right thing, and just do what your heart wants. I want to know you, Ashlin, not the person you think you should be."

"I don't want to be myself; I don't care for that person that much."

"I fucking do!" Jesse shouted.

"You don't even know her," she shouted back. "You think you like me, you think you want to be with me? You don't know the first truth about me…what my life has been like."

"Because you won't fucking tell me!"

"Because you're too damn perfect." She started to pace. "I mean, damn it Jesse, what guy wants to get to know a girl first before he has sex? What guy goes out of his way to just court someone? What starting quarterback in the NFL has a body like yours and a heart as good as gold? It's impossible to measure up to you."

The admission coming from Ashlin shocked Jesse. He didn't know she felt that way. Didn't she know that, despite what she thought were her shortcomings, she was perfect? How could she not see that?

He stepped forward and grabbed her hand to pull her to his chest. "Listen carefully. I don't want you measuring anything when it comes to you and me. I want you to be yourself, because despite what you think, I know you, and I like everything about you. I don't go around dating people, Ashlin. I'm a picky bastard, and when I see what I like, I got for it. You're the perfect fit for me, in so many ways. I just wish you could see it."

"I don't have a very good self-image, hence all the makeup, hair, and Photoshopping."

"Stop. You're gorgeous, and do you know when I like you the best? When your hair is up, showing off your beautiful face and you're in a comfy shirt and a pair of sweats. You're so damn beautiful like that, that the mere thought of you sporting that style brings me to my knees."

"You're sweet," she said, while snuggling into his chest.

"I want you to know that I understand what your job entails. Do I like it? Hell no. I want to be the only man that ever touches you, but do I get it? Yes, I do, but that doesn't mean I have to like it." He kissed the top of her head and continued. "I don't want you ever to use sex as anything other than us connecting in the most intimate way. I don't need you to prove anything to me. If I didn't trust you, I wouldn't be with you. Okay?"

She nodded her head, stood on her toes, and kissed his chin. "Did we just have our first fight?" she asked.

"I think we did," he smiled down at her.

"You know what that means then, right?" she asked, while wiggling her eyebrows.

"What?"

"Make up sex."

"Wow, you're persistent."

"I am when I know what I want."

"Me too," he said, as he squeezed her ass, making her squeal.

"Five minutes, Ashlin," came someone from the hallway.

"Hmm…what can we do in five minutes?" Jesse asked as he rubbed her back with his hands.

"Make out?"

Jesse looked to the ceiling like he was really pondering it when she grabbed ahold of his head, pushed him against the door, climbed up his body, and started making out with him. To get better balance, he spun around and pushed her against the wall for better support.

"So good," she mumbled as their tongues met in the middle.

He had to agree…it was so good with her.

Hannah

"You're going to have to let go of me at some point," Hannah said, as they sat in a chair together, watching people make the final touches to the set. Assistants scrambled around them, trying to get everything ready for the shoot, while makeup artists tended to Ashlin, who was sitting close to them with Jesse at her side. Their hands were connected, just like Ryker's and hers, but where Ryker was attached like a moth to a flame on Hannah, Jesse was confident as he looked down at Ashlin.

"Yeah, but I don't have to just yet. Hey, maybe if I ask, you can take Ashlin's place. Now that would be hot."

"No way," Hannah replied quickly. Me in lingerie is only meant for your eyes."

Ryker pressed a kiss against her lips and said, "Do you know how fucking happy that makes me to hear you say that?"

"Language," Hannah reminded.

Ryker chuckled and said, "Sorry, but you bring it out in me when you say things like that."

"Are you blaming me for your crudeness?" Hannah teased.

"I am. You're too damn good; it's hard not to use swear words when you make me so happy. I just want to shout from the roof tops how amazing you are."

"You're just saying that…because of what we did in your dressing room," she blushed.

"Say it," Ryker poked her side, making her laugh and shake her head no. "Say it, Hannah."

She leaned over to his ear, brushed her lips against his lobe and said, "You're just saying that because we just had an hour of sex."

"Mmm…music to my ears," he leaned over and kissed her cheek softly.

"Alright, Ryker and Ashlin, we're ready."

"Duty calls," Ryker said as he got up, placed Hannah in the chair, and leaned over her so his hands were on the armrests, hovering over her. "Give me a kiss to tide me over."

Not being able to say no to him, she grabbed his cheeks, kissed him lightly on the lips, and then patted his cheek and sent him on his way before he could deepen it.

"You are getting away with murder, you know that? You can kiss way better than that."

She laughed and said, "When you're done, I'll give you what you want."

Ryker shook his head and pushed away from the chair as he muttered, "Ball buster."

Ashlin walked over to him and he put his arm around her shoulder as he said, "You ready for this, kid?"

"Just like old times," she responded, and they both laughed.

At that moment, all of Hannah's insecurities resurfaced, even though Ryker had just made love to every part of her body for an hour in his dressing room. A mere comment from Ashlin that they had a history pained Hannah because she was still trying to get to know Ryker; she didn't know him like Ashlin did.

From a distance, Hannah saw Ashlin drop her robe, showing pretty much her entire body...her magnificent body, and Ryker removed his, showing off his ripped physique and small boxer briefs. They stood next to each other as they talked to the director, while he described what he was looking for. There were a lot of hand movements from the director and a lot of nodding from Ryker and Ashlin. Occasionally, Hannah would hear words like, hot and sexy and she wondered if it was her selective hearing or if the director just kept saying those words over and over again.

Ryker clapped his hands and said something as they both headed to the bed.

A strong presence casted over her as she looked at Ryker, who was now positioning himself in the bed.

"It won't be very long," Jesse said from behind her.

Hannah looked up at him and replied, "It will be the longest couple of minutes of my life."

"There's nothing to worry about."

"I keep telling myself that..."

"But..." Jesse made her continue.

She blew out a heavy breath and said, "They just have so much history together. It's hard to just sit back and watch them practically have simulated sex in front of us."

"Then why did you come?" Jesse asked mater-of-factly, not even acknowledging that his girlfriend was practically naked in front of a bunch of people and currently straddling another man.

"Because he told me I could."

"And you were curious?" Jesse asked, as Ashlin threw her

head back, her hair floating around her shoulders. Camera flashes started erupting around them and the shoot was off.

"Maybe," Hannah confessed.

"Do you not trust him?"

Hannah looked at Jesse. He was normally a nice guy, but right now, she felt like he was being an ass, and she wondered if it was because he was showing his own insecurities, but in a different way. It was a tough positon to be in, as a significant other.

"I trust him, no doubt about that, but I'm just worried that…" Hannah trailed off as the director told Ryker to sit up more and press his lips against her neck, which he did automatically, making Hannah feel ill, because those lips were just all over her neck.

"What are you worried about?" Jesse pushed.

Ashlin's hands ran over Ryker's chest as Ryker's hands did the same to hers. He cupped Ashlin's breast, making her mouth drop open, giving the photographer the perfect shot.

"Hannah…"

She shook her head and looked at Jesse as she said, "I'm worried that he is going to be with Ashlin and then come back to me and finally realize that we are so different. He should be with a girl like Ashlin, a super model."

"Why's that?"

The director called out to Ryker and Ashlin, who stopped mid silent moan and then looked at each other. They shared a knowing smile, and then Ryker undid her bra, letting it fall to the side of her arm. He flipped her on her back, like it was something he did every day, and hovered over her. His arms flexed as they held up his body and his lips were attached to hers. Right in front of Hannah and Jesse, they were kissing.

Bile came to the edge of her mouth, threatening to come out, as Ashlin arched her back when Ryker's hand palmed her breast. The photographer cheered and started moving all around them, while clicking. Hannah didn't know how long they were in that position, but it was way too long for her liking.

She looked over at Jesse, who was done talking to Hannah, because his gaze was focused on the same thing she was seeing. Ryker was hovering over Ashlin, but there was a definite bulge happening, and Hannah knew Jesse wasn't happy about it from the tick in his jaw.

The director said something to Ashlin, which made her nod her head and laugh. Her foot came up to Ryker's waistband and her toes grabbed ahold of his boxers and pulled them down until a part of his butt crack was showing. She smiled up at Ryker, who smiled back, and then pressed his lips against her neck. Her eyes closed tightly shut as her back arched off the mattress again, but this time, her hips went right into Ryker's. The minute their hips met, Hannah noticed the flex of Ryker's back muscles, taking in the impact of having Ashlin wrapped around his waist.

All the telltale signs that Hannah knew were Ryker's "I'm excited" tells were coming out right in front of her, but instead of having them with her, he was sharing them with another woman. It slowly tore her heart apart as her body went numb and into fight or flight mode. The pain was almost too much; she couldn't take one more moment of this.

Instead of sticking around, which she knew she should have done, she got out of the chair she was sitting in, passed a seething Jesse, who was trying his best to be cool, but Hannah knew better, and went back to Ryker's dressing room. She could have waited for him there, but she needed to get away from that place. So, she grabbed her purse, called a cab, and took off to where she could think.

CHAPTER NINETEEN

Ryker

"Why the hell did you not stop her?" Ryker asked Jesse, as he drove his car from Hannah's apartment to his. The moment she left, he could feel her retreat away from them, but they had to finish the shoot; he didn't have a choice. He couldn't chase after her right away.

Once he was done groping Ashlin, he tore off of her and went to his dressing room. When he saw that all her things were gone, he got dressed quickly, tried calling her, and when she didn't pick up, he started driving to her place while calling everyone he knew, but no one knew where she was. Now he was on the phone with Jesse who had watched Hannah walk right out of the studio.

"Sorry, I was a little busy watching you have your hands all over my girlfriend, dickhead." Ryker could hear Ashlin in the background, trying to calm Jesse down.

Yes, they had to touch each other; they had to do things that should really only be happening between a committed couple, but that was what they were signed up for. When they first signed the contracts with C.C. Morris, they were both single, so there was no harm in what they were doing; it was just awkward. But now that both he and Ashlin were with other people, it made the situation significantly more awkward and uncomfortable. They were both done with C.C. Morris after this shoot, because they didn't feel comfortable doing the same kind of work when they both had someone so important in their lives.

"It was a job," Ryker gritted out.

"Whatever," Jesse hung up the phone, acting completely out of character. He couldn't blame the man, though, because if he ever saw Hannah making out with someone else while they played with her breasts, he would see red. Ryker was surprised he was able to get out of the studio unharmed.

He continued his search, but after two hours of driving around, he gave up and went back to her place, where he expected her to show up. Luckily, he had a key and let himself in to wait for her.

He sat on her couch and took in her surroundings. Her place was so comfortable, so homey. She had throw pillows, afghans, pictures…everything that made a house a home. On the side table, there was a picture frame and it was the two of them at Jesse's house. They were both holding cups of hot chocolate with Ryker's arm around Hannah's shoulder, pulling her in closer. Her head was tilted into his shoulder and they both had giant smiles on their faces. Ryker was right about the first assessment he made when he first saw Hannah, she was going to be his wife one day, no doubt about it. She was everything he needed.

The day turned into night as Ryker lay on Hannah's couch, clutching the picture. It wasn't until Hannah walked into her apartment at midnight that Ryker looked at the time and saw that it was so late. He sat up automatically and forced his eyes to adjust to the light Hannah had just turned on.

"Where the fuck have you been?" Ryker swore, not even caring about what he said.

Hannah's hand flew to her heart as she screamed from being startled.

"Ryker, what are you doing here?" she breathed heavily.

"Looking for my girlfriend who walked out on me."

"I didn't walk out on you," she said, as she set her purse down on the side table. "I just couldn't watch anymore."

"Nothing happened," Ryker said between clenched teeth.

"Don't, Ryker. I don't want to relive it. I know what I saw."

"And what exactly did you see?" Ryker stepped forward, feeling heat and anger burst through his veins.

"I saw you groping another woman, touching and kissing her like you kiss me," Hannah's voice caught on a cry. "You were…excited, Ryker," she continued softly, as a tear slipped down her cheek.

"It's called acting, Hannah."

"You're a football player, Ryker, not an actor. Plus, I'm pretty sure you can't act out the kind of excitement you were having."

Ryker ran his hand over his face. "Hannah, it was acting, and I'm sorry that I sported a minor boner while I was picturing my girlfriend as I had to be on top of another woman."

"Don't give me that excuse. You were not picturing me…"

"The hell I wasn't," Ryker shouted. "You can ask Ashlin…before we got on set, we both told each other we'd be picturing someone else to get through our last shoot. It's so beyond awkward being with her that picturing you with me made it so much easier to get through. Why don't you trust me?"

"I do trust you," she shouted back. "I just know I'm not good enough, okay?"

Ryker stepped back from the force in her voice. He had never seen Hannah liked this, with fire in her eyes.

"Who's to decide who is good enough for me?"

"I…"

"No, Hannah. That's my job. I get to decide who's good enough for me, and I choose you because you are, by far, superior to me, but I love to aim high, I always have." She went to respond, but he stopped her as he grabbed her hands and pulled her down on the couch. "I'm so sick of you putting yourself down and being insecure. Where is that girl I first met?"

"She's gone," Hannah said, as she lowered her head and tears fell from her eyes.

"Why?"

"Because," she cried. "Because I wasn't good enough for Todd; I was only good enough to be the other woman. He spent his life with someone else and only used me when it was convenient for him."

Realization hit Ryker that she was still reeling from what Todd did to her. He knew it was hard on her, but for some reason, he thought that she had gotten right over it, probably because Ryker thought Todd was a total douche burger.

Wanting to comfort her, he lifted her chin so she was looking at him. Tears filled her ice blue eyes as she searched his face for what he was going to say. His palm pressed against her cheek as his thumb rubbed away her tears.

"Hannah, I'm sorry about what happened to you with Todd. You never deserved to be treated like that, but I'm going to be honest, I'm not that sorry." Confusion crossed Hannah's face as he continued. "I'm not that sorry, because it gave me the chance to finally be with you."

She shook her head. "It's too hard, Ryker. Seeing you with Ashlin; it's just too much."

"Listen, that was the last time…ever. You won't have to see that anymore. From now on, I belong solely to you and you alone, boo."

She nodded her head as she wiped her tears away.

"I want to be strong for you, Ryker. I want to be the girl that you need. It's just going to take some time for me to get past all my insecurities. Todd really hurt me, but I want to get over this…"

Ryker's heart was beating fast as he listened to Hannah. Something possessed him in a matter of seconds, because he found himself cradling Hannah into his chest and asking her a question he had never asked before.

"Move in with me," he stated.

A gasp escaped Hannah's lips as she looked up at him with big eyes.

"What?"

"Move in with me," he repeated. "Be with me, Hannah. I've waited a while to have you in my arms, and now that I do, I don't want you to be anywhere else. Move in with me."

Her face was priceless as she tried to figure out if he was serious. Her lips parted slightly and her breath hitched as she tried to figure out what to say, and her eyes glistened.

"You're serious."

"So fucking serious."

"Ryker…"

Laughing, he said, "Just answer the question."

"It's so soon."

"It's not," Ryker replied. "Hannah, can't you see the connection we have? We're meant for each other." He paused for a second before he took a deep breath and said, "I love you, Hannah. More than anything. From the moment I first saw you at the bar, I knew you were it for me. Please, move in with me."

That did it, tears started running down her face that Ryker tried to catch with his thumbs.

"I love you too, Ryker."

Warmth spread through Ryker's body as he held on to his girl and listened to the words that came out of her mouth…words that he never thought would affect him, but they did…they turned him into a crumbling mess.

Wanting to be closer to her, he grabbed her face and pressed his lips against hers. She met the stroke of his lips with hers, and when her tongue entered his mouth, he lost it. He pulled her down so she was lying on the couch and he was on top of her. Her little body fit perfectly under his, making him realize that this was it…this was all that he needed in life; all he needed was Hannah.

He kissed up her neck and made his way to her mouth. Before he kissed her lips, he stared into her eyes and asked again, "Will you move in with me, boo?"

A smile spread across her face as she nodded her head and said, "Yes, I would love to."

She didn't get a chance to say anything else, because his lips were covering hers in seconds. His hand glided under her shirt, making her let out a little moan of pleasure.

"Ahh, you're killing me, boo," Ryker mumbled.

"Take me to the bedroom, Ryker."

Not having to be asked twice, he bounced off the couch, grabbed Hannah by the waist, threw her over his shoulder, and sprinted to the bedroom, making her laugh the most delicious laugh he had ever heard.

Ashlin

Thanksgiving rolled around, and not only was Ashlin feeling awkward about being at Jesse's family Thanksgiving, which was just his brother and his family, but Jesse had been very cold toward her ever since the photo shoot with Ryker. He wasn't being rude or avoiding her, but the way he interacted with her, the lack of touching on his part, was noticeable. When she asked him if everything was alright, he always said yes, but as she sat in the kitchen and watched Jesse prepare food all morning, she knew he wasn't being himself.

"Ouch," Johnny said, as he shook out his hand. "Dude, you don't have to slap me, I was just taste testing. I don't want you serving up shitty potatoes."

Jenny sidled up next to Johnny and placed a kiss on his hand before saying, "Baby, if your daughter picks up on that potty mouth of yours, your hand is not the only thing that is going to be hurting."

"Is that right?" he wiggled his eyebrows.

"Ugh, men," Jenny threw her hands up in the air and turned to Ashlin. "Please tell me you got the better end of the deal when it comes to the Rutledge brothers."

Ashlin peeked a glance at Jesse, who was busy carving the turkey and avoiding eye contact with her, making her stomach sink to the ground. She didn't like the idea of Jesse being upset with her;

it was slowly eating away at her.

"Well, I don't know Johnny very well, but from the way he just cried like a little girl, I'd say I did get the better end of the deal," Ashlin winked, trying to joke around so she could fit in.

Both Johnny and Jenny stared at her for a second before laughing hysterically. Jenny poked Johnny in the side and teased him, as Johnny told Jesse not to let Ashlin go.

"Mommy!! I got the bwue cwayon on my dwess," Daisy called out, as she came running into the kitchen holding up her dress so everyone could see her underwear underneath. Ashlin laughed to herself, as Jenny told her ladies don't hold their dresses up like that.

"Tide stick?" Jenny asked Jesse.

"In the laundry room," Jesse's voice rang out, making Ashlin feel week in the knees. She missed his voice; he wasn't much of a talker lately, and it was almost warming to hear him speak. He looked up at Johnny and said, "Set the table for me?"

Johnny nodded his head, grabbed all the items he needed, and went into the dining room.

Watching Jesse in the kitchen was such a turn on. The man knew how to cook and entertain, while looking sexy as hell, with his fitted grey jeans and forest green sweater that was practically painted on him. His sleeves were pushed up, showing off his tattooed forearms, and if she watched closely, she could see the outline of his abs through the sweater. All she wanted to do was take him upstairs and finally have him the way she wanted, but with the way he had been so quiet, she didn't think that was the best idea.

"Do you need any help?" she asked shyly, waiting for him to turn her down.

"I'm good; you can go in the other room," Jesse replied, without looking up at her. His forearms flexed as he continued to cut the turkey and place it on a plate.

Ashlin's throat started to get tight from the way Jesse was being so standoffish. The holiday was rough on her as it was, because when she was young, her family either didn't celebrate the holiday or they fought the entire time. The cold façade Jesse was putting on toward her was a deep reminder of what she went through as a child. Instead of pushing it, she excused herself and went to the bathroom upstairs to gather herself.

With a pounding heart and an aching chest, she sat down on the closed toilet and tried to catch her breath as sour feelings ran through her body. Her dad's face kept popping up in her head, visions of him reprimanding her mom with not only his words, but his fists, flashed through her eyes. Mashed potatoes sliding down the wall, broken glass all over the floor, and spoiled food that was thrown on the floor after her dad threw the table upside down ran through her mind as she gripped onto the sides of the toilet, trying to steady herself. She hadn't had flashbacks in a while, but the combination of seeing Jesse's family together and the cold looks she had been receiving from Jesse the past couple of days was throwing her for a loop.

There was a light knocking on the door, which brought her out of her thoughts as she realized she must have been in the bathroom for a long time for someone to come check on her; but she wasn't sure how long she was there, because she was lost in her past.

"Ashlin, are you in there?" Jesse's voice called out.

Not being able to answer from her throat being too tight from not crying, she just kept silent as she put her head in her hands.

There was another knock at the door, this time a little more forceful. "Ashlin, I'm coming in." He didn't give her a chance to reply before he barged in and filled the bathroom with his muscular frame. He looked so delicious, and the concerned look in his face did her in. She broke down, right there in the guest bathroom, on Thanksgiving.

Jesse was at her side in seconds, sitting on the tub next to her and grabbing her hands.

"What's wrong?"

She choked on a sob as she tried to reply, but she couldn't get out the words.

"Ashlin, you're scaring me. Is everything alright?" She shook her head no, as tears ran down her face. "Why? What's going on?"

"You," she squeaked out.

"Me what?"

"You're….you're mad at me," she cried into her hands.

She heard Jesse exhale next to her, and then he sat down on the floor as he grabbed her and put her on his lap.

"I'm not mad at you," he said, while trying to get her to look at him.

"Yes, you are, and don't lie to me. You've barely touched me since the photo shoot, and whenever you look at me, you have this look in your eye as if you're disgusted with me."

"I'm not disgusted with you…" he paused.

"Yes, you are," Ashlin said, as she tried to get up, but he wouldn't let her. "Let go of me," she said, rather sternly.

"Stop," Jesse scolded, trying to still her. "Just give me a second."

"What do you need a second for, Jesse? Are you trying to figure out the best way to get rid of me while sparing my feelings? Just respect me enough to say it without sugar coating it."

The room filled with an unpalatable tension as Jesse pinched his nose, trying to figure out what to say.

"I don't want to break up with you," he said evenly. "I'm just having a hard time dealing with everything."

"What's everything?" she asked, as she finally gave in and looked him in the eyes. At that moment, she saw pain, but she didn't understand. Was he really that hurt from the photo shoot?

"I don't think this is the time to get into this. My family is downstairs waiting to eat."

"Oh," she replied, as she wiggled to get up. "Well, that's fine. I'm just going to head home."

Standing up as well, Jesse said, "Don't be like that, Ashlin. Come have Thanksgiving with us."

Have Thanksgiving with them? Was he crazy? She could barely talk she was so upset, how was she supposed to stuff her face?

Shaking her head no, she stepped away from him and said, "Thanks for the invite, Jesse, but honestly, I can't even think about eating right now. My stomach is twisted in knots; anything I eat will just not settle well, if I eat anything at all."

"You're not just going to leave," he said, while grabbing her arm.

The action was nothing harmful, nothing rough, just concern to reach out to her, but her mind played it as something else as a weak cry escaped her lips, and she yelled at him, "Don't touch me!"

Quickly pulling away, Jesse pulled his hands off of her and looked at her with total confusion crossing his face.

"Ashlin, what the hell? Did I hurt you?"

"No," she said, as she opened the door and went down the hallway toward the stairs. She had to get out of his house before she lost it. Luckily, the dining room was on the other end of the house, away from the entryway. She flew down the stairs, Jesse trailing behind her, grabbed her purse and jacket, and went out the front door. Thankfully, her car wasn't blocked by Johnny and Jenny, since they'd been staying with Jesse for the past couple of days.

When she got to her car, she opened the door quickly, but it was shut automatically as Jesse hovered over her.

"Will you please stop? I don't want to keep chasing you around."

"Then don't," she replied, as she tried to pull at the door. But Jesse was too strong for her, and she couldn't make the door budge, which only threw her into another round of tears as she sank to the ground.

"Ashlin," Jesse said, as he squatted in front of her. "For the love of God, what is going on with you?"

"You are," she said, as she wiped her eyes. "You're so cold toward me; you're treating me like someone you don't even know. It's killing me, Jesse, because last thing I knew, you were fine with me doing my job, but I guess I've come to find out that you can't handle it. You can't fucking handle it."

"You're right," he shouted. "I can't handle it. I can't handle seeing you touched by someone else, kissed by someone else, and aroused by someone else. That photo shoot totally destroyed me! I'm not mad at you, I'm just…frustrated."

"At me."

"No, I'm frustrated at myself," he shouted back, as his chest heaved from the level of heat running between them. "I'm fucking livid at myself for waiting so long."

Ashlin's head perked up from his words. "Waiting for so long for what?"

Jesse buried his head in his hands as he rubbed his face. "For fucking you."

Well, she thought he was going to say something like that, but she wasn't expecting to hear such pain in his voice when he said it.

"Then why did you wait?"

"Because I still don't know you. You're still a giant question mark to me. I don't know anything about your family…"

"That's because you don't need to," she interrupted him.

"Yes, I fucking do," he replied, eyes blazing now. "I fucking deserve to know you if we're going to make this work."

"You don't want to know me, Jesse. I'm not like the perfect little family you have waiting in the house for you. I'm fucked up."

"Who isn't?" he replied.

"Oh, really? You think you're fucked up? Did your dad beat your mom almost every night until, one night, he finally killed her? Is that what happened to you?" Jesse's mouth was agape as she spoke to him. "That's what I thought. We grew up in two different worlds, Jesse. My world was full of trailer trash drug addicts who would rather beat their wife for a fix than support their family. That is not the kind of girl you need or deserve. I told you I was bad news, and now you finally know why."

Without giving him a chance to respond, she opened her door, slammed it shut and locked the doors, and took off out of his driveway. As she looked in her rearview mirror, she saw Jesse still standing in the driveway, not even looking at her, but looking down at the ground, as if he couldn't believe what she'd just said. She didn't blame him; she was one fucked up girl with a car full of baggage that was almost impossible for someone to deal with. He was better off without her. If only he could have realized that before she became accustomed to having him around, to welcoming him into her heart and stealing her breath away.

Piper

"Are you doing alright, babe?" Mason asked as he walked in behind Piper who was bringing dishes in from the dining room table. They'd just finished eating Thanksgiving dinner with Mason's parents, and even though they were the nicest people she had ever met, she was feeling a little overwhelmed by how nice they really were. The whole family atmosphere was almost too much for her to handle.

"Yeah," she breathed out, as she turned to find Mason staring at her with concern lacing his eyes. But that wasn't what caught her breath…it was the man in general. If his parents weren't with them, she would have had Mason on top of the counter, and she would have been riding him like a banshee. He was wearing a pair of well-worn jeans that cupped his ass perfectly, a navy blue long-sleeved shirt, and his scruff was a little longer than normal…making him look dark and dangerous. Piper's lower half squealed in appreciation.

"Did I tell you how beautiful you look today?" he asked, as he played with the purple wrap dress she had on. She felt fancy, but compared to Mason's mom, who was sporting her pearls and heels, Piper looked like a commoner.

"Only a few times," she answered, as she allowed Mason to pull her into his arms.

Pressing a kiss to her forehead, he said, "You seem mellow. Is everything okay?"

"Yeah, your family is just so…loving."

Her confession made Mason chuckle. "What did you expect? Should we be biting each other's heads off?"

She laughed and said, "No, it's just a different atmosphere for me. Hard to get used to, you know?"

"I get it," he said, as he played with one of her curls. "They like you a lot. My mom was just telling me how pretty you are."

"Was she?"

"Yeah, she was saying that I should really just take you back to our bedroom and have sex with you."

"She did not!" Piper said, while playfully hitting his chest.

He shrugged his shoulders and said, "Worth a try."

"Is my son being inappropriate again?" Mason's mom asked, as she brought in some dishes to be cleaned off.

"I'm afraid so, Mrs. Dashel," Piper said, as Mason squeezed her side at her confession, making her jump in place.

"Traitor," he whispered in her ear, making her arm hairs stand on end. He did that to her with just his voice; he made everything stand at attention from the brush of his scruff to the deep whisper of his voice.

"It's true," she whispered back, as she placed a light kiss on his cheek. She wanted to do more, a lot more, but there were prying eyes in the room.

"You two are adorable," Mrs. Dashel said, as she started the water in the sink.

Feeling embarrassed by the thoughts that were running through her head while Mason's mom was in the room, she turned toward the living room and said, "I'm going to get the last of the dishes."

She walked into the dining room and saw Mr. Dashel with his hand on his flat stomach, a glass of water to his mouth, and a content look on his face. Mason definitely got his looks from his dad; his mom was beautiful, but his dad was ruggedly handsome with a light spray of grey at his temples and laugh lines caressing his eyes. He was built just like Mason, but there was a little extra fluff on him…but not much, because the man still had a body, just not one like Mason's.

"Dinner was fantastic, sweetheart." The term of endearment was sweet; it was something her dad had never called her, so to hear a father figure speak to her with such affection was comforting and odd at the same time.

"Thank you, Mr. Dashel. I was happy to help Mrs. Dashel in the kitchen. She is quite a lovely woman." As the words escaped her mouth, she felt like she was having an out of body experience. Was she really speaking pleasantries with her boyfriend's parents, while wearing a dress that was made for meeting the parents? This was so not her, but she didn't care because she was changing; she was changing for the better.

"You need help, babe?" Mason asked, as he crutched up next to her.

With one eyebrow in question, she looked at him as if he was crazy. "And how do you expect to help?" Feigned innocence crossed Mason's face as he tried to figure out what to say, but Piper wasn't stupid. "Just go watch football; nice try, though, with the offer of help."

With a quick kiss to her cheek and a fist pump to his dad, both of the men were off to the living room while talking about the games that were playing today. She shook her head, grabbed the last of the dishes, and took them into the kitchen where Mason's mom had already made a dent in cleaning them.

"Wow, you're fast," Piper said, as she grabbed some Tupperware for the leftovers.

"Not my first time, and honestly, I think this is the smallest Thanksgiving I've ever been to. It's been nice, just spending time with Mason and getting to know you."

"I've had a nice time too," Piper admitted, even though she felt awkward around Mason's parents.

The water turned off as Mrs. Dashel grabbed a towel that was hanging off of the stove handle and started wiping her hands. "I want to thank you for taking care of Mason while we were on vacation. I'm glad he had someone he could count on."

Piper waved it off as if it was nothing, because honestly, she was grateful Mason's parents were on vacation. If they hadn't been, Piper might not have ever had the opportunity to be with Mason again.

"It was no problem at all."

"I know you two weren't together when you offered," Mrs. Dashel said with sensitivity.

Well, Piper wasn't prepared for an awkward conversation, but apparently Mrs. Dashel was.

"Doesn't matter now," Piper said, trying to dismiss the topic that was now gnawing at her stomach. "You have to give me the recipe for those sweet potatoes; they were so good."

Yes, it was a lame attempt at changing the subject, but she couldn't think of anything else to say.

"He was pretty hurt after Brooke broke off their engagement," Mrs. Dashel continued.

There went Piper's attempt to change the subject right out the window. Strapping on her big girl pants, Piper turned to face Mrs. Dashel and prepared herself to have a conversation that seemed less appealing than swallowing a jar full of razor blades.

Mrs. Dashel continued, "After Brooke left, there was something dark that took over my Mason. He barely talked to us, we never saw him, and deep down I could see that he was hurting, dying to talk to someone, but the stubborn ass wouldn't let anyone in…until you."

"What do you mean?" Piper asked, as her breathing started to pick up.

"A couple of months ago, Mason called us to tell us about this redhead that had taken control of his life. He told us all about her quick wit and sassy sense of humor. He, of course, told his dad about her, how did he put it? I think it was, 'kick ass body'." Piper chuckled to herself, hearing Mason's mom swear. "He sounded alive again; he sounded like my goofy, fun-loving Mason again, and I couldn't have been happier…" Mrs. Dashel's voice silenced, and Piper knew what was coming next. She liked Mrs. Dashel a lot, and the fact that she knew Piper hurt her son, killed Piper. She hated the fact that Mrs. Dashel had a tainted view of her, but then again, she'd brought it upon herself.

"Well, you know what happened next," Mrs. Dashel said honestly, as she turned toward the sink and started washing dishes again.

Awkward was not even close to what Piper was feeling. What the hell was she supposed to say? Sorry that I was a complete whore bag and screwed over your perfect son? That didn't seem fitting. So, she just settled with a simple apology.

"I'm sorry, Mrs. Dashel."

"What happened is between you and my son, but when he's around you now, he lights up. His eyes are full of love, and I will tell you this, as a mother, that is one of the most amazing things to see in your child…to see love pouring out of them. Not every relationship is perfect; you're bound to have your ups and downs, but as long as you are able to fight, to hold on when things get tough, then you'll be just fine." She turned and looked Piper in the eyes. "Mason is worth fighting for."

Piper couldn't agree more. Mrs. Dashel nailed it on the head. Mason was worth fighting for.

They spent the rest of the time in the kitchen, cleaning in silence as Mrs. Dashel let her words sink in. When they joined the boys back in the living room, they all watched football, listened to Mason and his dad yell at the TV, and enjoyed some pie. It was one of the best Thanksgivings Piper had ever had, even including the awkward conversation in the kitchen.

That evening, once Mason's parents had gone to bed and she and Mason were lying in their bed, together, holding hands, Piper finally let out the long breath that she'd been holding in. She'd made it through her first holiday with Mason's parents, and for the most part, it was successful.

With a gentle gesture, Mason leaned in and placed a kiss on her lips. "Thank you for making dinner with my mom. She said she had a great time getting to know you."

"I had a nice time too," Piper admitted. "I like your parents, and I would be lying if I said your dad wasn't hot."

A shocked look crossed Mason's face as he took in what Piper said.

"You think my dad is hot?" His nose scrunched as he asked his question.

Nodding, she replied, "Hell yeah. Makes me think, why should I be with you when I could have the original?" A teasing smile crossed her face.

Playfully squeezing her side, Mason said, "Maybe because I have a dick that makes your pussy weep."

"You got that right," she said, as she traced his tattoos. The man was a god with his bare chest, sleeve tattoos that told a story, and his well-defined muscles. Even with being out of commission for a while, he was still able to keep up his physique; the man was not normal.

Her hand traveled from his tattooed chest down to his navel, where she dipped her fingers just below his waistband, all the while looking him dead in his eyes.

"Trying to get yourself in trouble?" he asked in a husky tone.

"Maybe."

His hand trailed up and under her shirt, landing right on her bare breast. A little hiss escaped her lips as he pulled on her nipple.

"Mason…"

"Does that feel good?"

"You know it does," she whispered, as she could feel herself start to get lost in his touch.

As he stroked her nipple, her fingers fell below his waistline and made contact with the tip of his cock that was already erect and ready to go. His body jumped from the contact, making her giggle.

"Do you think that's funny?" he asked, as he shifted his body on top of hers, trying to be careful with his knee.

"No, not at all," she answered, as his lips ran up and down her neck.

His lips found hers and his head lowered even further so they could deepen their kiss. Her hands wrapped around his neck as they continued to torture each other with their lips. Sometimes in their frantic rush to get naked, Piper forgot to revel in the feeling and emotions a simple make out session could deliver. Mrs. Dashel was right, as Mason kissed her back with the same forcefulness she was kissing him with, she felt the love pouring out of Mason. It was hard to miss. The way he cupped her face, pressed his body against hers, and cooed in her ear, she knew she'd found her soul mate, the person she was supposed to be with for the rest of her life. The person worth fighting for.

Pulling away for a second, she cupped his face and looked into his eyes. "I love you, Mason."

A small smile crossed his gorgeous lips as he looked back down at her and said, "I love you too, Piper."

Even though they told each other they loved one another often, the words never grew old, especially coming from him.

They had been through a lot, but Mrs. Dashel was right; they were perfect for each other, and even though they'd had a rough start, they were going to have a smooth finish, Piper was determined to do so.

CHAPTER TWENTY

Ryker

"I can't believe you do this every year," Hannah said, as she tailed behind Ryker, dragging ass.

"Why wouldn't I?" Ryker asked, as he hurried up to get in line.

"Because you have to wake up at some God-awful hour, and the lines are ridiculous. There's a lot of pushing," she whined.

"Boo, have you forgotten my profession? A crazy, foaming at the mouth, stay at home mom with the need to get thirty percent off on a blender is not going to deter me."

Hannah leaned in to his ear as she looked around and said, "But they're crazy."

"It's all part of the fun. Plus, once you look at your receipt and see all the savings you got, you'll feel elated and re-energized."

"But you have money, lots of it," Hannah pointed out.

"Yeah, but might as well save it while we can. Plus, don't you want to make my apartment a place where we both can stay? Don't you want to make it our own?"

"I do," Hannah responded, as the doors opened to the retail store and women started screaming and pushing. "But I don't want to get killed while doing it."

"Don't worry, boo, you're with me. I won't let anything happen to you. Here, let's grab a cart." As Ryker reached for a cart, a lady came up from behind him, swatted his hand and hissed at him, literally hissed, making Hannah squeal and tuck her head into his shoulder.

"Shit, lady, it's a fucking cart, not a damn blue light special."

"Fuck off," she called over her shoulder, as she sprinted toward the back where all the major electronics were.

"Well, she was rude," Ryker responded, as he grabbed a cart, this time making sure to look over his shoulder for any hissing lady folk.

"She was terrifying," Hannah said, as they started walking through the store, watching dignified women lose their minds over half-priced items.

"She did have crazy in her eyes. We'll steer clear of her in case she decides to come after you," Ryker teased, as he kissed the side of her neck. Ryker positioned Hannah so she was in front of him and his arms were wrapped around her pushing the cart. She smelled like heaven, and honestly, he would do anything just to be close to her. He was well on his way to being totally pussy-whipped, but he didn't care, he had the love of his life wrapped in his arms and they were shopping for items for their place together.

A gasp came out of Hannah's lips as she pointed to a scuffle in the corner. "Oh, my God, it's the hisser, and she's fighting over a TV with some poor woman."

Ryker turned his attention to the corner where Hannah was pointing, and she was right. The hisser was hissing like a lunatic while yelling at another lady that she'd gotten to the TV first.

Laughing, Ryker said, "See, boo, and you could have missed all of this."

"Yeah, good thing I came out to watch people lose all of their self-respect," she said sarcastically.

The aisles were filled with frantic women, searching high and low for the sales they'd marked in their ads, and screaming at salespeople, trying to find out where the robotic ninja was located.

Must be the toy of the season.

Black Friday was something he got into one year when he wanted to see what the big deal was. After one year of marking off sales, finding out the times when each store opened, and making a plan of attack, Ryker was hooked. Every year, he went out and enjoyed the sights and sounds of ravenous women clawing their way through the stores to get a present for someone at an extreme discount. The first year he went, he bought items for his family, but the second year he went, he bought toys for kids who wouldn't be having a Christmas because their parents were down on their luck, or the kids just didn't have parents at all. This year, he would be doing the same, but Hannah didn't know that.

"Uh, linens are over there," Hannah said, while pointing behind them. As she looked forward, she noticed they were headed right for the tornado zone. "Ryker, why are we going toward the aisles where we'll be eaten alive?"

Chuckling, Ryker said, "I got you, boo. I just have to pick up some toys."

"Toys? For who? Do you have some kids I don't know about?"

"Actually, I do," Ryker said, while filing into the Lego section.

"What?!" Hannah spun around with eyes wide and a hurt look on her face.

Smiling, Ryker placed a kiss on the tip of her nose and said, "Every year, I sponsor at least five families who can't give their kids the Christmases they deserve. Every kid deserves to open a present on Christmas day."

Watching intently, Ryker saw Hannah's face soften and her tears well up. "Oh, my God, Ryker, you're so sweet."

He shrugged his shoulders, pulled out a list from his back pocket, and said, "Here's what we need to get, and then we can head over to the linens. Does that work for you?"

She took the list in her hand and said, "I get to pick out the Barbies!"

"They're all yours, boo." A giant grin spread across her face as she kissed him on the lips. "God damn, you're adorable," he said, while pulling her into a hug.

"Move it!" a lady called out as she bumped her cart into theirs. It was the hisser, and this time, she had the TV in her cart and her hair was pulled out of her ponytail on one side. Hannah was right, she was terrifying.

"You don't have to be rude," Hannah spat back, while clutching onto Ryker a little tighter as a shield.

The lady spun around and said, "If your husband had a tongue like a damn paddle board, and he refused to use it on your pussy until he got a flat screen, you'd be rude too. Now, if you don't mind, I have some board games to purchase for five dollars each." With that, she took off, leaving Ryker and Hannah to think about what she'd just said.

They looked at each other, and at the same time, burst out in laugher.

"Oh, my God," Hannah said, as her hand went over her mouth. "Did she just say that?"

"I think so," Ryker replied, as he looked after the lady. "Paddle board, huh? Does that seem appealing to you?"

Hannah blushed as she thought about it. He poked her in the side as he wrapped her in closer to his chest and whispered into her ear. "Apparently, I'm going to have to show you the wonder tricks I can do with my tongue when we get back to our place."

She smiled up at him and repeated, "Our place."

"That's right, boo. Our place."

They spent the next hour in the toy section, gathering everything needed, and actually had to grab an extra cart. Hannah had a wonderful time picking out all different kinds of Barbies, as Ryker flocked toward the Legos and bought the biggest sets he could find. Hannah also put a girl's set of Legos in the cart, as well, stating, "Girls can play with Legos too."

After they were fully stocked in the toy section, they went over to the home section and started looking at bed linens. Ryker could care less what was on the bed. As long as it was soft and easily washable, he didn't care what they slept on, but he knew he needed to add a touch of Hannah to his place, so he let her pick out what she wanted.

"Oh, look at this one, it's so pretty," Hannah cooed, as she held up a white quilt with pink flowers. Inwardly cringing, Ryker nodded and smiled, telling himself that this was for Hannah. The pink and white quilt was a stark contrast to his black comforter back home, but if it made her happy, he didn't care.

A half hour later, there were pink and white sheets and accents piled up in their carts, as well as the quilt and matching shams. Yup, he was losing his man card today, but the look on Hannah's face made it all worth it. He would do anything to see that bright smile and glow radiating off of her.

"You really like them, right?" she asked, as she practically bounced up and down toward the checkout counter.

"Love them, boo. And they pass the comfort test, which is the most important thing." Surprisingly, they did; they were almost too soft, as if the manufacturer was trying to pull a fast one on men. They knew what they were doing…draw women in with the daintiness of the fabric, and suck the men in with the comfort. Evil bastards.

"Yay," I can't wait to show Piper. Maybe we can paint the walls a blush color."

"Blush? Is that a fancy word for pink?"

"Light pink," she answered, as she started piling things on the conveyor belt.

Ryker stopped her and said, "Boo, I love you, but I don't think I can do pink walls. You have to let me have some kind of manliness in the room."

She thought about it for a second as she cocked her lips to the side and then poked Ryker in the chest. "We can keep the walls grey; that's a manly color, and it will look precious with the new quilt."

Rolling his eyes, Ryker said, "If the wall color is going to be the manly part of the room, can we refrain from calling it precious?"

Laughing, Hannah flexed her arms and said, "Fine, the color will be so macho against the quilt. The perfect match. Flowers and muscles."

"Just like us, boo."

Hannah squeezed his bicep and said, "Maybe, but you might want to hit the gym."

"You crush me," Ryker said, as he gripped his heart.

They spent the rest of the day unloading the presents in their home, wrapping them up, and setting them to the side for delivery. Ryker had never enjoyed a day more in his life. If he had to be thankful for something, it would be for Todd the fuck up, because without him, Ryker never would have had a chance at claiming Hannah as his.

Jax

Jax sat in his apartment, alone, going over film for this Sunday's game. He missed Brooke like hell ever since she'd gone back to San Diego for the holiday, but he was able to get some work done. They decided to spend the holiday apart, because they weren't quite ready to display their relationship to the public yet. Given Jax's status and Brooke, who was starting to become a rising celebrity in Denver, they thought it would be best to keep everything on the down low until they were fully prepared.

That being said, Jax spent his Thanksgiving volunteering at a homeless shelter downtown, while Brooke went back home to see mommy and daddy dearest. They weren't really able to talk on the phone, given the busy schedule Brooke's mom had for Brooke, visiting family and going shopping. She did text him at one point, a picture of multiple lingerie items that gave him many ideas of what he was going to do to her when she got home.

The thought that Brooke, Mason's Brooke, was the one who brought light back into Jax's life was almost mind-boggling. He remembered seeing Brooke on occasion, attached to Mason and thinking how gorgeous she was, but Jax never thought that he would end up with the beauty.

He was starting to get over the Piper whirlwind he'd fallen into, and was able to mend his heart back up in order to give it over to Brooke…who was doing an excellent job protecting it. They hadn't said it yet, but he loved her, no doubt about it.

People always said love is so hard, which Jax could see, but when it came to Brooke, love seemed like the easiest thing on earth. He couldn't get enough of the girl, and when she was around, he was happy. Simple as that.

The film he was watching cut out as it ended. He sat back in his chair, pulled his glasses off, yes he had to wear glasses, and massaged the bridge of his nose. Sunday's game should be an easy win, and then they would go on a long road trip. They'd been home a lot, but after Sunday, they would be away for the next four weeks. Their schedule was all kinds of fucked up.

He was taking a sip of his beer when his phone started ringing. Looking down at the screen, he saw Brooke's gorgeous face appear, making his insides warm immediately.

"Hey darlin'," he answered, feeling instantly comforted by her calling him.

"Hey, how are you doing?" her sweet voice rang through the phone. "How was your Thanksgiving?"

Slouching on the couch, Jax got comfortable to talk to his girl. "It was good. There were a lot of people who visited the shelter, some families. It made me sad, but I was able to make a great donation to the shelter, and pick up some families' names for Christmas. Ryker already took a couple to support, and the rest of the boys and myself will help support the others."

"You're so amazing. That is so sweet, Jax."

He shrugged his shoulders, not that she could see. "It's nothing. We're blessed to have the opportunity to play for the Stallions; it's only natural we give back." Wanting to change the subject, he asked, "So, how is your family?"

"Good. Daddy couldn't be happier that my clothing line is

launching, and mom and I went out shopping all day."

"I saw that," Jax said in a gruff voice. "Did you get anything for me?"

Giggling Brooke said, "I might have."

"Do you wear it?"

"Maybe," she responded, making Jax's entire body tense up at envisioning her in some of the items she'd taken pictures of.

"When do you get back again?"

"Not sure yet. But I'll be home before you leave for your away trip."

Jax groaned. "You better be, because we leave on Wednesday. Don't you have things to do here? I'm pretty sure you need to come back so you can take care of some clothing things."

"You're so full of shit," Brooke said, while laughing.

"Can you blame a guy for trying? I miss you."

There was silence on the phone for a second, making Jax sweat, but then Brooke responded in the most sincere voice he had ever heard.

"I miss you too, Jax. A lot."

"Darlin', you're not making this easy on me when you talk all sexy like that."

"Well, I'm in my room now; we can have a little fun..."

"Do you really think that's a good idea? Last time we had phone sex, or tried to, you just laughed the whole time."

"You said lady garden! How am I not supposed to laugh at that?"

Chuckling from his choice of words, he said, "I was confused, and my mind wasn't working. It was the first thing that came to mind."

"And pussy wasn't? Honestly, Jax."

"Yeah, I royally fucked that one up."

"You kind of did, but I would be willing to try again."

"Really?" Jax said with hope, as he shifted on the couch.

"Yeah, I miss you, and right now, I could really use a chance to relax and listen to your deep southern voice bringing me to climax.

"Fuck…that turns me on to hear you say that."

"What else turns you on?" she asked, as Jax could hear her shifting around. So, they were really doing this, fine by him; he was already turned on.

"Let's see, you in a white see-through bikini, wet as fuck, and not just from the water."

"I don't own a white bikini."

"You do in my head."

"Something I should have purchased, apparently."

"Yes. Purchase one, and we can hang out in my hot tub in the cold night air."

"It really seems like you've planned this all out."

"You have no idea, darlin'," Jax said, as he breathed heavily. "Ever since you left, I've thought about you in my arms, naked and wet."

"Mmm, that sounds go good," she replied.

"Not wanting to sound cheesy, but dying to know, what are you wearing?"

"One of your shirts…the blue one with the state of Texas on the front, and a pair of panties."

Smiling to himself, he said, "When did you steal my shirt?"

"Last time I was over. I knew we were going to be apart for a little while, and I wanted a piece of you with me."

This woman opened him up and buried her soul so far into his, he had no clue what to do about it, especially when she said things like that.

"You have no idea how great that makes me feel."

"Are you hard?" she asked in a sexy voice, changing the topic quickly.

"Now I am," he admitted, as he started to stroke himself while listening to her sweet voice.

"Is your hand wrapped around your hard cock?"

"It is."

"Are your pants down?" she asked in a husky voice.

"No, do you want them down?"

"I want them all the way off."

"Fair enough, but you have to do something for me."

"Panties or shirt?" she asked, not letting him give her a choice.

"Can I say both?"

"You can, but you'll owe me when I get back."

"Fine by me," he laughed.

They both shuffled the phone as they deposited their clothes. Jax should have felt weird, sitting in the middle of his living room with his erection poking the air and his hand wrapped around it, but with Brooke's hot voice blazing through the phone, he didn't have a worry or care.

"I'm naked and so wet for you right now," Brooke said into the phone, as Jax continued to stroke himself.

"How wet?"

"Soaked…"

At her admission, Jax felt himself grow even harder. The thought of Brooke testing how wet she was, was such a huge turn on.

"You better fucking be. Now, listen carefully, Brooke, I want you to rub your clit, and while you're teasing that delicate little nub of yours that I love sucking on, I want you to run your hands up your body until you reach those perfect tits of yours." He paused for a second and said, "Are you doing what I say?"

"Yes," she said breathlessly, making Jax rub himself out even harder.

"Good girl. Is your nipple hard?"

"Mmm…"

"Pull on it, darlin'. Pull on it hard, pinch it, and envision my teeth running along that tight nipple of yours. Can you feel my teeth?"

"Yes…oh, Jax."

"Feel my hand run down your stomach and then down between your thighs. Feel me exploring your wet pussy. I want you to slip two fingers inside of yourself."

"Jax…"

"Now, Brooke, I want you to fuck yourself with your fingers, don't make me ask for three."

"Oh, God," she sighed into the phone, letting Jax know that now she was finger fucking herself.

"How close are you, darlin'?"

"So close."

"Me too," he replied, as he felt his balls start to tighten at the moans that were escaping her mouth.

"I can't do this, I want to touch my clit, please let me touch my clit."

Grunting and holding back his own release, Jax said, "Why should l let you?"

"So I can come while screaming your name."

Fuck…that did him in.

"Touch yourself, Brooke, do it."

From his command, she screamed his name into the phone at the same time he pumped one out, throwing his head back on the couch and releasing himself.

"Ahh…fuck," Jax exclaimed as he finished himself off and tried to catch his breath.

Silence met both of them as they steadied their racing hearts. Jax knew she was still there, because he could hear her breathing heavily.

"Jax," she said weakly. The way she said his voice made his hairs stand on end and a knot form at the pit of his stomach.

He sat up on the couch and pressed the phone against his ear.

"Yes, darlin', is everything okay?"

"Yes, but…can I ask you something?"

"Anything."

"Can we…." she stumbled. "Can we be official?"

"What do you mean?" he asked, confused. Last he knew, they were official. She was his girlfriend, and they were exclusive; he hoped to God she was thinking the same thing.

"I don't want to hide anymore. I want to go to events with

you; I want to go out on dates with you and not hide away at our places, not that it isn't nice, but I want to be the girl that is draped on your arm. I want people to know that you're my man."

A giant smile spread across Jax's face as he pulled his shorts back on.

"I think that can be arranged."

"Really?" she asked in disbelief, as if he'd just promised her the moon.

"Yes, darlin'. I can't wait to show you off. I'm just sorry you have to be seen with such a fashion disaster."

A pure laugh filtered through Jax's ears. Her laugh was so beautiful.

"You're not a fashion disaster, you're just an athlete."

"Well, can you make this athlete look good so I don't look like a total ass when I have you next to me?"

"It won't take much; you just need some shoes other than Nikes."

"What's wrong with my Nikes?" Jax asked in shock.

"Nothing, babe. Nothing at all."

CHAPTER TWENTY ONE

Jesse

There was something seriously wrong with Jesse. On Thanksgiving, he'd watched Ashlin drive away from him and he didn't move, he didn't beat an eyelash; he just stood there and stared at the ground from her confession. A day later, he was still frozen, unable to figure out what to do. He knew he had to go to her, that he needed to wrap his arms around her and kiss away her pain, but he didn't know how to do so…and the longer he stayed away, the longer his chances of getting her back were growing.

He just couldn't find the words or the actions to comfort her. She had literally rendered him speechless. The past she revealed was terrible, but that wasn't what got to him; it was the pain of the little girl that projected from her eyes that gutted him. At that moment, in his driveway, he saw the Ashlin that Ryker had grown up with, the one he warned Jesse about, the one he was not ready to face. Call him an idiot, call him naïve, but he lived in a sheltered world, and seeing such hurt and pain come from someone was something he was not used to, and it showed, because his lack of response was a death warrant for their relationship.

He sat at the side of his pool, watching the moon reflect off the water with a blanket thrown over his lap. The Denver air was chilly as the stars shined against the dark night sky. It was on nights like this that he wished Ashlin was tucked up against him as he ran his hands through her hair and they talked about their day. It was a simple life, but it was what he craved.

"Are you really just going to sequester yourself out here and not talk to us?" Johnny, Jesse's brother asked, as he walked up next to where Jesse was lounging.

"Sorry, man, just doing some thinking."

"I've noticed. Ever since Ashlin took off, you've been doing a lot of thinking."

"What is that supposed to mean?" Jesse asked, as he looked up at his brother whose arms were folded across his chest.

"It means you need to stop thinking and take some action. Clearly, you like Ashlin, you've been talking about her for months now…and the minute she runs away, you let her? After what you told me she said, you let her?"

"I didn't know how to react. You should have seen the look in her eyes."

"Well, being silent and not talking to her is not the way to go. Out of all the times in your life to man up and deal with something, this is the time. Yesterday was the time, and the longer you wait, the longer she's thinking that she's disgusted you with her past."

"She didn't," Jesse said, as he stood up and ran his hand through his hair. "Do you really think that's how she feels?"

"Are you really that dense?" Johnny asked. "Come on, man. She goes and tells you that her dad beat her mom to death, and you just sat there in silence. She's not thinking you're all fucking rainbows and ponies about the news."

"Shit," Jesse responded, as his hands ran over his face. "I need to go see her."

"Yeah, Daisy, my three year old daughter, could have told you that."

"Fuck off," Jesse called over his shoulder as he ran through his house, grabbed his keys, and ran out the door. He was wearing sweats and a long-sleeved T-shirt, but he didn't care. He needed to go see Ashlin.

As he drove to her apartment, he thought about how he'd really screwed up royally. There was no excuse for his absence, none whatsoever. He just hoped that, when he got to her apartment, she'd let him in to beg for forgiveness.

To think that she would be afraid to tell him such important information about her life was a little upsetting…to find out that she didn't trust him, but with the way he acted once she told him, he didn't blame her. He had one opportunity to give her the reaction that she deserved, and he blew it. Now he needed to make it up to her.

Arriving at her place in no time, Jesse hopped out of the car, and climbed the stairs to her place. Taking a deep breath, he knocked on the door, and waited impatiently for her to open it. Spotting the peephole, he hoped and prayed that she didn't look through it, because given what an ass he was, he was pretty sure she wouldn't let him in.

Jesse's heart settled as the locks started to move and the door opened. He expected to see Ashlin in some casual pajamas and her hair in a bun, her usual late night garb, but what he didn't expect to see was Ryker, shirtless and in a pair of boxers.

"What the fuck?" Jesse roared, as he charged through the door and pushed Ryker up against the wall.

"Dude," Ryker replied, as he struggled to get out of his grasp.

"Does Hannah know you're here, cheating on her?"

"Jesse! What the hell are you doing?" Ashlin said, as she tore him off of Ryker.

With erratic breathing, Jesse took in the sight of the two of them. Ashlin was in short shorts, a thin tank top, and her hair was on the top of her head. Her body looked incredible, but her face looked angry, really angry. Looking back over at Ryker, Jesse's temper started to fume again as he saw who he thought was his best friend getting all snuggly with his girlfriend.

"I came over here to apologize to you, but apparently, I should have just stayed home. I knew the photo shoot looked way too comfortable for you two."

Ashlin's mouth hung open in shock at Jesse's low blow, but he didn't care. He might have hurt her, but she'd hurt him ten times more. Sleeping with his best friend, with someone who was supposed to be dedicated to another woman? That was unforgivable.

"I hope you tell Hannah, or else I will, because she deserves better." Jesse looked Ryker up and down and said, "I thought you were cool, man."

Shaking his head in disgust, Jesse opened the door and ran straight into a lump of towels.

"Oh, sorry," Jesse said, as he helped the person up who was covered in laundry.

"Not a problem," Hannah said, removing a towel from her head, revealing her silky brown hair.

"Hannah?" Jesse asked, as an uneasiness started to settle over him.

"Oh, hey…Jesse." She looked over Jesse's shoulder and tossed some clothes behind him. "Your clothes are dry now."

"What?" Jesse asked, as Ryker started putting jeans and a shirt on.

"He is such a slob," Hannah responded, as she gathered all the laundry. He spilled soda all over himself and I was luckily able to get any staining out before it set in, but that meant having to wait for his clothes to dry. Thankfully, we were with Ashlin, so we could use her laundry room downstairs."

A slow and drawn out "fuck" ran through Jesse's head as he turned toward Ryker and Ashlin, who had the look of death on their faces. If Jesse hadn't already buried himself in a six foot hole with Ashlin, then he just did.

"Ashlin…"

"Don't," she held up her hand and turned to Ryker. "I'm sorry your friend is such an ass. Thank you for coming over; I appreciate it, but it might be best if you and Hannah go. You still have to put together all the things you got for your place," Ashlin said, looking at Jesse during the last part, which let him know that his assumption was way off base.

"Are you going to be okay?" Ryker asked, as he pulled her into a hug.

"Yeah, thanks though." When she pulled away, that was when Jesse noticed her eyes were rimmed with red and looked rather puffy. Had she been crying?

"Come on, boo. I want to try out those new sheets of ours."

Hannah handed the laundry over to Ashlin, gave her a hug, and then laced her fingers with Ryker's. Jesse was a giant ass.

Before the two love birds walked away, Ryker leaned in toward Jesse and said, "You're a giant fuck stick. I thought better of you."

Pain ricocheted through Jesse's chest at the disappointment in Ryker's voice.

"I'm sorry," Jesse said faintly, as Ryker walked away. He owed his friend, big time.

Once Ryker and Hannah were gone, Jesse looked up at Ashlin, who had just started to shut her door on him, but he stopped her and pushed his way in. He may have been inviting himself in, but she wasn't screaming bloody murder, so he thought it was okay.

"What the hell are you doing?" she asked, as her hands went to her hips. She was adorable when she was mad.

Clearing his throat, he said, "I know you might not want to see me right now…"

"You can say that again," she interrupted.

"But, I wanted to talk to you."

"You lost that chance, Jesse."

"I know, but please let me explain."

"Why would I do that? You let me walk away…after I told you the darkest secret of my life, you just let me walk away. Then you didn't contact me, you didn't bother to see if I got home alright or see how I was doing. Finally, when you pulled your head out of your ass, you come over here and instantly accused Ryker and me of cheating. Don't you know by now that you are the only man I have ever been interested in? I think that should have been clear."

"I'm a dickhead," he confessed, which made a slight smile crack at the corner of Ashlin's lips.

"That pretty much sums it up."

"I need to talk to you, Ashlin. Please."

She weighed her options as she looked him up and down. Her light perusal of his body made a wave of heat take over his body.

"Fine," she succumbed, as she stepped aside, placed the laundry on the floor, and went to the couch.

Taking a deep breath, Jesse followed her to the couch and sat next to her, close enough to hold her hand, which thankfully, she allowed.

He looked down at their joined hands and he said, "I can't tell you how sorry I am, not just about today, but mostly about not going after you on Thanksgiving. The moment you confided in me, I froze. Not because of the information you told me…that doesn't bother me. What bothered me was the look in your eyes, the hurt, and the pain you went through. I read it all in your one confession, and I was so upset, so overwhelmed, I didn't know how to react. I still don't, but what I do know is that you need to know I don't care about what happened in your past. I care what happened to you, but I don't judge you for it; I never will. We all have our demons, our hidden secrets, but those demons are what made us into who we are today."

Ashlin was looking down at their hands as Jesse spoke, and at that moment, he needed to see her eyes…he needed to see how she was feeling. Gently, he pressed his finger to her chin and lifted it so her eyes met his. A glassy sheen fell over her light green eyes, which cut Jesse to the core.

"I'm so damn sorry, Ashlin."

She nodded her head as two tears fell down her cheeks.

"Please, don't cry." He moved in closer, wanting badly to place her on his lap, but he didn't think it was a good idea just yet.

"You hurt me, Jesse. Out of everyone, I thought that you would accept me the most, but after I told you, after I shared, I have never felt so unwelcome in my life."

He was disgusted with himself. He could throw a ball while four, three hundred pound men chased after him, but when it came to gathering someone up in his arms and telling them that everything was going to be okay, he froze.

"And you don't deserve that kind of treatment, Ashlin, because you didn't do anything wrong. You are so bright, so beautiful, and so smart that you should feel welcomed and accepted by everyone. It kills me that I was a total dick. I was just so lost. I wish I'd reacted differently, but I can't take it back now; all I can do is hope to move forward and hope that you will move forward with me."

"Why did you think Ryker and I were together?" she asked sincerely.

Shaking his head, Jesse said, "Because I'm a giant douche bag, because I like to fuck everything up in my life at the same time, because I was so blinded that the first thing I did was jump to conclusions without trusting the fact that you care about me, that you want to be with me, or wanted to be with me, for that matter."

A small chuckle came out of her plump, gorgeous lips. "You're honest, I like it. I'm glad you know you're an ass."

Laughing as well, Jesse said, "It's not hard to see when you fuck everything up."

"Not everything," Ashlin said, as she leaned a little closer.

"No?" he raised his eyebrow at her.

She shook her head no and straddled his lap. That was when he noticed she wasn't wearing a bra, because her nipples were hard as hell and staring him in the eyes.

She leaned down to his ear and said, "I want to be mad at you, but when you come over here and beg for my forgiveness, looking all sexy, it's hard to stay away from you."

He felt his cock start to twitch and bang at his boxers as she shifted on his lap.

"Would you say the sexiness saved me?" he asked jokingly.

"I would say you're pretty damn lucky you have muscles and know how to wear some pretty revealing clothes."

"Sweatpants and a shirt are revealing?" he asked, as her finger started to drift up and down his chest.

"That shirt is so tight on you, I'm pretty sure I can see your abs."

"It's not that tight," he chuckled.

She continued to stroke his chest, and once her finger slid under his shirt, his hand stopped hers. Her eyes widened as she looked at him to see what was wrong.

"I need to know that we're okay, that you forgive me for being an ass."

"I do," she said honestly. "I'm not going to lie, I was hurt, badly, but seeing the sincerity in your face and how upset you were, I can tell that you meant it. I just need you to know that I'm not perfect, not even close to it. I have a different background that has shaped me into the person I am today, but meeting you has shaped me differently. Normally, I wouldn't have trusted to tell you, to let you back in, but I know, even if at some point we disappoint each other, we will always come back, even if it's a day later."

"You're so right," Jesse said, as he slipped his arm around her waist. Cupping her face, he looked her in the eyes and said, "I can't tell you how sorry I am, and how grateful I am that you have such a big heart, and that you let me in it. I promise, moving forward, I will treat it carefully and make sure to never break it."

Her smile danced across her face as she brought her lips to his. "You make me happy, Jesse."

"You make me happy, Ashlin."

Ashlin

Jesse was spread out on the couch, with his arm propping up his head as Ashlin finished rinsing the dishes from their take-out dinner. He offered to help, but she told him to relax. After he

315

explained himself and said how sorry he was, she knew she couldn't stay mad at him...there was no way. She had finally opened her heart to someone, and she wanted it to stay that way. She felt cared for when Jesse was around, and she reveled in the feeling.

She wiped her hands and headed over to Jesse, who was watching sports highlights on the TV. When she was straddling his lap earlier, she really wanted them to finally have sex and connect in a way they hadn't before, but he stopped her, and asked if she was hungry. This time, she wasn't going to let him distract her. She was going to grab him by the balls and take what she wanted. They were in this together...they were in a relationship, it was time.

As she walked into the living room, Jesse smiled up at her and eyed her up and down.

"What's with the sly grin over there, beautiful?"

"Just taking what I want," she replied, as she played with the hem of her shirt.

Completely oblivious, he asked, "And what is that?"

Not giving him a second to further question her, she took off her shirt, exposing her breasts to him. She knew he was instantly excited by the way his eyes heated and the way the bulge in his sweatpants grew. Yes, she was definitely not letting him distract her from what she wanted.

Clearing his throat, he said, "Uh, what are you doing, Ashlin?"

"Shut up, Jesse," she said, as she straddled his lap on the couch and ran her hands up his shirt, which he was forced to take off once she rode the hem over his head. His chest was now bare, exposing his finely chiseled muscles and his colorful tattoos that had no rhyme or reason, but they were sexy as hell. She loved Jesse's art, because on the outside he was kind and caring; you would never know the man had sleeve tattoos unless they showed, but when they did, he was sexy as hell.

Leaning down, she kissed his taut abs, which jumped at her touch. She could feel him harden quickly under her, which only made her smile. She loved the fact that she could affect Jesse so easily. Kissing his stomach, she made her way up to his chest, where she kissed his pecs and found out first-hand just how muscular he was.

She peeked up at him and noticed his eyes were closed and he was biting down on his lip. She poked his face with her finger and said, "What's going on? Am I disgusting you?"

"Fuck no, are you kidding me? I'm just trying to be…"

"If you say you're trying to be good, I am going to pinch your nipple right off." Her fingers hovered over his nipple.

He laughed uneasily and said, "You're so beautiful, Ashlin, I'm just…nervous."

"Nervous?" She cocked her head to the side. "Why?"

"I've only been with one other woman, and that was a long time ago."

Her heart melted instantly. If she hadn't already known she was in love with the man, she did now. He was a strong, confident, starting quarterback on the field, but a little cuddly teddy bear in person. She was head over heels in love.

Not wanting to use her words, she ran her hands from his chest to his face, and rubbed his cheeks with her thumbs.

Taking a deep breath, she said, "I love you, Jesse, and I don't care about your past sexual history. All I care about is you and me."

She had never seen his face so bright. "You said you love me," he teased, while poking her side.

Blushing, she said, "So?"

"You love me," he sing-songed and teased.

Propping herself off his chest she said, "Don't be a jerk about it."

Within seconds, he'd scooped her up over his shoulder and run through her apartment. Once they were in her bedroom, he placed her on her bed and hovered over her.

He leaned in close and looked her dead in the eyes as he said, "I love you too, Ashlin. I love you too."

She was lost after that.

Slowly, Jesse grabbed the edges of her panties and slid them down her legs, making her completely naked for him.

"You are so damn beautiful."

She just smiled as he leaned forward. She stopped him with her foot and said, "I think you're forgetting something," she looked down at his boxer-clad crotch.

"Alright, but don't stare," he said shyly, making her laugh.

He turned his back and shucked his boxers, giving her a great view of his tight ass. She'd be biting into that later. When he turned around, her breath caught in her throat as she saw Jesse...all of Jesse.

Propping herself up on her elbows, she stared at his erection, and then swallowed hard as she looked back up at him.

"I hit the fucking king of all cocks motherload," she exclaimed, as she licked her lips, sat on her knees, and pulled Jesse close to her. Marveling at his thick size, she started stroking his long length, and watched as he continued to grow. "Does Mason know about your dick?" she asked, dick-struck.

Laughing, Jesse said, "I'd rather not have you talk about my teammates while I'm aroused and you're stroking me. It just confuses Boris."

"Boris?" her eyebrows raised as she tore her eyes off of the giant dick in her hands.

"That's his name."

"Oh. My. God!" She laughed as she fell back on the bed.

He was on top of her in an instant with Boris poking at her pussy, begging to be let in. The feeling of him pressing up against her had her laugh falling from her lips and her body heating up all over again.

"Think it's funny now?"

"Nope," she shook her head furiously, as she felt her breath start to pick up.

"Good. Now open for me...wide."

Jesse was pretty easygoing and a fun guy, but right now, he wasn't anything like that. He was demanding and sexy as sin, something she loved to know that he kept for only the bedroom.

Wanting to listen to his demands, she spread her legs as wide as possible, which allowed the tip of his cock to rub against her clit. A moan escaped the back of her throat as he started to move his dick up and down along her slick pussy. The feeling was incredible, especially since he was owning her mouth with his lips and running his hands up her stomach.

His lips worked down her neck, right to her breasts, where they stopped to peruse. He kissed around her nipple until she was moaning and thrusting her chest into his mouth. With a smile, he grabbed one of her breasts and took it into his mouth. He lightly bit down on her nipple at the same time that he entered her just with his tip.

"Ahhh, Jesse. You're killing me."

"I'm killing you? Then I need to stop," he said jokingly, as he pulled out of her, eliciting a small cry from her. "Sweetheart, you sound so sad."

"I don't want to play games, please, make love to me."

"Well, when you ask like that…" he looked around and pulled out her bed side drawer. "Condoms?"

"I'm on some serious birth control. Don't worry about it. Please, I just need you."

He smiled down at her and spread her even further.

"Ever since I saw you hanging out with Ryker, I knew I wanted you, needed you. I just had to find the right time to make my move," he confessed, as he steadied himself right above her.

"I thought I was the one who made the move?"

"You going to be sassy now? Well, I can either let you be sassy, and I go back to my place, or you can be a good girl, stop talking, and listen to me."

"I'm listening," she said breathlessly. She really, really liked sexy alpha Jesse.

"Good, normally I would have you flip on your stomach so I could take you from behind, but right now, I want to see your face as my cock enters that sweet hole of yours."

Nodding, she spread her legs more, put her hands above her

head to grab onto the headboard, and waited for his next move.

His fingers ran up and down her stomach and sternum, making her wetter than she thought possible. She could feel the weight of her arousal and she was afraid that she was going to come just from him touching her, but she didn't dare say a word...she just let Jesse work his magic.

"You're so soft...everything about you is so perfect."

"I'm not perfect," she mumbled.

He grabbed her face and made her look him in the eyes. "You're my kind of perfect, Ashlin."

And she melted.

He kissed her lips softly, grabbed her legs, and put them on his shoulders. With a deep breath, he slowly moved his cock into her entrance. There was need lacing his eyes and self-control pouring out of him, but he never once let go. He continued to ease into her, even though the veins in his neck pulsed; his cock twitched relentlessly as he entered her. Once she felt his balls hit her ass, she knew they were fully connected. They both breathed deeply as they felt each other connect in the most intimate way possible.

"You're perfect for me," Jesse gritted out, as he started easing himself out, slowly.

The pace he was going at was torturous, but in the most magnificent way ever. He was definitely the most well-endowed man she had ever been with, and she could feel him stretching her in the best way possible.

"Are you doing alright?" he asked, as he started pushing back in again.

"Yes," she hissed. "But if you could pick up the pace, that would be appreciated."

Laughing, he did as he was told, and started moving faster. The friction and sounds that he was starting between them were so hot, so erotic, that Ashlin couldn't help but get lost in his touch, in his weight, in the way he made little grunting noises every time he entered her.

"Fuck," he mumbled as his head lowered and he pulled on his bottom lip with his teeth. "I'm not going to fucking last."

"Me either," she said, as his hand went to her clit and started rubbing tiny little circles over it.

A feral scream escaped her mouth as he took her over the edge. She didn't even see it coming, but with the way he was moving in and out of her while his fantastic fingers moved over her, he had her screaming his name at the top of her lungs.

As she tried to rein herself in, she saw Jesse above her bite down on his lip and grunt as he released himself into her. Seeing the poised man lose control was such a huge turn-on that she would be seeing him like that, in her head, for days. The image would be helpful when she was all alone on a photo shoot and was in need of a little Jesse loving.

He gently set her legs down and pulled her into his chest. They both breathed each other in as their hearts steadied.

Life would never be the same for her. The gentle giant that was now holding her to his heart had forever changed her, and she couldn't be more grateful for his persistence in knocking down her walls and making her his.

CHAPTER TWENTY TWO

Piper

Mason was at the stadium, getting in some Saturday physical therapy, as Piper went to visit with Hannah. Apparently, Hannah had some big news. Mason told Piper that he would get a ride home with one of the guys, so not to worry about him. She didn't know how long she would be hanging out with Hannah, so she might as well pick Mason up if he was done, but she would figure that out once she got to the stadium.

As she walked into Dick's Last Chance, she thought about how much her life had changed and so quickly. It was only a couple of months ago that she had hit rock bottom and had to crawl back to her parents for help. One lucky day, she ran into Mason, the love of her life, something she never thought she would say, and then they were swept up together in a whirlwind. There was always the nagging feeling in the back of her mind that everything was too good to be true. He'd let her back into his life too easily, but then again, he loved her, and the way he looked at her proved it.

Piper instantly spotted Hannah behind the counter at the bar and went over to her. When Hannah looked up and saw Piper, she squealed and ran over to her. She wrapped her arms around Piper's waist, since she was so much shorter, and gave her a big hug.

"Hey," Piper said while laughing. "What's going on that has you bouncing up and down like a lunatic?"

Grabbing ahold of her hands, Hannah swung them back and forth as she said, "Ryker and I are moving in together! We bought some things on Friday for our place. I'm so excited!"

"Wow, Hannah. That's amazing. I'm so happy for you. So, I'm assuming that means things are going very well for you two?"

"Yes, I couldn't be happier," she said, as she walked back around the bar. "He is so perfect, Piper. He puts up with my insecurities and calms me down when I go all psychotic on him. He is sweet and funny, and he is…" she paused and looked around before saying, "he's fantastic in bed."

A laugh escaped Piper as she watched Hannah's face blush.

"So, he knows how to pork you like a champ?"

"Piper!" Hannah admonished. "Honestly, I don't know how Mason puts up with that dirty mouth of yours."

"He likes it dirty, Hannah. You should know that by now."

Hannah held up her hand and said, "Let's not go there." She started drying some glasses and stacking them as she said, "So, how was meeting the parents?"

Sitting down on the bar stool and leaning her elbows on the counter, Piper said, "It was interesting. Of course, Mason has the best parents ever." Hannah nodded her head. "His mom totally called me out for my, how would you say it? My slutty ways."

Hannah snorted and nodded her head. "God, that must have been embarrassing."

"Mortifying is more like it, to know that your boyfriend's mom knows that you fucked her son around, yeah, I wanted to melt into the cranberry sauce, but she didn't seem to care or, at least she didn't show it. She told me that she can truly see that Mason loves me and that he is worth fighting for, which I completely agree with. He is worth fighting for."

"Well, I guess that was a good conversation then, right?"

"It was just a little awkward at first, but in the end, everything was great. We had a good time, and his parents gave me big hugs when they left this morning. I feel like it might take a little bit for his mom to truly accept me in Mason's life, given my pathetic history, but we did bond, and she is going to be sending me some recipes that Mason loved growing up as a kid. It was kind of cute."

"Well, that's sweet. I'm glad you had a good Thanksgiving."

"Yeah, it was one of the best ones I think I've ever had, and I have Mason to thank for it. It's so weird…" Piper trailed off.

"What's weird?" Hannah asked, as she pulled out the bowls of nuts, once again prepping the bar for the patrons.

"Mason, it just seems like something is going to happen, you know? Life can't be this easy."

"It can when you're in love," Hannah responded honestly. "I think the same thing about Ryker sometimes, you know? This amazingly handsome professional football player walks into this bar and says that I'm going to be his wife one day? That never happens, but it did. It has taken me a while to get to where I am today, and I'm still struggling with my self-confidence where love is concerned, but with the way Ryker treats me, touches me, and even looks at me, I know he is in this for the long run. Sometimes I'll catch him just looking at me, and when I do, he has the most loving look on his face. I know, at those moments, that we are meant to be. He would never hurt me like Todd did, and for that, I'm the luckiest girl ever."

Joy filled Piper's heart for her friend as she patted Hannah's hand. "You deserve happiness, Hannah, after everything you've been through, and I'm so glad you've found it with Ryker. He really is such a good guy, even though he can be a pain in the ass."

"He can be, but that's why I love him."

They spent the next two hours talking about the men in their lives and sharing stories about how they acted behind closed doors, when it was just them alone together. Ryker likes to dance around in his boxers and, apparently, he has some really good moves, according to Hannah. Piper told Hannah that Mason is notorious for singing into a wooden spoon when making dinner, and his song of choice is always, "My Heart Will Go On." Hannah nearly split a gut when she heard that confession.

It was just about the time that Mason would be getting done with PT, so she said her good bye to Hannah and drove the short distance to the stadium. Luckily, she was on the approved list for player access into the stadium. She didn't know if Mason was done with PT, but when she called him to find out, her call went straight to voicemail. She didn't really want to go into the stadium, but Ryker's car was still in the parking lot, and that was who Mason was probably going to get a ride from, so she put her car in park and headed into the stadium.

The familiar scent of the stadium washed over her as visions of Mason pressing her up against the painted cinder block walls ran through her mind. She was still with Jax at that point, but her heart had been slowly falling into Mason's hands.

As she walked through the tunnels of the stadium, she kept her head down, not really wanting to make eye contact with anyone...not that her hair wouldn't give her away; it was quite noticeable.

When she turned the corner to the PT room, she ran straight into a man's chest, a very familiar man's chest. As she looked up, she saw those brown eyes and white hat that used to star in her dreams.

"Oh sorry...Piper?"

Catching her balance, so she didn't fall over like a pathetic mess, she looked him in the eyes and said, "Hi, Jax."

"Why the hell are you here?" He looked angry. She didn't blame him, but as she tried to answer him, her heart hammered in her chest, and she couldn't think of what to say.

"Listen, I don't know why you're here, or walking toward my office, but I'm going to have to ask you to leave." His office? Did she make a wrong turn? She hadn't been in the stadium in a while; she might have made a wrong turn at some point.

"I'm sorry. I must have gotten lost."

He gave her the "I'm sure you did" look, which only

possessed her to open her mouth to apologize.

"I'm sorry, Jax. I didn't mean to hurt you."

"Yes, you did," he replied, matter-of-factly.

Piper felt her face twist as she took in what Jax said. "No, I didn't," she said back, feeling a little fire brewing in her. "I honestly loved you, Jax."

"Wow, well I feel bad for whoever you love in the future, because that is one shitty way to love. You don't cheat on the people you love, Piper. You don't sneak around behind their backs and fuck their players. You don't tell me that you love me, and then go to sleep in another man's arms. Just admit it…for what it's worth, you're a giant whore, and you have no purpose in life other than to fuck with people."

Well, she knew Jax was mad and had an issue with their break up, but she never knew he would be so hurtful…not that she didn't deserve it, but still. He was being a little harsh.

"I'm sorry…"

"Save it and get the hell out of here."

Not even bothering to fight back, she grabbed her phone out of her pocket and tried dialing Mason again, as she tried to find her way back to the PT room. As she turned another corner of one of the all-too-similar-looking hallways, she peeked up to see Brooke walking toward her. Her entire body went stiff as they eyed each other.

What the hell was Brooke doing in the Stallion's stadium? There was no other purpose for her being here besides visiting Mason. He was the only connection she had to the Stallions. Then, everything hit her…the sinking feeling she'd had in the back of her mind started to come forward. Mason didn't want to have Piper take him home, and now she knew why…because Brooke clearly was.

Her heart was aching from the words Jax spat at her, but now, it was broken as Brooke eyed her with venom and walked right past her, not even giving her a second glance. Piper hated to admit it, but Brooke looked good, really good, and for some reason, Piper got it. This was it, this was what she had been waiting for...for someone to blow over her house made of cards.

Not even needing to fight it, she cut her losses, and went back to her car. Mason was worth fighting for, but when it was clear that he was only putting up with Piper until he could screw her over like she screwed him over, there was no point in fighting. She would only embarrass herself. It was time to move on...again.

Brooke

Deciding to come back home to Denver was one of the easiest decisions she had ever made. After her little phone sex escapade with Jax, she knew she needed to see him; she missed him and she'd had enough visiting time with her parents. Plus, she was ready to get her relationship out in the open with Jax; she wanted everyone to know that the southern gentleman was all hers.

When she went to the stadium to surprise Jax, she was not expecting to run into Piper...the last person she ever wanted to see again, especially coming from Jax's office. Instinctively, Brooke wanted to rip Piper's head off, and then beat it against the wall, but she knew that wouldn't help the situation. Then, she thought of just leaving, because clearly, if Jax was going to be hanging out with Piper when she was gone, he didn't need Brooke anymore. However, the inner bitch in her came to life, so she gathered herself and stomped her way down the hall and straight into Jax's office.

The door was open to his office and he was just sitting down as she charged in and placed her hand on her hip. She was in full bitch mode and ready to raise hell.

He must have felt the whirlwind of her anger, because he looked up and a look of shock washed over his face. She wasn't quite sure if it was shock or guilt, but whatever it was, he was surprised to see her.

"Hey, darlin'," he stood up and walked over to her. "Isn't this a surprise..." he reached for her, but instead, she pushed him away.

"Hey, what's going on?"

"You mind telling me about your little visitor while I was gone?"

Confused, he asked, "What are you talking about?"

"Don't act stupid, Jax. I saw her, okay? How convenient that the minute your girlfriend is out of town, visiting her family, you can call in the redhead and have some fun. I'm so stupid." She pressed her hand against her forehead as she paced. "I should have known you weren't over her, but no, I go and give you the benefit of the doubt and trust you."

"Which you should still do, Brooke," he spoke sternly. "I had no clue she was coming over here, and I have no clue why she was here."

A maniacal laugh escaped her lips as she looked up at Jax. "Please, Jax. She can't just come in here without a pass. You and I both know that."

"I didn't give her one!" he said, raising his voice.

"Then who the hell did?"

"I don't know…Mason?"

Brooke laughed even harder. "You're insane! They would never get back together. You didn't see the looks on their faces when they broke everything off, when they said those awful things to each other. They're both too stubborn to even try to make that work again. I know Mason; he would never take her back. Once he's burned by someone, they're out of his life forever."

"You seem like you're talking from experience," Jax said coldly.

"Of course I am, you idiot. He was my boyfriend before you…he was my fiancé."

"And you want to be with him?"

Brooke felt like her brain exploded at Jax's comment.

She threw her hands up in the air and said, "Are you fucking insane? No, I don't want to be with him. Holy shit! We've talked about this…"

"I know. I know," Jax apologized, as he tried to walk closer, but Brooke kept her distance. "That was not the right thing to say. I'm just overwhelmed right now. I have no clue why Piper was here…"

"Well, she was here for a reason, and I want to know the fuck why. Did you talk to her?"

Jax's face told her everything she needed to know.

"Unbelievable." She flung her purse and started walking away.

"I told her to leave," Jax said, as he chased after her. "I didn't want her here, and she wasn't in my office, she was in the hallway."

"Oh, okay. That makes it so much better. You know I hate her Jax, and there is no reason for her to be here other than visiting you."

"It could be Mason," Jax shouted.

"What about me?" Mason asked, as he crutched up the hallway. The minute he saw Brooke, he stopped and his face contorted. She'd thought about the moment she'd see Mason again, and she never thought that she would feel absolutely nothing for the man, but right now, right here, the only man that was distracting her was Jax…even though she hated to admit it at the moment.

"This doesn't concern you, Dashel," Jax dismissed him.

"I think it does when my ex-girlfriend is here. What are you doing here, Brooke?"

Silence fell between all of them as Mason looked back and forth between them. Realization hit him as his mouth opened and Brooke silently confirmed what he was thinking.

"Oh, my God, you guys are together?"

"Like I said, this doesn't concern you, Dashel."

"It sure as hell does when you're yelling my name up and down the hall."

"Just leave, Mason."

"Not until you tell me why you were saying my name." He was a stubborn ass.

Brooke exhaled as she said, "I saw Piper walking around here, and Jax is trying to tell me it has nothing to do with him."

Brooke watched as a million thoughts ran through Mason's face in a matter of seconds, as he tried to calculate what Brooke was saying. Finally, he looked up and said, "Piper was here and she saw you?" His voice had a slight panic to it.

"Yeah…"

"Fuck!" he shouted, as he ran his hand through his hair and grabbed his phone out of his pocket. He turned it on and stared at the screen.

"Soo…"

Mason looked up at them and said, "Whatever is going on between you two, I really don't give a shit about, but it has nothing to do with Piper. She was here for me." Mason put his pone back in his pocket and started crutching away. He turned around quickly, and the Mason from college, the Mason Brooke fell in love with looked her in the eyes and said, "Brooke, even though I don't like him, Jax is a good guy, and he wouldn't fuck you over like I did. Don't make a mistake now for something I did to you in the past. Be happy." With that, he took off down the hallway at a rapid pace.

Looking back at Jax, she saw the pain in his eyes. She didn't know what to think, what to say, how to broach the awkwardness between them. If Jax didn't look so hurt, Brooke would be contemplating the insane reality that Mason was talking to Piper and concerned about her. The man must be bat-shit crazy in order to put up that red-headed waffler.

"I…I don't know what to say," Brooke stuttered, as she shifted in place.

"Me either," Jax replied, as he pushed his back up against the wall, turning away so he was looking down the hallway and not at her.

"I'm sorry. I thought you were here with Piper. It's just that…I feel like I can't trust anyone in this fucked up love triangle." Brooke shook her head as she waved her arms about. "I mean, look at us, I'm running into an ex-fiancé, you're running into your ex-girlfriend, we're all confused as to who is with whom. I feel like someone is above us fucking around with our lives; I can't get one ounce of peace. One second, Mason wants me, and then he doesn't, then he does, and then it's over. Piper is in love with you, but then she's not, and then you're engaged....like, what the fuck?!" Brooke could feel herself losing her mind, but she didn't care anymore, she just let loose.

"I finally get my life back on track, I get away from the black hole that was sucking us all in, and then I run into you." Her voice softens as she continues. "I meet you and you turn my world upside down. You give me something to look forward to, to wake up to. You make me believe in love again, but it can never be that easy, can it? No, we have fucking Mason and Piper running around ruining everything, plus my inability to trust one God damn living thing. Ahh!" she screamed, as she sunk to the floor next to Jax.

She felt him sink down to the ground with her. His hand grabbed hers, and when she looked at him, he was smiling brightly.

"Why are you smiling?"

Then he did something that she never expected, he started laughing, hard. She was confused. Was Jax losing his mind as well? Was he going crazy? Did she need to check him into an institution? Because the way he was laughing so hard, with tears were springing from his eyes, she was pretty sure she might have to check him in somewhere.

"Jax, what is going on?"

He wiped his eyes and said, "Seriously? Think about it; think about what you just said. We are living some serious TV drama right now...you can't help but laugh. Next thing we know, Kiera, my wife, will appear and tell me she never did die, but was hiding from the government for years because she was part of some kind of body selling business."

A small giggle escaped Brooke's lips as she thought about it. "You're so right. Our life is a soap opera."

"It really is." They both laughed as they held hands in the hallway of the stadium. It felt good to just laugh, to look at their lives and laugh, because what else could they really do? They couldn't control anything that happened, especially in the situation they were living with Mason and Piper being so close to them.

Jax kissed Brooke's hand and said, "I despise Mason, but the man is right, please don't let what he did to you affect our relationship, Brooke. Remember, we're starting new? Just you and me darlin'. Fuck the redhead, fuck the douche, and fuck everyone else. It's just you and me."

Brooke rested her head against his shoulder and agreed. "I guess you're right, it is just me and you. I'm sorry Jax."

"I'm sorry you had to see our two favorite people in the whole world." At that, they both laughed again as Jax wrapped his arm around Brooke and pulled her in closer. "You in this for the long haul?" Jax asked out of the blue.

Looking up at Jax, she smiled and nodded her head. "Yeah, I kind of am."

"Good, because so am I."

He kissed the top of her head and they just sat there in silence, in the Stallions stadium, relishing the feel of their bodies connected in knowing that in the twisted world they lived in, they would always have each other. They would always be there for each other.

"Thanks for coming home early."

She buried her head in the crook of his neck and said, "You're the only home I have; of course I wanted to come home early. You're everything, Jax.

"You're everything too, Brooke."

Mason

"Drive fucking faster!" Mason yelled, as he looked out the car window and clenched his fists together, trying not to throw his fist through the windshield out of anger.

"Dude, I can't drive over the semi-truck in front of us. Chill the fuck out."

"How can I chill the fuck out when Piper is not answering her phone, and I know that, right now, she is going to run. She is going to fucking run, and I'm going to lose her again, all because of a damn misunderstanding."

Ryker was silent as they drove, because he knew Mason was right. Piper was a runner, always had been, and even though she said she was done running, she had more than enough ammunition to run now. Why would she think Brooke was at the stadium for any other reason than seeing Mason? And it didn't help that Mason told her that he could get his own ride home. What a clusterfuck.

"Fuck!" Mason shouted, as he pounded his fist into the dashboard.

"Jesus, dickhead, don't beat the shit out of my car, alright? We're almost there; just calm the fuck down for one second."

"What if she's not there, Ryker? What the fuck am I going to do then?"

"We'll find her."

"Yeah, okay, because it was that easy last time. Lexi didn't even know where Piper was."

They pulled up to Mason's condo, and he flung the door open to get out.

"Crutches, asswipe. Use your crutches; I would like to see you playing next season."

Even though he wanted to sprint up his stairs, Mason knew Ryker was right. He couldn't hurt his knee anymore. Physical therapy was already hard as it was; he didn't need to reinjure himself.

It took him longer than he wanted, but when he got to his front door, he quickly opened it and started searching around his condo. He went straight to the bedroom, where he looked for Piper's clothing. It was all gone.

"Fuck!" his voice caught in his throat as he looked around the bedroom while running his hand through his hair.

What the hell was he supposed to do? Where was he supposed to go from here? If only Ryker had driven faster.

Mason went back into the main living area, and when he spotted Piper sitting in the corner of the room with her bags next to her, his breath caught in his chest. She wasn't gone.

Fuck crutches; he hobbled over to Piper and dropped to the ground in front of her. Her head was in her hands as he tried to peek up at her. When he took her hands away from her face, he saw her tear-stained cheeks and red-rimmed eyes. She was hurting, and he didn't blame her.

"Piper…"

A sob escaped her throat, as she put her head in her hands again.

He got up and pushed her to the side of the chair, so they could share it. Once he was on the chair, he lifted her up and placed her on his lap. Instantly, her head went to his shoulder, as she continued to cry.

"Shhh," he cooed, as he rubbed her arm. His throat was tight as he thought about how she hadn't left yet, she was still here. "You didn't run," he said in a whisper.

She shook her head and said, "I was going to, but then I remembered that I promised you I wouldn't, so I figured I at least owed it to you to say goodbye and explain why I was leaving."

"You don't need to explain, because you're not going anywhere."

"Mason, don't do this to me, okay? I get it. Payback is a bitch. I deserve it, I did the same thing to you, so it's only fitting that I get a taste of my own medicine."

"What are you talking about? Piper, I love you."

"Mason, don't say those words if you don't mean them. I saw Brooke, okay? I saw her at the stadium…"

"Visiting Jax," Mason interrupted her.

Piper's head flung up in surprise. There was a light sheen under her nose that Mason thought was adorable. God, he must be hell over heels in love to think Piper's snot was adorable. Mason wiped his sleeve under her nose, and smiled when she crinkled her nose.

"Why was she visiting Jax?" Piper asked, as she wiped her eyes frantically.

"Apparently, the two of them are an item."

Piper didn't say anything as she tried to soak in the information Mason had just told her. He didn't have much time to digest the information when he first found out because he was so concerned about Piper, but now that he thought about it, the whole idea of them together seemed like some sick and twisted love story. Not only was Mason now dating and in love with his coach's ex-girlfriend, but his coach was now dating his ex-fiancé. Like, what?

"So...Brooke wasn't there for you?"

"No, baby. She was there for Jax. When I told you I loved you, I meant it. I love you Piper, more than anything."

Her face looked so confused as she thought about his words. "You really love me," she stated, making Mason laugh.

"I do, I really love you."

"Oh."

"You seem surprised. Don't you love me?" His chest started to hurt at the thought of Piper not truly reciprocating his feelings, but when he searched her eyes, he knew that wasn't the truth. Her eyes were boring into his and they were full of love and heat for him and only him.

"I'm so in love with you, Mason. I just thought..."

"What did you think?"

"It just seemed too easy. I had this feeling in the back of my head that you were just waiting to pull the trigger on me, just waiting to drop the bomb and tear me apart. When I saw Brooke, I thought my suspicions were true."

Mason shook his head. "I guess I haven't done a good enough job of showing you how much I really love you." He grabbed her face and made her look him dead in the eyes as he pressed their noses together. "Piper Shores, you are, by far, the craziest, most beautiful, yet smart-mouthed girl I have ever met. You bring joy to my life and you challenge me like no one else ever has. When I met you on the airplane, hung over as hell, I knew, at that moment, when you introduced yourself as Jojo, that I was starting to fall in love. You didn't put up with my shit and you handed it right back to me.

"Then I got the opportunity to get to know you better, you let me in after a lot of persistence, and once I spent that first day with you, at the ballpark, touching your hand and talking, it solidified it for me that you were the one for me, even if I didn't show it at the time. We've been through so much, and I have fought from the fucking pit of my stomach to have you in my life, and there is nothing in the world that would deter me from making that happen. You're mine, Piper. You're fucking mine, you hear me?"

She nodded her head as she pressed her salty lips against his and welcomed his tongue into her mouth. His body shook as he took her in, as he allowed himself to go over that last step, to fall completely into her arms. This was it; they were either going to make it or break it, and by the way she ran her tongue against his, sending shivers down his spine, he knew they were going to make it…no doubt in his mind.

Pulling away, she pressed her thumbs against his cheeks and smiled at him.

"I'm so in fucking love with you, Mason. You're mine too. Forever."

"Forever, baby. There will never be anyone else but you."

"Not even Jake," she joked.

"It'll be hard on him, but he'll make it, I just know it…but you do know that Ryker still has viewing rights of my dick."

Piper threw her head back and laughed as she said, "Naturally. I would never take that away from him."

"Come here," Mason said, as he grabbed the back of her neck and brought her lips back down to his.

Life was going to be one hell of a roller coaster when it came to Piper, but hell if he wanted to be on any other ride. He was one stubborn mother fucker, and Piper was the one thing in his life that he would forever be stubborn about, because hell if he was ever going to let her go again. They might have hurt each other, they might have done some serious damage, but not being together wasn't an option. Their only choice was to move forward, and moving forward was what they were going to do.

Easing out of the chair, they grabbed his crutches and walked back to the bedroom, where Mason slowly, but deliciously, pulled every article of clothing off of her body and made the sweetest love he knew possible to the girl who had captured his heart on an airplane headed to his best friend's wedding.

EPILOGUE

Mason

"Heads up!" shouted Ryker, as the ball dropped just short of the little gaggle of children and women.

"Ryker Lewis!" stated Hannah, as she stood up with the ball in one hand and her other hand on her hip, getting ready for a lecture. "What did I tell you about playing near the children? If you and Mason are going to try to see whose junk is bigger, then do it away from the kids."

Mason watched as a smile spread across Ryker's face. He always loved it when Hannah got riled up; he said it was the biggest turn on ever.

"Don't smile at me like that."

Ryker swooped in and cradled Hannah in his arms. "You're so intimidating, Mrs. Lewis. I'm shaking in my boots."

"Put me down," she laughed, as Ryker bounced her around the yard.

"Daddy, daddy, can you carry me around too?" Birdie, Jake and Lexi's three year old daughter asked, as she pulled on Jake's shirt.

"Anything for my little girl." Jake scooped Birdie up in his arms and started spinning her around the yard.

"Jake Taylor, be careful. She just ate, and she is bound to..."

Before Lexi could finish, Jake had regurgitated lunch spilled all over his shirt. He held his daughter out at arm's length as he dry-heaved and Birdie giggled.

"Serves you right," Lexi said, as she continued to breast feed their son, JJ. "There are spare clothes in the coat room. Maybe if Jesse is nice, he'll let you borrow one of his shirts."

"Did I hear my name?" Jesse said, as he came up from behind Ashlin and wrapped his arms around her.

Ashlin pulled Jesse's head down and kissed him on the lips. "Jake needs a shirt, babe. You want to get him one?"

"Sure, you need anything while I'm in the house?"

"Nope, I'm good," Ashlin said, as she sat down in a lounge chair. She was three months pregnant, and Jesse was the most irritating fuck when it came to taking care of his girl. He didn't understand how Ashlin was able to put up with his hovering, but then again, the look in her eyes when Jesse was around spoke volumes. She was in love, and no matter what, she was going to love the man.

As Jake, Jesse, and Birdie walked into the house to clean up, Mason sat down on the blanket that was spread across the grass and grabbed a spare piece of paper and a couple of crayons.

"What are you drawing?" Mason asked Logan and Shane, Ryker's twin boys.

"Baseballs!" Logan shouted as he held up his picture. They were four years old, and they ate, slept, and drank baseball...to say it bruised Ryker's ego was an understatement. Ryker didn't take too much time in putting a ring on Hannah's finger, marrying her, and then getting started on a family...and now he had twin boys infatuated with a sport that wasn't his. Just thinking about it made Mason laugh.

After they won the Super bowl after the year Mason recovered from his injury, Hannah gave birth to Logan and Shane. They were the first kids to enter their group of friends, and they set the standard for kids to follow. Hannah and Ryker were amazing parents. Hannah was now a stay-at-home mom, and would occasionally go to the Stallions' away games, but for the most part, they stayed at their ranch on the outskirts of Denver, where Ryker had reluctantly put in a baseball field in their backyard. It may not be his sport, but Ryker would give the boys the moon if it would make them happy.

"Did you see this?" Lexi asked, as she showed everyone

the magazine she was reading. "Jax and Brooke finally tied the knot, and look at that gorgeous dress!"

"Ooh, let me see," Hannah shoved everyone aside to see what it looked like. "Oh, she looks gorgeous. I'm so happy for them."

Mason glanced at the picture, but didn't pay too much attention. After they won the Super bowl, Jax was picked up as head coach for Seattle. Was Mason happy about it? Fuck yeah! The moment he heard the news, he rejoiced, and actually bought Jax a goodbye present. He gave him a flask and told him he was going to need it when the Stallions took out his team next season. They had a good handshake, but then parted ways. Neither of them were interested in being in each other's lives, and they kept it that way, but Mason would be lying if he said he wasn't happy for Brooke. She deserved happiness, and he was glad she was able to finally find it in Jax, even if the thought of their little love triangle still made him confused as hell.

Jake, Jesse and Birdie came back out shortly. Birdie was wearing a new shirt and some tights, and Jake was wearing a Property of Stallions shirt. Once everyone saw him walk out with a defeated look on his face and a giant smile on Jesse's, everyone busted out laughing.

Waving his hands around to calm everyone down, Jake flexed and said, "At least I fill his shirt out better. Check out these pipes."

Lexi rolled her eyes, but she wasn't kidding anyone, because she was also licking her lips and staring at Jake with a heated gaze. Even after so many years of marriage, they were still madly in love. It felt like only yesterday that Mason was lecturing Lexi in her dorm room about giving Jake a chance, about allowing him to be let into her little world. Now, when he looked at them, he knew that even though they'd had their ups and downs, love always prevailed. Just like him and Piper, love always prevailed.

They had their ups and downs. They were both stubborn and had their own opinions, which made for an interesting living environment at times, but what Mason could count on was that there was a never dull moment between them.

The happiest day of his life was when he saw Piper walking toward him on the beach, wearing a silver dress like the one she wore at Jake and Lexi's wedding, with her hair blowing in the wind and a bouquet in her hand. They had a small ceremony, only their close family and friends were invited, which was perfect for them. Mason could not be happier. After college, after Brooke left him, he thought that was it for him, that he would never find love again, but then Piper showed up on the same plane as him, in her hung over and drooling state. She turned everything he thought about love into a lie and showed him exactly what it meant to have a soul mate, to be a part of someone else. She was his…forever.

"Where is that wife of yours?" Lexi asked, as she patted her son's back, trying to get the little guy to burp.

"She went to the bathroom. I swear, her bladder is the size of a pea."

"Well, that's what happens when you're nine months pregnant," Lexi commented back.

"Yeah, and it turns into a grain of salt when you have twin boys pressing against it," Hannah added, making everyone laugh.

"I should go check on her," Mason said as he got up, but once he stood, he saw Piper waddling, yes waddling, she was at that stage now, walking toward him. Her eyes were bright with shock and she looked almost pale.

Rushing to her side, Mason grabbed her by her waist and said, "Baby, is everything okay?"

Tears welled in her eyes as she nodded and said, "My water broke, Mason. It's time."

"Holy shit!" Mason shouted, making everyone scold him for his language. Now that there were kids around, they had to keep the swear words under control, but at the moment, Mason didn't care. He was going to be a dad.

"Piper is in labor," Mason shouted, as he started ushering Piper to his car. Everyone wished them well, and Lexi said they would figure out what to do with the kids and then be right over.

Mason didn't care; all he cared about was getting his wife to the hospital.

He buckled Piper into her seat, and then looked her in the eyes. He had never loved anyone in his life as much as he loved her, and at that moment, he knew these were the last moments where they would be truly alone together before they became a family of three, so Mason leaned in and kissed her lips.

"I want you to know, Piper, that I love you so much, and there is no doubt in my mind that you're going to be the most amazing and beautiful mom I've ever met. I could not be prouder to be called your husband."

"Thank you, Mason. I love you, too, more than life itself."

He pressed his forehead against hers as his hand cupped the back of her neck. He kissed the tip of her nose and said, "Are you ready to meet our baby girl?"

"More than ready."

"Let's do it, Jojo," Mason teased, as he closed the door and drove through the streets of Denver, preparing for another new chapter in his life.

Thank you for reading Three and Out! I hope you enjoyed it. If you did, please help other readers find this book:

1. This book is lendable, so send it to a friend who you think might like it so she can discover me, too.
2. Help other people find this book by writing a review.
3. Come like my Facebook page: Author Meghan Quinn
4. Find me on Goodreads
5. Don't forget to visit my website: www.authormeghanquinn.com

ABOUT THE AUTHOR

I grew up in Southern California where I was involved in sports my whole life. I was lucky to go to college in New York where I met the love of my life and got married. We currently have five, four-legged children and live in beautiful Colorado Springs, CO.

You can either find my head buried in my Kindle, listening to inspiring heart ripping music or typing away on the computer twisting and turning the lives of my characters while driving my readers crazy with anticipation.

Made in United States
Troutdale, OR
11/05/2024